UNDER DARKENED SKIES

H.E. BAUMAN

Copyright © 2023 by H.E. Bauman

First paperback edition April 2023

Cover design by MiblArt

Map by Cartographybird Maps

ISBN 978-1-7354553-6-5 (paperback)

ISBN 978-1-7354553-4-1 (hardcover)

ISBN 978-1-7354553-5-8 (ebook)

www.hebauman.com

Content Warning

Thank you for picking up *Under Darkened Skies*. This is a fantasy novel that follows Astrea Sovna, a 24-year-old librarian and mage, as she navigates an increasingly dangerous city. The story includes themes and events that may not be suitable for some readers:

- Fantasy and magical violence, including death

- References to past parental death, war and imperialism, gambling, and drug use

- Alcohol consumption

- Panic attacks and anxiety

- Stalking

If you need to put the book down at any time (including now), please do so and take care of yourself.

THE NORTH SEA
THE WESTERN SEA
TALMARIS
GRAND DUCHY OF NOVARIA
ZINDIR
THE ZAIKUD EMPIRE
MACADIAN MOUNTAINS
POSAN
FORT AVALON
NARIZON
CORSYCA
FORT BLACKROCK
FORT IRONWING
KINGDOM OF DELIA
SAPOI
CAPITAL CITIES
CITIES
NOTABLE TOWNS
FORTS
MEMATOS
ILESOURIA

THE LOST ISLES

IRVINA

MOUNTARES MOUNTAINS

THE
HELOSIAN
EMPIRE

THE
ADLANDS

REPUBLIC OF
TORNAMA

RING OF
FIRE

TINALE BAY

KALAMA

SEZIA

THASIA

KATAVENA

TAIPOLI
ISLANDS

THE EASTERN SEA

THE SOUTHERN OCEAN

To those who have tried to make themselves small and play it safe

CHAPTER 1

Astrea Sovna hated deviations from her routine. She looked up from where she was digging around in her satchel, a handful of coins jingling in her closed fist. "What do you mean you don't have any pancakes?"

Carmella's narrow auburn eyebrows lifted. "Sold out yesterday," the café owner said. "I haven't gotten a shipment of cinnamon in over two weeks."

"No shipment?" Astrea echoed.

"Another blockade by the Delians. Sorry, Astrea. I can get you something else if you'd like."

The pastry case to Astrea's right was filled with everything from miniature lemon tarts to flaky chocolate-filled croissants to sweet raisin buns. None of them were as good as the delicately fried cinnamon pancakes she loved so much.

Astrea's stomach rumbled. She sighed, then said, "Two raspberry turnovers, I guess."

"And your usual coffee?"

"Yes, but make it two, actually." Whenever Astrea went on these coffee runs for herself, she liked to bring something back for her boss.

"That'll be four lire."

Astrea handed the coins over to the café's owner, then moved toward the opposite end of the counter so the next customer could order.

1

The White Lily smelled like it always did on Thursday mornings: the sharpness of espresso, the sweetness of sugar-laden pastries, and the never-ending wisteria blooming outside. It was Astrea's favorite café in the Helosian capital of Kalama, nestled right in the heart of the Market District but away from the more crowded tourist traps that served watered-down versions of the coffee the city was famous for. It was even beautiful inside, a mix of creamy whites and lush brown accents. Wide windows spanned the front and rear walls of the shop, and the door at the back led to a private garden with a few extra tables for customers.

She'd been coming here since starting university, and even though she'd graduated two years prior, Astrea couldn't help but stop in at least a couple of days a week. In fact, she loved The White Lily so much that she'd chosen it for her birthday lunch a couple of months before. Her best friends had said a twenty-fourth birthday required more flair, but Astrea liked celebrations better when they were quiet.

Astrea reached into the pocket of her linen skirt, fishing out a silver pocket watch on a delicate chain. She popped the lid open. If she left here within the next ten minutes, she could still get back to the Great Library before her boss left for her meeting.

One of Carmella's employees, a young woman with dark curly hair styled in two poofy buns, smiled as she handed Astrea a crisp white bag. "The coffees will be ready in a minute."

Astrea wasn't sure who the employee was; Carmella always had a rotation of university students working for her. All that mattered was that she seemed to know her way around an espresso machine. The copper machine glittered in the late morning sun peeking through the windows, steam shooting out of a valve as the woman began making Astrea's order.

"Did you see this?" a rough voice muttered.

Astrea glanced toward the line of customers. A pale man dressed in a fitted tan suit—the style Kalama's businesspeople favored—tilted a newspaper toward his companion. Bright red pulsed around his friend twice.

People projected their emotions into the world differently, and sometimes it came across Astrea's Lightbringer magic as color, sometimes as a taste or physical sensation. Sometimes she even experienced several of the indicators simultaneously. The stronger the emotional reaction, the stronger it was to her magic. Whatever the man read in that paper, it upset him.

His rage reached her a moment later, fiery heat burning across her skin. Some days, Astrea liked being a Lightbringer—a healer and an empath. After all, it was useful to get a real sense of what people were feeling. But she hated being in crowds, in settings where she couldn't control what she experienced. It was so much easier to focus on the negative emotions than on whatever joy people around her were feeling. Negativity lingered longer, washing over her magic for twice as long as anything good ever did.

"We had no business getting into another war," the man in the tan suit said. He scoffed as he folded up his newspaper. "Another five hundred Helosians dead. What a waste."

"It's just going to make taxes go up," his companion said, running a hand over his dark, tightly coiled hair. "Do you think they'll expand the draft? Both my sons are already enlisted, but my daughter's about to come of age, and her magic is strong."

Astrea pushed back against the frustration rolling off the two men. The Helosian Empire had been in some kind of war for as long as Astrea could remember. In the last year, Emperor Aelius Auris had gotten into a war with the Delians and Zaikudi over Corsyca, a small territory to the northwest. The emperor's war machine was no small thing.

And though it wasn't unusual to hear people talking about their concerns over various imperial policies, it was less common for Astrea to feel such a volatile reaction when they did. Though many people disagreed with the Corsycan war, many others supported whatever conflict the emperor got them into. She'd never understood why.

"Astrea?" The barista slid two white paper cups emblazoned with a lily design toward her. "Enjoy."

"Thanks."

After tucking her bag of pastries into her satchel, Astrea picked up the coffees and skirted past the line of customers. She held her breath as she passed the two men with the newspaper, but they'd lowered their voices, and it seemed their moment had passed. No more auras, no more negativity. Just the midmorning sunshine warming Astrea's skin as she stepped outside.

The streetcar rumbled through the Scholar's District, its bell tingling as a passenger pulled the cord to request a stop. Pastel-colored storefronts stretched down the wide, tree-lined streets. Most of the shops in this part of Kalama were bookshops, antique stores, and vendors offering supplies for artists and scientists alike. A few cafés and restaurants were sprinkled in, though they weren't nearly as crowded as those downtown.

Astrea bit into one of her raspberry turnovers just as the streetcar started up again, the sticky sweetness clinging to her lips as she contemplated her to-do list for the day. There were books to be reshelved, which could take hours in the Great Library. It was the largest library in all of Kalama—and the entire empire, for that matter. With her boss out for the afternoon, Astrea would also need to keep an eye on the circulation desk. Hopefully Felix, Serra, or Lena would be working too, but there were no guarantees of that these days.

They passed a hotel on her right, the driver following the curve in the road. They were almost to her stop. Ahead, at the far end of a large piazza, towered the Great Library. The white marble facade shone in the late morning sun, and the glass dome at its top seemed especially shiny as the streetcar edged closer. From here, it looked more like a temple than a government building, but that was how many of the imperial government buildings looked: relics of a time long gone but beautifully maintained and repurposed.

Astrea tugged the red cord above her window. The bell tingled again, and when the driver stopped, Astrea hopped off the rear exit. After a short walk, she was climbing the wide, shallow stairs leading to the library.

Up and up she went, sweat beading at her brow and sun warming her back. There were exactly seventy-four steps; she'd counted after her first week at the job, and they were the only thing she didn't particularly love about working at the Great Library. But as soon as she reached the top, a breeze wafted through the covered colonnade.

One of the wide glass doors opened ahead of her, and Astrea stepped to the side, eyes trained on the ground as someone passed. Professors, students, and government officials were always going in and out of the library, but she didn't want to look too closely at anyone. If news of the war was on the front page today, what else might she encounter? People's emotions would be running wild with news of that many casualties.

Five hundred dead, she thought. It was terrible. It always was when such news came in from the front, and it seemed like those stories came in almost daily now.

The lobby was, thankfully, empty when Astrea walked inside. Empty and blissfully cool compared to the early summer heat.

The library's interior was all Kalama with its beautiful stone floors, rich colors, and elaborate architecture. Several sitting areas broke up the space near the front of the lobby, a combination of settees, overstuffed armchairs, and sturdy wood coffee and side tables.

Astrea headed toward the rear of the building. The lobby opened all the way to the ceiling five stories above, where sunlight filtered in through several large skylights. A staircase loomed at the far end of the lobby, and to its left were the elevators.

She passed under the stairs. This part of the first floor always felt claustrophobic to her; the lights were dim, and the bookshelves made narrow rows that she hated going down. Beyond that were a few private meeting rooms as well as the staff offices.

Staff offices. Astrea almost rolled her eyes at the thought. Being the library's director, Raela was the only one who got a real office. The two senior librarians they'd had on staff had been let go a few months prior due to budget cuts, and their offices had been converted to storage. Astrea and the three library pages all shared a small workroom, which they really just used as a drop space for their bags and coats.

Astrea stopped at the end of the narrow hallway and knocked on the door to Raela's office.

"Come in!" Raela called, and Astrea pushed the door open.

Raela Zornovski was a middle-aged woman, the touch of gray in her black hair and the fine lines around her eyes the only true signs of her age. She was slender and graceful, taller than most people in the capital, and had warm bronze skin covered in freckles that betrayed how much time she spent in the sun when she didn't have to be at the library.

This may have been Raela's private workspace, but it wasn't spacious or beautiful like the rest of the library. It barely fit three bookshelves on the back wall and a desk. Of course, the parts of the library the visitors couldn't see were lackluster. They could barely get the funds they needed to keep senior staff around—ironic considering the emperor loved to brag about their collection of books and artifacts. How he expected them to run an entire library with one director, a junior librarian, and three pages, Astrea still didn't know. They were drowning in work.

"Oh, Astrea!" Raela exclaimed as she looked up from her desk. Though she'd lived in Kalama for most of her life, Raela had never lost the subtle lilt in her accent that hinted at her hometown in the northeast of the empire near the Tornamian border. "Good, you're here. I just sent Felix home; he seems to have come down with something. He was just coughing all over the place! As soon as I saw him, I knew he couldn't stay."

"Are Serra or Lena here today?" Astrea set the second coffee cup on Raela's desk and slid it toward her.

"Unfortunately, no." Raela took a sip of coffee and nodded. "You'll be alone until I get back. Will you be alright?"

Astrea wasn't actually sure she'd be fine by herself, but what was she going to do, insist a sick man come back? Hopefully he'd be able to see a healer. Guilt settled in Astrea's stomach, heavy but not impossible to push away. She had plenty of experience doing that. "I'll be alright," she said. "What do you need me to do while you're gone?"

"Watch the front desk," Raela said as she stood. She smoothed her short salt-and-pepper hair away from her face. "That's priority. I'm expecting a delivery today."

"New books?" Astrea asked.

Raela smiled. "Even better than that."

"What could be better than books to a librarian?"

Her boss waved a dismissive hand as she laughed. "Just wait until you see it. A friend of mine—he's an antiquities and art dealer—found something he was sure the government would be interested in. I convinced them to purchase it for the collection."

Warm excitement danced its way from Raela to Astrea's senses. It was the genuine kind of joy few adults in the city seemed to experience, the kind that made Astrea's heart beat just a bit faster.

Astrea smiled. "Well, I'm certainly curious what they'd be willing to spend money on."

"You and me both, if I'm being honest." Her blue eyes met Astrea's. "But don't tell them I said that."

Astrea could only think of one person to tell, but she had no reason to. Eliana already knew all about the staffing problem at the library and would surely be livid if she knew what the imperial bureaucrats were willing to spend money on instead.

"Do you want me to put it anywhere in particular?" Astrea asked. "Should I unpack it?"

"Have the delivery crew bring it to the basement, please. You can leave it in its box for now." Raela reached for her leather bag, then stuffed a thick folder inside. "If I'm not back by the fifth bell this afternoon, close up without me."

By the fifth bell? The library was usually open until the sixth bell, and they often stayed until the seventh or sometimes even ninth bells to make up for their staffing shortage. But who was Astrea to argue when Raela was the one in charge? An early night sounded great.

"Sure," Astrea said. "Anything else?"

"What time is it?"

Astrea looked at the clock over her shoulder. "It's—"

"Oh, skies damn it, I'm late!" Raela grabbed her bag and her coffee, then rushed past Astrea into the hallway. "Remember, delivery in the basement. I'll see you tomorrow, alright? Get home safely!"

Raela rushed down the dim hallway, her long skirts fluttering as she disappeared around the base of the stairs. Though she was often late and forgetful, Raela more than made up for it with her quick thinking and ability to keep patrons happy.

Sighing, Astrea looked down at the coffee she was still holding. "Well," she murmured as she started toward the lobby, "I might as well enjoy this before it gets any colder."

Checking books back into the library was one of Astrea's least favorite tasks. It was one that usually fell to the library pages, but seeing as she was the only one around *and* stuck at the circulation desk, it was Astrea's only option if she wanted to be productive.

The last few hours had ticked by slowly. Some of the library regulars had come in to return or pick up new books, and chatting with them helped ease some of Astrea's boredom. But no one had come in for the last twenty minutes.

Sighing, Astrea reached for the stack of books to her left. The first one, a heavy thing with a faded blue cover, was about old Helosian architecture. The next was a novel. The rest were a mix of history and fiction, the most popular books for patrons to check out. She took her time, carefully pulling out the thick checkout cards and filling in the necessary information before she set the books aside.

As she pulled the checkout card from a heavy book, it sliced her thumb. "Shit," she muttered, watching as red blood bloomed on her pale skin.

She yanked open one of the desk's drawers. Inside were a few pencils, random checkout cards, scissors, and brass paperclips. A small white box was lodged near the back, and Astrea pulled it out. There should have been bandages inside, but all she found was a mini bottle of antiseptic and some kind of ointment.

Astrea shoved the box back into the drawer. Papercuts weren't severe by any stretch of the imagination, but skies, they hurt while working with books. They always seemed to catch on pages no matter how much she tried to avoid it.

She *could* heal it herself if she went back to Raela's office for a moment.

Just as she stood, the library's front door swung open. In walked a young man dressed in a white shirt and black pants. His calm disinterest met her magic instantly, steady but light as it pushed against her. Astrea sat back down. She'd deal with her thumb later.

"Excuse me," the man said as he walked up to the counter. "I've got a delivery for . . ."

"Oh!" Astrea smiled up at him. "Perfect. Raela wants it in the basement. Is your crew outside?"

A sheen of gray confusion wavered around the man, his light eyebrows pulling together. He set something on the counter. "You want me to take a letter to your basement?"

A letter? Raela had said she was expecting something large. Larger than a letter, anyway.

Astrea forced a laugh and tucked a strand of dark hair behind her ear. "Sorry, I assumed . . . never mind. What's this about?"

"I'm looking for Miss Sovna," the man said.

Despite the fact that no malice met her magic, Astrea's stomach sank. She peered up at the man. He didn't look familiar at all. His blond hair was pulled into a short braid, and his simple but expensive clothes gave away nothing.

Not nothing, Astrea realized. At the top of his shirt was a golden pin she'd almost missed, a phoenix surrounded by rays of the sun. *Oh no.*

"Uhm." Astrea swallowed. "That's me."

"Perfect." He slid the letter closer to her. "Have a nice day."

Before Astrea could ask any more questions, the man left. Why would a messenger from the Palace of a Thousand Suns be at the library? Had something happened to her uncle? Or Eliana? Hands trembling, Astrea reached for the letter, careful not to get the blood from her thumb on the thick, smooth envelope. Only her name was scrawled across the front in neat cursive. The gold wax seal on the back told Astrea everything she needed to know, though.

This wasn't just from the Palace of a Thousand Suns. This had come from someone in the imperial family.

Her mind jumped back to Eliana. There was no way she'd send a letter. Princess Eliana Auris was one of Astrea's closest friends. The youngest of the four imperial siblings, Eliana had befriended Astrea when she moved to Kalama with her uncle, Saros, fourteen years prior. Astrea had been just ten years old at the time; Eliana had been nine. Thanks to her uncle's position as the Imperial Stargazer and part-time tutor to the emperor's children, Astrea grew up on palace grounds and still lived at the old imperial observatory with her uncle.

And in all their years of friendship, Eliana had never been one for letters. She preferred phone calls or in-person visits when she was in the capital, and when she was away on business, she sometimes sent telegrams. But rarely, if ever, did Eliana mail letters. Astrea doubted it was any of the three imperial princes, either. Which left just one person.

Emperor Aelius Auris himself.

Astrea wanted to throw up. She set the letter back on the circulation desk and stared at it.

You don't know it's from him, her mind argued, but her gut was certain. It was the only logical explanation. But that begged the question of why the emperor would be sending her a letter. Had he found out about her magic?

When they'd moved from the Grand Duchy of Novaria—a small country to the north—to the Helosian Empire's capital city, Saros had instructed Astrea to hide her magic. At the time, she hadn't understood why, only that she might have to leave Kalama if anyone found out. As she'd gotten older, Saros had explained it was to prevent her death on the battlefield, a future he'd foreseen with his Stargazer magic. The imperial army was always in need of healers, so Lightbringers and Purifiers were both required to serve.

Saros had only been trying to protect her, but now Astrea had this impossible burden to carry. She couldn't actually use her magic to help people like she wanted to. Magic was a source of joy and strength for many mages, but not Astrea. No, she was stuck hiding it from the world. If she ever got caught by the government, she'd either end up on the front lines or thrown in jail for dodging the compulsory military service shouldered by healers.

Astrea sucked in a deep breath. What would Cressida say? Her other best friend, Cressida Nikaphoros, was almost always able to pause and think clearly. *She would tell me there's no way the emperor knows about my magic. If he did, he wouldn't be sending a letter.*

If he'd learned her secret, Emperor Aelius would send the city police or his palace guards to arrest her. Nobody crossed the emperor without coming to regret it. Even the smallest infractions were punished.

Astrea pulled open the top drawer of her desk, removing a silver letter opener from inside. She slid the metal under the wax seal and blew out a sharp breath as it lifted easily. Inside was a single page of thick parchment.

Miss Sovna,

His Imperial Majesty has invited you to a meeting tomor-

*row, the eleventh day of the sixth month of Year 1020, at his
private office in the Palace of a Thousand Suns.*

Kindly arrive by the ninth morning bell.

Sincerely,
Edouard, Secretary
Office of His Imperial Majesty Emperor Aelius Auris

Astrea set the letter on the circulation desk. She still had a few hours before she could close up for the night. That meant she had a few hours to figure out what to tell her uncle.

CHAPTER 2

Astrea's key ring dangled from her fingers as she trudged up the stairs toward the observatory's second floor. The four-story tower deep within the imperial palace gardens was both her uncle's workspace and their apartment, and it was after long days like today that Astrea truly despised the stairs.

Although she'd gotten to close up the library early, Astrea had barely been able to focus after receiving the emperor's letter. She'd barely even paid attention when the Earthmover crew brought in Raela's delivery an hour before closing, and Astrea loved when the library got deliveries.

When she finally reached the second floor, Astrea stepped off the winding staircase to a narrow landing. She unlocked the door and pushed inside.

"Uncle?" she called as she slipped off her brogues and picked them up with her free hand. She padded past the kitchen and down the hallway toward her room.

When they'd first moved to this tower fourteen years prior, she'd claimed the bedroom at the back of the apartment on the side of the tower overlooking Tinale Bay. It wasn't a large space, but it had every-thing she needed, and she loved the view. After setting her shoes next to the mint green wardrobe on one wall, Astrea crossed her bedroom to the windows. As she threw the window and shutters open, the evening sea breeze rolled in, the tang of sea salt and rain heavy in the air. Thunder rumbled in the distance, dark clouds looming over the bay.

"Uncle?"

Still getting no response from Saros, Astrea closed her bedroom door and slipped her satchel off her shoulder. She set it on her bed. Saros wasn't supposed to be working this late, but maybe something had come up. Something always seemed to be coming up lately. Regardless of if he was working, she really needed to show him the letter.

Astrea opened the flap of her bag. The envelope was tucked safely inside, stuck between two of her notebooks to prevent it from bending or tearing. What would her uncle think about this development? She'd had the last couple of hours at the library to mull over what it might mean, but the only thing her mind could come up with was that, somehow, this was a trick.

Astrea knew it wasn't logical, but she couldn't help it. Her mind did that sometimes, following conclusions that made no sense and ended up being entirely false.

Sighing, Astrea pulled the letter from her bag and retraced her steps through the sitting room and into the kitchen. A familiar form hunched over the counter.

"Uncle?"

Saros jumped as he turned to look over his shoulder. "Oh, there you are. I was wondering when you'd be home." He returned to whatever he was doing, and as Astrea stepped closer, she realized he was pulling boxes of food out of a woven bag.

At least he isn't up in his office.

"Do you need some help?" she asked.

He shoved the now-empty bag toward her. "Put this away for me, would you, my dear? I'll get the plates."

Astrea took the bag, hanging it on a brass hook in the hallway before moving back to the kitchen. "Do you need—"

"Sit, sit! I don't need any more help."

Pressing her lips together, Astrea moved to the kitchen table on the opposite wall. It took all of four paces to get there. She smoothed the pastel floral tablecloth before sitting down and placing the envelope at the edge of the table.

"Do you want me to—" she started, but he cut her off again.

"Astrea," Saros said, his back to her as he plated whatever food he'd brought home, "you need to learn to relax for five minutes. I know you had a long day. Now, what would you like to drink?"

Relax, right. Rich, coming from you, Astrea thought. Saros always overworked himself, spending longer than necessary in his observatory. He knew the consequences of using too much magic. And though he'd always been prone to overworking, it had gotten worse in the last six months. Now, Saros usually spent at least fifteen hours a day in his observatory. What could possibly be so important?

"Whatever you're having is fine."

That earned her what could only be described as an exasperated sigh. "White wine, then?" he asked.

"Chilled, please, if we have it."

Saros moved two steps to his right to the short, narrow refrigerator in the corner of the kitchen. The Nikaphoroses had gifted it to them a few years prior, right when the invention first hit the Kalamian market.

"Already ahead of you." Saros grabbed a bottle of wine, then brought it to the table with a corkscrew. "Open this for us?"

Astrea made quick work of the task and slid the bottle to the middle of the table. After setting a plate of food and an empty wine glass in front of her, Saros dropped into his chair. The fried rice balls on her plate smelled incredible, a light mix of spice and sauce greeting her nose.

"I thought a dinner from The Saffron Garden was in order tonight." Saros grabbed the bottle of wine and poured some into both of their glasses. It was his favorite restaurant in the city, one he almost always picked when they ordered in.

"How did you know I had a long day?" Astrea asked as she cut into her food. "You didn't even know I was home."

"Call it a parental sixth sense."

"Well, it was right. I got a letter from the emperor at work today."

As the silence stretched on, Astrea looked up from her meal. Saros was staring at her, a light gray aura of confusion filtering around him as his fork hovered near his mouth. Sometimes it unnerved her how similar they looked. There was no mistaking they were related, both sharing the Sovna silver irises, moon-pale skin, round faces, and dark wavy hair. Saros was her mother, Roxana's, younger brother. He'd been just sixteen when Astrea was born and twenty-six when he'd become her sole guardian.

"What did the letter say?" he asked, voice low as orange anxiety blossomed around him.

It wasn't unusual for Saros to go quiet when discussing their lie. Astrea was sure nobody could hear them in the observatory tower, but Saros was more paranoid than she was.

"It's an invitation to a meeting tomorrow morning."

Saros's fork and knife clattered against his plate. "A meeting?" He ran a hand through his shoulder-length hair. "What do you mean by a meeting?"

"I don't know. That's all it said." Astrea slid the letter across the table to her uncle. "Here, you read it." Bringing her wine glass to her lips, Astrea waited for Saros to finish reading. "Well?" she asked, heart thundering in her chest when he still didn't say anything.

She just wanted clarity from someone, some logical explanation for it. Astrea did her best to go unnoticed around the city and the palace.

Taking a job as a junior librarian was supposed to keep her away from the emperor. Her friendship with Princess Eliana was the only exception, and even then, it didn't bring Astrea into contact with Emperor Aelius. He wasn't one for socializing.

Saros crossed his arms and sighed. "I don't know, honestly, Astrea. I don't know."

"What do you mean you don't know? Can't you . . . can't you stargaze and see what he's planning?"

The hard lines around her uncle's mouth softened. "You know that's not how it works."

What good is being a Stargazer if you can't reliably see the future? Stargazers were seers, but their glimpses of future events were unpredictable, ever-changing, and up entirely for interpretation. They were better at predicting crop output than victors of war, despite what many people thought. As Saros had explained several times over the years, people's choices changed every day. The future was never set in stone.

She sighed. "I know."

"Did you show anyone else the letter?" Saros asked, finally picking up his silverware again.

"No." Astrea had wanted to show it to Cressida, but calling her in the middle of the workday wasn't ideal. The Nikaphoroses were the only other people in the city—the world—who knew about Astrea's magic. "I was alone when I received it."

"Good. Don't show it to anyone."

"But what do I do about the meeting?" Astrea asked.

"You have to attend," Saros said.

Astrea slowly cut another rice ball into four equal pieces. Of course she had to *attend* the meeting. But knowing she had to go and actually being prepared were two entirely different things.

"I wish there was time for the alternative," Saros continued. "We really need to reconsider it."

A few months prior, Saros had approached her with an idea: leave Kalama. Since then, they'd only talked about the idea twice, and Astrea still wasn't sure how she felt about it.

"And how am I to leave Kalama when neither of us have enough money for me to start over somewhere else?" she finally asked. "I don't even make enough to move into my own apartment."

That was the problem she always came back to. They may have lived on the palace grounds, but the emperor didn't pay Saros much of a stipend, and Astrea didn't earn that much as a junior librarian. No place in Helosia would be safe for her to use her magic when they'd lied to the emperor's face. She could go east to Tornama, or maybe south to the Taipoli Islands, but it would take thousands of lire to get out of the city, let alone the country, and start over.

But she also couldn't leave everyone she loved, could she? Cressida and Eliana both had lives and homes here. Balthazar and Sarsali Nikaphoros—Cressida's parents—were important to Astrea, too. And even though Saros frustrated her sometimes, Astrea couldn't bear to live thousands of miles away from him. He was her only blood family.

Saros cleared his throat. "It's something to think about. We'll find a way. Just make sure you don't reveal anything in your meeting."

She wanted to say something else, to ask her uncle what he thought about her leaving, or the emperor's letter, or if he could foresee her in some far-off city, far away from this place. But Astrea didn't move, and Saros remained quiet. As he continued to eat his dinner, Astrea followed his lead, managing to eat her entire meal and drink two glasses of wine in record time.

"I'm going to bed," she said, already pushing her chair away from the table. Why didn't her uncle have something more to say about this? "Thanks for dinner."

Astrea stood, then pushed her chair back into its usual place. No response. She grabbed the letter and left her dirty plates on the table. No response. But finally, as she neared the kitchen door, Saros spoke.

"Astrea."

She turned.

"I love you, my dear. I hope you know that."

"I know." And she did know. Saros had sacrificed so much for her over the years. "I love you, too."

"Everything's going to work out as it should."

"How can you be so sure?"

"Because I trust the stars, and so should you. Now go on, get some rest."

Shadows burned all around her as a low, grating laugh came from somewhere in the dark. "Oh, little Lightbringer, where are you?"

She had to hide. She knew she had to hide. But she couldn't make her legs move. The shadows pressed in around her, all-consuming.

"Where do you think you're going, little Lightbringer?" A hand yanked her hair as searing pain blasted across her shoulders. "I've been looking everywhere for you."

Hot and cold licked her arms again. Astrea screamed. More heat. More screaming. And she couldn't stop.

Astrea gasped as she sat up in bed, chest heaving and tight. Lightning flashed outside her window, casting a strange, distorted pattern from her shutters onto the bedroom walls. Thunder clapped a second later.

"Just a dream," Astrea muttered as she flopped back into her pillows again. "Just a dream."

A recurring dream from her childhood, one she hadn't had in years.

Astrea slipped out of bed and grabbed her silk robe from its hook on the back of her door. She needed a drink of water. She needed to move—to run, like in her dream—otherwise, she'd never go back to sleep.

The hallway outside her room was dark. To her right, Saros's bedroom door was wide open. She didn't need to peek in to know he wasn't in there. The ceiling above her creaked, then footsteps shuffled overhead. He was still in the observatory.

What could he possibly be doing up there in the middle of the night? It didn't matter. He probably wouldn't tell her anyway.

They'd been so close for much of her life, Saros being something between an older brother and an uncle to her after her mother died. He'd always told her what he could about his work, and in return, he'd always asked about her own life. But everything had started changing six months prior, right around the winter solstice.

"Whatever," Astrea muttered as she crept toward the kitchen.

She'd asked him at least a dozen times since then if something was bothering him or if he needed help. He was always tired, and he wouldn't let Astrea heal him even when she insisted. Sarsali Nikaphoros knew many healers in the city; it didn't have to be Astrea's own magic that helped Saros. Eliana had plenty of connections if he needed something else. But Saros said there was nothing wrong, that he 'simply had work to do.'

"You're just like your mother, and she would be so proud," he'd told her. *"But you have to stop worrying about me."*

Astrea retrieved a glass from the cabinet to her left, filling it with cool water from the faucet. Just as she swallowed her first sip, a dark figure towered to her left. Her pulse jumped. She swore red eyes peered out of the darkness at her, but they were gone just as quickly as they'd appeared. A moment later, the floor creaked, and Saros rounded the corner into the kitchen.

"What are you doing up?" he asked.

"Storm woke me," she lied. If Saros had finally come downstairs to go to bed, she didn't want to tell him about the dream. It would worry him too much. "Night."

"Goodnight," he said as she passed him and slipped down the hallway to her room.

Astrea closed her bedroom door, but instead of climbing back into bed, she waited. Saros hadn't followed her down the hall. It was dead silent except for the low rumbles of thunder.

And then she heard it. Footsteps overhead as the floor creaked.

She sighed as she slipped off her robe and crawled back into bed. Maybe someday she'd figure out what was bothering Saros, but it wouldn't be tonight. Tonight, she needed to focus on going back to sleep. She needed to focus on being rested so she would be sharp for her meeting with the emperor.

Chapter 3

Astrea hadn't been able to go back to sleep, and that fact was evident on her face as she stared into the mirror mounted above her vanity.

She had to be at the palace in an hour. The walk from the observatory to the palace itself would take all of fifteen minutes, but she needed to figure out what was both appropriate to wear for an audience with the emperor and not too formal for work. Was that even possible?

After waking up from the dream, Astrea had been kept up by the endless thunderstorms rolling in off the bay and her own incessant thoughts about the meeting and its implications. As much as she wanted to tell herself it was just about work, her mind wouldn't be convinced so easily.

Astrea dabbed on moisturizer, then lined her upper lash line with kohl and swiped on some blush. She went to her wardrobe next and flicked through the various dresses, blouses, and skirts she typically wore to work. They were nice, but they didn't feel right. Astrea skimmed through the handful of more elegant dresses she owned, pulling out a purple dress with wildflowers embroidered along the skirts. The hem fell mid-calf, and the transparent sleeves were definitely in fashion. It was one of the nicest dresses she owned. *Good enough.*

Slipping the dress on, Astrea smoothed the skirt over her wide hips, then pinned the top layers of her dark hair back with silver crescent moon clips. After finishing the outfit with a pair of white brogues and grabbing her satchel, Astrea took one last look in her vanity mirror. It was a little excessive for her long day in the stacks, but she'd just have to make it work.

Before stepping out the door, Astrea opened her bag. Her notebooks for work were there, as was the invitation from the emperor. She let her fingers skim the top of the envelope before buckling her satchel closed and flinging her bedroom door open.

The apartment was quiet. Saros must have already been up in the observatory; his bedroom door was open, and he wasn't in the kitchen.

After grabbing her key ring from the hooks near the apartment door, Astrea started down the spiraling stairway outside. She went down one flight to the ground floor, then stepped out into the morning sunlight. The sea breeze was surprisingly cool despite the puddles left over from the night's storms.

She started down the gravel path, passing the lake across from the observatory tower. It was her favorite spot on the palace grounds, and there was even an island in the middle that housed a beautiful stone gazebo. It was a spot she used to play in with Cressida when they were children, and Eliana joined them whenever she was able to slip away from her governess.

The Palace of a Thousand Suns came into view as Astrea rounded the bend. She should've been used to it by now, but the sight was always startling. The cover of the wide weeping willows and towering palms ended suddenly, giving way to the more manicured formal gardens filled with hedges and bushes covered in fragrant flowers. Everything from delphinium to roses to begonias and more were in bloom. The gardens still had a slightly wild look to them—a popular aesthetic among Helosian nobility and the wealthier businesspeople—but were nowhere near as overgrown as the sections near the observatory.

The imperial palace was anything but unkempt. The marble structure shone under the bright morning sun, a beacon. Three golden domes sat atop the palace—one on each wing and one in the middle, which was the public part of the imperial seat. Wide terraces stretched the lengths of the building, and the one in the front was covered by a roof held up by pillars. It really was beautiful, but it was still a shock amid the sea of green.

From here, the rest of the walk to the palace was easy. Three lefts, two rights, another left, and Astrea was out of the hedge maze on the eastern side of the compound. One summer when Astrea was twelve, she, Eliana, and Cressida had spent the mornings before lessons figuring out exactly how to navigate the maze, and Astrea had never forgotten.

She continued west, approaching one of the terraces. Even though there were only a few stairs from the garden up onto the landing, Astrea took them slowly, controlling her breathing as she went.

It was real now. She was really going into the palace, not to meet with her friend or find her uncle, but to speak with Emperor Aelius.

Stop panicking. Nothing's going to happen.

Astrea's right foot hit the terrace first, and she continued without missing a beat. Two young men walked out through the double doors ahead. She stepped to the side, but one held the door open for her.

"Busy morning?" he asked.

Astrea glanced up at his face, taking in his dark brown skin and eyes. He was young, perhaps a few years older than herself. She recognized him from somewhere. His well-tailored suit, gold jewelry, close-cropped hair, and perfect posture all screamed nobility. His friend was equally well-dressed and well-postured, though his pale complexion almost blended in with the white palace exterior. Eliana had surely pointed them out at some party or function, but Astrea didn't know their ranks or names.

Rather than risk offending someone, she simply nodded. That might still offend someone, but the wrong title was worse than no title at all.

The man holding the door open gestured for her to go through, and Astrea ducked her head.

"Thank you, sir."

She didn't stick around to hear whatever the two men said. Instead, Astrea scurried into the cool palace interior.

Just inside was a large sitting room, then a corridor beyond. She wasn't exactly sure where the emperor's office was, but she could check the throne room first. That would be toward the middle of the palace.

"Miss Sovna?"

Astrea stopped. She'd just gotten to the hallway when the man spoke her name. She turned. A palace guard stood behind her, dressed in the standard red structured uniform trimmed in gold.

Breathe.

"Yes?" Astrea asked.

"I'll escort you to your appointment."

The man was unfamiliar to her. She knew most of the palace guards; it was hard not to meet them when she was their neighbor. He was pale, taller than most of the guards by at least a few inches, and his nearly snow-white hair was cropped close to his head. His amber eyes were the most normal thing about him—some kind of fire or earth mage. Every palace guard was a mage. So what was his specialty? Astrea wasn't sure she wanted to find out.

"Oh." She flashed a quick smile. "Thank you. That would be lovely."

"Follow me." The unfamiliar guard didn't smile back.

In fact, Astrea couldn't sense anything from him at all. Although her Lightbringer magic allowed her to sense other people's emotions and even feel their physical pain if it was strong enough, some were good at keeping things close to their chest. She thought of it as a wall or mask.

She could always feel that strange block, and Astrea could even imagine her magic moving around it as if it were a physical thing.

Astrea followed the man down several corridors, none of which she was familiar with. At one point, they crossed through the main atrium of the palace, the heart of imperial court activity. The massive hall was bustling with well-dressed businesspeople, a handful of courtiers Astrea recognized, and even diplomats from the Delian embassy. How many of these people were here to see the emperor and how many were here to liaise with his children and advisors? She'd have to ask Eliana later.

Astrea didn't see her royal friend as the guard led her through the throng of people. Nobody even seemed to notice Astrea either, all of them too busy discussing whatever business they deemed so important. The guard led Astrea down a wide main hallway on the other side of the palace, then turned down several smaller ones.

As they approached the end of the hall, Astrea actually recognized where she was. They'd just passed Eliana's office door, which was shut. Was she supposed to know the emperor's office was right here? It was so . . . unassuming, something the emperor never was. It was just a plain brown door with the imperial seal etched in it, a mirror image of Eliana's and the other two offices here. Astrea had always assumed they were the four offices of the emperor's four children.

The guard stepped toward the door. "Wait here."

You don't have to tell me twice.

The guard lifted his fist, but the door opened before he could knock. Out stepped a surprisingly familiar face. Willowy figure, dark spiraling curls, smooth wide nose, and warm copper skin—what was Cressida Nikaphoros doing here?

Lavender surprise exploded around her friend. Astrea almost called out to her, but Cressida simply shook her head once and mouthed 'gardens' as she passed. Then Cressida was gone, and the guard was motioning for Astrea to follow him. Sucking in a deep breath, she followed him into the office. *Later,* she promised herself. She would find out what Cressida was doing there later. *Just focus.*

"Your Imperial Majesty," the guard said as Astrea stepped up next to him, "may I present Miss Astrea Sovna."

"Have a seat, Miss Sovna."

Astrea turned to look at the guard, but he was already closing the door behind him on his way out. She turned back toward the emperor and smiled, dipping into the curtsy Eliana had taught her years ago.

"Thank you, Your Imperial Majesty."

Even before she'd met him as a child, Astrea had heard of the Helosian Emperor and his armies. He lived up to his reputation as a handsome leader: tan skin, a striking jawline, straight nose, thick black hair even in his middle age, and the second most brilliant pair of golden eyes Astrea had ever seen. He hadn't changed much since she first met him fourteen years prior. Even his suit made of rich black brocade was no different.

Emperor Aelius motioned for her to sit in one of the plush chairs in front of his massive oak desk. She took a few steps forward until she was next to the chair on the right. She sat, careful to gather her skirts before doing so and setting her satchel in her lap. *Breathe.*

The emperor leaned back in his chair behind his desk, fingers steepled in front of his lips. Should she say something? Astrea didn't think so. She might risk offending the young nobleman who held the door open, but the emperor? Absolutely not.

"Would you like some tea, Miss Sovna?" Emperor Aelius asked. Before she could respond, he tapped a button on his desk. The sound of a radio crackled to life. "Bring tea to my office for me and my guest."

She didn't realize he had an intercom, but the palace always had any new technology before the rest of the population, thanks to Cressida's father's company. Cressida had been telling her about the invention a few weeks before.

"Thank you, Your Imperial Majesty," Astrea said. "Tea sounds lovely."

"Your Majesty."

Astrea knew she was staring at the emperor wide-eyed, but she didn't know what to do with the correction. All she sensed from him was cool curiosity. No malice, no anger, no rage. Not even annoyance. She hated that she couldn't control this part of her magic, that she could still read him. Nobody could tell she was an empath; she didn't glow, nor did any light spill from her fingers like it did when she healed.

All night, she'd been awake imagining all kinds of versions of this moment. A big reveal that he'd discovered her secret. Guards dragging Saros into the office to face punishment with her. Questioning about her friendship with Eliana. A warning to stay away from his daughter, even. But being offered tea? The calm the emperor now exuded? This was not how Astrea imagined this meeting going at all.

"I find," Emperor Aelius continued, the corners of his thin lips pulling up, "that my full title is a bit of a mouthful when having a simple conversation."

Astrea held his gaze. Was this some kind of test? It didn't seem to be, even if it was unexpected. "Of course, Your Majesty."

He smiled. "My daughter tells me you've grown into your role at our city's beautiful library. You have worked there for . . . ?"

Thank you for this, Ellie, Astrea thought ruefully.

"For just over two years, Your Majesty. I started after graduating university."

"And you studied here in Kalama, right?"

"I did."

"Very good. The best university on the continent. Eliana mentioned that you started studying there when you were just sixteen?"

"Yes, Your Majesty." Saros had encouraged Astrea to start taking part-time university classes earlier than normal; whatever her tutors had for her to work on was never challenging enough. She'd received two degrees, one in Helosian literature and one in Tornamian language studies.

The office door opened, and Astrea turned. Emperor Aelius was already on his feet and moving toward it, each movement measured and graceful. The same snowy-haired guard from before had rolled in a cart laden with tea and small breakfast pastries.

"Thank you, Caliban. That will be all," the emperor said.

The guard—Caliban—bowed before leaving the room again. Then the emperor did the unthinkable. He poured his own tea.

Did he do this every meeting just to surprise his guests? At the handful of palace functions she'd attended with Eliana in recent years, Astrea had never seen the emperor pour anything.

"How do you take your tea, Miss Sovna?"

Astrea would have loved to see the look on her own face in that moment. "Two spoonfuls of sugar, Your Majesty."

"Ah, a sweet tooth." He laughed, a warm sound.

I don't think I've ever heard him laugh like that.

"I believe it runs in my family, Your Majesty."

The emperor laughed. Again. At something she said.

"Hopefully this is to your liking," he said, and Astrea stiffened when she realized he was placing a tea cup on his desk in front of her. "You were telling me you studied here in Kalama. Do you like being a librarian, Astrea?"

Reaching for the teacup and saucer, Astrea balanced it carefully in her hands. "I do, Your Majesty."

Emperor Aelius nodded, sipping his tea before setting the cup back down on his desk. "I'm glad to hear you're already serving the empire.

The task I ask of you is in even greater service to the people of this nation."

What was *that* supposed to mean?

"Your Majesty?" Astrea swallowed hard. "I'm afraid I don't understand."

Pushing his chair back, the emperor stood again and strode to the right side of his office. Maps of differing sizes, countries, and colors decorated the wall. Emperor Aelius paused in front of one, his suit jacket wrinkling as his arms crossed behind his back.

"Astrea, I know you are in my daughter's confidence. Surely you recognize that we are fighting wars on multiple fronts: our attempts to overcome unruly neighbors, and of course, unruly groups within our own borders."

Astrea knew about the war and the so-called rebellion. Who didn't? The newspapers had a new story about the war every day and about the rebels every week. At the very least, they published speculation about which nobles and senators had been caught dissenting in public.

That was really all the rebellion was: talk. People gathered in salons in the city to discuss ideas about government and policy. They opposed the Corsycan war. They tried to sway Senate representatives to their side—not that it mattered. The Senate was purely ceremonial. Though its sixty-five members were elected, they had no influence over imperial policy. Emperor Aelius was the one who actually made the laws.

The rebels also wanted Eliana to be named heir, or at least that was the rumor. Emperor Aelius had yet to formally declare which one of his four children would take over for him someday. Kaius was the favorite pick. But the rebels certainly weren't violent. They weren't 'unruly,' as the emperor called them.

Besides, what did the rebellion have to do with her? Or the emperor's war, for that matter?

He doesn't know about your magic, Astrea reminded herself. *He isn't sending you to the front. He's not making you a soldier.* That didn't stop her heart from racing wildly.

Emperor Aelius kept his back to her as he continued, "So in an effort to bridge some gaps between our nation and another, I'm organizing an exhibition about the Grand Duchy of Novaria for the autumn equinox festival. A delegation from Grand Duchess Ysabel's court will be here, and it's important they see how much we value them as friends."

Astrea stiffened. She and Raela had assisted with exhibits and galas around the city before—mostly helping bureaucrats with research and logistics—but nothing of this magnitude. This would be an enormous job.

"With that in mind, I would like you to immediately begin preparing to work with Prince Varojin on this when he returns to Kalama next week."

It felt like a Tempest had sucked all the air out of the emperor's office. This was not what she had expected, not in the least.

Prince Varojin Auris was returning to Kalama, and Astrea was going to have to work with him.

Perhaps this was worse than whatever she'd anticipated. Perhaps being thrown in jail would be better. In fact, being sucked into the void—that very cold, very empty part of the night sky—would be the best possible outcome right now. But she wouldn't be so lucky. Awkward and uncomfortable situations didn't usually result in one's death.

"Your Majesty," she started slowly, "I would be honored to help, though the library doesn't usually—"

"This is of the utmost priority," he said, voice sharp as he turned to face her. Anger flashed through the room, hot on Astrea's skin. But when Emperor Aelius spoke again, there was no longer an edge to his words. "I want to host a gala and present the exhibition to the Novarian delegation in the autumn. This must go well, Miss Sovna."

Astrea nodded. "Of course, Your Majesty. What . . . what exactly about Novaria would you like the exhibition to include?"

Dozens of possibilities ran through her mind. Part of her was excited to have something specific to study and work on. But mostly, she was confused about why the emperor would choose her and Prince Varojin to work on this project. She was a librarian; he was a soldier. Neither of them were diplomats, not like Eliana. Wasn't the princess a better fit for the job?

And why would the emperor suddenly choose to show favor to Novaria? While they weren't enemies, the two countries weren't exactly allies either. Novaria and Tornama both tried to stay neutral despite Helosia, Zaikud, and Delia constantly fighting.

"For now, gather whatever you think is interesting or relevant from Novarian history," Emperor Aelius said. "I will send for you again when I'm ready to hear what you and my son have learned in your research." He walked back to his desk, and Astrea took another sip of tea to keep from watching him too closely. "There will, of course, be bonus payment for your work on this, an additional ten thousand lire."

Astrea nearly choked. "Your Majesty, that's very generous—"

"As I said, this job is of the utmost importance." Light green focus and marigold excitement bubbled up around the emperor. "Tell your superiors about this project, and my secretary will send a message to them by the end of the day that gives this project priority over your other assignments."

Sucking in a deep breath, Astrea nodded. "Of course, Your Majesty. I'll get started right away."

"Excellent. You may see yourself out."

Astrea stood on shaking legs, curtsied again, then walked toward the door as quickly as she could without being suspicious.

Skies, did she have a lot to tell Cressida.

CHAPTER 4

Astrea didn't know what to think as she hurried out of the emperor's office and down the empty corridor. *Ten thousand lire?* That was nearly double her yearly salary, and the autumn equinox wasn't for another three months. The summer solstice was still a week away.

Perhaps this is a good thing, she reasoned. *Ten thousand lire in just three months.*

Yes, the emperor's behavior was odd, and she still didn't know why she'd been assigned to this project, and she really didn't want to work with Prince Varojin, but that much money would help her leave Kalama. It was enough that she might be able to invite Cressida or Saros along with her.

Astrea's breath caught in her throat as she turned down another hallway. The thought of leaving anyone she loved behind hurt, but she couldn't stay in Kalama forever. *Maybe I could just leave for a year or two, until the Corsycan war is over.*

"Astrea," a familiar voice called out as she reached the main atrium. All of the diplomats and aristocrats from earlier had disappeared.

"Hi, Nicos," Astrea said.

Though he was just a couple of years older than Astrea, Nicos Masalis was one of the youngest palace guards. He was one of the few Astrea actually liked, a Fireweaver who had grown up around the empire—including Kalama—thanks to his family's long history of military service. They hadn't spoken much when Nicos first joined the imperial guard, but now that he was close with Eliana, Astrea considered him a friend.

"Her Imperial Highness is in a meeting," Nicos said as he walked up to her. He looked the same as he did every day: auburn hair pulled back into a neat bun, close-cropped beard hiding none of the many freckles covering his pale face, and perfectly pressed crimson and black uniform. "I can pass along a message if you need me to."

"Uhm, that's okay," Astrea said. "I was just . . ." Should she say anything about her meeting with the emperor? She didn't think so. Two more guards stood at the far end of the atrium—the entrance to the throne room—but they didn't seem interested in the conversation. "Well, I actually need to find Cressida. She's waiting for me."

"Oh, sure." Nicos glanced past her toward the palace's front doors, then nodded. "I'll let you get to it, then."

"Thanks, Nicos," Astrea said. "I'll see you later. Let Her Highness know I'll call on her this weekend."

Nicos grinned and waved as Astrea hurried back through the palace. She exited through the same door she'd used to enter, then started back through the hedge maze. Cressida wouldn't be waiting just anywhere for her in the gardens.

Though she passed by it every day on her way to work, Astrea hadn't been to the gazebo in months. It sat on a small island in the middle of the lake next to the observatory, vines crawling up its white marble facade. It had always been a favorite spot for Astrea and her friends when they were children, a secret spot since few people ever ventured so far into the palace compound. Thick trees surrounded the lake, and the only bridge leading to the island made it easy to spot any adults who might've dared try to wrangle Eliana back to the palace.

And now, Cressida was pacing on that very same bridge. Her brilliant jade eyes locked with Astrea's. Orange anxiety spiked around Cressida, followed by gray confusion and green curiosity. That couldn't be good. Cressida was rarely anxious.

As soon as Astrea reached the bridge, Cressida pulled Astrea into the gazebo. "What were *you* doing going into his office?" she hissed.

"What were *you* doing coming out of his office?"

The colors surrounding Cressida shrank and faded to nothing but a low hum of nervous energy that prickled the hair on Astrea's arms. Reaching into the pocket of her white wide-legged trousers, Cressida fished out an envelope. Sighing, Astrea pulled out her own identical letter and shoved it toward her best friend.

"Well, skies damn me," Cressida muttered as she took the envelope. "Let me guess, a new work opportunity?"

"Of course. What's yours?"

The fact that Astrea wasn't the only one being given some special assignment made her feel marginally better. Maybe the emperor was just showing them favor as Eliana's friends.

Cressida's full lips pressed together as she stared down at the envelopes. "Classified."

Astrea laughed. "Classified? What, are you some kind of spy now?"

"Even my father can't know about this one."

That sobered Astrea quickly. Balthazar Nikaphoros was one of the best inventors in the city. He'd built his business, Lodestar Industries, as an engineer and inventor, and now Cressida worked with him. Someday, she'd inherit the business for herself. Both were powerful Metalli—mages who could manipulate earth and metal—and both were fond of experimenting with new technology. Balthazar did plenty of work for the government. If Cressida couldn't tell her father about it, then it had to be serious.

"Not even a hint?" Astrea asked.

"Just . . ." Cressida dropped onto the narrow marble bench in the middle of the gazebo. "A change in my schedule. I'll be spending half my days working on this."

Astrea could make an educated guess about what this was. Emperor Aelius was probably making Cressida work on something for the military. A new explosive, maybe? A new gun? Just the week before, Eliana had told Astrea that the emperor was trying to bolster their armory for the many non-mage soldiers in the army.

"But what about you?" Cressida asked. "Also classified?"

"He instructed me to tell Raela, so I suppose not." Astrea took one last deep breath, then in hushed tones, she told Cressida everything that had happened in the last day: the angry people at the café, the palace messenger, how she'd spent half the night awake. "I was worried Emper—*he'd* found out about . . ."

Cressida nodded. "And I assume that secret is safe."

"It is."

"Then what did he want?"

"He wants me to organize an exhibition about Novarian history ahead of a diplomatic summit and gala at the autumn equinox festival. With Jin."

Cressida held her tongue, though her raised eyebrows gave away her surprise even before it reached Astrea's magic.

"I mean, I can do it, but I don't understand why the emperor chose *me*. There are hundreds of people in the city who could do this. Raela could do this."

"You're smart and capable, that's why. You're one of the smartest people I know."

"Thanks, Cress." Astrea blew out a harsh breath. "I just . . ."

"I know that tone. Out with it."

"I assume you're being paid for whatever you're working on," Astrea said, and Cressida nodded. "I am too. And I know what I want to do with the money, but I don't think you're going to like it."

Astrea had been dreading this conversation. Months before, when Saros had first suggested the option of moving away, Astrea hadn't told Cressida or Eliana. Leaving hadn't seemed possible, so what was the point? But now it was a very real possibility, and Astrea still didn't know what she wanted to do.

Cressida and Astrea had been friends for over half their lives. Saros had known the Nikaphoroses long before Astrea was born. So, too, had Astrea's mother. That was part of why Saros brought Astrea to Kalama all those years ago. Not only had he been able to procure a stable job as imperial tutor and Stargazer, but he'd had friends here.

"Don't tell me you're going to try to buy The White Lily from Carmella."

"No, nothing like that."

"Then what?"

"Saros wants me to leave Kalama."

"On a holiday?"

"Permanently."

Deep blue sadness flashed against the gazebo's white stone. Cressida frowned. "You want to move away?"

"If it means—"

"But what about me?" Cressida asked. "And my parents? Saros? Ellie? We're your family, Az. You can't just leave."

Heavy, oppressive regret overwhelmed Astrea's senses.

"Shit, I'm sorry," Cressida added hurriedly. "I am. I know how impossible your position is. I mean, even yesterday . . . I get it."

"Do you?"

"As much as I possibly can without being in the same position." Cressida offered a tight-lipped smile. "I just don't know what I'd do without you here."

"I know." Astrea smiled, too. "That's the problem I always come back to. I love living here." She didn't need to explain the one thing she didn't like: hiding her magic. Teal understanding blossomed around Cressida. "You could come with me, you know."

"Only if you promise we can go someplace warm."

"Warmer than Kalama?"

"Well, I certainly don't want to move to the Macadian Mountains."

"Fine, no mountains."

Cressida slung her arm around Astrea's shoulders. "Then let's revisit this conversation *after* we get paid, and we can decide exactly where we're going. Who knows, maybe I'll even open that bakery I've always talked about."

Astrea nodded. "Decisions for later."

There was so much that Astrea had to think about in the next few months, but first, she needed to focus on just getting through them in one piece. She didn't even know if Cressida was serious about leaving with her—there was so much she would be leaving behind, too—but it was fun to entertain the idea.

"And what about working with Jin?" Cressida asked. "We haven't even touched on that yet."

"It's something I'd rather ignore for now."

For the last eight years, Astrea had tried to forget everything about Prince Varojin. Everything. And while she couldn't ignore him for the next few months, she at least had a few days before she had to see him. That meant she had a few more days to keep ignoring him.

Cressida pushed herself off the bench. "Fine. So, how about we go out tonight? I think we could both blow off some steam."

"I don't know . . ."

"Oh, come on. You need to have some fun."

There were plenty of places to go on any given night in Kalama: restaurants, bars, clubs, gambling dens. Cressida had always been the more extroverted of the two of them, and she loved getting out of the house. Museums, shopping, cabaret clubs, bars—it didn't matter as long as she was having fun. "Living" was what Cressida called it, though Astrea wasn't so sure she agreed with that assessment. It was often loud and crowded when they went out after work.

Heavy anxiety settled in Astrea's gut. The project. Jin. Leaving Kalama. Saros's odd hours. It was too much for one morning. Maybe Cressida was right. Maybe she needed to do something fun.

"Alright," Astrea said. She took Cressida's outstretched hand and let her pull her to her feet. "Where do you want to go?"

"Just meet me at my house after work. I'll plan everything."

"Nothing excessive," Astrea warned as they started over the bridge.

"Nothing excessive, I promise."

They wound their way back through the palace gardens in comfortable silence and headed for the palace's main gates. Cressida needed to get back to Lodestar's office on the far side of the district, and Astrea had to get to the library.

"Tonight!" Cressida called as Astrea started crossing the road to get to her streetcar stop. "Don't be late!"

CHAPTER 5

Despite the crews setting the city up for Solstice Night, Astrea made decent time on her commute. With the summer solstice festival just a week away, city staff were out decorating buildings, streetlamps, and the parks with all manner of banners, floral arrangements, and posters.

She'd spent the better part of her trek trying to focus on this temporary new job she had and on its benefits, but Astrea couldn't shake the nerves buzzing in her bones. This project was going to be a burden if she still had to do all of her other library work on top of it. Astrea hustled up the last few steps outside the library and pulled open one of the front doors.

Would Raela be frustrated by the development? Or would the library pages be mad at Astrea for having to pick up more of her usual duties?

"Astrea!" Raela called as she hurried toward the door, her white skirt billowing around her like a cloud. "There you are. Are you alright?"

She's not upset? The cold shock of Raela's worry raced over Astrea's skin. *Or she doesn't know yet.*

"I'm fine," Astrea said. "I just got caught up at the palace. Didn't you see my note? I'm sorry, I'll—"

"Oh, no, it's quite alright." Raela waved a hand in the air. "You said you left a note?"

"I told you about the note this morning!" The voice belonged to Serra, one of the library pages. She shuffled out from behind the grand staircase, pulling a cart half-full of books behind her. "I left it on your desk."

"You did?" Raela looped her arm through Astrea's and pulled her toward circulation.

"I did." Serra stopped when she reached the desk, pausing to push a strand of straight, glossy dark hair from her eyes. "You had a meeting this morning, right, Astrea?"

"Yes." Astrea glanced at Raela, her shock still cold and sharp. "What's going on?"

"Didn't you see the paper this morning?"

"The paper?" Astrea asked.

Raela strode around to the other side of the desk, then slammed a newspaper on the top counter. "There's been an attack!"

"A what?"

"A murder!"

When Astrea caught Serra's eye, the page shrugged. Astrea genuinely had no idea what her boss was going on about. Like every city, Kalama had its crimes, but most of them were financial. Some were violent, of course, but murder? She could only recall a couple of murder trials in all the years she'd lived in the capital.

Looking down at the paper, Astrea read the headline: *Woman Found Dead Near Nobleman's Hill . . . Rebels at Fault?*

"This is terrible," Astrea said. Raela perched on the stool behind the desk, her eyes wide. "But . . . why were you worried about me?"

"Isn't that near your streetcar stop?"

She skimmed the rest of the article. It wasn't 'near' her streetcar stop, but it wasn't as far away as Astrea would've imagined either. Nobleman's Hill was heavily patrolled by the emperor's guards and police, so to have someone murdered near the district border—and no suspect in custody—was surprising. Terrifying. The city police and palace guards were supposed to be the best of the best. Kalama was, after all, the seat of imperial power. Not only was most of the royal family here, but so were many other families with power, including those serving in the Senate and on the Imperial Council. And they all lived in or near Nobleman's Hill.

Could it really have been the rebels? Astrea peered down at the newspaper again.

"Just promise me you'll be careful, alright?" Raela asked.

"Yes, of course I'll be careful," Astrea said as she set the paper down.

"Good." Raela nodded, but the orange anxiety sparking around her didn't dissipate. "I want both of you leaving before sundown tonight, workload be damned. Give yourselves plenty of time to get home."

"I have to leave soon anyway, remember?" Serra said. "I have classes."

"Right! Is it Friday already?" Raela sighed. "Leave when you need to, Serra. Astrea and I can handle things here this afternoon."

As Serra abandoned the cart of books and made her way to the back offices, Raela straightened a handful of pens and notepads on the circulation desk.

"So, my note," Astrea said. "The one I left you last night. I have news."

"News?" Raela asked.

"It's actually related to my work here."

"You're not quitting on me, are you?" Raela paused, then groaned. "Oh, please don't tell me they've cut the budget again. I can't run this place without you. We're barely surviving as it is."

Astrea shook her head. "No, nothing like that. The emperor invited me to a meeting."

"Emperor Aelius?" Raela's narrow eyebrows shot up.

Who else? Astrea thought. "Yes," she said. "He'll be sending you more information, but he wants me to start researching Novarian history for some diplomatic gala and exhibition he's hosting in the autumn."

Raela was quiet for a moment, but she finally said, "A gala and exhibition in the autumn?"

"He said it was about a Novarian delegation that's coming—"

"Emperor Aelius has *rarely* been interested in our work, let alone exhibitions and such," Raela said. "I wonder why he's so interested in this."

Astrea had been contemplating the same question since she left the palace. Emperor Aelius was not known for attending cultural events in the city, typically sending his children in his place. Eliana loved a good party, and Prince Kaius could never be outshone by his younger sister. Prince Apelo, the eldest of the four imperial siblings, was rarely in Kalama long enough to actually attend now that he was married with children. And there was, of course, Prince Varojin, but he didn't live in Kalama anymore.

The emperor hosted monthly dinners and the occasional party at the palace, but this was different. This exhibition was publicly political, somehow related to Helosian-Novarian diplomatic relations. It was nothing like the groveling and politicking that went on behind closed doors. Astrea heard about most of it from Eliana, but she'd attended a few such events with both Eliana and Cressida in the past.

"Well, I suppose it doesn't matter why he's interested now," Raela continued. "It's not our job to ask *why,* simply *what* and *how* and *when.* Did he give you any other constraints or have any particular requests?"

Astrea shook her head. "No, just that he wants me to begin researching and that he'll want another meeting down the road."

"Then research you shall," Raela said. "Get started whenever you're ready, and let me know if you need any help. I can have Lena or Felix pull some books for you this weekend."

"I will, thank you."

"And Astrea?" Raela called as Astrea started toward the staircase to put her bag in her office.

She turned. "Yes?"

"I'm serious about you going home early tonight. You shouldn't be out after dark."

As it turned out, working in a library could be incredibly boring sometimes.

Astrea had managed to find several books on Novarian history, but the Great Library's collection didn't include that much on the small country. That probably shouldn't have surprised Astrea, considering that the diplomatic relations between the Helosian Empire and the Grand Duchy of Novaria had been fraught for the last several centuries. Things had improved somewhat with ongoing trade agreements in the last few decades, but Novaria and Helosia's mutual history was . . . bloody. War didn't seem like an ideal topic for what was supposed to be a friendly event.

Instead, Astrea had spent most of the day reshelving books. Patrons were always leaving tomes scattered around the library, and then there were the carts of books being returned from their loan out. Important to keep the library organized? Definitely. Often repetitive and boring? Absolutely. She hadn't even gotten to see what was in that crate Raela had ordered.

So when Astrea finally stepped out onto the library's massive front steps and into the early evening breeze, she closed her eyes and sighed. Blush pink and dusty lavender painted the sky. She still had a good hour before darkness settled over the city, and she could make it back to Cressida's house in less time than that.

The plaza outside the library was quiet, as it usually was at this time. A few university students sat on the benches surrounding the ornate fountain in the middle of the plaza, and Astrea spotted a handful of people exiting the stores on the other side of the street. Somehow, the Scholar's District was always peaceful, especially compared to the rest of the city. Despite her work in the library being boring sometimes, Astrea loved how quiet this part of Kalama was. It was a chance for her magic to take a break and her mind to stop trying to sort through what everyone else was feeling.

As Astrea reached the sidewalk, a sleek emerald car pulled up to the curb, the gold-tinted hubcaps flashing despite the sinking sun. Astrea took two steps back. Who would be coming to the library this late in the day? Raela was inside locking up for the night.

The car's rear passenger window rolled down, revealing a pair of bright golden eyes. "Az!"

Princess Eliana Auris flung the car's door open and stepped out, the dark waves of her hair fluttering in the evening breeze. She was several inches shorter than Astrea, and though they both had curvy figures, Eliana was nearly a perfect hourglass shape. Besides, what Eliana lacked in height she made up for in sheer presence alone. Whether she was walking into a crowded ballroom or quiet café, Eliana could command anyone's attention. Her driver had just hopped out of the front seat to get the door for her, but she waved him off.

Cressida grinned as she slid out from behind Eliana. "I figured Our Highness here could help us get to our destination in style."

Astrea's eyes narrowed. "And what, exactly, is our destination?"

"The Whiskey Dream."

"And before you say anything," Eliana added, cutting off Astrea's groan, "Cressida already told me everything. My father's an ass, but let's forget about all of that and get you drunk."

"Cress, when you said we'd go out tonight, I thought you meant for dinner," Astrea said. She had no plans to get drunk, though it was a favorite pastime for many Kalamians. So were gambling, dancing, and revelry in general. "Don't you think I'm a little underdressed for this?"

"Oh, nonsense. You're dressed perfectly for the occasion," Eliana said, slipping her arm through Astrea's.

Eliana's dress was similar to Astrea's from its transparent sleeves to the skirt falling halfway down her shins. Where Astrea's was lavender with embroidered flowers, though, Eliana's was a bold crimson dusted with sparkles. And though Astrea was in flat brogues, Eliana wore delicate gold heels that glinted in the setting sun. As always, she looked amazing. Cressida was wearing her own signature style for a night out: half a dozen glittering stone bracelets at her wrists and a sleek sleeveless dress in a deep blue that popped against her copper complexion.

"I didn't even wear jewelry," Astrea said, a halfhearted attempt at changing her friends' minds. Once Cressida and Eliana came up with a plan, it was hard to convince them to change course. "And my hair is probably a mess."

"Here," Cressida said, sliding two bracelets from her left wrist. One was silver studded with a row of polished amethyst stones, and the other was a delicate gold chain dotted with opals. "Take these."

Astrea fastened the bracelets on her wrist, then pinned Eliana with a look. "You're fixing my hair on the way."

Eliana squealed. "Deal!"

Cressida was already climbing into the back of the car, Eliana following. Astrea glanced over her shoulder at the library. Raela's warning about going home before dark whispered through Astrea's mind, but she tried to push the worry away as she climbed into the car. If she was going to be safe with anyone, it was with one of the heirs to the throne.

CHAPTER 6

In the heart of the imperial capital, the Whiskey Dream club was the place to be on a Friday night. The dimly-lit space was a sea of bodies dripping in silks and glittering jewels. Chandeliers sparkled above, but the heavy red drapes and black-painted walls absorbed the little light they gave off. The smell of blue lotus—the expensive, potent drug popular among the upper echelons of Kalamian society—choked the air, a guarantee that, one way or another, the patrons' heads would be swimming before the night ended.

"You alright?" Cressida asked as she followed Astrea through the crowd.

"Yes," Astrea replied over her shoulder. "Fine."

A woman at a nearby card table shouted, though whether it was an excited or angry sound, Astrea couldn't be sure. She flinched and focused on Eliana ahead of them. Nicos had joined them outside the Whiskey Dream as soon as their car pulled up, and he was now clearing their way toward the bar.

Crowds were a challenge for Astrea's magic. Emotions coming at her from every direction weren't easy to manage, sift through, and understand. She wanted to shut it down, to rein her magic in until she felt nothing at all, but the few times she'd tried had given her a headache. There was no stopping it.

"You sure?" Cressida asked.

"I'll be fine." The little control Astrea did have over her magic let her block out a portion of the room. She'd always imagined it to be a sort of bubble, one she could expand and contract if she tried. Though Astrea couldn't shut out everything, she could pull that bubble in toward herself until she only experienced the emotions of those within a ten-foot radius.

"Come on," Eliana said, turning around to grab Astrea's hand. "Let's get you a drink."

The crowd parted as club goers realized who was in their midst. The Whiskey Dream, with its shared border of Nobleman's Hill and the Market District, attracted a certain crowd; it was a high-end club for big spenders. Most of the other people here were either noble by birth or marriage, or their families simply had money. Astrea had only been here a handful of times, but the other patrons respected Eliana's space and presence. They were her peers, after all. Getting on her bad side could mean their downfall at court.

Astrea followed Eliana to the oval-shaped bar set near the back half of the club. A wall splitting the middle of the bar was lined with shelves of liquor bottles in every color and size imaginable. Several bartenders dressed in crisp black and white uniforms circled the bar, taking orders and making drinks. Eliana waved at one, a heavyset man with sand-hued skin and curly blond hair. He smiled, nodded, and pulled out three cocktail glasses.

"Did you just order for us?" Astrea asked, half-amused as a few patrons bowed to Eliana and vacated their seats. Nicos ignored the empty seat on Eliana's right, instead standing just behind her. Astrea and Cressida sat on her left. "How often are you here, Ellie?"

Eliana batted her eyelashes, then gathered her skirts and lifted herself onto her barstool. "You know my father encourages us to go into the city."

"And besides," Cressida said, leaning on the bar and twisting one of her bracelets, "it's the *perfect* place to meet with her contemporaries. The young, upcoming, and upstanding citizens of the Helosian Empire."

Cressida's voice was half-teasing, half-serious, but she wasn't wrong. The crowd was mostly made up of people around their own age, though a few seemed to be closer to Saros's generation, and some older still. Most people here were amused or eager, especially those sitting around the card tables to one side of the club. Next to that was a small stage where a tan woman in a glittering, short-hemmed dress was singing with a band, her voice deep and sweet. On the other side of the club were sofas, settees, armchairs, and cocktail tables, and beyond that were several doors and a set of stairs leading up to a mezzanine. The lights of an elevator lit up next to the stairs, then opened as a person in a wheelchair exited the lift.

As Astrea settled into her seat at the bar, she pulled her magic in closer toward her body and started to relax. Asking Eliana where Emperor Aelius had gotten the idea to hire Astrea and Cressida had crossed Astrea's mind, but now didn't seem like the time or place for that conversation.

"So, are you going with me to Solstice Night this year?" Eliana asked as she leaned over the bar.

"You think I wouldn't?" Cressida asked.

"I know *you* will." Eliana fixated on Astrea. "But what about you?"

Solstice Night. It was a night of celebration, with giant bonfires lit across the city and empire to welcome the official start of summer. As the imperial princess, Eliana always attended, as did Kaius and Apelo. The emperor even made an appearance most years, though he never stayed long. Astrea and Cressida usually attended as Eliana's guests.

"You must come so you can see my gown," Eliana continued. "I think it's the best one I've picked yet."

"Oh?" Cressida smiled. "Let me guess what color it is."

Eliana stuck her tongue out. "It's tradition for the imperial family to wear red," she said. "But I got something extra special this year."

"Are you going to give us a hint?" Astrea asked.

"No, because then you won't come to see it."

Astrea twisted the bracelets on her wrist and rolled her eyes. "You know I'm going to go, Ellie." She didn't love the festival—it was crowded, loud, and difficult to control her magic in—but if Eliana wanted her there, she could at least make an appearance.

"Well I'm still not telling you. Just know that it's going to be a show-stopper."

"Right," Cressida said, "because it wouldn't be a truly magical event unless the papers write a story about you."

"It's good for the economy," Eliana replied with a demure shrug. "I buy from Kalamian dressmakers, the newspapers report it, and then those same dressmakers get more business. Besides," she continued, a wicked smile spreading across her painted lips, "I can't very well let Kaius get the attention."

"Skies forbid Prince Kaius gets some press." Nicos had finally spoken up, and though his tone was teasing, Astrea knew what they were all thinking. Prince Kaius Auris didn't need any press attention; his ego was already bigger than was good for him.

"Your Imperial Highness."

Two men had seemingly materialized at Eliana's side. The one who spoke was handsome, and his dark brown eyes seemed familiar and warm. His companion, a man with copper eyes, looked on with cool indifference.

"Oh, Lord Diallo," Eliana said. Her shoulders pushed back slightly as she smiled. "Bernard. How are you? How's your father?"

That's where I know him from. Bernard Diallo, the younger son of the Duke Diallo. Bernard had held the door open for Astrea earlier that morning at the palace, and she was sure she'd met him here before. She still didn't know who the other man was, though she'd seen him that morning too. A well-dressed guard, perhaps? Or a rich friend?

Bernard smiled, one dimple appearing in his left cheek. "He's well, thank you, Your Imperial Highness. I wonder," he said, eyes darting to Astrea and Cressida, "might I pull you away from your friends for a moment? We have business to discuss."

To Eliana's credit, her smile never faltered despite the rusty annoyance spiking around her. That was Eliana, though, always playing the role of princess when she needed to. She was kind to everyone she encountered, and Eliana somehow both attracted attention and commanded privacy at the same time. Still, that kind of presence wouldn't stop an eager young nobleman if he saw an opening.

"Of course," Eliana said. She turned back to her friends. "I'll be back shortly, alright?" When Astrea nodded, Eliana looked up at Nicos, then back to Bernard. "Shall we?"

As Eliana, Nicos, Bernard, and the unknown man all disappeared into the crowd, Astrea finally turned back to Cressida. "Well, now what?" she asked, and Cressida grinned.

"First, we take our drinks."

The bartender had returned with three drinks in short-stemmed glasses. The liquid was a vibrant pink, and when Astrea lifted her glass toward the dim lights behind the bar, she saw gold floating in the cocktail.

"Just try it, miss," the bartender said, his thin lips pulling into a smile. "Her Imperial Highness orders it for a reason."

A bartender's word wouldn't normally inspire confidence in Astrea; she didn't drink much alcohol aside from wine at dinner. But Eliana had good taste, and Cressida was already bringing her glass to her lips. Astrea lifted hers, breathing in the lush scent of raspberries and clear liquor. She took a sip. It was surprisingly light and smooth despite the slight burn of alcohol.

"So," Cressida said as Astrea swallowed another mouthful of the cock-tail, "how are you doing, really?" She leaned against the bar.

Astrea shrugged. "Fine."

"Really?"

"Not great," Astrea admitted, then cringed. A few seats away, an umber-skinned woman with an elaborate crystal hair piece shrieked. Drunken glee skittered over Astrea's skin. "But I don't want to talk about it, please. Not now."

"You're right." Cressida tapped her short painted nails on the marble counter. The sparkles in the green lacquer nail polish caught the bar's dim overhead lights. "I said tonight would be fun, and I mean it. So what do you want to do? Do you want to play cards?"

Cards didn't sound fun. Astrea had never really bothered to learn the rules, and she was terrible at judging the hands she was dealt. "No, not cards."

"People watching?" Cressida offered. There wasn't much to do at a Kalamian club besides gamble, drink, smoke, or people watch. But it wouldn't require Astrea spending—and losing—the little money she had on her.

"Sure." Astrea turned in her seat. "You pick first."

They'd made up the game when they were still teenagers. One of them would pick a person from the crowd, then make up some kind of story about their day or life. The stories would get progressively more ridiculous until someone laughed, and whoever laughed first was the loser. When they were teens, the loser simply lost. But now that they were older, the loser had to finish whatever alcoholic beverage they had. It was a surefire way to get drunk in a place like this.

"How about . . ." Cressida trailed off. A bulky man dressed in a pinstripe suit headed straight toward them, waving a pale pink hand high above the crowd.

"Who's that?" Astrea asked.

"An old friend." Setting her drink on the bar, Cressida stepped in front of Astrea, blocking the man from her line of sight before Astrea could get a better look at him. "My dad's old friend, I mean. We've done some business with him."

"What business?" Astrea asked.

"A few things for the club. He owns it. I'll be right back."

Cressida spun on her heel, hurrying toward the man. He didn't look old enough to be Balthazar Nikaphoros's 'old' friend. The man couldn't have been past his midthirties, which would make him barely a decade older than Cressida and Astrea. They moved through the crowd, disappearing behind one of the doors on the far wall.

Now what? Astrea sighed. Eliana was nowhere to be found either. *How do my friends take me out after a long day and I somehow still end up alone?*

Gathering up the three drinks still sitting on the bar, Astrea carried them to a sofa and low cocktail table that had just opened up. If she was going to wait for her friends, she might as well be comfortable. After setting the drinks down, Astrea gathered her skirts around herself and plopped onto the middle of the couch.

Hopefully Cressida and Eliana wouldn't be long. She'd play her and Cressida's game in the meantime, just on her own.

Astrea picked the singer on stage first. The woman had just started a new song, this one in Delian. If anyone here was bothered by it, they didn't show it. All five continental languages and that of the Taipoli Islands were spoken in Kalama thanks to its diverse population and tourism industry, but people could also get defensive when tensions flared around the Corsyca issue. With Helosia, Delia, and Zaikud in all-out war—a real free-for-all according to the papers—it was a surprise to see everyone in such a good mood.

What's your story? Astrea asked silently, trying to direct her magic toward the woman. A mix of pride and concentration flowed from her, but other than that, Astrea came up short.

Maybe the singer was like many of the people who came to Kalama, someone searching for the opportunity and culture so abundant here. But like many of the people who came to the city, was she disappointed to find out it was hard to get ahead? That despite the wealth, glamour, and beauty of the city, there was also a lot of inequality and struggle?

Still no sign of her friends in the crowd. Astrea frowned. Eliana being gone didn't surprise her, though what Cressida might have to talk about with that man, she had no idea. It couldn't wait? She stood, her drink in hand, to get a better look at the space. As she turned, Astrea found Lord Bernard Diallo's friend waiting next to her. She jumped, her drink sloshing in its glass.

"Skies," she muttered, checking the front of her dress. At least her drink hadn't spilled.

"You're Astrea Sovna, right?" he asked.

"Yes . . . sir," she said, trying to remember her manners as she set her glass on the table next to her. "That's me."

"And your uncle is Saros Sovna, the Stargazer?"

"Indeed, he is."

The man stood so close she could make out the pores on his short nose, even in the club's minimal lighting. His breath didn't smell of alcohol or blue lotus.

"Do you think you might be able to secure me a meeting with him?"

What would this man want a meeting with her uncle for? And why didn't he just go through channels at the palace? Anyone could schedule a meeting with Saros.

"I'm sorry," Astrea said, "I don't believe I caught your name. You are . . . ?"

He didn't offer his pale hand for a shake as he said, "Victor Nazarov."

"You know, Mister Nazarov—"

"Lord Nazarov."

"I'm sorry?"

"It's *Lord* Nazarov."

"Apologies, my lord." Astrea cleared her throat and avoided his intense stare. "Anyone can request time to meet with my uncle. Just ask someone at the palace about it, and they'll point you in the right direction. I'm sure my uncle would be happy to speak with you." How Lord Nazarov didn't know that as a nobleman was beyond her, but Astrea really didn't care.

Nazarov's expression faltered slightly, but he smiled, revealing perfectly straight teeth as he somehow moved closer to her. Astrea tried to take a step back, but the sofa behind her blocked her path.

"I saw you earlier today, you know," he said. "At the palace. That was you this morning, wasn't it?"

She swallowed.

"Did you know who I was then? You didn't use my title this morning."

A heavy cold pressed against Astrea, unyielding. She couldn't place the feeling. Annoyance? No. Hate? That didn't seem right either. Goose bumps prickled her arms. Where were Eliana and Cressida when she needed them? *Skies damn both of you.* Astrea didn't recognize anyone else in the crowd.

"I didn't know who you were this morning, my lord," Astrea finally said, trying to keep her face neutral. "I apologize for any offense—"

"All could be forgiven if you help me get that meeting, and if you spend some time with me."

She didn't know whether to laugh or be offended, but Astrea was suddenly very, very tired. She didn't have the energy for this, not after the day she'd had.

"Play a few rounds of cards," the young nobleman continued. "Have a few drinks. Take a chance and see what happens, Miss Sovna. You might be surprised by what the shadows can offer."

Is he speaking in riddles now, or does he fancy himself a poet?

"My lord." Astrea edged away as subtly as she could, hoping he didn't notice her putting space between them. "Again, I apologize for any offense, but I need to be going. I'm sure Her Imperial Highness is looking for me. As I said, if you need help, just ask someone at the palace about a meeting with my uncle."

Astrea took another step to the side, turning without waiting for his response. Pain flared in her wrist. Nazarov pressed the bracelets Cressida had loaned her right into her skin as he yanked her back around. A flash of obsidian surrounded him. Astrea had never seen that color before, and again, she couldn't name whatever it was that Nazarov felt.

"You would deny me?" he asked, voice hardly above a whisper as the color dissipated and that cold returned. A lock of his dark hair fell into his eyes, but he didn't brush it away. "Do you forget your place, Stargazer's niece?"

Who was this man? She'd never met him before tonight, yet he was making demands? Astrea gritted her teeth together, but the warning in Nazarov's eyes made her think twice about her choice of words. He was a nobleman, and this man surely had connections. He could make her life—or Saros's life—miserable if he wanted to.

Astrea tried to pull away, but Nazarov's grip tightened. If she were any other kind of mage, she'd show some strength and draw attention to them both. She had a basic command over light with her celestial magic, but it wasn't like she could use it here anyway. So Astrea pulled back again, this time harder, as she held the man's gaze. That's when she noticed him looking over her shoulder.

"Is there a problem here?"

The last of her breath left Astrea's lungs in a whoosh. It couldn't be him, not here. Not tonight.

"Your Imperial Highness." Nazarov didn't stutter. He didn't even flush red as he let go of Astrea's wrist. "I didn't know you were back in the city."

Astrea's gut tightened.

"Get lost, Victor." That familiar, unwelcome voice was so close to her ear that Astrea could feel the breath tickling her skin. "Now."

Part of Astrea wanted to thank her savior, and the other part wanted to give him a long overdue kick in the shin.

Victor Nazarov simply inclined his head, then turned and retreated, never once looking back at Astrea as he melted into the crowd beyond.

Astrea sighed. She had no other choice. She had to turn around.

Sucking in a heavy breath, she shifted. She was met first by the sight of broad shoulders, then thin lips, as she slowly looked up into the most brilliant pair of golden eyes flecked with amber.

Prince Varojin Auris smiled. "Hello, Astrea."

CHAPTER 7

"Are you alright?" the prince asked, breaking the silence. "Was he bothering you?"

Astrea still couldn't believe what she was seeing. Prince Varojin—Jin, as she used to call him—standing in front of her, looking entirely relaxed despite the chaotic club around them.

"I'm fine."

She stole another glance at Jin. He wasn't wearing his military uniform, though she should've expected that. After all, Jin was here in Kalama, not wherever he was currently stationed with the imperial army. Where many of the club goers were wearing rich fabrics in a rainbow of jewel tones, Jin was astoundingly casual. He wore a black blazer over a black shirt with a low neckline. The rest of his outfit was equally monochromatic: black slacks and brogues. The only thing standing out was the gold chain at his neck and the gold rings on his fingers.

They hadn't spoken in years, and she'd only caught glimpses of him the few times he'd returned to Kalama since he left. His rich brown hair had the same soft curl it always had, and he now sported a close-cropped beard. He was no longer the awkward teenager he was years ago. Gone were the gangly limbs and too-tall height, replaced by a body hardened by his time in the military.

Jin had grown up, and it suited him.

"You look well." The words tumbled from Astrea's mouth before she had a chance to stop herself, and she was grateful for the low light in the club. Her cheeks were on fire. *Foolish,* she thought. *So foolish.*

"And you look even more beautiful than I remember," he said in that honeyed voice of his.

The rage she'd felt toward Victor bubbled just underneath her skin again. Jin may have been a prince, but he didn't get to just come back like this, after eight long years, and pretend to flirt with her.

"What are you doing here?" she asked, the words slicing the air between them.

One of his thick eyebrows quirked up. "I could ask you the same thing. This doesn't seem like the kind of place you'd go on a Friday night."

The woman on stage had changed songs, the lyrics now in smooth Helosian. A few in the crowd near the card tables started clapping as the band's tempo picked up.

"Your sister thinks it's the perfect place to unwind."

Jin smirked. "Yes, I suppose this is someplace she would like."

This was the last conversation Astrea wanted to be having tonight—or ever. On her list of people she wanted to talk to, Prince Varojin Auris was near the bottom.

"I'm told we're going to be working together on a project." As Jin said the words, Astrea thought he sounded unsure, but she couldn't tell. The crowd was too loud, the emotions of those around her too amplified. She couldn't focus.

"Yes, I'm aware."

Jin's eyebrows rose again. "You're aware?"

"I spoke with His Imperial Majesty this morning."

"His Imperial Majesty?" Jin smiled, that skies damned smile she used to adore. "Perhaps, if you're not busy, we could talk now—"

"I really need to go find my friends."

Astrea started in the opposite direction. She didn't even know if it was the *right* direction, but it was away from Jin, and that was good enough.

Talking to him at all was a bad idea, but talking to him about the project here, in a club filled with loud music, louder patrons, and blue lotus smoke was a worse idea. If they were going to do this and do this efficiently, then they were going to have to sit down in the quiet of the day and hammer out the details. She was not going to let him screw this opportunity up for her.

Jin's hand landed on her shoulder, his touch featherlight. It was gentle, almost asking permission while Victor's grip had been demanding. Astrea stopped and glanced back at him.

"Astrea, please—" he started.

"Az!"

Astrea closed her eyes as Jin's hand dropped from her shoulder. She turned, already bracing for the many, many questions Cressida would be asking her when they were finally alone.

"Hey, Cress," Astrea said, trying but failing to smile as her best friend strode toward them. She was alone this time.

"Az, I—" Cressida cut herself off as she looked over Astrea's shoulder. This close up, it would be impossible for her to miss Jin.

After all, they'd also been friends once upon a time. All four of them.

Not anymore, Astrea thought.

"Hey, Cressida," Jin said.

"Well, skies damn me," Cressida muttered as Astrea pivoted to stand by her side. "You're the last person I expected to see tonight, and least of all in this place. How are you, Jin?"

"All things considered?" Jin shrugged. "I've had worse nights."

"Do you know where Ellie and Nicos are?" Astrea asked, putting all of her focus on Cressida. Curious as she was, Astrea wasn't going to ask him for any clarification. "I'd really like to go home now."

"Oh." Cressida looked from Jin back to Astrea. "I don't know, I haven't seen her since I left to talk to Osin—"

"Osin's here tonight?" Jin asked.

That must have been the man Cressida was talking to, but why would Jin have a mutual friend with Cressida's father? Sure, Balthazar did a lot of work at the palace, but that didn't actually mean he and Jin would share a social circle.

Balthazar's connection to the palace and the Sovnas was actually part of how Cressida had met the imperial siblings years before. He'd often brought Cressida on jobs with him, usually leaving her with Astrea and Saros while he worked. Because Saros tutored the imperial siblings in Novarian and astronomy, and because Astrea had been allowed to join those lessons, Astrea had met Eliana and Jin. And once Cressida had started spending more time at the observatory, all four of them became inseparable.

Too many questions for one day, Astrea thought. *And I shouldn't even care.* Who Jin was friends with and how he met them was none of her business.

"I think he went back to his office," Cressida said, her hand finding Astrea's. "Well, good luck, Jin. I'm sure Osin will be happy to speak with you. We'd better go find your sister."

Cressida steered Astrea away from the cramped seating area without waiting for Jin's response, but he did call out, "See you on Monday!"

The club seemed louder now, though Astrea wasn't sure if it was from being overwhelmed by the moment or if people were actually getting louder. It may have been the latter, as club goers were pressing in around the two of them as they walked.

"Where did Ellie go?" Astrea asked.

"I'm not sure." Cressida scanned the room. "Look for Nicos." The guard would be hard to miss in this crowd. Not only was he still wearing his crimson uniform, but he was taller than most.

Astrea searched the crowd as they headed toward the bar. She still didn't see either Nicos or Eliana, but she also didn't see Jin. That was something at least.

"What do we do if we can't find her?" Astrea asked. "We can't stay here all night until her impromptu meetings are done."

"Are you alright? You don't look so good," Cressida said.

"I'm fine." It was the second time Astrea had told that lie in just a few minutes. Her face was still on fire, and now her pulse thundered in her ears. "If we can find Ellie, we can go. Come on, we should split up."

"No." Cressida's hand on her forearm made Astrea pause. "What was going on over there?"

"I don't know."

"You don't know?" Cressida arched one perfectly sculpted eyebrow. "Astrea Sovna, you're a terrible liar." Her voice lowered as she continued, "Jin's back already?"

"I don't want to talk about this, Cress," Astrea warned, hoping there was as much edge to her voice as she wanted. "I'm *fine,* but I need to go. This place is . . . overwhelming." There was too much noise and too many people, too many emotions, too many colors. The club was caving in around Astrea, threatening to crush her into a million pieces. What little control she'd had over her magic earlier in the night was gone.

Cressida pressed her lips together, then nodded. "Go wait outside. I'll be right there, with or without Ellie."

As Cressida melted back into the crowd, Astrea made her way toward the club's front double doors. There was a small host station there, and a young redheaded man was writing on a notepad. It was a long shot, but she had to ask.

"Excuse me?" The man looked up at Astrea and nodded, so she continued, "Have you seen a man here in a red uniform? I came with him, and now I can't seem to find him."

The redhead's thin eyebrows raised. "Actually, yes, I believe he just stepped outside a few minutes ago."

"Thank you!" Astrea called, already hurrying out the doors.

The sidewalk outside the Whiskey Dream was empty. A handful of cars idled out front, their drivers either talking among themselves or leaning against the driver's side doors. No imperial uniforms in sight. Maybe the host had been mistaken?

An engine rumbled around the corner, and after two more cars had passed—one cherry red and the other blue—Astrea spotted what she thought was Eliana's emerald green car. It pulled up to the curb behind the line of other vehicles, then the engine shut off. Nicos climbed out of one side, Eliana's driver out the other. Astrea almost sprinted to them but forced herself to slow down.

"Nicos," Astrea said as she met him halfway between the club and the car. "Where's Ellie? Cress is looking for her, but we really need to be going—"

"You can't find her?" The guard shook his head, a smirk pulling at the corners of his lips. Tart amusement and bitter jealousy coated Astrea's tongue. "I knew she was going to do this."

"Do what?"

"You know how she is," he said, starting toward the building. "I ask her to stay put at the bar to wait for you and Cress, and she's probably off talking to some other . . . well, it doesn't matter. You know she can't resist entertaining a meeting even in the strangest of places."

That was true. Eliana never turned down the invitation to listen to her peers, the people she might someday lead. A night club didn't seem like the ideal spot for a meeting, but what did Astrea know of politics and courtly behavior?

"Can you go find them?" Astrea asked. "I can't go back in there."

Nicos frowned, his thick auburn eyebrows knitting together. "Why not?"

"I just can't."

She'd expected him to press the issue, but after holding her gaze for a few seconds, Nicos said, "Alright. Let me go find them. Why don't you go ahead and wait in the car?"

"Do I have to?" The cool night air sounded better than the car.

"You've seen the headlines, haven't you?" Nicos gazed over her shoulder, his eyes darting around. "I really think it's for the best."

Astrea turned, surveying the street as the headline Raela had shown her earlier in the day repeated in her mind. *Woman found dead near Nobleman's Hill . . . rebels at fault?*

Other than the nearby drivers and a few pedestrians on the opposite side of the road, she was the only one outside. It wasn't surprising for Kalama's streets to be quiet now that it was past the dinner hour. Everyone was either at home or at another restaurant or club. Still, something about the scene seemed . . . off, like the shadows were darker than normal.

After taking one last look at the Whiskey Dream, Astrea walked over to the imperial car, opened the door, and climbed into the back seat. She was more than ready to go home.

CHAPTER 8

Going to work was far from what Astrea wanted to do on a Sunday, but when Raela had called a half hour before and said Felix was still out sick, Astrea hadn't had a reason to not go in. She wasn't doing anything important. But now, as she found herself cutting through the palace gardens, Astrea almost regretted saying yes.

She was going to have to deal with the Great Library enough in the next few months as she worked on this project with Prince Varojin. Any time she could spend away from it might be a blessing.

Or, she reminded herself, *this could be a good opportunity to do some preliminary work ahead of tomorrow.* Any chance she had to do this right, she had to take it.

As Astrea passed the palace's main gate, its gold-painted details glinting in the brilliant sunshine, a high-pitched voice caught her attention. Eliana stood just outside the gate, Nicos and another familiar form nearby.

"Are you following me?" Eliana asked, jabbing her finger into her brother's face.

Prince Kaius scoffed. "I think I have better things to do than follow you."

"Oh really? Because you rarely leave the palace grounds unless it's to go out to a club, and now you just happen to be loitering nearby when I'm headed out?"

Astrea hesitated. She had no business interfering in imperial sibling drama, but she had to walk that way to go to her streetcar stop. A steady wave of annoyance rushed out from Eliana, heavy against Astrea's chest. What, exactly, was she so upset about?

"The world doesn't revolve around you, Eliana."

"No, but you seem to, *Kaius*."

"What makes you think you're so important that I care what you're doing?" Kaius asked. "You're not even the spare heir. You're the spare to the spare. Whatever you're doing doesn't matter."

Crimson rage exploded around Eliana. This was not good. Eliana and Kaius both had short tempers, and their fights never ended well.

"I do more than—" she started, but Astrea moved toward them.

"Your Imperial Highnesses!" Astrea exclaimed, plastering the biggest smile she could on her face. Whatever Eliana was going to say next died on her tongue. "I didn't expect to see you today."

"Miss Sovna." Kaius sniffed as he glanced in her direction, then looked back at his younger sister. "Don't be so paranoid, Eliana. I wasn't following you." Without so much as a backward glance, he shoved past Astrea and disappeared behind the palace compound's gates.

Kaius shared the Auris sibling's striking appearance: tan skin, dark hair, those golden Auris eyes, and the straight nose. He was nearly the same height as Jin. But that was where the comparisons stopped. Where Eliana was kind and eager to serve, Kaius was entitled and eager to take. He'd always been Astrea's least favorite of the four siblings, and she didn't even know Apelo that well.

"Is something going on?" Astrea asked when Kaius was out of earshot. "Are you alright, Ellie?"

"I'm fine," Eliana muttered. Nicos shook his head. "Are you going somewhere?"

"Work." Astrea gestured toward the streetcar, now rumbling down the road. She held back a sigh. "I was, anyway. One of the pages called out today, and Raela needs the help."

Eliana looked back at the streetcar, then to Astrea again, her perfectly shaped eyebrows drawing together. "I'm headed that way anyway. Walk with me."

The next trolley on Astrea's route wouldn't come by for a good half hour, and she could almost make it to the Scholar's District in that much time. Besides, she hadn't gotten to see much of Eliana lately. A walk would be nice.

"Alright, let's go."

Nobleman's Hill was one of the quieter districts in the capital, its neat streets of sprawling townhouses and upscale businesses less frequented than those in the Market District and beyond. Most of the wealthier citizens who lived here didn't seem to be out and about, though that wasn't unusual on weekends. They were probably all sleeping in after another night at the clubs.

"Are you really alright?" Astrea asked, keeping her voice low despite the empty streets. Nicos remained several paces behind them, the most privacy he could really offer Eliana when they were outside of the palace. "What Kaius said—"

"What he said doesn't matter," Eliana snapped. Then she sighed. "I'm sorry. I'm not angry with you. He just drives me absolutely mad sometimes."

Astrea hesitated. If Eliana didn't want to talk about this, she wouldn't push, but Eliana's emotions contradicted her words. The slow, deep burn of shame reached Astrea's senses first, but numbness seemed to be winning the battle for dominance.

"I hope you know it's alright if you're bothered by what he said. Your brother's an asshole."

Eliana snorted. "That's an understatement."

When Eliana offered no other commentary, Astrea decided to change the subject. "So, where are you going this morning?"

"I need to pick up my dress for Solstice Night."

"Ah, the infamous dress I'm not allowed to see."

"I'm perfectly serious about that." Eliana's red-painted lips pulled into a sly smile. "You're not allowed to see it until you come to the festival."

"And I was serious the other night when I said I'd go with you."

"Good, otherwise my plan would be ruined."

Eliana's gaze was trained on the empty sidewalk ahead of them. A few people had crossed the street, their surprise cooling Astrea's skin despite the sunny afternoon. Eliana went into the city often, but she was usually driven around. This wasn't the first time Astrea had seen something like this happen, though. Helosians respected the imperial family's privacy. Civilians generally left them alone and let them go about their days.

"What plan?" Astrea asked warily.

"Oh, nothing."

Looking over her shoulder, Astrea glared at Nicos. "What plan?"

He held his hands up in mock surrender. "That's none of my business."

"What plan, Ellie?" It was rarely a good thing when Eliana came up with secret plans for their friend group.

"I *may* have ordered you a dress for Solstice Night," she said slowly.

"You may have, or you did?"

"Maybe I'm picking up two gowns today." Eliana shrugged as they turned a corner. The streets here were still wide, but the gardens in front of the townhouses were smaller and less formal than those closer to the palace. "Consider it a thank you gift."

"A thank you gift?" Astrea echoed. A couple was heading toward them on the sidewalk, but the two men paused, then tilted their heads to Eliana before crossing the street. "Why are you buying me a gift? I haven't done anything."

"You're helping Jin."

Astrea had been dreading this conversation. She'd barely discussed it with Cressida two days before, and now Eliana knew, too. Over the years, both women had pressed Astrea for details about why she avoided Jin on the rare occasion he was back in Kalama. Eventually, they'd simply accepted that Astrea wasn't willing to talk about it.

"I don't need a gift, Ellie," Astrea started, but by the set of Eliana's jaw, she knew this was going to be a losing battle. "You're going to buy it for me no matter what I say, aren't you?"

"Trust me, Az," Eliana said, a spark of joy in her voice, "you're going to look incredible."

To Eliana Auris, incredible might mean elegant and understated or couture and attention-grabbing. Astrea just hoped the gown was the former. Her one consolation was that Eliana knew her preferences—and sensitivities—when it came to fabrics. Even if the gown was extravagant, there was no doubt it'd be comfortable.

"Well, thank you. I'll see it on Friday?"

"On Friday," Eliana agreed.

They walked the next two blocks in silence, passing beautiful home after beautiful home. The architecture was one of the things Astrea loved about Kalama. The large arched windows, terraces framed with delicate wrought iron trim, columns, tiled roofs, and bright colors all added to the city's charm. As they ambled by a few street vendors and their patrons, Eliana murmured her hellos. *That'll give them something to brag about to their friends for days,* Astrea thought.

As they crossed another road and turned onto a pedestrian-only street, Eliana asked, "You really have to work today?"

"You say that like you're one to take breaks."

"Fair enough."

"And how is work?" Astrea asked. "I feel like we haven't gotten to see each other in ages."

"I know, and I'm sorry," Eliana said. "It's been so busy around the palace. I'm still working on that trade agreement with Tornama, which I think is actually going well."

"Oh?"

Eliana had been working on the agreement with the Republic of Tornama since early spring, and it was proving to be a source of both constant work and headaches for the princess. She'd spent more than one night lamenting that fact to Astrea and Cressida over dinner or drinks.

"The council is likely to vote to approve it. I think my father will appreciate the terms."

"That's great, Ellie, really, after all these months."

"Well, you know how it is." Eliana sighed. "Everyone wants to get the best deal for themselves. Tornama has so many exports we can make use of here, especially with the Delian embargo, but agreeing on a pricing structure was . . . difficult. My father's been breathing down my neck about it."

It was easy to forget that Eliana's job was more than just going to galas and exhibition openings, more than the gorgeous clothing and accessories she sported. Eliana was one of her father's advisors and held a senior position on the Imperial Council, a group of nobles who advised the government. She was just twenty-three, so young to be in such a role. Though he was three years older than her, Prince Kaius was the only other person on the council remotely close to her age. Eliana had also been traveling more lately, another sign of her father's trust in her to act on his behalf.

"It sounds a bit exciting," Astrea said.

"Trust me, it's anything but. Everyone acts like your friend until you try to stand your ground on an issue." Eliana grew quiet as they passed a café, and a few of the customers waved at her. When they were alone again, Eliana continued, "I hate the politics. Like yesterday, I simply tried to *suggest* peace talks with the Zaikudi and Delians, and Kaius shot me down in front of the entire council."

That explains their fight outside the palace.

"I'm sorry about the meeting."

"Trying to create the *smallest* change and getting stonewalled at every turn is frustrating."

"I can only imagine."

Even with Astrea's job, even with her strange situation and her secret, Eliana's worries were far bigger. Her job came with bigger risks, bigger rewards, and more responsibilities. She was responsible for an entire empire where Astrea just had to worry about books—and now this exhibition and gala.

That wasn't entirely true anymore. The exhibition and gala *were* connected to the empire. The emperor had suggested it was all to strengthen Helosia's relationship with Novaria. Astrea swallowed hard. What if she screwed it up?

"It's faster if you turn up ahead," Nicos said as he drew closer to them. "And we can avoid that."

A mass of people had congregated near the border of Nobleman's Hill and the Market District, but they didn't seem to be creating anything more than a nuisance for the cars and trolleys that needed to get by. There were maybe two dozen people, and someone was cleaning bright red paint off the side of a tall building. Half of a star and circle were visible, but a Tidebacker splashed more water on the wall before Astrea could get a good look.

Confusion, anxiety, and frustration seeped from the crowd. Astrea pulled her magic back toward herself as much as she could. Despite the graffiti, those feelings weren't anything out of the ordinary in the city. Kalama was a vibrant place, the people passionate and welcoming, but it had its downsides. It was crowded, loud, and fast-paced. *Not* getting confused, nervous, or annoyed was impossible.

"What do you think is going on?" Eliana hesitated, green curiosity flaring to life around her.

"It's best we don't find out, Ellie," Nicos said, his deep voice dropping to barely more than a murmur.

"And why not?" Eliana asked. "Those are my people. This is my city. It's my job to make sure they're alright."

"And it's my job to make sure *you're* alright," Nicos said. "Whatever it is, the police will handle it."

"It could be a protest," Astrea offered as Nicos steered them down a pedestrian-only street. Protests weren't unusual in Kalama, especially near some of the embassies and hotels that housed diplomats and foreign dignitaries when they were in the city.

"Perhaps a really talented street performer?" Eliana suggested.

"Oh, I doubt that," Nicos said, and Astrea agreed. This wasn't the part of the city street performers frequented. They stuck to their usual spots downtown, in the parks, and near the docks and train station to attract tourists' attention.

Thankfully, the crowd didn't seem to notice Eliana's presence, and they made it to her shop after just a few more turns down side streets.

"Here we are." Eliana stopped in front of an unassuming building. The first floor was white-washed brick, the second and third stories were pink stucco like the surrounding buildings. Wind rustled through the leaves of a few nearby oak trees.

"I should be going," Astrea said. "I need to get to the library."

"Don't work too hard," Eliana teased.

"Only if you don't, either."

Eliana stuck her tongue out, then waved as Astrea started down the road. Going back past the crowd was actually the fastest way to get to the Great Library from here; this part of Kalama was full of side streets, awkward roads, and roundabout ways to navigate the city. She didn't love the idea of passing by the crowd again, but it would be faster by at least a quarter of an hour.

It didn't take Astrea long to backtrack. The crowd was still there, and the paint the Tidebacker had tried to wash off just a few minutes before was smeared across the tan brick building. Confusion and disgust drifted through the crowd, and Astrea found her steps slowing until she stopped at the back of the group.

"Skies damned rebels," one woman loitering at the edge muttered. She flicked her long blonde ponytail over her shoulder.

"It wasn't the rebels," a man next to her said. His back was to Astrea, but his harsh accent suggested he was originally from the northwestern part of the empire. "It had to be the Zaikudi after our victory over them yesterday. Emperor Aelius needs to go to their embassy and arrest them."

"You think the Delians wouldn't do something like this?" another person asked, their voice rising. Unlike the man from out of town, this person was Kalamian through and through, from their accent to their crisp linen suit. "They're always causing trouble. Always have been since we defeated them a few years back."

Wave after wave of emotion rolled over Astrea, and she gritted her teeth. She knew she should be on her way, but what if the crowd was right? What if the rebels were escalating? Or what if the Delians or

Zaikudi were bringing the war to Kalama? Fighting was currently limited to Corsyca, hundreds of miles away to the northwest, but surely it wasn't a stretch to think they could get to Helosia's capital.

"The lot of you are fools if you don't think this has to do with the—" The fourth voice, a tall, pale woman, was cut off by the blast of a police horn.

"You need to disperse!" The staticky voice of an officer came over a bullhorn somewhere in the crowd. "Leave the area immediately!"

Despite the raging emotions pouring off the crowd, people started to disperse one by one. Whatever was going on wasn't anything Astrea needed to be involved in. She needed to be focused on impressing the emperor and exceeding his expectations, not city gossip and graffiti. And so Astrea hurried past the edge of the crowd and toward the library, ready to get some real work done for the afternoon.

CHAPTER 9

Laughter echoed through the Nikaphoroses' dining room, a balm to Astrea's soul.

Even though Astrea had to work earlier in the day, this dinner more than made up for it. It had always been tradition for her and Saros to join the Nikaphoroses for dinner on Sunday evenings, but this was the first time they'd managed to get together in a month. Astrea didn't even know what they were laughing about, just that Balthazar had said something to earn a chuckle from even her stoic uncle.

Astrea's mother, Roxana Sovna, had died over a decade earlier from a sudden-onset illness. Astrea had never known her father, and her mother hadn't shared his identity with Saros. He was her only blood family left in the world, but the Nikaphoroses were family, too. While Balthazar was Cressida's match—strong, fierce, outspoken—Sarsali was more Astrea's speed. A Greenkeeper, she worked in gardens all around the city, encouraging new life to bloom all year long. She was gentle, soft-spoken but firm in her beliefs, patient. She was everything Astrea wanted to be.

Sarsali clutched a glass of wine to her chest with one hand, the corners of her lips pulling up into a sly smile that highlighted her high cheekbones. Though she was well into her middle age, her deep bronze skin remained smooth and bright. "Cress, my dear, didn't you try that new recipe today?" Sarsali brushed a dark, glossy curl out of her eyes. She typically wore her long hair in a braid down her back, but she'd left it loose tonight. "What was it again?"

"Tarts, Ma." Cressida took a swig of her wine. "Melon tarts."

"Melon tarts?" Saros asked.

"Don't knock it until you try it." Grinning, Cressida pushed her seat back and disappeared into the dark hallway beyond the dining room. The floor creaked. Cabinets slammed. Then Cressida returned, a pink and blue ceramic platter in hand. "Go ahead, try them."

Astrea never questioned Cressida's kitchen creations. She somehow knew what combinations of ingredients would work best, and the tart was no different. Subtle, sweet, and light, Astrea ate two of them before Saros even finished his first.

"Decent," he said, setting the half-eaten tart down in the remnants of spicy red sauce left on his dinner plate. Cressida and Balthazar had cooked a Taipoli dish for dinner, one passed down from Cressida's maternal grandmother, who still lived in the southern islands. "But I prefer the strawberry ones."

Cressida rolled her eyes, but peach amusement colored the air around her. "I'll make sure I bring some by the observatory later this week."

"I would appreciate that very much, my dear," Saros said.

"Speaking of the observatory." Balthazar ran a hand over the smooth dark brown skin of his head. He'd had curls tighter than Cressida's for many years but had recently taken to shaving it all off. He crossed his arms and shifted in his seat. "How is your new assignment going, Astrea?"

"How, exactly, is that speaking of the observatory?" she asked.

He offered her the smallest of smiles. Balthazar was tall with broad shoulders and impressive musculature even in his middle age. But where his physical size was intimidating, and though he was a titan in the Kalamian business community, Balthazar was also one of the gentlest people Astrea knew. He'd always been the first to offer the girls a fresh-baked cookie or patch up scrapes when they were children.

"I don't know how it is," Astrea said. "I'm supposed to meet Prince Varojin tomorrow to get things started."

"Why would the emperor give Jin this assignment?" Sarsali asked as she swallowed the last bite of her dessert. Her jade eyes—the exact same shade as Cressida's—flicked to Astrea, then Saros. "He's been away for so long. Why now?"

Astrea shifted in her plush dining chair. She watched Sarsali as casually as she could, but the Greenkeeper's emotions were calm curiosity, nothing more. Astrea had barely told Cressida what happened between her and Jin years ago, let alone anyone else at the table. The Nikaphoroses had always welcomed both Eliana and Jin with open arms, though Jin was given far more freedom than his sister. He'd visited this very house on birthdays and a dozen other occasions, and the Nikaphoroses were no strangers to the palace. Of course they were curious about what he was up to.

"Does it matter why he's back?" Saros asked, rusty annoyance bursting to life around him. "That boy is nothing but trouble."

"He's hardly a boy anymore, Saros," Balthazar replied, his broad nose and the corners of his rich brown eyes wrinkling slightly. "None of the Auris children are, well, children anymore."

Astrea still had no idea why her uncle disliked Jin so much. Saros had never been fond of him, not even when they were all still children. That had left Astrea walking a tightrope as she got older, trying to balance her uncle's boundaries with her and Jin's friendship. Astrea's chest ached. That wasn't something she had to worry about anymore.

"Maybe not," Saros agreed. "But I don't like that he's back, nor do I like that his father is recruiting him for this . . . work."

"Why?" Astrea heard herself ask. "Did you foresee something?"

The rusty annoyance bouncing around Saros died as dark green concern took its place. His thin lips pressed into a line, then he shook his head once. "I saw nothing. I simply do not trust the bas—prince."

"But you trust Eliana, do you not?" Sarsali asked.

"I do."

"And Prince Kaius?"

"I believe Prince Kaius has the training necessary for tasks like diplomacy," Saros said after a long inhale. "As does Princess Eliana. Prince Varojin does not. This exhibition is an awfully big task."

"Lighten up, Saros." Cressida tore off another bite of tart, chewing quickly before swallowing. "Jin's smart. Astrea's smarter. It'll all work out."

"It'll be fine, Uncle," Astrea said, even if she didn't fully believe it herself. She'd been asking herself the same question as Saros: why was the emperor giving this task to Jin, and why was he giving it to him now? The only thing keeping her going was the knowledge that she was getting a big paycheck, and a big paycheck meant she would have options. She could decide what she wanted to do, if she wanted to leave.

"You act like he's a monster, Saros," Balthazar said with a chuckle. "Like something from those bedtime stories we used to tell the girls."

"Because torturing small children with warnings of monsters and madness is the best thing before they go to sleep," Cressida muttered.

"I warned your father not to tell you those." Sarsali clicked her tongue. "Never does any good to scare children before bed."

Parents all over the continent used stories of monsters to convince children to behave and go to bed at a reasonable hour. But those were just old stories from centuries past.

"I know he's not a monster," Saros finally said, his pale cheeks burning red. "Monsters aren't real. But I do not trust the imperial family with my niece. I cannot."

Astrea huffed. "I'm sitting right here."

"Well then, you know the truth. I don't trust them with you."

"And whose fault is that?" Astrea asked.

This was an argument they'd had several times in her teenage years. Once, when Cressida and her parents were in Sezia for a summer holiday, then-fourteen-year-old Astrea had snuck both Eliana and Jin into the observatory. They'd just been going through the books in the observatory's small collection, but when Saros had found them, he'd sent the imperial siblings home and warned Astrea against her friendship with them. All because of the lie he'd forced her into.

He'd softened up again on Eliana in recent years, but Astrea knew he still didn't like the princess as much as he liked Cressida.

Saros opened his mouth to reply, but Sarsali pushed her chair back and stood. "Would anyone like coffee?" she asked. "Or tea? I could make tea."

"I'm fine, thank you, Sarsali." Saros stood too, then set his napkin on the table next to his plate. "In fact, I think I'm going to head home. I have some work I need to do."

Astrea held back a sigh. This was what always happened. They'd start an argument about this situation—the secret, their living arrangement, something—and then Saros would retreat almost immediately. She hated that it happened like this, but she didn't know how else to talk to him about it. And it was hard to hide her resentment, even if she understood his reasons.

"Make sure you're careful out there tonight," Balthazar said. "Both of you."

"Was there another attack?" Astrea asked.

"No, but between that and the war, the whole city's on edge," he replied. "Best to be mindful."

"Are you coming home now, Astrea?" Saros asked.

"I was going to stay." She'd actually planned on going home early, but walking back to the palace with Saros was just going to be awkward now. She'd much rather stay put.

He nodded, the dark waves of his hair bouncing. "Alright."

"I'll drive you home tonight if you'd like, Astrea," Balthazar offered, and Astrea agreed.

Sarsali left for the kitchen, and Saros and Balthazar disappeared into the dim hallway without another word. After one last look at Astrea, Cressida headed for the kitchen, too. Astrea sank back into her chair.

Why did this always happen? Sometimes it felt like Saros was speaking a different language, or maybe it was Astrea. Maybe they just didn't understand each other anymore. It hadn't always been like this, but for the last six months, they'd been getting into more arguments, more disagreements.

Had she changed? Had her behavior become too bold for her uncle's paranoia? Not that she considered herself bold—far from it. Cressida and Eliana were bold. Astrea was just . . . sliding by.

The front door closing made Astrea sit up in her chair. Cressida returned first, then Sarsali and Balthazar trailed in after their daughter. Sarsali poured coffee for everyone, and Astrea spooned sugar into hers.

"Do you want me to talk to him?" Balthazar asked. "I don't know why he's being like this. He's never been this obtuse."

Astrea sucked in a breath. An idea tickled at the back of her mind.

"He wants me to leave." Astrea took a sip of her coffee, grimacing at the bitterness and adding in some cream. "He wants me to leave Helosia."

Sarsali frowned. "That seems extreme."

"He's brought it up several times in the last few months," Astrea admitted as she looked up at the Greenkeeper. "The emperor is paying me a bonus for working on this project. I was actually considering taking Saros's advice and leaving when this is over."

"Is that what you want?" Sarsali asked, hints of her worry whispering across Astrea's skin like a breeze.

"Maybe."

"Then it's something to consider," Balthazar said. "You have time before this is all said and done. You don't have to make a decision tonight."

Astrea swirled her spoon through her coffee even though the sugar had surely dissolved by now. "The more I think about it, the more I realize it might be nice to get away, even just for a year or two. I mean, I haven't left Kalama since we moved here."

"We could travel together if you want, Az. Might be fun to see some more of the world." Cressida glanced toward her parents, then added, "If you'd be alright running Lodestar by yourself for a while, Dad."

"We can talk," Balthazar offered.

"Is it wise?" Astrea asked, looking first at Balthazar, then Sarsali. "Do you think Saros is right for wanting to send me away? Am I foolish for considering it?"

Sarsali took a sip of coffee, then set her cup on the table with a soft clink. "I think he's trying to keep you safe, my dear. Saros has always been willing to do anything for you."

"Including lie to the emperor," Astrea murmured.

"Including that," Balthazar echoed. "Right or wrong, it's done. And you're grown now, and you get to decide what your next steps are. Stay in Kalama and stay on the sidelines, or leave the empire and live whatever life you truly want for yourself."

"And those are my only choices?" Astrea asked, hating the bitterness clawing up her throat. She had so much in Kalama: her friends, her family, her job. No, her position at the library didn't pay her much, but she had everything she needed. Why couldn't she stay in Kalama *and* live the life she truly wanted? Why couldn't she live here *and* be a Lightbringer openly? She hated hiding.

"They're two paths, but where you end up at the end of that journey is up to you." Balthazar smiled when Astrea peeked up at him.

"What if I'm not sure what I want?"

"It's alright to not know what you want," Sarsali said gently. "But when you don't, the people around you may try to make those decisions for you instead. They often think they're helping and sometimes don't even realize they're doing it."

Astrea swirled her coffee in her cup as she turned Sarsali's words over in her mind. "And if I know I don't want other people making those kinds of choices for me?"

Sarsali smiled. "Then you just have to be willing to take a step back and figure out what you truly desire."

"You have time," Balthazar said. "Stay here and work on this project. Decide where you want to go and what you want to do when it's done. And whatever choice you make, we'll be here to help you. Whatever you need, just tell us."

"We'd do anything for you, Astrea," Sarsali said. "After all, you're practically our daughter, too. And that's what family's for."

Astrea swallowed hard, tears burning the backs of her eyes. The Nikaphoroses had been part of her life for so long, always filling in the cracks left behind when her mother died. Family dinners, birthday parties, even all the summers Sarsali had spent trying to teach Astrea more about gardening. Now this. She didn't know what she'd done to get so lucky.

"Thank you," she whispered.

"Once you finish your coffee," Balthazar said, "I'll drive you home, alright? Take your time. I'll be in the parlor whenever you're ready."

CHAPTER 10

Though her weekend had wrapped up with Saros locking himself in the observatory, Astrea was feeling more confident in her decision to stay in Kalama for the time being. Balthazar, Sarsali, and Cressida were going to support her no matter what she decided, and Astrea was sure Saros would too, if he would take a few minutes to think about it.

Now, she was starting her morning in one of her favorite places: the library basement. Astrea loved when Raela received shipments of new books to add to the library's collection, and a few new crates had come in earlier that morning.

"Fetch the crowbar, would you, Astrea?" Raela asked as she headed down the basement hallway. Six enormous wooden crates lined one wall, and they were easily as tall as Raela's hip. She sighed. "You'd think they could have chosen smaller boxes to ship these in."

"We'll be fine," Astrea said. She opened the door to the storage closet on the far end of the hallway and searched three of the cluttered shelves before she found the crowbar. The metal was cold in her hand as she met Raela at one of the crates. "Shall we start here?"

"Yes, let's get this over with."

"I thought you liked this part of the job." Astrea used all her strength to get the lid of the first crate to crack free. The nails holding the box together shifted, then the lid popped up.

"Speaking of this part of the job," Raela said as she reached inside and started removing the newspapers used as packing material, "I finally got that call from the emperor's office."

"You spoke to Emperor Aelius?"

Raela chuckled. "No, dear, not directly. His secretary—a man named Edouard. Do you know him?"

Astrea shook her head as she grabbed a wad of crumbled newspaper. "No, I've never met him."

"I'm surprised."

"Why?"

Raela shrugged her slender shoulder, then started gathering up the discarded papers. She placed them on the lid of the crate farthest from them. "I thought you would know almost everyone at the palace."

"You've known me for two years, Raela. You know I'm only close to the princess." She grabbed the last few pieces of newspaper and carried them to the pile Raela had made.

"Well, you've apparently made quite the impression on Emperor Aelius. He's instructed me to give you twenty hours a week to dedicate to the initial research phase of this pet project, and then we'll increase your time on it as needed. And this Edouard said you can expect a sizable deposit in your bank account this week and another when the project is complete."

Astrea hadn't expected any part of that ten thousand lire before the autumn. Her heart jumped, and she tried to keep her face neutral as she asked, "How should I plan my time around this new project?" Leaning into the crate, Astrea began sorting through some of the books. She'd think about the money later. "I don't want to slack off on my other duties. I know we're already struggling here."

Raela clicked her tongue as she walked to the other side of the crate and pulled out a stack of books. "I'll take care of anything you can't get done, and I'm sure the government will expand our budget to bring in Serra, Lena, or Felix a few more days each week since you're doing this for the emperor himself. Spend your time however you see fit. Focus on doing a good job for him."

"Of course. I just don't want you to work too hard."

"Then help me open this box!"

Raela had moved on, abandoning the books she'd picked up and the ones still left in the first crate. She was motioning to a larger one, and as Astrea walked toward it, she realized it was the very same one she'd organized the delivery for the week prior. She'd nearly forgotten about the damn thing.

"You haven't opened this yet?" Astrea asked, leaving the crate behind and picking up the crowbar.

"I thought you'd like to be here for the grand reveal," Raela said, and Astrea handed the tool over. With practiced ease, Raela pried the lid off the crate. She leaned over the side, then removed some of the padding and tossed it on the floor. "Just look at this."

Astrea stepped forward and peered inside the box. A worn, white stone bust of a man returned her stare. A crown circled his long hair, and his long, straight nose had been perfectly sculpted.

"Who is it?" Astrea asked as Raela removed more of the packaging. They were going to need an Earthmover just to get the thing out of the box; there was no possible way that she and Raela could lift it themselves. It had to be at least two feet tall and pure stone. "Is it Helosian?"

"I'm not sure who it is, actually." Green curiosity danced around Raela as she continued, "But my friend says it's a rare find. From the northeastern parts of the empire, but I'm not sure if it's originally Helosian."

Land in the northeast had once belonged to Novaria and Tornama both, so the likelihood of it being truly Helosian was low.

Raela picked up the tool and moved to another box of books. "That friend will be by with his team within the next week to look at the bust more closely, then we'll get it logged in to special collections. I'm sure there will be a line of professors just clamoring to get a look at it." She sighed. "In the meantime, why don't you help me take some of these books upstairs?"

All of that excitement for an anonymous statue? It was surely someone royal based on the crown, but there had been dozens of generations of monarchs from all over the continent. Centuries earlier, there had been dozens of countries, not just the five that now made up the continent. There was no easy way for her to solve that mystery. Why had the government agreed to purchase it?

"Alright," Astrea said, shoving her questions away as she moved back to the first box of books. "Where do you want them?"

"Just set them on the circulation desk to start."

As Raela went back upstairs, Astrea focused on the books. They were all in beautiful condition, a mix of cloth and leather covers in a variety of colors. She turned one over in her hand and read aloud, "*The History of the Great Wars, Volume I.*"

The Great Wars had started over six hundred years earlier, but they were still a popular topic among the city's noblemen. And though Astrea wouldn't normally see the appeal, that certainly fell under the emperor's specifications for Novarian history. All of the continental powers had been involved in those wars, and they'd spanned a century and a half.

Astrea leaned back into the crate and pulled out another ten books, then set the *Great Wars* tome on top of that stack. The more she could carry at once, the better. She didn't feel like walking up and down the stairs more than she had to. At least the elevator worked for the other floors.

She gathered the books in her arms, balancing them carefully as she started down the basement corridor and back up the stairs to the main floor.

"Raela!" Astrea called, trying to peer around her stack as she reached the lobby. "You said the circulation desk?"

"Do you need some help with those?" That voice did *not* belong to Raela. A pair of large, calloused hands brushed against Astrea's as the books were pulled from her arms. As her line of vision cleared, Jin smiled. "Hello, Astrea."

Though she'd seen him at the Whiskey Dream a few nights before, this was different. This was in the light of day, when the sun was up and she could make out his features more clearly. And now here Jin was, in her space and looking just as good as he did at the club despite it being a Monday morning.

She let Jin take the books.

Jin was handsome, of course, as all of the Auris children were. He had tawny skin, the unmissable Auris golden irises they all shared, and the same straight nose as his siblings. His hair was a shade lighter and curlier than his royal siblings', the only sign that he didn't share the same mother as the rest of them.

It wasn't fair that he looked so good.

"Oh, Prince Varojin!" Raela's shrill exclamation snapped Astrea out of her stupor. "Your Imperial Highness, we weren't expecting you, were we? I would've been prepared for your visit."

Astrea blinked. Jin was smirking at her, the same irritating smirk he'd had when they were children. Two could play at that game.

"Oh, no, ma'am, you weren't expecting me at all," Jin said, his voice smooth. "I hope I'm not inconveniencing you."

Astrea glared at the back of his head as he turned and carried the books to the wide circulation desk. *Liar.* She had technically been expecting him, though his promise to see her had hardly been specific, nor had he tried to get in touch with her any time since she'd last seen him. *Which is incredibly rude if you ask me.*

"Though it looks like I've come just in time," he continued. "Do you need help moving some books? Please, use me."

Raela glanced at Astrea.

"His Imperial Highness is here to see me, Raela," Astrea said as she took a few steps toward the pair. Jin's jaw tightened. "He mentioned he might be coming by for assistance with that special project, but I assure you, no other preparations were necessary."

"No preparations at all," Jin echoed.

Astrea's magic stretched toward him, then stopped, slamming into some kind of wall. Was that why she hadn't been able to read him at the Whiskey Dream? She'd chalked it up to the chaos of the night. Regardless, it was odd. Different. Her magic had always been able to connect with Jin.

"All I need is a place to work and Astrea's help," he continued. "I hope this isn't a burden to you or your team, Miss Zornovski."

Raela's blue eyes widened, but she nodded. "Of course not, Your Imperial Highness. You're welcome here any time. We have a private study room you can use for as long as you need. I'll make sure you aren't disturbed. Astrea will show you where to go, and please do not hesitate to ask for our assistance."

"That would be lovely, thank you."

"Follow me, Your Imperial Highness," Astrea said, stalking off through the lobby.

As Jin caught up to her, he leaned down and asked, "What about the books?"

"I'll move them later."

She hurried past the massive staircase. At the first break in the book-shelves, Astrea turned right, leading him through the stacks and down a bright hallway. There were several private rooms, and beyond that were the archives where they stored whatever daily newspapers they had. A water leak a decade prior had destroyed most of the older papers, but they still had the last ten years on file.

Pulling a set of keys from her deep skirt pocket, Astrea unlocked the door to one of the private studies. She opened it, then moved to one side so Jin could enter. He nodded as he surveyed the room. It was the nicer of the private studies they had on the first floor, the one that had just been renovated. A long solid oak table ran the middle length of the room, eight chairs with high backs tucked in around it. A few bookcases housing encyclopedias sat on one wall, and maps of the empire hung in frames on the other. Two potted indoor palms sat in one corner, and a chandelier dangled over the table, its lightbulbs buzzing as Astrea flicked the switch on.

"I hope this will suffice, Your Imperial Highness."

Jin turned toward her, his lips pressed together. "Astrea, I know I'm probably the last person you want to see—"

While that was true, this was also the last conversation Astrea wanted to have. She needed to keep things moving along. There could be no distractions.

"It's no trouble, Your Imperial Highness," she interrupted. His jaw tightened again. "Whenever you want to begin our work together, we can. Do you have time today, or is your schedule full?"

"My schedule?" He scoffed. "This *is* my schedule while I'm in town."

Perfect, Astrea thought. *Just wonderful.*

"I can bring in some coffee for while we work if you'd like, Your Imperial Highness."

"You don't have to do that." Jin motioned toward the chairs. "Sit down, please. Let's just get started."

Astrea closed the door behind her, then crossed the short distance to the nearest chair. She dropped into it and pulled a small notebook out of the pocket of her skirt. This wasn't going to be pleasant, but maybe Jin knew it, too, if he wanted to 'just get started.'

Jin settled into a chair a few seats away from her. He watched her carefully for a moment, then crossed his arms. "So . . . how exactly does this work?"

"We can start with some questions, Your Imperial Highness." Whenever they helped with projects like this, Raela always started with a list of questions for the host. Astrea flipped her notebook open to a blank page. "His Imperial Majesty said he would like us to research Novarian history. Do you have any ideas?"

"No, I have no ideas. History never was my best subject."

History hadn't been Jin's best subject, nor had mathematics, geography, or most sciences. He'd liked reading novels—not studying them—and he'd been a natural at picking up other languages. He'd liked astronomy, too, but he'd never taken studies seriously when they were children. Jin was so smart—far smarter than Kaius—but he'd never *tried*. She'd often helped him with his assignments so he didn't get in trouble with his father or his tutors, Saros included.

Astrea sighed. "Then what about venues, Your Imperial Highness? The emperor didn't mention any specific locations to me."

"I have no ideas for that, either."

This was going to be harder than she thought.

"I do, however, have one idea," he added.

"I would love to hear your thoughts, Your Imperial Highness."

The silence stretched on between them, almost tangible, as Jin's jaw tightened again. "Damn it, Astrea. You know I don't like that title."

"You seemed to have no problem when Raela called you that a few minutes ago."

"Raela isn't you."

As Jin stared at her, Astrea stared back. Somewhere in the back of her mind, she knew she was being petty. She was pushing a button few people knew Jin even had, and she was pushing it hard. Besides, he wasn't exactly falling back on old nicknames. He'd always called her Az. Hearing him say her full name was almost more foreign than the sight of him at the library table.

"Maybe not," she agreed, "but if I'm remembering correctly, only your friends have the privilege of foregoing the title."

Astrea regretted the words as soon as they left her mouth, the truth now laid bare before them both. But the hurt and understanding on Jin's face almost made it worth it. Almost.

"What, are we strangers now?" he asked.

"It's been a long time."

"It has."

"Then I don't see what the problem is."

Her heart beat wildly in her chest, but Astrea managed to hold Jin's gaze. It was unsettling how much Jin looked like his little sister when he was angry. But what right did he have to be angry with her when he was the one who left?

"I appreciate your help on this, Astrea. The private workspace will be enough, though I hope you'll stop feeling the need to use my title soon. Could I ask one more favor of you?"

"Of course, Your Imperial Highness."

Astrea had to stop herself from smiling as Jin's frustration visibly returned. She didn't need to be a Lightbringer to know just how annoyed he was. She would need to stop trying to get a rise out of him, though. It was distracting her, and it really was unprofessional. The sooner he was done with his project, the sooner he could leave Kalama. And the sooner Jin was gone, the sooner Astrea could get on with her life and leave the past behind.

"Perhaps you could leave me with a list of questions you need me to answer and ideas you need me to come up with. Since I don't seem to have a clue what I'm doing, I could stop wasting your time and go think about this at home."

"I'll write them down for you."

Astrea scribbled a list of questions into her notebook. Venue, ideas for the exhibition, whether or not they needed catering for the gala, relics and objects they might want to include—that would be enough to get him started, and getting Jin started on this would give her a better direction, too.

Astrea tore the page out of her notebook and slid it across the table toward him. "Bring your answers back to me when you can, and then I'll get started on everything."

"*You'll* get started?" Jin asked as he reached for the paper.

"It's a lot of work for me to do, but I'll manage."

Understanding dawned across his features. "You're going to take my answers and do this yourself?"

"That's why I'm here, Your Imperial Highness. I am at your service."

"That's most certainly not why you're here. This is *my* assignment. I'll not let you get cornered into this by my father."

"I—" Astrea started, but Jin cut her off.

"I'm not just going to sit back and approve whatever it is you come up with on your own. I want to be involved. I *need* to be involved."

Wonderful.

"Fine," she snapped. "Then bring your answers to me tomorrow, and we can start working on this, Your Imperial Highness." Jin flinched as his title left her mouth again. "We can keep this simple and organized."

"Simple and organized." He nodded. "Fine. Good."

Astrea pushed her chair back and stood. "You may use this room for whatever work you want to do here. I'll leave the key at circulation with Raela."

Astrea turned on her heel so quickly that her long skirt billowed around her. She hurried out the door, trying only to slow down enough to not make it completely obvious that she was avoiding him.

Why did it have to be so hard to see Jin again? Some tiny, foolish part of her had hoped it wouldn't be like this. That she wouldn't have such a hard time looking him in the eye or relaxing around him. That maybe she wouldn't still be mad at him. Astrea shook her head once as she passed the staircase. *Of course it's going to be like this,* she thought.

Raela was still in the lobby, though more piles of books now sat around the circulation desk. Astrea took the study room key off her key ring and set it on the desk.

"I told Prince Varojin I'd leave this here for him," she said. "Is it alright if I go work on my project for a while?" Even if she was waiting on Jin to answer those questions, Astrea could start researching things on her own.

She knew Raela was looking at her, so Astrea forced herself to meet her gaze. She needed to appear like everything was fine.

"You look like you saw a ghost," Raela quipped. An uncomfortable mix of curiosity and concern swept over Astrea's skin.

Astrea ignored her. "So, my project?"

Raela nodded. "Of course. I'll be right here if you need anything."

Without waiting for Raela to say anything else, Astrea turned and crossed the lobby. She stopped when she reached the elevators, pressing the 'up' arrow several times. It wouldn't make the damn thing come any faster, but she could try.

After all, she had things to research and plans to make.

CHAPTER 11

Raela's high, crisp laugh echoed through the lobby as Astrea strode through the library's front doors the next morning. She looked at the circulation desk to find her boss grinning and swatting at Prince Jin's arm. The woman was old enough to be Jin's mother, but she seemed to be enjoying whatever story he was telling her. A deep blush spread over Raela's bronze cheeks. Marigold excitement and peach amusement danced in the air around the librarian, light and warm and almost contagious.

Jin pivoted toward Astrea and smiled. "Good morning."

Despite the warmth of Raela's feelings fluttering over Astrea's skin, her stomach sank. "Hello, Your Imperial Highness." Astrea offered him a tight-lipped smile before turning to Raela. "I hope you're not running late for your meeting at the museum?"

Jin's expression didn't falter as he glanced at the librarian. "I didn't mean to keep you from a meeting."

"Oh, it's not a problem, Prince Jin," Raela said. Astrea didn't miss that Raela was now using his nickname. Jin always had been good at charming people. "Astrea, I'll be back in a couple of hours, alright? Lena and Felix are upstairs. Your Imperial Highness, it was a pleasure to see you today. I hope I'll see you again tomorrow?"

"I'll be sure to say hello when I get here."

As Raela crossed the lobby, Astrea turned to watch her leave. The hair on the back of her neck stood on end, and she knew Jin was staring at her. She pretended not to notice as she said, "I trust Raela has set you up with everything you need, Your Imperial Highness?"

"Can we please talk?" Jin paused. "In private?"

Now she'd have to turn around, but instead of looking at Jin, Astrea moved around the circulation desk. "Of course." She picked up the little wooden sign that read 'staff will be back shortly' and motioned for Jin to go first. "Lead the way, Your Imperial Highness."

He headed back down the hallway she'd shown him the day before, silent as they walked. What could he possibly want to talk about?

As he slid the key out of the lock, he opened the door and motioned for her to enter. "Please, go first. I insist." Astrea slid past him and into the room. "Please, have a seat."

She chose a seat near the middle of the table, the bookcases to her back. Only once she was seated did Jin select the chair directly across from her. He sat down and sighed.

"What would you like to talk about, Your Imperial Highness?"

Jin rolled his eyes, but he pulled a piece of paper out of his pocket and placed it on the table. "I did my homework assignment."

"It wasn't a homework assignment," Astrea muttered, but she reached for the paper anyway. Jin's neat handwriting contrasted the messy strokes of her own, his answers clear. "Why is this something we needed to speak about in private?"

"I'm not sure who in the general public is supposed to know about the project, and I didn't want word getting back to my father if I fucked this up so soon."

Good choice. Astrea looked back down at the paper. He'd listed a few ideas for venues, and he had two neat columns of topics for the exhibit itself. History, mythology and literature, fashion, art—he'd covered all of his bases. Astrea had been hoping Jin would offer some more specific examples, but this was a start.

"Do you have any preferences on what we focus on for our research?" she asked.

"It would be easier if my father would tell me what he wants to see, but he won't. I was thinking we could start with a bit of everything . . . if that's not too much work."

It was absolutely more work than they should be doing, but if the emperor wasn't playing nicely, they had no choice. *Ten thousand lire,* Astrea reminded herself. *Ten thousand.*

"We'll make it work, Your Imperial Highness."

"Then where do we begin?" Jin asked.

Astrea stood and started toward the study door. Jin's footsteps were his only response. She led him back to the lobby, then up the stairs to the third floor. Jin kept pace with her, but she supposed that wasn't hard; he was nearly a foot taller than her and had never had to try to keep up with her before.

The library was quiet. Weekday mornings were the quietest time, but there would be a steady trickle of students and professors in the afternoon, then businesspeople and nobles toward the end of the day. That was how it always was at the library, and Astrea loved the predictability of it.

"Here." Astrea stopped when they reached the third floor. Rows of bookcases stretched out before them, a single wide aisle leading to the back of the building. "Follow me."

Astrea led Jin several rows back, then turned right. Down a few more aisles, then she turned left.

"This is a lot of books," Jin whispered.

"It's the history section." She pointed left, then right. "All this area."

"Again, this is a lot of books."

Astrea tried to tamp down her annoyance. She didn't even know why she was annoyed at him. Jin wasn't doing anything wrong, though he didn't actually need to whisper. "This section should have both Novarian and Helosian history."

Jin glimpsed at her briefly, then turned back at the shelves stretching out before them. "And we have to look through all of them?"

"You can start here."

He hesitated. "Where will you be?"

"I'll be downstairs going through the catalog to see if I can find titles more quickly."

"Why don't I help with that?"

"Nobody touches Raela's catalogs except for me."

The corners of Jin's mouth twitched, but he nodded. "Alright, I'll start up here."

Astrea left Jin in the history section and returned to the library's first floor, then made her way to the basement. It had plenty of space for the extensive card catalog that detailed the library's collection of books and other artifacts.

As Astrea unlocked one of the doors in the long basement hallway and flicked the lights on, she sighed. There were thousands of cards here, but Raela, thankfully, kept this organized despite not being able to keep track of time.

In fact, if Raela were here, this would be a million times easier. Raela had practically every book in the building memorized, or at least that was how it seemed. So had the senior librarians before they were all laid off. Now, Astrea was left trying to play catch-up, desperate to build up years' worth of knowledge in the six months since she'd become the sole librarian there besides Raela. And Raela wasn't even really a librarian anymore. Half of her time was spent in meetings as the library director rather than overseeing day-to-day problems.

Astrea spent the next half hour combing through four drawers of the catalog, searching for any books that were marked for Novarian history. There were still plenty more cards to look through, but Astrea managed to find two books. And two books would be enough for them to read through that afternoon.

There was also the book she'd unpacked the day before, the one about the Great Wars. Jin hadn't asked for anything about war, but history was history. There might be something useful in it.

Astrea copied the titles' information onto a spare piece of paper, then slid the card back into the drawer. After locking up the room and heading back to an empty lobby, Astrea sighed. She'd been hoping Felix or Lena would be there. One of them needed to be; professors were bound to be making the rounds soon. But where were the two pages?

She checked the second floor first, but there was no sign of either of them. As she ventured up to the third floor, Astrea had her answer. Felix's light laugh, followed by Lena's giggle, told her everything she needed to know.

In the history section, where she'd left Jin alone, Astrea now found three people: Felix's tall, lanky form and bright red hair; Lena's short, curvy frame and signature blonde braid; and Jin. Orange anxiety, peach amusement, and teal approval tangled in Felix and Lena's auras as Jin regaled them with a story from his—and Astrea's—teenage years.

"Next thing I knew, both Astrea and my sister were pulling me out of the bay. I was soaked through and had absolutely ruined the outfit I was supposed to wear to one of my father's—Oh, hello, Astrea."

"Your Imperial Highness," Astrea muttered as she stalked toward the trio. "Felix, Lena."

"Why did you never tell us you knew His Imperial Highness?" Lena asked, blue eyes wide as she looked between Astrea and Jin. A delicate blush that matched her pink dress spread over Lena's pale cheeks. "I knew you lived at the palace, but I didn't know you were friends."

"We're not—" Astrea started, but Jin cut her off.

"I'm sorry if I've kept them from their work," he said. "That's my fault. Don't blame them."

"I'm not blaming anyone. But I do need one of you to go watch circulation while I help His Imperial Highness up here."

"I'll go," Lena offered. "I'm tired of shelving anyway. It was a pleasure to meet you, Your Imperial Highness." Lena curtsied before she scurried back through the stacks, her braid swinging with her quick steps.

Jin's smile was tight, uncomfortable.

"Felix," Astrea said, turning her attention to the redheaded page, "have you by chance seen a book about the Great Wars? One we unpacked from the shipment yesterday."

Felix paused, then smiled as he pushed his glasses up the bridge of his long nose. Dark brown freckles covered his pale cheeks, though he didn't have nearly as many as Nicos. "Actually, I believe I have. I'll go look for it."

As Felix disappeared down a nearby aisle, Jin turned his attention back to Astrea.

"I really didn't mean to overstep my bounds," the prince said. "They were startled to see me when they came down one of the aisles, and I just started speaking with them."

"It's fine." Astrea didn't love that he'd been telling them a story that included her, but it sounded like it was more embarrassing for him anyway. "Did you find any books, Your Imperial Highness?"

"No . . . did you?"

"Two."

"Do you know where they are?"

"I will in a moment."

Astrea went down one of the aisles, locating the first book after a couple of minutes. When she turned, she found Jin loitering at the end of the aisle. *Is he more uncomfortable with this than I am?*

She shoved the thought aside, instead meeting him at the end and handing the book to him. "There's one for you to start reading."

Jin turned the book over in his hands, its blue cloth cover fraying on one corner. "*The Cultural Influence of the Grand Duchy of Novaria: A History?*" He sighed. "This sounds incredibly boring."

"You say that about every book," she mumbled.

And he did. The only thing he liked to read were novels, but that had never gone over well with Saros or Jin's other tutors.

Jin started to reply, but Felix returned at that moment and held up two books. "I found both volumes, Astrea."

"Thanks." She took the books from him. "You may go back to what you were doing before."

"Shelving, got it."

Felix rarely complained about whatever tasks he was given at the library, and Astrea appreciated him for it. He'd taken the job and budget cuts in stride, offering to help in whatever extra ways he could.

"And what are those about?" Jin asked when Felix was out of earshot.

"War."

Jin sighed. "Alright, I'll take them with me."

"You can't get through three books by yourself, Your Imperial Highness."

"But if I take these, you can start reading whatever else you find. Organized and efficient, right?"

She hated when Jin was right. But he was. Raela would be back in a few hours, and she would know where there were more books on Novarian history. Astrea hadn't even had a chance to look into the mythology or arts topics Jin had suggested.

"Fine. I'll take the next three. Come on."

"Now where are we going?" Jin asked as Astrea started back toward the stairs.

"You may be a prince, but you still have to check those out if you're taking them home, Your Imperial Highness."

"Taking them home?" There was genuine question in his voice, but Jin nodded. "Right, taking them home. I will read these at the palace."

If he'd expected to spend his days in the library, Astrea couldn't technically stop him, but she was glad he'd agreed either way. She needed to focus, and Jin distracting Lena, Felix, and Raela with his stories would only distract Astrea too.

When they got to the circulation desk, Astrea found it empty, but Lena was speaking with a tall, well-dressed woman loitering near the front door. Jin handed Astrea the books without another word, and she made quick work of checking them out in his name. He could probably take whatever he wanted from the library—it was technically his father's library—but Astrea wasn't taking any chances.

"Thank you for the help finding these," Jin said when she slid the books across the counter to him.

"You don't have to thank me," Astrea said. "It's my job."

Jin watched her for a moment before nodding. "I'll be back tomorrow."

Astrea busied herself with straightening out the pens and cards Lena had left strewn across the workspace. "Enjoy your evening, Your Imperial Highness."

He tapped the desk with his palm, and Astrea looked up at him. "I'm sure I have no right to say this, but make sure you're home before dark, alright? Ellie filled me in on what's been happening, and apparently, there's been some unrest."

Unrest . . . like the crowd she'd seen on the edge of Nobleman's Hill and the Market District just a couple of days prior? Astrea wished she could read Jin's emotions now, but all she could do was try to decipher the strange look on his face.

"Yes, so I've heard," she finally said. "You don't need to worry about me, Your Imperial Highness."

Blue, purple, and white light swirled around Astrea's right hand, the brightness growing in the tiny room. It had once been a closet, but Saros had emptied it out save for a few boxes stacked on one side. Windowless and tucked away in the corner of the observatory apartment, it was a good place for Astrea to practice summoning her light.

Concentrate.

The light dancing around her right hand flared out, illuminating the darkness. Light burst to life over her left hand, and Astrea's arms began to tremble. Sweat beaded on her forehead.

Just a little longer.

"That's enough for today, Astrea."

Saros's voice cut through her thoughts like a knife. The starlight subsided as she blinked and refocused on the now-open door to her left. Saros leaned against the doorframe.

"You'll tire yourself out if you push too hard."

"I know." Two months prior, Astrea had collapsed in the observatory after pushing her magic too far. The headache she'd had for days afterward had been punishment enough. "You don't need to remind me."

"Might I ask what, exactly, you're doing?" Saros asked.

"I was just practicing." Summoning light was something both Stargazers and Lightbringers could do, but it wasn't easy for Astrea.

Where her empathic senses and healing talent came naturally, this felt impossible, like she was trying to push a boulder uphill.

She'd shared her Lightbringer magic with her mother and had learned the basics of everything before she'd died. But over the last fourteen years, Astrea had to teach herself most of what she knew, either through practice or the couple of books she'd managed to find on Lightbringers. Saros had never been keen on giving her lessons, and as a Stargazer, there wasn't much he could teach her anyway. Though she'd turned twenty-four a few months prior, Astrea was years behind on where a mage should be for her age.

"And why were you practicing?"

"No reason," Astrea muttered as she pushed past him.

The air in the apartment was cooler thanks to the ceiling fan spinning lazily in the living room. She sucked in a deep breath as she continued to the kitchen.

"Astrea," Saros said as he trailed in after her. "What's wrong?"

She ignored him, instead heading straight for the refrigerator and opening its door. Reaching inside, Astrea pulled out a glass pitcher full of water, then set it on the counter.

Saros blocked her path as she went for the cupboard where they kept the drinking glasses. She glared at him, and his stare matched hers.

"What's wrong?" he asked again, this time more forcefully.

"Nothing." There was plenty wrong, but Astrea didn't want to talk to Saros about it.

"You've been acting strange since you came home the other night. What happened that's put you in such a bad mood?"

She didn't know what to tell him. The obvious answer was the emperor's request, but it was more than that. It was Saros's strange behavior for the last few months and Prince Jin's return, too. That was why she was practicing so hard with this other side of her magic. It tired her out, and if she was tired, she couldn't be worried or angry or upset.

"Can I at least get a glass of water?" she asked, forcing her jaw to loosen. Astrea wasn't mad at her uncle. Annoyed, maybe, but not mad.

Saros finally broke their staring contest, turning around to reach into the cabinet and pull out a tall glass for her. She filled it halfway with water, then took a long drink.

When her uncle finally spoke, his voice had lost its edge. "Do you want to talk about it?"

"Not really."

He nodded. "Well, you know you can talk to me any time, right?"

Cressida and Eliana were her confidants of choice nowadays, but Astrea appreciated her uncle. He tried. Really, he did, in his own ways. And he'd been trying his best since her mother died. Even if it was his fault that she was forced to hide her magic, Astrea knew that deep down, this was better than the future he'd seen for her.

"Yes, I know." As Astrea's uncle watched her, with those dark half-moons under his eyes and the hunch in his shoulders, she added, "Actually, there is something I'd like to talk about."

"And that is?"

"Why you're staying up so late in the observatory every night."

"I told you," he muttered, "that I've got work I need to do."

"The emperor doesn't allow you to sleep anymore?" she challenged.

Saros ignored her. Instead, he simply turned toward the kitchen cupboards and started rummaging through them.

"Surely he's aware that mages need to sleep too," Astrea said. "Even he can't use his magic endlessly."

Still, Saros didn't reply. He pulled out a box of crackers, then shouldered past Astrea.

Crossing her arms, Astrea turned and took half a step toward him. "I thought you said we could talk."

Saros pulled a block of cheese out of the fridge. "I meant we could talk about *your* problems." He put the cheese back and bent down to look on a lower shelf.

"Your problems are my problems." She knew she was pushing him. Saros's fatigue, anxiety, and frustration all rolled toward her. "This is at the emperor's request, right?"

Steel pain, cobalt regret, and dark blue shame all jumped to life around Saros as he straightened. The emotions made her entire body itch, but Astrea willed her hands to stay at her sides. What could have him feeling so bad?

"Is this about the war?" she asked. "Or some trade agreement Eliana mentioned to me the other day? It has to be important if he's forcing you to work this much."

"Do you want something to eat?" Saros asked. "I hate to dirty any utensils if I'm the only one eating."

"I want answers, not a snack."

Saros's jaw tightened, then he slammed the fridge door shut. Hot and cold rolled over Astrea's magic as the colors around him brightened. Saros wasn't holding back, not like he sometimes did.

"I'm trying to do what needs to be done, Astrea. Now, if you'll excuse me."

What is that supposed to mean? She wanted to ask, but the words stuck in Astrea's throat. She simply watched as Saros grabbed the box of crackers from the countertop and headed down the hallway. The apartment's front door clicked shut, and sure enough, the floorboards overhead creaked a few moments later.

Something was wrong with Saros. And as Astrea headed back to her bedroom, she had a sinking feeling it had everything to do with the emperor.

CHAPTER 12

The ladder underneath Astrea was sturdy, but she was still worried about falling. The massive bookcases in the Great Library required ladders to reach the top shelves, and though they were well-built, Astrea always felt like she was going to fall backward.

Reaching for the green-spined book titled *The Rebuilding: Post-War Recovery in the Grand Duchy of Novaria,* Astrea pulled it off the shelf and tucked it under her arm. She didn't breathe steadily until both feet were back down on the floor.

Saros hadn't come down from the observatory after their argument the night before. Astrea had lain awake half the night listening for the occasional shuffle of feet or scratch of chair legs on wood, her mind dancing around every possibility for what could be keeping her uncle up there. Eventually, she'd fallen asleep, only to find Saros still wasn't downstairs in the morning.

Just focus, she scolded herself. Raela had been kind enough to pull a few book suggestions, and this was the last of them. Astrea had more to worry about than Saros's sleep schedule, like the fact that almost every book she'd found so far continued to cover the topic of war. Helosia and Novaria had a bloody history, just as Helosia had with Zaikud and Delia. Even this one, about the recovery after the Great Wars, was surely going to touch on that dark history.

As Astrea sat down on the floor and leaned back against one of the bookcases, she sighed. There were a few things she thought the emperor would like that *didn't* involve war: old Novarian mythology and literature, a handful of accomplished artists from several centuries prior, and the elaborate clothing from Grand Duchess Ela's court two centuries earlier that had influenced fashion on the entire continent.

Those were hardly controversial topics. They were certainly friendly. But was it enough? Astrea didn't want to disappoint him. She wasn't sure when he'd be calling on her again, but she was sure it would be soon.

The book opened with a crack. Astrea winced. She flipped back to the front cover where the checkout card was located. Only a few names and dates were scrawled on it, the last one being over a decade ago. She couldn't read the name, the ink faded and handwriting messy. It was no surprise that Helosians weren't regularly looking up the influence of Novaria. Many were too focused on their own country's history to care.

As she started scanning the table of contents, she let out a sharp breath. Maybe this book *would* be helpful. It appeared to cover the country for the last few hundred years. She grabbed the notebook she'd brought up to the fourth floor, then started outlining her notes. If the chapter titles were correct, she'd have information about fashion, gardening techniques, architecture, art, and even trade.

Astrea smiled, then jumped.

At the edges of her vision, she saw a black-clad shape leaning against the end of the bookcase. She looked up. Jin smiled at her.

"You hungry?"

"What?" she asked.

He lifted a white box, a purple ribbon tied into a neat bow at the top. He held a thermos in his other hand. "I brought coffee and pastries as a thank you."

"A thank you for what?"

"For making sure I've had everything I need to get started on this project."

"I haven't done that much, Your Imperial Highness," Astrea mumbled as she closed the book and set it in her lap. "Raela's done just as much as I have."

"And she already got her thank you pastry and tea, as did Felix and Lena," Jin said. He straightened, then sat down on the floor across from her, right next to the ladder. "Besides, I wanted to apologize for distracting both Felix and Lena yesterday. As I've already told Raela, I don't want to be a burden to anyone here."

"You don't have to apologize. They're basically your employees."

Everyone in the skies damned empire was technically under Jin's station, even if he was the product of the emperor's affair twenty-six years prior. If he wanted to distract Felix and Lena, he had every right.

"They're most definitely not my employees."

This was the trouble with Jin. It always had been. He didn't seem to understand the power and position he held. Or rather, he wanted to pretend it didn't matter. But it did matter, especially now. Jin wasn't just a prince anymore; he was an officer in the military. If he found out about Astrea's magic, he'd have to report her to his father. She supposed that had always been a threat hanging over her head. But that was before. And this was *now*. Things were different.

When she still didn't reply, Jin motioned toward the books on her right. "What have you been reading? Raela said you've been up here for hours."

The stack of books next to Astrea had all been pointless for her research. *Battle of the Endless Storm*, *The Siege of Jamiah*, and even *Battle of the Molten Mountain*. That last one had actually been interesting, a story about some ancient queen and her army of mages. It had happened at the beginning of the Great Wars.

"Just more books on the wars, Your Imperial Highness."

"Oh, skies," Jin muttered, then lifted the thermos. "I didn't think to bring cups for the coffee."

"Where's it from?" Astrea asked. She *had* been up here for hours, and her eyes were starting to hurt, but she couldn't risk using her magic here to make up for the dim lights hanging overhead. Coffee would help. "Please tell me you didn't go to one of the tourist traps."

"One of the tourist traps?" Jin exclaimed. "Astrea, I may not have been in Kalama much for the last eight years, but I would *never* get coffee from a tourist trap, for skies' sake."

"Then where's it from?"

"The White Lily. That's your favorite one, right?"

"Yeah." Astrea swallowed hard. "And . . . what's in there?" she asked, tilting her chin toward the box.

Jin's long fingers made quick work of the ribbon, then he opened the box. The smell of cinnamon flowed out, and Astrea's stomach rumbled in response.

A sudden wave of emotion washed over her, and she barely stopped the words about to tumble from her mouth. Skies, she wanted to know what he was feeling, but there was that damn wall again.

How could he remember her favorite treat from her favorite café in the entire city but still have ignored her for all those years? Astrea didn't know whether to be frustrated or grateful. Maybe she was both.

When Jin didn't say anything, she peeked up at him. He was watching her, expression unreadable. When she dared to meet his gaze directly—just for a second—he didn't look away.

"So, I was thinking," Jin said, sliding the thermos and pastry box toward her, "as much as I enjoy reading alone in my apartment, there's something more productive we can do."

"What is that, Your Imperial Highness?" Astrea asked, taking one of the pancakes out of the box. She couldn't resist. The outer layer of the flaky pastry was perfectly crispy, and as she bit into it, the cinnamon filling melted in her mouth. They'd been her favorite since Saros bought her one when they first moved to Kalama, a comfort she sought out after hard days or when nothing else sounded appetizing.

Leaning forward, Jin reached into the box and snatched one of the pastries for himself. "I thought we could go look at a potential venue today."

Astrea unscrewed the lid on the thermos, then brought the container to her lips. The coffee was perfectly warm and sweet, like he even remembered her coffee order. This was going to be harder than she'd anticipated.

"Alright. Which one did you want to view first, Your Imperial Highness?"

A flash of steely gray pain lit up the space around Jin, followed by an ache Astrea was familiar with. The feeling spread out over her limbs in a thin coat, almost the same as that sadness she'd felt so keenly eight years ago. But within a heartbeat, it dissipated into nothing, the heaviness of his wall returning.

"If you're going to insist on going back to titles," Jin said, voice strained, "would you at least consider calling me Captain?"

This was *definitely* going to be harder than she'd anticipated. As angry as she might have been with him once upon a time, Astrea couldn't make herself use that title anymore if it hurt him like that. Causing Jin real pain was different than simply annoying him.

"Captain?" she asked. The new title felt heavier on her tongue than his royal one, strange and unfamiliar.

"I was promoted a while ago."

She nodded. Captain. She could call him that. "So, which venue did you want to visit . . . Captain?"

"I was thinking we could view the art museum first."

"When did you want to go?"

"Now, if you're able," he said. "I don't want to keep you from your other work."

"This is my other work," she said. "It's my only work until we're done. Let's go."

Astrea hadn't expected to walk all the way from the library to the art museum. Eliana liked to take her car most places, and Astrea had just assumed Jin would've had a car waiting for them, too. She should've known better. Jin avoided protocol like it was a plague.

The walk had taken them a half hour, and it had been the worst half hour of her week so far. Paranoid someone would recognize Jin, she'd been on edge, but if anyone had noticed him, they didn't show it. Prince Varojin was the least public-facing Auris sibling, even less recognizable than his reclusive eldest brother, Prince Apelo. She supposed Jin's absence from Kalama and his casual outfit—black slacks and a white collared shirt with the sleeves rolled up—helped him go unnoticed. Even so, all it would take was one civilian recognizing Jin to attract unnecessary attention.

Why did things have to be so different? They used to do everything together. They'd been to this museum before, walked these same streets. And instead of the easy laughs and inside jokes they'd once shared, now all they had was awkward silence.

Thankfully, Kalama's museum of fine arts came into view. It towered above them, its dove-gray exterior muted compared to the colorful rows of shops and restaurants on every other side of the piazza.

"Ready?" Jin asked.

"Yes, Captain," Astrea said. His new title was still heavy and awkward on her tongue; she didn't even know why she was bothering to use it. It would be easier to just skip the formalities. Even if they weren't friends anymore, it wasn't like he was a stranger.

Astrea followed Jin up the sweeping staircase on one side of the building, his pace quick. A small group of students loitered on the stairs and nearby ramp, but the museum was otherwise quiet despite the nice weather. Jin held one of the wide glass-paned doors open for Astrea and ushered her inside.

Everything about this museum was soft, from the gray walls to the white tile floors and muted sunlight streaming in through the glass dome that hung over the main atrium. A docent near the entrance stepped forward, and even his blue-gray suit seemed to fit in with the decor.

"May I help you—Oh, my." Lavender surprise flashed once around the docent as he bowed at the waist. "Forgive me, Your Imperial Highness. I almost didn't recognize you. It's been so long since you last visited."

"That's quite alright," Jin said, smiling. "I believe Lady Romolo is expecting us."

"Let me fetch her." The docent disappeared around the corner, his footsteps quieting as he moved deeper into the building.

"You set up an appointment?" Astrea asked.

"People have more important things to do than tend to this little project my father assigned me. I didn't want to arrive unannounced."

It was anything but a 'little' project. Perhaps it wasn't important to Jin, but it was important to Astrea. It didn't matter if he was the emperor's least favorite child. If she didn't do a good job—if she didn't help Jin do a good job—then the emperor would be placing the blame on her shoulders.

"Well, Captain, I'm sure other people would disagree with that. We're here to serve the emperor."

Something unreadable flitted across Jin's expression, his mouth half-open to reply, but the docent returned. A short, rail-thin woman with light brown skin—Lady Romolo, Astrea assumed—waddled behind him, her graying hair nearly the same color as the building's exterior. Her pine green skirt and coordinating blouse were chic, unlike what many of Kalama's elderly nobles wore.

"Your Imperial Highness!" Lady Romolo exclaimed. "You're right on time. I must say, I was surprised when I received your call. I haven't seen you here in years."

"Hello, Milena." Jin smiled at the elderly woman. "I wish I had more time to enjoy the arts, but my father does like his wars."

Astrea blanched, but nothing except genuine amusement fluttered from Lady Romolo.

Milena touched a wrinkled hand to her collarbone and laughed. Then she wagged her ring-laden finger at Jin as she added, "Oh, you always were a cheeky one, Prince Varojin."

Jin's hand touched the spot between Astrea's shoulder blades as he nudged her forward, and she tried not to blanch again. "Allow me to introduce my colleague for this project," Jin said, "Miss Astrea Sovna. She works at the Great Library and will be working with me for the foreseeable future."

My colleague? Jin wasn't wrong, but it sounded so strange.

"How do you do, Miss Sovna?" Milena asked, her small brown eyes searching Astrea's face. "You work with Raela?"

"I do, my lady," Astrea said.

"I don't believe I've seen you stop by with her before."

"No, my lady, though I've been a visitor here many times."

If Milena was looking for the right answer, that was apparently it. She nodded, then looked back up toward Jin. "Right this way, Your Imperial Highness. I'd be happy to show you and Miss Sovna around the space."

Without waiting for a reply, Milena waddled back into the depths of the museum, her heeled shoes clicking on the floor. Jin followed the woman. Astrea hurried after them both, pulling her notebook out of her satchel as she did.

They examined the atrium first, and Milena explained how they might set up different tables and areas for the gala the emperor wanted to host. Then they made a quick pass through the museum's existing exhibits, ones Astrea had seen a dozen times before with Cressida. They circled back into the atrium and ascended the grand staircase to the second floor.

Astrea had been upstairs before for other special events—a year earlier, there'd been an exhibit on Tornamian paintings from the Rebuilding Era—but there wasn't much in the space at the moment. The wide walkways overlooking the atrium and galleries could accommodate six people across, maybe more, and a massive room at the top of the stairs would be perfect for whatever Jin decided he wanted to do for the event.

"And this," Milena explained, "is where we can put the bulk of your showing, Your Imperial Highness."

"How many people can you accommodate here, Lady Romolo?" Astrea asked, heat crawling up her neck as Jin glanced at her.

"The museum has a capacity for several hundred people," she said. "Upstairs, here, perhaps eighty at a time"—Astrea scribbled the number down in her notebook—"depending on how you organize everything. We can also make space downstairs for any additional displays you might have in mind."

"And do you have a preferred caterer," Astrea asked, "or would the palace staff be welcome to come take over?" It was a question she'd heard Raela ask a handful of times before, and even if Astrea didn't know Jin's plans for this event yet, she might as well get the answer.

"Whatever His Imperial Highness and His Imperial Majesty want, of course," Milena said. "The palace staff are welcome to do whatever they need."

Milena answered the rest of Astrea's questions about everything from museum staff to display cases to how they could hang artwork if they needed to. The woman's curiosity tickled Astrea's skin, her gaze flicking between Astrea and Jin.

"And when do I need to reserve the space by?" Jin asked.

"If you decide you want the space, it's yours, Your Imperial Highness. We only need a short time to get things organized if it comes down to it."

"What if someone already has it booked?"

"That won't be a problem."

Jin hesitated, but Milena didn't seem to notice. "It sounds like a problem."

What was he not getting? Milena was saying that she would kick out anyone who booked the space if Jin decided he wanted it. He was, after all, an imperial prince. Whatever the imperial family wanted, they got.

"Your Imperial Highness," Milena said slowly. "If you decide you want the space and it's already been booked, we'll move other events around to accommodate yours. Assuming they aren't ones already organized by your family, of course."

"That won't be necessary, Lady Romolo," he said. "I'll let you know by the end of the week."

"Very well." The curator gave a curt nod before turning back to Astrea. "Do you have any other questions, Miss Sovna?"

She shook her head. "No, my lady."

"Then I'll let you two look around the space. I look forward to your call, Your Imperial Highness." After a small curtsy, Milena waddled down the stairs and out of sight.

Jin took a few steps toward the center of the room. His shirt wrinkled as he clasped his arms behind his back. "So . . . what do you think?"

"I think it's fine, Captain."

He turned to face her. "Just fine?"

"I'm sure your father would be pleased with the choice."

"I'm not asking what my father would like. I'm asking your opinion."

Astrea sucked in a breath. Wasn't what the emperor wanted what ultimately mattered here? Her opinion was not important; she was there to assist with research and logistics. What did Jin not understand about her role in all of this? Or his role, for that matter.

"If he doesn't like it, that won't reflect well on me or Raela, Captain." She didn't want to get into the library's budget issues or how anything that went wrong would be her fault. "I'm concerned about what your father wants. What you want."

"What I want," Jin repeated, once again turning in a circle to look at the room. That steely pain was back, flickering to life in one breath and dying again in the next. "None of this is what I want, but here we are. So sure, whatever my father wants is what we'll do. I'll run the option by him."

It was Astrea's turn to hesitate. She'd never known Jin to have an interest in imperial life or government. When they were younger, he'd grumbled about protocol, been late to events, and ignored some of the palace rules. He'd never done anything outrageous, but it had still been a problem. In Kalama, everyone had their roles to play, and even after all these years, Jin didn't seem keen on playing his.

"Let me know what he says, Captain, and I'll get things organized." Jin smiled tightly. "Shall we go?"

Wordlessly, Astrea followed him down the stairs. Lady Romolo was nowhere to be found, but the docent from before offered his goodbyes and another bow as Jin led the way out of the building. The air outside was warm, the sun bright and harsh compared to the soft light of the museum.

"I'll finish reading through those books tonight," Jin said as they reached the bottom of the stairs outside. "Will you be at the library tomorrow?"

"I work all week."

"I don't know if I'll be able to stop by, but I'll try. There's still a lot of work we need to do."

Indeed, there was much for them to do. But as Astrea said her goodbyes to Jin and watched him walk away, she sent a small thanks to the stars that he at least seemed to be taking the project seriously.

CHAPTER 13

Astrea hated running late. The clock on her bedside table showed it was already a quarter past the ninth morning bell, and she was supposed to be at the library by half past eight.

Of course she'd oversleep today of all days. She had a thousand things on her to-do list, not just for her project but other tasks that needed to be handled at the library.

All night she'd been up, thinking about her uncle's suggestion to leave Kalama when this project was done. The thought of leaving Cressida and Eliana behind made Astrea sick to her stomach, but the idea of being able to live without fear of imperial punishment was tempting. Intoxicating, even. She'd spent hours imagining what it would be like to travel to the Tornamian capital or the Taipoli Islands, the kind of life she'd live there.

Daydreaming didn't get her to work on time, though. Astrea smoothed the front of her aubergine dress, slung her satchel across her body, and hurried out of the apartment. She took the stairs two at a time, landing hard on the tiles decorating the first floor. As she flung open the front door, she ran into something—someone—hard.

"Hey!" Nicos grabbed Astrea by the shoulders, stopping them from toppling over. "Where are you off to in such a hurry?"

"I'm late, Nicos." Astrea tried squeezing past him, but his wide frame blocked the exit. "Can you move, please?"

"Jin sent me to get you."

"Jin?" Astrea paused, the only sound the ducks splashing in the pond next to the observatory. "Why?"

"A meeting with his father."

Nothing was going according to plan.

"I—" She couldn't say no to this. This *was* her job; Raela had told her to do what needed to be done for the foreseeable future. "Alright, sure."

Nicos stared at her for a moment, then nodded and turned back to the palace. Astrea quickened her pace to keep up with his long strides.

"Was I supposed to know about this meeting earlier?" Astrea asked.

"I don't think so. Even Jin seemed surprised when he stopped me in the hall."

Great, Astrea thought ruefully. Surprise meetings with Emperor Aelius and Jin. This was just what she didn't need. "Do you know how long it's going to take?"

"Jin didn't say."

They finally reached the formal gardens, and Nicos started through the hedge maze. Dark green concern pulsated in the air around him, his shoulders tightening. A few gulls cried out as they circled overhead.

"You're quiet this morning," Astrea said. Nicos was usually the chatty type when they were away from the prying eyes of courtiers and would often talk about anything from the weather to sports to restaurants. The gardens were quiet, and as Astrea stretched her magic out, she confirmed nobody was nearby. "You feeling alright?"

"Oh, fine." Nicos ran a hand over his auburn hair, smoothing the top and fiddling with his bun. "Just have a lot on my mind."

You and me both, Astrea thought. "Anything you want to talk about?" she asked.

"Well . . . I'm just a little worried about Ellie."

That concern continued dancing around Nicos, the emotion rough like sandpaper against Astrea's skin. "What about her?" Astrea asked. "Did something happen?"

"She's just overworked, though she'd never let on to that. I know her . . . job . . . is important, but she's just one person."

Astrea frowned. She'd felt that fatigue from Eliana when they'd gone to the dress shop at the start of the week, had seen the way Kaius taunted her. Eliana usually hid her fatigue and anxieties well from others; that was part of her job. But based on what Astrea knew, Eliana was just running into obstacles lately.

"I know she is," Astrea said as they started up the veranda's shallow steps. "I could try talking with her if you want me to."

"Do you think she'll listen to you?"

As they reached the palace door, Astrea stopped. "Honestly? No, I really don't think she will, but it's worth a try." Astrea didn't even know if princesses got the day off, but surely Eliana could take an hour or two for herself.

"Well, thank you." Nicos's voice was tight, but mint relief tangled with that dark green concern. Then he looked at the door and nodded. "Let's get you to this meeting, shall we?"

While Nicos's news about Eliana was concerning, Astrea tried to focus on the matter at hand as they moved through the palace halls. She was on her way to a meeting with Jin and Emperor Aelius both. A meeting where they had basically no information to share. *Just great.*

The emperor's now-familiar office door came into view at the end of the next hallway. Nicos wasted no time in walking right up to it. The emperor's personal guard, Caliban, stood on the right side of the door. He glanced at Astrea, cool emptiness crossing the distance between them. The hairs on Astrea's neck prickled, and she forced herself to smile at the man. He didn't smile back. Instead, Caliban raised his pale fist and knocked twice, then opened the door for Astrea.

"You cannot be serious, Father," Eliana said. Her back was to the door.

Astrea hadn't expected Eliana or Kaius to be in the room. She turned to look at the door again, but Caliban had closed it. Nicos was nowhere to be seen.

"Watch your words, Ellie," Kaius hissed. He leaned against the emperor's desk and faced the door, arms crossed as he stared at Astrea. "You may not think this is important, but it is."

"Then explain why it's important!" Eliana exclaimed. "Father, you cannot keep diverting funds like this. At least a third of the council is against this move. What is so important about the Ring of Fire that you need two hundred thousand lire just for this expedition?"

Two hundred thousand lire? Astrea hesitated, her feet unmoving as she stood just inside the office's doorway. Finally, though, Jin looked over his shoulder and tilted his head. It was an invitation, but to what, Astrea wasn't sure. Should she be overhearing this?

"I do not need to justify this to you or the council, Eliana." Emperor Aelius's voice sent a chill through Astrea's spine. "Tell the council I will be pulling the money from the military's budget to cover this. Some of the troops can skip a paycheck this month. And tell the council it's not up for debate, either."

Eliana's hands tightened into fists at her sides, crimson rage igniting around her. "Fine." Snatching a file off the emperor's desk, Eliana turned on her heel and strode toward the door. She looked at Astrea for only a second, but her tight expression told Astrea everything she needed to know. Eliana needed time to cool down.

"Leave us, Kaius," the emperor said as he settled into his desk chair.

"But—" he started.

"Leave us."

Kaius looked at his father, then his brother, then Astrea before he followed Eliana out of the room. Only when the door clicked shut did the emperor turn his attention to Astrea.

"My apologies, Miss Sovna. Caliban should not have let you in while I was meeting with my children. Please, have a seat."

"I didn't mean to intrude, Your Imperial Majesty," Astrea said, trying to keep her voice soft as she made her way toward his desk. "I should be the one apologizing."

The emperor smiled as he motioned to the chair. Astrea sat.

"No matter," he said. "You know how Eliana gets."

If Astrea was supposed to agree with him, she didn't. Eliana had a temper, but she rarely got angry without good cause. And based on what Astrea had just heard, Eliana had every right to be mad. Instead of saying anything, Astrea simply offered what she hoped came across as a sympathetic smile.

"The real reason I wanted to speak with you two," the emperor said, his gaze drifting to Jin, "was to see how our project is going. Tell me, what have you found so far?"

Jin hadn't brought any substantial information or decisions to Astrea. She'd found a few interesting stories from Novarian history, but what was the appropriate step here? She looked toward Jin, who had taken the seat next to her.

"I actually have a few questions for you, Father," he said, voice steady. "Miss Sovna's been trying her best to get the answers out of me, but I simply didn't know what to tell her." He produced a paper from his jacket, then unfolded it and read the questions aloud to the emperor. They were the ones she'd written down for him days ago.

The emperor leaned back in his chair, the wood creaking with his movement. "Have you looked at venues in the city yet?"

"We visited the art museum yesterday," Jin said.

"That won't do." Emperor Aelius shook his head. "No. Something larger. Grander."

"Perhaps the palace," Jin suggested.

"Not the palace." The emperor reached for a trinket on the edge of his desk, a bejeweled egg. Its ebony exterior shone under the room's chandelier, the rubies that studded the silver filigree edges sparkling. "I want to remind our neighbors to the north of our shared history and culture. Go to the Great Hall of History, and perhaps even the Great Library"—he looked at Astrea—"before checking elsewhere. Those both have a grand but neutral presence."

The art museum also has a grand but neutral presence, Astrea thought. But she wasn't going to argue.

"And ask if there are any artifacts and items we may pull from the city's museums and archives for this event," the emperor added.

"Do you have further instructions on what Miss Sovna and I should be researching?" Jin asked. "Or is all of our 'shared history' on the table?"

"Limit yourselves to the last five hundred years," the emperor said as he set the egg back down on the corner of his desk. "Art, culture, history, mythology." Emperor Aelius paused and nodded again.

Astrea swallowed a sigh. Whenever Raela handled these kinds of events, people knew what they wanted to include. This was all over the place, and though there would be overlap in these subjects, that was a ton of information to research.

"Are you serious?" Jin asked.

Just as rage had flared around Eliana, it burst to life around the emperor. He leaned forward in his seat, sneering as he snapped, "You question me, son?"

"I would never question you, Father."

Astrea braced herself. Why, *why* would Jin provoke his father now? When she was in the room? She was going to kill him if the emperor didn't first.

But where Astrea expected the emperor's rage to grow, the crimson surrounding him died down, replaced by nothing. "Once you've done some more research, Varojin, we can narrow it down further. What other questions are you incapable of answering yourself?"

"Who do you want catering the gala?" Jin asked. He was focused on the paper, the muscle in his jaw tightening. "And how long is the exhibit going to run for?"

"The palace staff will cater," Emperor Aelius replied. "And we will open it to the public for a month. Is that all?"

"Those are all of our questions for now, Your Imperial Majesty," Astrea said quickly. She was as eager to leave as he apparently was to get rid of them, and Jin didn't need to say anything else they might both come to regret.

"Then you may both leave."

Though it was worded like permission, Astrea knew a command when she heard one. She was on her feet in seconds, curtsying to the emperor. He simply nodded. Jin guiding her toward the exit was actually a relief. She forced herself to breathe as they crossed the last few steps to the door.

Although the hallway outside the emperor's office was empty now, raised voices caught Astrea's attention. Her chest tightened again as she kept her magic pulled as close to herself as she could.

Jin sighed. "Come on."

They started down the hallway. The argument continued, growing louder as they got closer. When they turned a corner, the source became obvious. Eliana stood toe-to-toe with Kaius, jabbing her finger into his face. Nicos watched from a distance, his cold horror slamming into Astrea.

"You think you know better than the rest of us," Eliana hissed, "but you're just propping up Father's poor decisions. You *know* this is a bad idea, Kaius. You know that. Why are you still supporting it?"

"Oh, Ellie," Kaius cooed, "Father knows what he's doing. He's been running the empire for three decades. You're practically still a child."

"Still a child?"

Oh, skies. This was not going to end well.

"Still a child?" Eliana repeated, her voice rising. The hairs on Astrea's neck and arms prickled as lightning flickered around Eliana's fingertips. Nicos, still a few paces away from Eliana, pressed his lips into a thin line, that same cold horror leaking from him.

Jin finally stepped forward and wedged himself between his siblings. "That's enough from both of you," he said. But he was facing Kaius, their eyes level. "Especially you. If you can't see that Ellie's right, then you have no business being in this palace. Get lost."

Astrea had seen the siblings argue plenty of times when they were all children. Kaius had always picked on both Jin and Eliana, but this was different. Going at each other's throats over imperial policy, especially openly in the palace hallways, was . . . new. Bad.

To Astrea's greater surprise, Kaius simply backed away from his brother.

"Fine," Kaius snapped. "But that expedition is happening one way or another. The army will be fine without a paycheck for a month." Then he turned and strode down the hallway, shoulders back and head held high.

"Why did you intervene?" Eliana asked once Kaius was out of sight. "I had it handled, Jin."

How many times had Astrea heard them have this conversation before? Jin had always stood up for Eliana when they were kids, had always separated her and Kaius before their fights got too serious.

"Kaius deserves whatever you were going to do to him, but that's not going to get you support, Ellie." Jin turned and grasped Eliana's shoulders. "Go to the council and try to convince them to convince Father."

"What do you think I've been trying for weeks?" Eliana shrugged Jin's hands away. "You don't get it. You don't know what it's like trying to fight Kaius and half the council."

"Ellie," Astrea said gently. She didn't even know what to say, but the soft gray of numbness wove its way around Eliana. "Can you take the day off? You've been working so hard—"

"No. No, I cannot." Eliana's reply was quiet, but her jaw was set. "I'll be fine. I have meetings to attend. I'll see you both later."

Without looking at either Jin or Astrea, Eliana turned in the opposite direction and started down the long hallway. Nicos glanced over his shoulder at Astrea and mouthed 'see?' before he followed Eliana out of sight.

Now what? Astrea hated seeing Eliana like this. Could she and Cressida do something to help? They couldn't solve Eliana's political problems, but maybe they could help another way.

"Astrea?" Jin's light touch on her shoulder made Astrea jump. "Sorry, didn't mean to startle you."

"It's fine." Astrea stared down the empty hallway. "Do you think she'll be alright?"

"I hope so. And I hope she finds a solution, because no part of our army should be going without pay right now. Not with the situation my father's forced them into."

"I hate the war," Astrea whispered, finally daring to meet Jin's gaze. It seemed like no family was untouched by it in some way. Soldiers came back from the front every week, replacements sent in so those too traumatized to fight could recover. But they weren't recovering, not the way the government surely expected them to. And what was all of it even for? Resources the empire didn't need?

Even as much as Astrea hated the lie Saros had forced her into, she was grateful she hadn't been drafted because of her magic. Both options would put her in a cage, but at least this cage was a little more comfortable, if not one that left her drowning in her own guilt. She could be out there, helping people. Healing people. She wasn't.

Jin opened his mouth to say something, but a clock down the hallway chimed the tenth morning hour.

"I need to get to the library," Astrea muttered.

"Of course." Jin straightened. "I'm sorry this took so long."

"Raela will understand." Understanding and keeping up with library tasks were two different things, but Astrea wasn't going to lay that at Jin's feet. It wasn't his fault his father was calling them at his whim. "Are you coming with me?"

"No." He sighed. "Unfortunately, I think I need to go speak with the council. Maybe I can get them to see reason."

Disappointment curled in the pit of Astrea's stomach, but she shoved it away. She couldn't even begin to process that feeling. Instead, she said, "Yes, please, go help Ellie. I'll get started on the topics your father mentioned."

"I'll try to stop by later if I can," Jin said. "If you want me to, I mean."

"I can handle it today if you're busy."

"I don't mind coming by later if I have time."

Astrea forced a smile. "Really. It's fine. Go help your sister, Captain."

Jin searched her face for a heartbeat, then two, before he finally nodded. "Alright. I'll see you tomorrow."

"The library's closed tomorrow."

"What? It's never closed."

"Solstice Night, remember?"

Government institutions always closed on major holidays, and Astrea was grateful she was going to have the day off. Eliana likely wouldn't have the full day off, but she would at least get a few hours to prepare for the night's events.

"Oh. Right." Jin nodded. "I suppose I'll see you at the festival then?"

"Yes, I'll be there."

A ghost of a smile passed across his face. "You don't sound excited."

"Ellie wants me to go."

If he needed more of an explanation, Jin didn't ask for one. He simply smiled again. "Bye, Astrea."

"Bye, Captain."

As Astrea wove her way through the palace hallways and stepped back out into the morning sun, the earlier disappointment she'd pushed away clawed its way back into her belly, making its home there as she finally started for the library.

CHAPTER 14

Astrea closed the book in front of her and ran a hand through her hair.

After that near-disastrous meeting with the emperor, she'd taken the books Raela had helped her find up to the quiet of the library's fourth floor. She knew this was going to happen, but there was simply too much information for them to parse through for the emperor. Painting styles that originated in Novaria, fashion influences still seen across the continent, monsters and heroes from old myths, and so many battles. Dumping these books on Jin for him to sort through would be better, but he'd gone to help Eliana. Astrea needed to do this herself.

Bringing them home seemed like the best option. She'd never get through them before the library closed for the holiday weekend, and Astrea didn't want to go three days without working on this.

An outline, she told herself as she took the elevator to the lobby. She could create an outline and give that to Jin to review, then he could decide what to do with the information. *Good.*

As the elevator doors opened to the lobby, Astrea caught sight of Raela walking toward the basement door. A short man followed her, his curly brown hair streaked with gray. They disappeared downstairs, Raela's tinkling laugh echoing in the stairwell.

"Who was that?" Astrea asked Serra as she approached the circulation desk.

The dark-haired page glanced up from her book. "Oh, some antiquities dealer."

"What did he want?"

"I didn't ask." Serra nodded toward the books cradled in Astrea's arms. "You taking those?"

"Yes, could you check them out to me, please?"

As Serra filled out the paperwork, Astrea went back to the staff office and grabbed her satchel. Only Serra's belongings remained, and Astrea flipped the lights off before she headed back to the front of the building.

"Here you go." Serra slid the books across the counter to Astrea. "Do you have plans for Solstice Night?"

"I do, actually," Astrea said.

Serra's cerulean eyes widened, green curiosity dancing around her. "Are they with Prince Varojin?"

"Why . . ." Astrea huffed. "Why would you think I have plans with Prince Varojin?"

"Felix was telling me that you're *friends* with the prince," Serra replied. "And with Princess Eliana. How did you meet them? Are you going to the festival with both of them?"

Of course Felix had told Serra all about that. Felix loved to chat, even when he was supposed to be working. "I'm going with my friend Cressida," Astrea said. It wasn't a complete lie. "And Prince Varojin and I aren't friends. I'm just helping him with something."

"That's not what Felix said," Serra replied, eyebrows raised. "He said Prince Varojin had all of these stories about when you were kids—"

"Don't believe everything Felix says," Astrea muttered. "Enjoy your Solstice Night, Serra. I'll see you next week."

Astrea didn't wait for a reply. She didn't even wait for Raela to re-emerge from the basement to say goodbye. She simply grabbed her books and left the library, reveling in the cool sea breeze rolling in off the bay.

She didn't want to go back to the observatory. Saros was still barely making his presence known in the apartment, even though she could sense his turmoil through the floors separating them. Sitting there worrying about him sounded like the worst way to spend her evening.

Astrea also didn't want to go to dinner alone. That would be just as bad as eating alone at home.

There was one person Astrea could go see, though.

The Nikaphoroses' home was nestled on the end of a row of colorful townhomes, theirs a cheerful mint green with white trim and the most abundant garden of all. Tall shrubs, cypress trees, and a mix of snapdragons, wildflowers, and large peony bushes bordered the wrought iron fence. Astrea pulled out her key to let herself inside, but as soon as she climbed up the front steps, Cressida flung the door open.

"Good, you're here."

"How'd you know it was me?" Astrea set her books down on the narrow table near the front door, then hung her bag on the iron coatrack next to it.

"I heard the front gate. Come on in, I just made dinner."

As Astrea followed Cressida into the dining room, she realized how quiet the house was. The Nikaphoroses were not a quiet family. "Where are your parents?" she asked.

"They've gone and abandoned me."

"Are they out of town?" Astrea pulled out the chair she always sat in and plopped down. "Are they missing the festival?"

"Not out of town, but both of them had work to do in Crescent Park to finish setting up for said festival."

Astrea nodded. This wasn't the first year the Nikaphoroses had helped set up for the celebration. Lodestar Industries usually sponsored one of the many flashy games added to the festival in recent years.

"Well, I hope I get to see them tomorrow night," Astrea said as Cressida started spooning pasta onto her plate. The shell-shaped noodles and simple red sauce were a staple in Kalama despite the variety of cuisines and restaurants available. Astrea loved the spicy Taipoli food Cressida often made, and she often craved the savory southern Tornamian dishes Balthazar made, where his mother's side of the family was from.

"Speaking of tomorrow night," Cressida started. She finally sat down and took a bite. "Do you think Ellie's going to want us to go over early to get ready?"

"I hope so. She has my dress, and besides that, she needs a break."

"A break?" Cressida set her fork down. "What do you mean she needs a break?"

Astrea sighed and shoved a forkful of the pasta into her mouth. The red sauce, though it looked the same as always, had a slightly different flavor Astrea couldn't name. Cressida was always experimenting with whatever produce and herbs Sarsali had grown in the garden out back. It was different, but it was good. She chewed slowly, trying to decide how much to tell Cressida.

"Nicos showed up at the observatory to collect me for a meeting with the emperor and Jin."

"Oh, skies," Cressida muttered. "That must've been fun."

Astrea shrugged. "That's not even the bad part, honestly. On our way to the palace, Nicos was telling me he's worried about Ellie, and when we got to the meeting, Ellie was arguing with her father *and* Kaius." At the mention of Kaius, rusty annoyance flashed around Cressida. "And after

Jin and I finished up our own meeting, we found her and Kaius arguing right in the open in the palace. It was bad, Cress. Jin had to intervene, and honestly, I'm worried about Ellie."

"No shit?" Cressida set her wine glass back on the table. "What was she going to do to Kaius? Something he deserved, I'm sure."

"Oh, he did."

"What were they fighting about?"

This was probably something Eliana would talk to them about anyway, so Astrea explained the argument about the Ring of Fire and pulling funds from the military budget to cover the cost of the expedition.

Cressida suddenly found her pasta very interesting. "The Ring of Fire, huh?"

"Do you think that's odd?" Astrea asked.

"I just . . ."

"It's something you can't talk about?"

Cressida nodded.

"And how's that project going for you?"

"Well . . ." Cressida tucked a curl behind her ear, where she wore several small silver hoops. "All I can say is I don't know why the emperor's going back to the Ring of Fire. I have everything I need to do the work he wants me to do."

Back? Astrea had assumed this was the first expedition.

"Does Ellie know why her father's going out there?" Cressida asked.

"No." Astrea reached for one of the airy rolls sitting in a basket in the middle of the table. "I know she's got to work hard, Cress, but it's eating her alive."

Cressida was quiet for a long moment. She moved what was left of her dinner around her plate with her fork, then sighed. "Don't tell anyone I told you this."

"I won't."

"I'm serious. Not even Ellie can know I told you this. I don't want it getting back to the emperor."

"I'm being serious, too. I won't tell anyone."

Cressida nodded. "He's trying to exploit a resource he found a few months back. I don't know if it's even possible, but that's what he's got me looking into."

A resource? What resource could the emperor have possibly found in the Ring of Fire? All that was out there was volcanic ash and rock.

"Is your work dangerous?"

"Dangerous? No." Cressida shrugged. "Figuring out what the emperor is doing doesn't solve Ellie's problem, though."

"Maybe we could do something nice for her," Astrea said.

"Nice how?"

"I was hoping you had an idea."

"Well, I know *something* that would take her mind off things," Cressida said, grinning as the tight orange knot of anxiety around her loosened. "Do you suppose Nicos would be up for some overtime—"

"You're ridiculous." But it was a little funny, and Astrea had wondered for months now if something was going on between Eliana and her guard. They were close, and Nicos clearly cared deeply for her, but did it cross the line from professional to personal? She wouldn't ask if Eliana didn't want to tell just yet. "Surely you have more ideas than that."

"Being serious, no, I have no ideas. All we can do is try to support her."

Astrea sighed. She was afraid that was the case. Maybe Eliana would be more open to support if she wasn't fresh off an argument with Kaius or her father.

"Speaking of taking your mind off things, how are things going with Jin?" Cressida asked.

Astrea nearly spit out her water. She coughed, then asked, "How is that taking my mind off things?"

"Is it as bad as you imagined it would be?"

"Straight to the point."

"Sorry," Cressida said, her smile soft. "I just expected you to be in worse shape, considering how upset you were last week."

Astrea wouldn't call herself not upset, but working with Jin wasn't what she'd expected either. "It's awkward," Astrea admitted. "And even though he's still kind, I'm well aware of his position as a soldier and prince and what he'd have to do if he learned my secret."

"As if Ellie isn't also in that position?" Cressida asked. "Why is Jin a bigger threat?"

Astrea opened her mouth to respond, then snapped it closed. Why *was* she so much more threatened by Jin? Cressida wasn't wrong. Eliana would also have to report that information to her father, bound by duty and station. But that thought rarely crossed Astrea's mind when she was with Eliana.

"You never told me what happened, you know," Cressida finally said.

Sighing, Astrea let her eyes flutter closed. Eight years. Eight years and she'd never actually told Cressida what happened between herself and Jin. Part of that was because even Astrea wasn't exactly sure what happened or why things ended the way they did.

"It's so silly, Cress," Astrea finally said. When she opened her eyes, she found Cressida staring at her.

"Try me."

"He didn't say goodbye when he left."

Astrea sighed again. She didn't know why she'd waited so long to tell her best friend, but she hadn't told anyone. It had been easiest to avoid the topic, and Eliana and Cressida had soon realized *something* had happened. It wasn't like Jin came back home often anyway; he didn't even return to the capital on a yearly basis. It was always so easy to make herself scarce, to not be around when he was in the city.

"When he left for the military?" Cressida asked, and Astrea nodded. "That's not silly. He owed you more than that."

"He didn't owe me anything." Even as she said the words, the lie pierced her deeply. "When he left for his military training . . ." Astrea swallowed. "He didn't even tell me he was going. Ellie said he'd known for weeks. How was that supposed to make me feel?" She didn't know why she felt like she had to defend herself. Her voice trembled as she continued, "No call, no letter, no visit. We were friends for so long, and he just . . ."

"He disappeared on you."

"And he's never tried to contact me since. Eight years, Cress! He's made it clear he doesn't want to be my friend anymore."

It had never made sense to Astrea. Though he was a couple of years older than her, Jin had been around since the day Astrea and Saros set foot in Kalama. He'd shown her the best places for hide-and-seek and how to get the palace chef to sneak them extra cookies when they were kids. As they'd gotten a little older, he'd shown her how to navigate the streetcar system—much to his governess's dismay. He'd always attended the birthday parties Cressida's mom put on for Astrea.

Astrea would sneak Jin into the observatory when they were teenagers because he insisted he wanted to learn about the stars and that she was the best teacher. They'd raced each other through the gardens, and he'd always let her win despite being much faster than her. They'd snuck to the beaches below the palace with Cressida and Eliana, and they'd both been there to support Eliana when her mother, the empress, died.

Eliana and Cressida were Astrea's best friends now, but Jin had been her best friend back in those days.

How could he just leave and never talk to her again?

Astrea blew out a sharp breath as she stared up at the dining room's box beam ceiling, willing herself not to cry as memories flooded her system. "It's foolish, I know. Childhood friendships don't always carry over. He didn't owe me anything."

"Az, look at me." Cressida's voice was as steely as her eyes when she spoke. "He does owe you something. Maybe he has no decent explanation, but he should at least apologize for being an ass."

"I guess."

"I'm going to kick his ass next time I see him," Cressida muttered. "I'll do it, I swear."

"It's fine, Cress. He'll leave Kalama in a few months, and then I can go back to pretending he doesn't exist."

"Well, you need to figure out how to work with him in the meantime," Cressida said as she started tearing into one of the leftover dinner rolls. "Maybe you two need to talk about it."

"Because that's what I want to do. It's already awkward enough."

"You don't have to if you don't want to, but I know Jin just as well as you do. There must be some explanation."

If Jin did have a reason for abandoning her all those years ago, Astrea wasn't sure she wanted to know. Her mind already had a dozen possibilities, ones she'd run through over and over again. That she was actually his little sister's best friend, not his like he'd told her many times. That he'd only been friends with her because she could help him with his studies. That he was simply being polite and had never really considered her a friend at all. That she'd been his only easy option for a friend within the palace compound's walls. Getting confirmation that one of those was true would hurt more than never knowing in the first place.

"I should get going," Astrea said as she stood. The sunset, a brilliant mix of pinks, purples, and oranges, was slowly building outside, visible through the windows that overlooked the Nikaphoroses' garden. "I want to get home before it's dark."

They walked to the front door in silence, and Cressida pulled Astrea into a quick embrace.

"You really don't want me to kick his ass?" she asked as she pulled away.

Laughing, Astrea grabbed her books. "No, thank you, but if I change my mind, I'll let you know."

"Fine. Want me to drive you home?"

"That's alright. I could use the fresh air."

Cressida nodded as she opened the front door. "Well, call me when you get there."

"Bye, Cress." Astrea trotted down the porch steps, willing herself to think about anything other than the memories of years past and what explanation Jin could possibly have.

CHAPTER 15

Going to the palace didn't usually stump Astrea this much, but she also didn't typically get ready with Eliana. What would she need besides makeup? Eliana had her dress, so there wasn't much else she could bring. *Jewelry*, she realized. Without knowing what her dress looked like, this might be impossible. Hesitating, Astrea plucked two silver bracelets, a handful of rings, and the crescent moon necklace Cressida had gifted her from her jewelry box.

When she had everything packed in her satchel, Astrea went into the living room. All she needed now were her keys, and she could be on her way.

"Are you ready for Solstice Night?"

Astrea jumped. Saros was sitting on the narrow blue sofa in their living room, a book open in his lap. Saros wasn't an old man—he was barely forty years old—but he'd aged visibly in the last six months. Strands of gray shot through his dark hair and beard. He'd always had fair skin, but now it seemed even paler. Even his cheeks, usually round and rosy like Astrea's, seemed sunken in. Astrea hated that he looked so exhausted.

They hadn't spoken much since their argument a couple of nights prior. If he was willing to engage now, she had to try.

Astrea leaned against the wall opposite the sofa. "Are you alright?"

He waved a hand at her but didn't look up from whatever he was reading. "I'm fine, my dear. Go, enjoy your time with your friends."

She knew he wasn't fine. Why would he try lying to her when she could sense his anxieties?

Astrea pushed off the wall and moved to one of the armchairs across from him. She rested her hand on its back as she said, "Uncle."

He raised an eyebrow but still didn't look up. "Yes?"

"Will you please look at me, especially when you're trying to lie to me?"

Saros tilted his head up. "What is it, Astrea?"

"Why are you so tired?" she asked. "Would you tell me if I could help you in some way? With your work, I mean. You've been working so much, and I've barely seen—"

"I don't need your help," he said, his words sharp.

"Is there something you've seen, then?" she pressed. "Something that's bothering you?"

"I'm simply tired."

"Are you ill?" Astrea moved toward her uncle's spot on the sofa. Something had to be wrong with him. He wasn't usually this grumpy. "Should I call a healer?"

Saros shook his head, closing his book with a thud. "Go, please. I'll be fine."

Astrea pursed her lips. Saros hated it when she used her magic at all, let alone to help him. Several years prior, he'd broken his arm and had refused to let Astrea heal him for a good half hour before he finally gave in. He'd only agreed to it because finding another healer would've taken too long. That was the last time she'd healed him.

She sucked in a breath and placed a hand on his shoulder. Her palm tingled, a faint white light illuminating the room. Fatigue washed over Astrea, like she'd had just a few hours of sleep. It wouldn't hurt her, but this was just like healing an injury: mirror pain then, mirror fatigue now. Most times, it faded quickly, but the greater healing energy she poured into another person, the longer the symptoms lingered in her body.

"You can't keep going on like this," she whispered. If this was how her uncle felt, no wonder he looked so tired.

"Do not heal me, Astrea," he warned. "Do not heal anyone. It's not safe, nor is it good for you."

She never told Saros that she healed the Nikaphoroses whenever they needed her to. She'd eased illnesses, healed broken bones, and taken care of all kinds of wounds for them over the years. Just a couple of months prior, Cressida had broken her finger, and Astrea had been able to heal it but not without suffering herself. It was a pain she would gladly take on if it meant her friend wouldn't be in pain for weeks—or have to pay another mage healer. The Purifiers and Lightbringers in the city typically charged a fortune for their services.

"I'm fine," Astrea said. "I'll feel better in a few minutes, and maybe you can have a day where you feel normal. Nobody's going to know."

He pressed his lips together. "Just don't make a habit of it, my dear."

"I won't, I promise."

"Thank you." Saros smiled, the corners of his eyes wrinkling. "Go, enjoy your time with your friends. You deserve to have some fun."

Astrea took her time walking to the palace. The dizziness that had accompanied the fatigue she'd taken on from her uncle had faded, but she barely had half of her normal stamina. How did Saros live like this? What could possibly be so important to the emperor that he would ask Saros to do this to himself? Maybe that extra money from her special project could get them both away from the city for a while.

The gravel crunching under her sandals turned to cobblestones as Astrea entered the main segment of the palace gardens. Another ten minutes, she reasoned, and she should start feeling like herself again. Her head felt a little clearer already. If she circled around to the opposite side of the palace, that would give her enough time to recoup before meeting Eliana and Cressida.

Astrea had no idea how to make Saros open up about what was going on in his role as Stargazer, what he was seeing, and what the emperor was demanding. Would Eliana know? Should she ask, or would that be an invasion of her uncle's privacy? Sighing, Astrea pushed the thoughts from her head. There was no use worrying about it right now. She could figure out some kind of solution later.

As she strolled down the rear side of the palace, Astrea gazed out over Tinale Bay. The palace was raised above the city thanks to the magic of Earthmovers, and that extra height provided a magnificent view of the bay that stretched to the horizon. The water glittered in the late afternoon sun, and a seagull crooned into the breeze. Somewhere in the bay far below, a cargo vessel sounded its horn.

While the eastern side of the palace compound housed the observatory and greenhouses, the northwestern side was home to barracks, training rings, stables, a massive garage, and an airship mooring station. The expanse of buildings broke up the carefully unkempt foliage, and there was a lot more life here. Instead of nobles and courtiers walking the pathways, there were just palace guards and military officers. It was lively, especially now. A small crowd had gathered around one of the sparring circles, creating a sea of red and maroon uniforms.

Astrea rarely saw anyone spar unless it was Eliana at one of her training sessions, and seeing what other mages could do was exciting. It was also an opportunity to study what they did. Her mother may have taught her how to heal, but Astrea had never learned to fight.

As she loitered a few dozen feet from the edge of the crowd, a familiar freckled face turned and waved at her. Nicos.

"Astrea!" he exclaimed as she went to his side. A few of the guards who had been standing with him nodded at her, but they turned and walked back toward the palace. "What are you doing here?"

"I was just trying to waste a little time," she said. "I'm meeting Her Imperial Highness and decided to take the long way. What's going on here?"

Astrea finally looked down into the sparring circle. It was more like a wide pit than a circle, the ground covered in well-worn grass and moss. The sides sloped down gently. Below, two men circled each other.

"An epic sparring session," Nicos said, his attention trained on the figures below. "Have you ever seen him fight before?"

One man's back was to her, and the other she didn't recognize. He had dark brown skin and short black hair and, if she had to guess, was close to her age. He kicked up and out in a circular motion, and a chunk of earth the size of Nicos's head flew toward his opponent.

"The Earthmover?" she asked.

"Well, him too, but I meant Prince Varojin."

Just my luck. He was going to think she was purposefully seeking him out, but if she turned and ran into the palace, Nicos would think that was odd.

"Uh, a bit, when we were children," she said. Astrea fought to keep her eyes on the Earthmover, but a blast of fire from Jin's fist caught her attention.

He was moving so differently than she remembered and even differently from Eliana. They shared the same base magic—fire—but Jin's motions were fluid like a Tempest in one moment and then strong the next, almost like the Earthmover across from him.

"Come on, Adi!" Jin shouted as they circled each other. "I can take it!"

Adi—the Earthmover—laughed, the sound echoing. "You sure about that, Captain?"

Even from this distance, Astrea could see the sweat pouring off Jin's face. His hair was matted to his forehead, and his sleeveless black shirt clung to his abdomen. Adi didn't look to be in any better shape.

"How long have they been going?" Astrea asked.

"Oh, I showed up about fifteen minutes ago when Her Imperial Highness sent me out for a 'break,'" Nicos said. As rough annoyance scraped over Astrea's skin, she pressed her lips together and focused on the sparring. "I think she just wanted to get rid of me. But I'd reckon they've been here for at least twice that long."

Though it was just training, that had to be difficult. Astrea couldn't imagine healing someone for thirty minutes straight.

A piece of earth the size of Adi's head shot toward Jin. Astrea's entire body tensed. Jin rolled to one side, getting off a shot of his own. Adi dodged the flames, peach amusement sparking in the air around him.

"I thought for sure that one would land!" Adi called, grinning.

"And I think we're both done for the day," Jin replied. "Truce?"

A good-natured chuckle came from Adi as he straightened. "If that's what you have to tell yourself, Captain. I could keep going."

The two men met in the middle of the pit, clapping their palms together and shaking hands.

"Aw, come on!" Nicos called. "That's it?"

A few of the guards still watching laughed, and Jin, who had started to walk off toward the barracks on the opposite side of the sparring pit, turned. He smiled at Nicos, his expression faltering only for a second as his gaze fell to Astrea. She forced herself not to turn and leave. Jin waved, his shirt clinging to his well-muscled chest.

The Earthmover turned around then. He caught Astrea's eye and waved, too, so she waved back. Then she turned to Nicos.

"Well, that was fun," she said, "but I should be going."

"And I should be getting back to duty. Come on, I'll walk with you."

Astrea followed Nicos toward the palace. The late afternoon sun beat down on them relentlessly as they left the training grounds and moved back into the gardens.

"So, you ready for Solstice Night?" Nicos asked when they were alone. "Ellie didn't tell me you were coming by today."

There was a lot Eliana probably didn't tell Nicos, but Astrea wasn't going to tell him that. The poor man was already worried.

"She probably just forgot," Astrea said instead. "She's got a lot on her mind lately. Is she feeling any better?"

Nicos shrugged. "Maybe a bit."

"A bit is better than not at all."

Nicos scratched at his neatly trimmed beard. After a moment, he nodded as if this were some great revelation. "Yes, I suppose it is."

Astrea sincerely hoped Eliana was more than a 'bit' better, but knowing the situation in the palace, that was unlikely. Something was going to have to change, whether that was Eliana's approach or the emperor's politics. Hopefully it would be the latter.

The veranda that lined the palace's western wall was a mirror image of the eastern side, though this one had a portico, offering temporary refuge from the sun. Astrea took the steps quickly, Nicos matching her pace. When they reached the landing, he opened the door for her.

"Do you need me to walk you upstairs?" he asked as she stepped into the palace.

"No, I'll be alright. Are you on duty tonight?"

"Of course." More of that annoyance pressed into Astrea as Nicos continued, "I've got a few things I need to do before I come collect you ladies. I'll see you soon."

"Bye, Nicos."

As he stalked off through the garden sitting room and down the corridor, Astrea watched him for any other emotion. But all that was there was that rusty annoyance, harsh against the palace's white walls. What was bothering him?

Astrea trailed after him. But instead of disappearing to the right, she veered left. The narrow hall had a marble staircase tucked in one corner, and Astrea followed it up two floors.

The upper levels of the palace were always quiet. There were five floors in total, but much of the fifth floor was storage, and the fourth floor contained additional sitting rooms, several guest suites, and the emperor's chambers.

Maroon rugs embroidered with subtle suns—part of the imperial crest—stretched the length of the third-floor hallways and muffled Astrea's steps on the marble tiles. Tapestries, paintings of Kalama, and portraits of long-deceased Auris dynasty monarchs decorated the walls. There were just a few doors, all spread far apart.

Astrea crossed through the middle of the corridor where the grand staircases from below continued their ascent. The murmurs of courtiers two levels below floated up the stairwell, and Astrea kept moving. Toward the opposite end of the floor, Astrea finally got to the hallway containing Eliana's apartment. The other Auris siblings all had rooms on this floor, too. Would Jin be coming back here before the festival? Astrea pushed that thought out of her mind as she knocked on Eliana's door.

After several seconds, it opened and Eliana waved Astrea inside. It had always been this way with her; the emperor was surprisingly relaxed about what his children did and who could see them. There wasn't even a guard outside Eliana's door, though Astrea was sure Nicos would return soon.

"Oh, good, you're here!" Cressida called as Astrea and Eliana passed from the entryway into the sitting room.

A settee and four heavy armchairs took up half of the room, and on the opposite wall, near the closet door, was Eliana's desk. Another door was open, revealing a view of Eliana's four-poster bed. The room was decorated in a vibrant mix of jewel tones, and though it was too bright for Astrea's taste, she had to admit it looked good.

Cressida was stretched out on the settee, her ankles crossed as she popped some tiny sandwich into her mouth.

"Sorry I'm late," Astrea said. "I got distracted."

"You certainly didn't miss anything," Cressida said as Astrea sat down in a chair opposite her. "Ellie's been faffing around since I got here."

"I'm not faffing," Eliana muttered. She crossed from the sitting room into her bedroom. "I'm puttering."

"Because that's so much better." Cressida hefted herself off the settee with a groan. "Want coffee, Az?" Astrea nodded. "Ellie was *supposed* to tell me about a conversation she had with Count Lorenzi," Cressida continued as she approached the credenza against the far wall. She poured coffee from a copper pot into two cups, then started adding cream and sugar to both. "But then she started puttering."

Eliana exited her bedroom and strode toward her closet with several gowns draped over one forearm. "I loathe the man, but apparently, he has some connection to the rebels."

Astrea sat up straighter, turning to look at Cressida. Why was Eliana talking with a potential rebel?

"I thought your father wanted to squash the rebels!" Cressida called toward the closet. "Why the skies would you be speaking with them?"

"Believe it or not," Eliana said as she walked back into the room, "my father does sometimes try diplomacy before sending his tanks and aircraft in. I don't think Count Lorenzi knows much, anyway. He has strong opinions, but people are allowed to have those. Nothing that would suggest treason. And frankly, both he and the rebels have some good points."

Cressida's eyebrows shot up, and Astrea was sure her expression mirrored the Metalli's. Astrea had never given too much thought to the rebels. It wasn't that she wasn't curious; she was. They wanted reforms, and based on everything Astrea knew, reforms were desperately needed. Eliana fought for reforms nearly every day. But taking on additional risks, like associating with those very same rebels, was a terrible idea. Hiding her magic already put her in a precarious position.

And to hear Eliana admit that she thought the rebels had 'some good points,' even just to the two of them, was . . . surprising. Potentially dangerous.

"Princess Eliana Auris, agreeing with the rebels," Cressida mused, amusement thick in the air around her. "This wouldn't happen to be because of the rumors, would it?"

Emperor Aelius Auris had not formally declared which of his children would be his heir. Logically, Apelo, the eldest, would claim that spot, but rumors had been circulating for years that he'd abdicated to marry his wife, Lady Thana. Astrea was sure Jin wasn't even being considered for the spot, which left just Eliana and Kaius.

And the rebels wanted Eliana on the throne.

"No," Eliana demurred. "Though I happen to agree with them on a lot of things, particularly that Kaius isn't fit to rule."

"Nobody in their right mind thinks he's fit to rule," Cressida quipped.

While Astrea agreed that Kaius would make a terrible emperor, most people didn't see the side of Kaius they did. Most people didn't see how nasty and downright mean he could be. A lot of Helosians probably supported him becoming heir simply because he was the older of the two.

"It's not just about quelling so-called rebellious reforms," Eliana continued as she plopped into the seat next to Astrea. "My father thinks the recent murders are connected to the rebels."

Astrea took the cup of coffee Cressida handed her, then asked, "Could that be true?"

"I doubt it." Eliana drew her legs under her body and curled into the corner of the sofa. "It would be awfully out of character for them. But if there is a connection, the police will find it."

Astrea opened her mouth to ask another question, but Cressida waved her hand. "Enough about politics and intrigue." She handed Eliana her coffee, then sat down next to her. "Are we ready for another Solstice Night?"

"I've got my and Astrea's dresses hanging up in the closet," Eliana said before swallowing some of her coffee. "It's going to be perfect. Come, let's get ready while Oskar brings up our dinner."

Cressida jumped to her feet, taking her cup with her as she walked toward a bag near Eliana's bathroom door. The princess herself was taking her time standing, smoothing her skirts despite the fact that she'd be changing into something else soon.

"Oskar?" Astrea asked, and Eliana raised an eyebrow. "Where's Nicos?"

Rusty annoyance flickered around Eliana. "Hopefully taking a walk like I told him to."

Nicos had definitely taken his walk, but what did Eliana have to be annoyed about? Had she and Nicos had a fight? Astrea was about to ask when Cressida's gasp from the closet drew her attention.

"Wow, Ellie!" Cressida called. "You've really outdone yourself this year."

Eliana wiggled her eyebrows at Astrea. "Let's get you dressed, shall we? And hurry; I really need to have some fun tonight."

CHAPTER 16

Bonfires shimmered all around the city, music and dancing accompanying each smaller party the imperial car drove past. But the largest bonfire of all, and the one traditionally attended by the imperial family, was in Crescent Park, the massive park bordering Nobleman's Hill and the Market District.

As they stepped out of Eliana's car, Astrea smoothed the bodice of her dress. Eliana had made the best possible choice. The silver beaded flowers winked in the setting sun, the midnight blue fabric a sharp contrast to Astrea's pale skin. Even the voluminous skirts and tulle straps that tied in delicate bows at her shoulders were perfect.

Cressida and Eliana looked even better. Cressida's slinky emerald dress embroidered with large gold starbursts was at the height of fashion, the color popping against her warm copper complexion. And if Eliana had gotten Astrea's gown right, her own was perfect. She was a vision, a flame come to life. It was more stunning than Astrea had imagined it would be. The top of the dress was gold, fading first into a deep orange and then crimson at the bottom of the skirts. Not only were the colors beautiful, but it perfectly highlighted Eliana's curves.

"After I talk to some of the more 'important' guests," Eliana said, ushering Astrea through the stone archway marking the park's entrance, "I want to dance!"

"You, dancing?" Cressida quipped. "I never would've guessed."

Eliana leaned around Astrea, who was walking in the middle of the trio, and stuck her tongue out at Cressida. "And let me guess, Cress," she shot back, "you want to drink."

"One of the many benefits of adulthood," Cressida replied smoothly. "We all need to let off some steam, and now I can do so on your father's dime. What could be better?"

Eliana laughed, and Nicos cleared his throat behind them. When Astrea turned to look at him, she caught the hint of a smile pulling at his mouth. Even his usual uniform had been traded out for a more elevated version, and though Nicos still wore crimson like the rest of the palace guards, the brocade jacket and black slacks almost made it look like he was purposefully coordinating with Eliana.

"You two go ahead and drink and dance to your hearts' desires," Astrea said as they walked deeper into the park. "I'm just here for the food and the people watching."

The sun was still sinking below the horizon, giving way to a brilliant sky of magenta, violet, and cornflower blue. Once night truly took over, the park would surely become a sparkling landscape. Hundreds of people spread out over the grassy expanse in the middle of the park, all dressed in their finest outfits. Their jewels glittered in the firelight cast by the four enormous bonfires being tended to by imperial Fireweavers. To Astrea's left were large white tents filled with tables piled high with food and drinks. To her right, crowds lined up for the next dance of the night. A wooden dance floor had even been laid out for the occasion. Beyond that were stalls with games and dazzling lights, a cacophony of laughs and shouts already coming from that direction.

"Don't just stand there with your mouth open," Cressida teased, lacing her fingers through Astrea's. "Come on!"

As she followed her friends deeper into the crowd, Astrea tried to focus on anything but the waves of eagerness, amusement, and even frustration that pressed heavily against her skin. A smell caught Astrea's attention first. She turned in time to see a man walking by, his ring-laden hands carefully balancing a plate piled high with food. Her stomach rumbled. They'd spent so long getting ready for the evening that they'd barely touched the dinner brought up for them. But Cressida tugged on her arm again, and Astrea stumbled toward her friends instead of the tents of food that man had just come from. She frowned.

"I need to go check in with my family before I can do anything else," Eliana said. She held a hand out to Nicos, who produced a tube of lipstick and a pocket mirror from somewhere in his uniform. Eliana checked her makeup, applying a fresh coat of red lipstick before handing the items back to Nicos. "Do you want to accompany me, or shall I go alone?"

"We can go with you," Cressida offered, then glanced at Astrea. "Or I can go with her, if you'd rather . . . ?"

Astrea didn't miss the unspoken question. Was she alright seeing the rest of the imperial family given, well, everything? "Sure," Astrea said. "We can all go."

As Eliana and Nicos started off in one direction, Cressida held on to Astrea's hand, slowing their pace. "Are you sure this is a good idea?"

"Wouldn't it be odd for me not to go with the two of you?" Astrea countered. "The emperor knows we're her friends. We're here with her every year." She might not want to spend any extra time around Emperor Aelius, but purposefully avoiding him might raise questions. Besides, Eliana's meltdown the day before didn't give Astrea confidence the princess could handle Kaius. "We'll only have to go for a few minutes."

"Alright." Cressida nodded, her curls bouncing around her shoulders.

Eliana led them along the edge of the festivities, heading north toward a wide dais flanked by imperial guards. Only one of the three ornate chairs facing the crowd was occupied. Prince Kaius was sprawled out in his seat, a few attendants and guards rushing about behind him. Several men chatted in a circle nearby.

"Ah, sister." Kaius stood slowly, almost lazily. "There you are. I was wondering if you'd ever show up." He looked her up and down, only glancing at Cressida and Astrea for a moment. "You look . . . well."

Prince Kaius's outfit, a red silk shirt paired with white pants and plenty of gold jewelry, wasn't out of place among the rest of the festival goers. But next to Eliana's flame-inspired dress, he looked plain.

"Don't get jealous, Kaius," Eliana said, voice low. "Where are Father, Jin, and Apelo?"

He shrugged. "Father's on his way, I have no idea where Varojin is, and Apelo couldn't make it. One of his brats is sick."

Rough annoyance scraped Astrea's skin, so suddenly it made her flinch. Eliana adored her two nieces, Velia and Nina. Astrea was sure Eliana would lash out at Kaius for the dig. But Eliana simply smiled and turned her attention to the men loitering nearby.

"Councillors, hello," she said. "I hope you're all having a lovely evening and that my brother is being accommodating."

"Actually, Your Imperial Highness," a man with deep brown skin said, his emotions unreadable. Streaks of gray speckled his otherwise thick black hair. "I was hoping to speak with you about the budget issue. There were some things we didn't get to discuss at this morning's council meeting."

Eliana's shoulders tightened, but she smiled. "Of course, Duke Pompilio. I'll be with you in just one moment." Then Eliana crossed the dais again and kept her voice low as she said, "I'll meet you two by the food tents within an hour."

"Always at work," Cressida murmured as Eliana hurried off to speak with the duke, Nicos hot on her heels. "Now what?"

"I don't believe you've said hello to me yet, Miss Nikaphoros." Kaius sniffed. "Nor have you, Miss Sovna."

Astrea had almost forgotten Prince Kaius was there, which was actually an accomplishment.

"You *must* forgive us, Prince Kaius," Cressida said, her tone laced with false sincerity.

"Oh, fuck off, Cressida," he muttered. Kaius peered over his shoulder at Eliana, sighing as he turned back around. "Has my sister mentioned any recent meetings?"

Cressida's eyes narrowed, the shimmer of her gold eyeshadow sparkling in the bonfire light. "Why are you asking us?"

Green curiosity and rusty annoyance mingled around the prince, but that was a good question. Why *was* Kaius asking them? Was this about Eliana's meeting with Count Lorenzi? If so, why not just ask the emperor about it since he apparently sent Eliana on his behalf?

Astrea fingered the skirt of her dress. "She doesn't tell us much, Your Imperial Highness."

He raised an eyebrow. "You're her best friends and have been for years, and she doesn't tell you much?" Kaius scoffed. "I know she went to visit Count Lorenzi, and I know why."

"If you already know, then why are you asking us?" Cressida asked. "Just talk to your sister."

"Don't be smart," he warned.

Cressida smiled. "Then don't pry for information and pretend it's because you genuinely care, Your Imperial Highness."

"Apologies, Prince Kaius," Astrea said quickly as she gripped Cressida's elbow. This was neither the time nor the place. "We need to be going now. Enjoy your night."

Cressida stuck close to Astrea as she marched down the dais steps and back onto the grass below. Astrea didn't turn around until they'd disappeared into the crowds beyond, hopefully too far for Kaius to see.

"What was that?" Astrea hissed as she spun around to face Cressida.

"You have to admit, he deserved it. He always deserves it."

"That's . . ." Astrea sighed. "That's not the point. Let Ellie antagonize him if she wants to. Intervene if she asks for our help, but it's not our business right now."

"Maybe not." Cressida shrugged, her eyes roaming the crowds. It was getting louder, people cheering as the night's band struck up another song. The drums started first, then the brass instruments joined in. "What do you want to do until Ellie gets back?"

"Let's eat," Astrea said, "and then maybe I'll even join you for a dance or two."

Grinning, Cressida grabbed Astrea's hand. "You won't regret it!"

She'd only danced to two songs, but the crowd pushing in around Astrea and Cressida was getting to be too much. Everything from jubilation to anger to lust smashed into Astrea's body, and her head was swimming. Besides, the fatigue she'd taken from Saros still lingered at the edge of her consciousness. She needed to check in with him when she got home.

"I need a break!" Astrea half yelled into Cressida's ear as the band transitioned to their next song.

Cressida nodded, but her eyes were drifting over Astrea's shoulder. She turned and found what—or who—her friend was looking at: A beautiful woman with warm sepia skin, glittering jewelry, and a shimmery bronze dress. She smiled at Cressida, and Cressida beamed back. Green curiosity and pink desire tangled between the two women.

When Astrea went out with Cressida, she sometimes ended up playing the role of wing woman. Astrea had never quite understood Cressida and Eliana's ability to be instantly drawn to a person; she'd rarely ever felt that kind of pull toward anyone. Certainly not in the physical sense, but not even that much in the romantic sense, either.

When it came to the physical, Astrea knew that was just how she was. There were lots of attractive people in the world, but that alone had never translated to physical desire for her. As for the romantic, she'd had exactly two relationships in her twenty-four years of life. They'd been nice young men she met while at university but ultimately not partners she saw herself with long-term. Part of that had simply been because, in the end, neither was the right person for her. But perhaps part of that had also been the secret Astrea and Saros were trying to keep. How could she be involved with someone and keep a secret like that?

Maybe someday she'd find someone she could trust with that, but that certainly wouldn't be happening with a stranger from Solstice Night. That wasn't even what was important. What mattered now was that Cressida was happy, safe, and enjoying herself on the biggest holiday of the year.

"Oh, just go have fun," Astrea said, laughing as she pushed at the small of Cressida's back. "You know where to find me."

"See you later!" Cressida called over her shoulder as she moved toward the other dancer.

Weaving her way through the crowd, Astrea finally made it off the dance floor and back onto the soft grass. She took her time passing the bonfires, letting the evening sea breeze cool the warmth still lingering on her skin from all of the dancing. It had been fun, and she actually felt lighter. For almost half an hour, she hadn't thought about the assignment, the library, or her uncle.

As she passed the second bonfire, she spotted Sarsali's slender form first, then Balthazar's large one. Both of them had dressed in a mix of greens and blues. They were speaking with another couple, so Astrea just caught Sarsali's eye and waved.

Astrea went back to the food tents next. She wanted a drink and to see if Eliana had shown up earlier than expected. As she paced down the row of tents, Astrea found everything from grilled meat on skewers to fresh fruit spooned over ice cream to tiny, personal-sized cakes. There was lemonade, iced tea, wine, and liquor in almost every color imaginable, but there was no Princess Eliana.

A few off-duty palace guards greeted Astrea as she passed them, and she smiled but kept walking. When she got to another tent with drinks, Astrea helped herself to a glass of lemonade.

"Oh, there you are!"

Astrea turned. Nicos was standing behind her, Eliana emerging from the crowd behind him as she spoke with a woman in a stunning rose gold suit. Even her flashy headband and the cane she leaned on coordinated with her outfit.

"Hi, Nicos."

"Az!" Eliana exclaimed as she approached alone. "Alright, let's get started. Where's Cress?"

"Dancing," Astrea said, motioning across the field. "With a very beautiful woman, I might add."

"Oh?" Eliana's eyebrows lifted as she grinned, but unease crawled over Astrea's chest. "Well, shall we go introduce ourselves and perhaps see if she has any friends?"

The grate of jealousy was rough against Astrea's magic, almost like someone was dragging bark against her skin. *Maybe Cress was right about Nicos working overtime.*

"How about you and Nicos take Cress a drink and go have some fun by yourselves?" Astrea suggested instead. The thought of going back into the crowd, where she didn't have even an ounce of control over her magic, exhausted her. "I need a break, but I'll be around here whenever you're done."

"You'll be alright alone?" Eliana asked. "I don't want to leave you . . ."

"It's fine, Ellie." Astrea smiled, and she hoped her sincerity came across. It would be nice to have a few minutes to herself. "I just need to clear my head and eat something."

"Well, alright. If you're sure. I just don't want to abandon you like we did at the club."

"Consider me *not* abandoned." Astrea turned back to the drink table behind her and plucked up two wine glasses. "Here, one for you and one for Cress."

That was all it took to get Eliana off toward the dance floor. Nicos followed her closely, as usual, the tall guard the only way Astrea could still find them among the crowd until they'd truly disappeared beyond sight.

Astrea exchanged her empty lemonade glass for a full one, then scanned the park. Though the festival area was packed, there were plenty of smaller sections she could wander off to. Her favorite was back by the other end of the food tents, one that Sarsali had actually designed during a remodeling project several years earlier. Cressida would know to check there for Astrea if needed.

As Astrea set off in that direction, she couldn't help but think about Saros. Should she find Balthazar and ask him to go check on her uncle? All she had to do was ask, and the older Metalli would run the errand for her.

"Oh, come on, have another, Captain!"

Astrea looked up. That voice was familiar, and at the edge of the crowd, she spotted Jin. He was unmissable in his black and gold floral-print jacket, black pants, and dark red shirt. The three people circled around him were dressed in vibrant colors. Adi, the Earthmover she'd seen earlier in the day, was dressed in green and white. A tall woman with cool brown skin and long white hair wore lavender, and the short pale woman next to her was in teal.

"You need to relax," the white-haired woman said. She handed Jin a shot glass filled with a clear liquid.

Jin murmured something, but it was too low for Astrea to hear. Whatever he was feeling, she couldn't tell. His wall was up, just as it had been for days.

"Lighten up, Captain," said Adi. "Zephyrine's right. You deserve to have a night of fun. We all do!"

Jin tipped the shot back, shaking his head once as he swallowed.

Astrea sighed. If she wanted to go to her spot, she'd have to walk past his group unless she wanted to double-back and go the long way, and she definitely didn't want to do that. Smoothing the bodice of her gown with her free hand, Astrea skirted past the group, but she found her eyes moving without her permission. She met Jin's intense stare, like he was tracking her.

But instead of calling out to her, he simply nodded.

Astrea returned the gesture, and as she looked away, the white-haired woman's gray eyes caught Astrea's attention. The woman's eyebrows rose a fraction, almost like she recognized Astrea. And just like Jin, this mystery woman was unreadable.

As much as Astrea hated to admit it, maybe she wasn't as invisible as she hoped. She was friends with *the* Eliana Auris, after all. It shouldn't really surprise her if people recognized her. The woman said nothing, instead turning her head to speak to Jin in hushed tones.

Astrea hurried away, the ground changing from soft grass to crunchy gravel as she crossed a wide park path. The smell of wisteria, peonies, and roses greeted Astrea's nose as she passed a tall, manicured hedge. This part of the park was quiet, more overgrown, but Astrea still had a clear line of sight to the bonfires.

After heading a bit farther into the garden, Astrea sat down on one of the iron benches. Nobody else was around, though she was sure other parts of the park had plenty of amorous couples sneaking off for time away from the crowd. Solstice Night was famous for that.

Why did everything have to get so complicated in such a short time? She tilted her head back, looking up at the stars just starting to show themselves in the sky. She'd always had a fascination with the night sky; Saros claimed it was her celestial magic calling to her. And tonight, her magic hummed just under her skin, overwhelmed by the intensity of the crowds.

Would it be worth it to try to leave Kalama? Would she miss nights like this with her friends, dressing up in ridiculously fancy dresses and drinking this exceptional lemonade?

The constellations were almost too faint for her to see, but Astrea strained to pick them out anyway. The Serpent, the Archer, the Queen, and the Dove—those were easiest to find this early in the night. The North Star, too, winked its hello to her.

Astrea sighed. How was she supposed to know what to do? It felt like either way, there was no right choice, if the choice was even really hers at all.

"You alright?"

Astrea jumped. Jin stood a few feet away, two wine glasses in hand.

"Sorry," he said. "I didn't mean to scare you."

"It's fine."

"Just thought you might like some more wine." Jin held out one of the glasses as he approached her bench.

She raised her lemonade glass. "I'm actually not drinking tonight."

"Let me guess," he said, "trying to avoid the inevitable Solstice Night hangover?"

"Something like that." It was actually because of the lingering fatigue. It had been hours since she'd healed Saros, and still, Astrea couldn't shake the feeling. But she couldn't tell Jin that.

"Is something on your mind tonight?" he asked after a long stretch of silence.

"Nothing you need to worry about."

Jin sighed, a harsh noise, as he sat down on the bench across from her. "Astrea, we need to talk," he said as he set the second wine glass down next to him.

"About?"

"About this." He motioned between them with his free hand. "I know I screwed up our friendship, and I want to apologize."

How was it that for the last two times she'd gone out to have fun, both nights had taken wrong turns? Part of her desperately wanted this apology from Jin, wanted to hear what he had to say. But the other part didn't want to hear any of it.

"I don't want to talk about this."

"But I just want to—"

"I don't want to talk about it!" Astrea exclaimed. "Save your halfhearted apologies for another night, Jin."

"Oh, so you'll see me again, then?" he asked, eyebrows quirking up dramatically as he smiled.

She blew out a breath. There was that glimpse of who he used to be, just like at the library, the museum, and even the hallway after Kaius and

Eliana's fight. That made it so hard to not at least hear what he had to say.

To Astrea's left, gravel crunched and a bush rustled. Jin glanced that way just as Astrea stretched her senses out. She tensed, but the steps started again, retreating in the opposite direction. Astrea shook her head as she pulled her magic back. Probably just a drunken couple in search of some privacy.

"If you don't want to talk about that," Jin finally said, "will you at least tell me why you're out here all by yourself? You should be having fun with your friends."

She swirled the lemonade around in her glass, watching the ice cubes dance. "I'm just tired. It's been a long week."

"Astrea," Jin murmured, but she didn't look at him. "I know we haven't seen each other in years and that we have a lot to discuss, but . . . if something's bothering you"—he swallowed—"you can tell me."

Astrea didn't know how long she stayed silent. The sound of Solstice Night—drums and brass instruments and cheers from the crowd—were distant here in this dark corner of the park. Maybe the lemonade was spiked, or maybe it was the memories of years past, because she was actually considering his offer.

She used to tell him everything. She missed the walks they used to take, the conversations they used to have, the meals they used to share. She didn't want to be mad at him anymore. And most of all, Astrea simply missed *him*. She always had.

Was she a fool? Probably.

"My uncle," Astrea finally said. "I'm thinking about my uncle."

Jin sat up straighter, holding her gaze.

"He hasn't been feeling well lately," she continued, "and he says he's fine, but I don't believe him. I don't think he wants anyone to know he's so burnt out, and I haven't even told Cress or Ellie, but I just . . . I don't know how to help him."

Silence reigned again, Jin's face and emotions unreadable. "Would he go see a healer?" he finally asked. "Do you want me to ask my father to lighten—"

"No." The word cut the air between them. "That's the last thing I want you to do. I shouldn't have said anything."

"I won't tell anyone, I promise." Jin held his hands up in surrender. "But thank you for trusting me with that."

"Trust is a heavy word," she said, and Jin actually laughed.

"Perhaps," he agreed. "Would it help if I tell you a secret of mine?"

Astrea held her breath. Did she want to know one of Jin's secrets? And it probably wasn't just his; it was probably related to the military or his family. Would that be worth knowing, or would it just bring her more stress?

Still, Astrea heard herself saying, "Sure."

"What do you want to know?"

"It's your secret. You figure it out."

He smiled, but his face sobered quickly. "Being gone for so long has left me feeling a bit out of place now that I'm here. I don't really know what to do with myself half the time."

Astrea swallowed hard, but she said nothing. She wasn't sure she could speak even if she knew what to say.

Jin breathed a laugh. "I mean, I never really fit in here with all of this"—he gestured toward the bonfires—"but you . . ."

"There you are!" Eliana rounded the corner, her footsteps quick and emotions bright against the night sky. Rusty annoyance, red anger, midnight blue grief, marigold excitement, tangerine fear, and even . . . raspberry lust?

Skies, Astrea thought just as Nicos joined them. His emotions nearly perfectly mirrored Eliana's, his expression hard. His chest heaved, almost like he was trying to catch his breath after a run.

Glancing between Astrea and Jin, Eliana smiled. "I've come to make you dance with me." She grabbed Astrea's hand and hauled her to her feet before Astrea could say a word. "Tonight's about having fun, remember? And I really, *really* need to have some fun."

"Just don't have too much fun, Ellie," Jin said. "We've got that council meeting tomorrow."

"Yeah, whatever," Eliana said as she tugged on Astrea's hand.

Astrea half stumbled after Eliana, but just before they rounded the corner, she looked over her shoulder at Jin. He sat unmoving, though he watched her closely. What, exactly, was he going to tell her before Eliana showed up?

CHAPTER 17

"Are you finally done dancing?" Astrea asked with a laugh.

Though the band was still playing, most of the other dancers had started trickling off the dance floor, likely headed back to the food tents for one more drink, finding their chosen afterparties, or even waiting for the impending fireworks show. After getting Astrea back to the heart of the festival, Eliana had kept her entertained with dancing, playing the carnival games, eating, and stories as the princess introduced her to all sorts of people. They'd only taken one break for Eliana to join her father and Kaius on stage for the emperor's short speech; Jin hadn't joined them. Emperor Aelius's speech had been the same as every year, an incredibly brief recitation of the history of the festival and how he wanted people to remember the troops they'd lost during the war. Besides the speech, the night had been so fun that Astrea had almost forgotten about everything. Almost.

Sighing, Eliana handed off her empty wine glass to a nearby attendant. It was her fourth glass in the last hour. "I suppose it's over now, isn't it?"

"Done for another year, unless you plan on staying for the fireworks," Cressida said, throwing her arm around Eliana's shoulders.

"No fireworks," Eliana groaned, then hiccuped. "Kaius always stays for those, and I don't want to see him."

Cressida nodded. "Then let's go home, shall we?"

"I can get the car," Nicos offered as he approached the group. He'd been sidelined by Eliana earlier in the night, sent to stand near the band's stage since he'd refused to dance with her while on duty. That had just made those volatile emotions around the pair spike higher, and Nicos's annoyance still scraped against Astrea's skin. "I'm sure Chesare is nearby. Let me go find him."

"Sure, go find him." Eliana nodded, waiting until Nicos was a few dozen yards away before she smirked. "Except we won't be here when he returns."

"And you plan on going where, exactly?" Astrea asked. "The only place to go is home."

"I'm *walking* home." Eliana started toward the imperial dais on the northern edge of the field, but Cressida grabbed her forearm. "I'm sick of Nicos following me around."

"You're not walking," Cressida said, voice low. "Have you lost your mind?"

"I want more fresh air, not a stuffy car." Another hiccup escaped Eliana's mouth with the last word. "I'm tired of doing everything *right* just because I'm told to! Kaius gets to do what he wants, but nobody ever listens to me. I want to walk."

Eliana was usually reasonable about things. Solstice Night tended to continue long after the official parties ended, and though Kalama loved their princess, walking all the way back to the palace after dark was simply a bad idea right now. Even with Eliana's heavy drinking, there was no way she'd forgotten about the recent murder or the growing unrest over the war, right?

"We could wait for Nicos to walk back with us," Astrea said.

"I don't want to see him right now," Eliana muttered. "I didn't even tell you what he said to me this morning."

"What did he say?" Astrea asked as Eliana yanked free from Cressida's grasp. She stalked off at a surprisingly quick pace, her balance steady despite the endless flow of wine earlier in the night. "Ellie!" Astrea ran a hand over her face, then looked at Cressida. "Can you stop her? Root her to the ground or something?"

"Yes, I'm sure the guards here will have *no* questions about why I've basically imprisoned one of the emperor's children," Cressida replied.

There had to be at least a dozen guards loitering nearby, and the imperial Fireweavers were still tending to the bonfires. Hundreds of guests still milled around the park in anticipation of the fireworks show, but they didn't seem to be paying attention.

Astrea watched Eliana's retreating form again. One of the guards was speaking with her, and lavender surprise flared bright around the guard before they bowed and stepped away. *Just great, Ellie.* Of course she would order the guards to leave her alone. They'd have to follow her orders.

"Well, we can't let her walk home by herself," Astrea said. Where was Jin? He'd always been able to talk some sense into Eliana when she stopped thinking things through. Even Kaius might be a welcome sight right now. Astrea didn't see either of the princes, though.

"You said she's been having a tough time with the council and Kaius," Cressida said. "Maybe this is how we can help her. Let her have a few supervised moments without Nicos hovering over her."

"And just how much have *you* had to drink, Cress?"

"Not even half of what she did."

"You cannot be serious about this." There was no way Cressida was seriously considering this, right?

Cressida rolled one shoulder. "We'll be halfway to the palace by the time we leave the park's northern exit. Nobody's going to bother her, and I'm sure the other guards will tell Nicos where we went."

Astrea sighed. This was probably the most foolish plan Cressida and Eliana had ever devised—if it could be called a plan—but Astrea didn't know what to do. She couldn't just let the two of them run off into the night. Besides, Astrea could sense if anyone was nearby. *Maybe I can steer her in the right direction if I need to.* Maybe Cressida was right. This might help Eliana calm down.

"Fine," Astrea said, "but I don't like this."

"Noted." Cressida grabbed her hand. "Come on, let's go get her."

Lifting up the hem of her dress, Astrea broke into a jog as she and Cressida tried to catch up with Eliana. She'd slowed down considerably and was meandering down one of the park's quiet paths.

"Took you long enough," Eliana said with a snort. "Thought you'd never come."

"Can't let you go off all on your own, now can we?" Cressida asked. "Let's get you home, Highness."

They passed through the park's quiet northern entrance. The occasional honk from an irritated driver several streets over nearly made Astrea jump out of her skin, but there wasn't anyone nearby. The only emotions Astrea could feel were Eliana's chaotic ones and Cressida's steady ones.

They didn't have to wait for any cars to pass before crossing the street. Every shop they passed was closed for the night, the shutters drawn and lights off. Streetlamps glowed around them, and it sounded like bars and restaurants were open somewhere nearby, the after parties already starting. They'd go well into the night, possibly even until daybreak.

"Why are we going this way?" Astrea asked as they turned down a side street. There were a dozen routes to get back to the palace, but she'd never been this way before.

Eliana rolled her eyes. "It's faster."

"It is," Cressida confirmed.

Astrea pushed her senses out as far and wide as she could, but doing so was almost disorienting. The faster they got back to the palace, the better.

The narrow pedestrian thoroughfare they turned down next was dark. There were no streetlamps, no lights on in the shops, nothing, just the glow of the crescent moon above. Behind them, the first fireworks from Crescent Park exploded in the air, loud booms resonating through the city streets. Astrea glanced back, watching only for a moment as brilliant blue and white designs sparkled in the sky.

"So, what did Nicos say to you this morning?" Cressida prodded as they walked.

"You wouldn't believe me even if I told you." Eliana sighed, her disappointment stinging Astrea's skin. "Why doesn't he understand?"

"Understand what?" Astrea asked. "You do seem really torn up about it, Ellie."

"Why I push so hard against the council. If I don't, nobody will." Eliana hiccuped. "It's like he doesn't get me at all. I thought . . . I mean . . . he and I . . ." She sighed again. "Does he even know me?"

"He's worried about you," Astrea said. Another round of fireworks went off, crackling and whistling as cheers erupted from the far-away crowds. "He sees how much of a toll the job takes on you."

"It takes a toll on everyone."

"Well, he cares about you, Ellie. He's going to worry."

"If that's true," Eliana said, voice cracking, "then why wouldn't he dance with me? Why wouldn't he—" She paused, then shook her head. "Never mind."

Astrea's heart ached. She wanted to tell Eliana about her conversation with Nicos, the way he'd been so obviously worried the day before, the jealousy and desire she'd sensed from him at the festival. But Eliana had gone quiet again, and it wasn't like Astrea could explain how she knew those things.

The road before them seemed to stretch on forever. There was a piazza at the very far end, the glow of streetlamps and a few passing silhouettes breaking up the night's darkness. From this distance, though, Astrea couldn't sense anything.

She'd always been scared easily. Once, when Astrea was fourteen, the empress had agreed to let her and Cressida have a sleepover with Eliana. It was all Eliana's idea, as was going down to the ancient dungeons underneath the palace. Jin had been waiting for them in the dark to scare them. Eliana had laughed hysterically, and Cressida had been both surprised and annoyed, but Jin had spent a whole day apologizing because Astrea got so spooked.

A particularly loud explosion made Astrea jump. She turned around, frowning as burst after burst of red and white fireworks lit up the night.

"How much longer—" Astrea started, but footsteps ahead made her cut herself off. She slowed, straining against her magic to find the source. But there was nothing other than Eliana and Cressida's steady presences.

The footsteps sounded again, one set ahead of them and one set to Astrea's left.

"Nicos?" Cressida called.

No response.

"Leave me alone, Nic!" Eliana yelled. "I'm still mad at you."

Two figures stepped out from the shadows. Into the shadows? The darkness lingering around the edges of the buildings seemed to stretch with the figures. Astrea couldn't make out their faces. Whoever this was, it definitely wasn't Nicos.

"We've been watching you all night," a masculine voice said, somehow both familiar and not. "We've been looking for you for a long time."

Watching us? Astrea thought as she cursed herself for going along with Cressida's plan. She should've known better, stuck to the main streets with other festival goers and city guards. She *did* know better.

Eliana stiffened next to Astrea, then raised her chin. "What do you want? Jewelry? Money?"

"Oh, Your Imperial Highness," said that familiar voice, "we're not here for your money. We're here for her."

It took Astrea a moment to realize both figures were staring at *her*. What could they want with her? This wasn't supposed to happen; she'd only agreed to this foolish plan because she'd been sure she could sense any bad intent before it reached them. But the men in front of them were unreadable, almost invisible.

"You don't want to fight me," Cressida growled, her sandals sliding on the cobblestones as she settled into a low fighting stance. The bracelets she was wearing had already shifted into a dozen tiny metal daggers. Few people could spar with Cressida and win, let alone take her in a real fight. She'd trained with special coaches for over a decade, having once wanted to pursue a career as a pro mage athlete. Cressida was tough, but Astrea didn't miss the tangerine fear bubbling up around her.

"Just come with us and we won't hurt your friends, Miss Sovna," said the other voice.

Eliana straightened. "What do you want with her?" All traces of her previous emotions shrank back except for the red anger. That jumped higher, as did dark green concern.

Now's not the time for negotiations, Ellie. The buildings around them were dark, the shutters drawn. If these were even homes—Astrea couldn't be sure—nobody would be home tonight, not yet. She looked behind her, hoping that perhaps Nicos or even another guard would walk by the street. Nobody came. Fireworks still whistled and popped.

"You mean you don't know her little secret?" the second voice scoffed. "Figures. Our boss wants to talk with her."

"Enough," snapped the first man. "We asked nicely. Don't make this harder than it needs to be, little Lightbringer."

Astrea shuddered. *Little Lightbringer.* Nobody had ever called her that outside of her nightmares from when she was young.

When Eliana turned to Astrea, her mouth open with the start of a question, Astrea noticed the fire in one man's palm. Except it wasn't fire. It was nearly black, like someone had covered it in shadows. That was also when she noticed Cressida lifting her fists.

"Don't—" Eliana started, lightning crackling around her fingertips, but Cressida struck first.

The cobblestones under the second man's feet began to shake, and he leaped back, landing low and bringing a wall of earth up just in time to block Cressida's daggers. An Earthmover. Black fire whizzed by Astrea's ear, and she turned to see the Fireweaver push another strange fireball her way.

Astrea ducked, turning to grab Eliana's wrist. "Come on," she urged, trying to get Eliana behind the stone wall Cressida had summoned. "Don't fight back, just—"

But Eliana danced out of Astrea's grasp, surprisingly quick on her feet. The electricity buzzing at her fingertips made the hairs on Astrea's arms prickle. Of course Eliana was going to try to fight back.

A massive chunk of earth broke through Cressida's wall, stone exploding in the air. Astrea ducked as Eliana hopped out of the way. Stretching both arms out, Cressida squeezed her fists, and the sound of metal straining echoed through the alley. An unlit lantern from one of the buildings flew right toward the Earthmover's head.

Eliana sent her lightning skittering down the alley, the blue light casting an eerie glow over them. Still, the two men seemed to be cloaked in shadows.

"I expected more of you, princess." The Fireweaver laughed as he sidestepped the lightning, Eliana's attack missing by several feet. She was definitely in no shape to fight.

These men already seemed to know Astrea's secret. Could she fight, too? She looked back at the buildings around them, the windows still dark and shuttered despite the sounds of the fight. Would Eliana remember this in the morning or chalk it up to a bad dream?

Maybe she just needed to go with them. Would they really leave Cressida and Eliana alone then? This wasn't their fight. This was Astrea's fault. This was Saros's fault. They shouldn't have lied about her magic. They shouldn't have—

"Watch out!"

Cressida's warning came too late. A chunk of cobblestone smacked into Eliana's shoulder, another crashing into her abdomen. Eliana lost her balance, falling backward with a gut-wrenching crack.

Time froze as Eliana hit the ground, a stream of blood flowing from the back of her head and into the cracks between the bricks. Pain exploded in Astrea's chest and head, an unfortunate side effect of her magic. It was only with great effort that she stayed standing. Eliana was still breathing, but if they didn't get her out of here soon . . .

No. Astrea could not let that happen. She would not let that happen.

Even with how careful she and Saros had been, even with everything they'd sacrificed, someone already knew her secret. They'd been fools, arrogant fools, to think they could keep it a secret forever. And now, if Astrea didn't do something, Eliana was probably going to bleed out in some skies forsaken alleyway. She didn't deserve to die here tonight because of Astrea's—Saros's—mistakes.

White light danced around Astrea's fingers. She willed it forward. Putting on a light show for the whole city would just expose her, but it would let someone know where they were. Surely Nicos was searching for them by now. Surely one of the other guards had told him where they went. Surely he would see it.

"What are you doing?" Cressida shouted as Astrea's light brightened.

"Just help me!"

Astrea didn't have the training Eliana or Cressida did, but she knew enough. Her emotions influenced her light, and now, she pulled on the utter panic pulsing under her skin. She pushed more light toward the Fireweaver, and he rolled left, narrowly avoiding it. But Astrea was faster, desperate, and was already aiming for his left shoulder. He grunted as Astrea's light burned through his shirt, exposing angry skin underneath. Astrea ground her teeth against the ghost pain pressing in on her own shoulder and the smell of burning flesh.

"You stupid little bitch," he growled. "Skies damned Lightbringer."

The Fireweaver charged. Dark flames snaked through the air as he headed straight for her. Astrea tried to dodge, but her gown only hindered her movement. Fire followed his punch. Astrea stumbled back as flames caught her shoulder. More pain washed over her—her own this time—and she thought she might vomit.

Cressida had forced the Earthmover back against a nearby wall, daggers hovering in the air and pointing at his throat. A thud behind Astrea made her whirl. The spot where Eliana had just been sprawled out on the ground was empty. *Where did she—*

A sharp burn on her wrist made Astrea turn back. The Fireweaver's grip on her tightened, burning her skin again.

"Don't make this harder than it has to be," he hissed.

Astrea did the only thing she could think to do. She brought her knee up right into the man's crotch, ramming it into him as hard as she could. His grip loosened. Astrea staggered backward, her burned forearm throbbing. The Fireweaver sank to his knees and wheezed.

A tall figure dressed in black and gold had come from skies knew where, bright flames engulfing his hands. *Jin.*

"Get out of here!" he shouted.

Cressida didn't turn. Instead, she simply called, "Took you long enough!"

"Talk later, Cress!"

The Earthmover roared and slammed his fists onto the ground, the cobblestones melting into magma. He wasn't just an Earthmover; he was a Tephran. Jin and Cressida jumped back, but the hot, molten earth spread too fast.

It was now or never, Astrea realized. It was too late anyway. Whoever had sent these men, she'd find a way to deal with them and the emperor, but first, she had to get out of there alive.

"Run!" Astrea shouted.

Jin and Cressida looked at her only for a moment. Then they moved, disappearing into the smoke steaming up from the mess of molten rock. Sucking in a deep breath, Astrea focused on her pain and her fear, then summoned the brightest light she could manage. The heat rising from the ground died as their attackers were blinded. Astrea was, too, and when she felt an arm wrapping around her waist and pulling her back, she resisted.

"It's me," Jin whispered in her ear. "Take my hand."

She took Jin's hand. A nearby door squeaked open, then there was darkness.

No, not darkness. Jin's flame illuminated the space around them. Besides a few crates, the narrow building was empty. Eliana lay unmoving in the corner.

"Ellie?" Cressida kneeled next to her, shaking the princess's shoulder. "Ellie?"

Pure white terror burst to life around Cressida, and from the corner of Astrea's eye, she saw that same white terror reflected around Jin.

Astrea dropped his hand and moved toward her friends. "Move," she instructed, and Cressida scooted over.

"Az, you don't—" Cressida started.

She knew what Cressida was trying to tell her. She'd already used part of her magic in front of the imperial siblings and those two strangers. They might be able to explain it away as stargazing. Healing Eliana would only expose her more. Healing Eliana would reveal the truth, the full truth.

"Lift her head up for me?"

"We can get her to my mother," Cressida started. "She has friends—"

Judging by the blood pooling on the building's stone floor and the pain exploding over and over again in Astrea's chest, Eliana didn't have that much time.

"If you're not going to help me, then get out of my way," Astrea ordered.

Cressida stared at her for a moment, lavender surprise spiking high around her. But then she lifted Eliana's head. Astrea lowered herself to get a better look. A long gash sliced the middle of Eliana's skull, the skin split wide and her dark hair matted with blood.

"Set her back down."

Cressida followed those orders too.

"Just hold her steady," Astrea instructed. Out of the corner of her eye, she saw Jin squat down, but he didn't come any closer.

"Are you sure you can do this?" Cressida's voice was low. "What you did out there—"

"What I did out there won't matter if her wound keeps bleeding or gets infected. And I don't think we can safely leave to find another healer."

"You're right." Cressida straddled Eliana's midsection and held her arms on each side. "Alright, I've got her."

Astrea settled behind Eliana's head, the ground cold through her dress. Placing her hands near Eliana's temples, Astrea sucked in one deep breath, then pushed it out. She repeated that a few more times, then reached deep inside herself, pulling on her magic. It rushed forward, eager.

It wasn't the glow around her hands but the pain that made Astrea close her eyes. All at once, the back of her skull burned, ached, and stung, so intense that even without her eyes open, black dots crowded the edge of Astrea's vision.

Whatever was brewing under Eliana's skin was bad. Astrea had healed a number of bumps on Cressida's head when they were younger, but this hurt a thousand times worse. Still, Astrea pushed her magic farther down Eliana's body. The pain in her abdomen was sharp and heavy, and Astrea's magic swirled in her mind's eye.

Astrea clenched her jaw tighter, trying to hold in the scream ready to tear free. She should've just gone with the men in the first place. Then Eliana wouldn't be so hurt. Then Astrea herself wouldn't be here, absorbing so much pain and risking everything Saros had ever tried to do for her.

If only she hadn't hesitated. If only she hadn't been so unsure.

"Az?" Cressida's voice sounded far away, like she was speaking underwater.

She was almost done. She was so close to finishing this, but Astrea couldn't get the words out of her mouth. She could feel the wound stitching back together on her own scalp, mirror healing and mirror pain.

"Almost . . ." Astrea tried to say again as she opened her eyes. All she could see was darkness.

CHAPTER 18

"Little Lightbringer," the voice whispered. *"You've made a terrible mistake. We will find you."*

Astrea awoke with a dry mouth and throbbing pain in her head. Her wrist and forearm burned, as did her shoulder. Footsteps shuffled on the hard, cool ground around her. For a few moments, all Astrea could think about was how exhausted she was, so bone-deep tired, but then she remembered.

She remembered everything.

Astrea scrambled to sit up, but her head swam with the movement. Wherever she was, it was dark. The stone floor underneath her was cold. Was she in the police station in downtown Kalama? In the emperor's ancient dungeon?

Astrea had never made a mistake this big before. Not a mistake—a decision. Saving Eliana's life, healing her wounds, and likely saving Cressida and Jin wasn't a *mistake.* But it was a decision that came at a heavy price. The life she'd worked to build for herself—the life Saros had tried to build for them—was over.

"She's awake." That was Cressida's voice, gentle and low.

"Az!"

Astrea flinched as soft arms brushed the burn on her shoulder. Eliana clung to her, her eyes puffy and face flushed.

"Are you alright?" Astrea tried to ask, but it came out as little more than a few scratchy syllables. It felt like she'd swallowed knives, though her vision had begun to clear.

Jin squatted in front of her, a flask in his outstretched hand. "It's water," he said as he searched her face.

Taking the flask, Astrea swallowed a few gulps and tried to calm her mind. The scene around her was the same as before: crates stacked nearby, a few shelves lining one wall, and an empty counter near the windows on the far side of the room. She wasn't in a dungeon or jail cell. She was exactly where she'd been before, the same closed-down store with the same people.

"How long was I out?" she asked.

"Ten minutes, maybe a little more." Jin took the flask when she handed it back to him. "Can you move? We need to leave."

Astrea searched the room again, finally focusing on Cressida. She was trying to peer through the slats in the shutters covering the front windows.

"They haven't come back," Cressida said, turning to walk toward them. "I don't even hear sirens. But Jin's right. We need to leave."

"I'm not going anywhere," Eliana said, her voice steady despite her tear-stained cheeks. "What the fuck happened?"

Astrea opened her mouth to speak, a defense—a lie—already forming on her lips, but what was the point? Even if Eliana didn't remember what happened, Jin had seen everything, as had those two men. Her secret was out.

"We were attacked," Cressida said simply. "I guess they ran off."

"You already told me that," Eliana said, "when I woke up. But what *happened*?"

"I'm a Lightbringer." Astrea's voice was surprisingly steady as she said it, but she didn't dare look up from the floor. "You got hurt, Ellie, really bad, and I had to heal you."

She could feel Eliana's stare burning a hole in the side of her head, but Astrea didn't look up. She couldn't. Her cheeks were on fire, and tears pricked her eyes.

"You're a Lightbringer?" Eliana's voice was barely a whisper, as if the secret couldn't be repeated aloud. "How . . . how long have you known you're a mage?"

"My whole life."

"And you didn't tell me?"

"Ellie," Cressida warned, "now's not the time. We can explain later. We need to leave—"

"And *you* knew?" Eliana said, voice rising and aura flashing red. "You've both been keeping this from me?" She jumped to her feet, the skirts of her gown rustling. "You didn't think you could trust me after all these years?"

"I'm sure Astrea has her reasons," Jin said as he rose to his full height. "You know who our father is. *How* he is."

Was Jin actually defending her choice? Did he . . . did he actually understand why she might hide this? Astrea glanced up, but Jin was focused on his sister, his expression and emotions unreadable.

"I know that keeping it a secret broke imperial law," Astrea finally said, breaking the tense silence between the siblings. "If you have to arrest me, I—"

"Nobody's arresting you," Jin said. "Your secret isn't leaving this circle."

"What about the men who attacked us?" Cressida asked. "They know."

"They already knew anyway," Astrea said. "They *already* knew, Cress." How they knew and who they were, Astrea had no idea. Her lungs tightened until they hurt. She could barely take a breath.

Jin looked back at the store's door, the one that led to the street they'd been attacked on. "It's only a matter of time before someone figures out something happened here. Let's get you two home, then we'll talk."

"No," Eliana said, taking a step back when Jin reached for her. "And just what were you doing here? How'd you find us?"

Astrea watched Jin. She'd been wondering the same thing, but then she remembered something from the fight. When he'd shown up, Cressida had said something to him. "*Took you long enough.*"

"Were you following us?" Astrea asked. "Did you somehow tell him to follow us, Cress?"

Astrea didn't even know why she was upset; things probably wouldn't have ended well if Jin hadn't come along. As much as she knew that to be true, she couldn't help the energy buzzing beneath her skin.

"I just assumed it was Nicos," Cressida said. "They're both so skies damned tall."

Jin ran a hand through his hair as he turned toward the door, shoulders stiff. "Yes, I was following you. I saw Ellie storm off and knew she was doing something reckless."

"I'm too drunk for this," Eliana muttered. She closed her eyes and sighed, a harsh sound. "Is this some bad dream because I hit my head?"

Sirens whined in the distance. Ignoring the pulsing at the back of her skull, Astrea finally pushed herself to her feet. "We need to leave."

Jin frowned. "Can you heal those burns?"

She couldn't. She had no energy left to give, but this skies damned sleeveless dress made her injuries obvious to anyone who might look at her. And there would definitely be palace guards who would look at them when they got back. Somehow, Cressida's gown was in better shape, as was Eliana's. Frizzy hair, dull skin, and smudged eyeliner were the only signs Eliana had gotten into trouble.

How had they gone from partying to *this?*

Astrea had been so foolish to agree to follow Cressida and Eliana. She'd known it hadn't been a good idea, but Cressida had seemed confident enough. They weren't *that* far from the palace. It should've been fine.

And maybe it would've been fine if Astrea had let Cressida and Eliana go alone. The men had been looking for Astrea, not her friends. *My fault.*

"No," Astrea finally whispered. "I probably can tomorrow."

"Can you cover up any evidence outside, Cress?" Jin asked.

"I'll do my best."

As Cressida slipped out the door, Jin shrugged off his blazer. "Wear this," he said, handing it to Astrea. "Please."

The thought of putting fabric against the burns made Astrea's stomach churn. She finally looked down at her forearm, *really* looked. It was red and starting to blister and bleed. Based on how much her shoulder throbbed, she assumed it was in similar shape.

"I don't care about the blood." Jin was looking down at the injury too. "We just need to get you home."

Astrea took the jacket, but Jin had to help her into it. She could barely move her bad shoulder, and the feeling of the fabric made bile rise in her throat. She swallowed.

"Ellie, will you be alright to walk?" Jin asked.

"I'll manage," Eliana said as she combed her fingers through her dark hair and straightened her gold headband.

Right, Astrea thought. Her hair. She was probably a mess, too. As she reached up to check, pain shot through her. Astrea dropped her hand immediately.

"Let me," Jin said gently.

He was so calm. So, so calm, especially compared to the chaos surrounding Eliana right now—crimson rage, icy shock, teal understanding, gray confusion. The colors undulated and danced in the darkness of the room, and Astrea wished more than anything she could shut her magic off. Her entire body was on fire, and Eliana's emotions just made it worse.

Astrea couldn't manage anything more than a simple nod. As she let Jin adjust her hair clips and long curls, she focused on breathing. *You will figure this out,* she repeated over and over in her mind. *You will figure this out.*

The door creaked open just before Cressida said, "Let's exit out the back. The next street over is much closer to Sunrise Way. I assume there'll be guards there?"

"There should be," Jin confirmed. He motioned for Eliana and Cressida to go first, then offered his arm to Astrea. When she hesitated again, he smiled. "It's going to be fine."

Astrea took his arm and let him lead her out the door.

Despite every fiber of her being screaming for Astrea to run, all she could do was continue walking. Cressida and Eliana were just a few paces ahead of them, weaving through the last couple of pedestrian streets before finally emerging onto Sunrise Way, the main road through Nobleman's Hill that led all the way to the palace.

They'd been so close to the palace. So close, and she'd put on her light show. So close, and they'd still been attacked.

They merged into the foot traffic leading back toward the palace. A few people said hello to Eliana and Jin. Astrea could barely pay attention to anything but her wildly beating heart, but she sensed nothing other than mild surprise and curiosity from the few who greeted the siblings. The crowd thinned as they traveled deeper into the district, people veering off onto side roads to return home or go to the well-lit restaurants dotting the surrounding streets.

As they approached the massive palace gates, Astrea held her breath, suddenly all too aware that Eliana or Jin could turn her in. It would be so easy. All they'd have to do was whisper it in one of the guards' ears as they passed.

Jin didn't so much as look at the guards saluting him, but his forearm flexed under Astrea's fingers. She almost pulled away; she hadn't even realized she was still holding onto him. She *shouldn't* be holding onto him. She should have just walked on her own. But Astrea couldn't make herself let go.

When they finally made it to the veranda on the eastern side of the palace, Astrea couldn't make herself look toward the observatory. She didn't want to go back. Saros would be ten types of livid when he found out what had happened. She still didn't know what she was going to tell him. If she was going to tell him.

"Eliana," a voice hissed. Nicos stood just inside the veranda door, red rage, dark green concern, and white terror spiking in the air around him. "Where the fuck have you been? I was looking everywhere for you."

Eliana flinched, and lavender surprise circled Cressida. All Astrea could do was stare at Nicos.

"Calm down, Nicos," Jin said. He finally pulled away from Astrea's grip. She let him go. "Come upstairs, then I'll explain."

Explain? Astrea thought as she followed the very angry Nicos and her friends into the palace. Jin wouldn't tell Nicos of all people, would he?

They walked to the third floor in silence. Astrea wanted to pass out right on the stairs, let the staff find her and simply carry her away. This was absurd, all of it. Still, she pushed down the rising panic and the pain and forced her legs to carry her the last few paces to Eliana's room.

"What the fuck is going on, Jin?" Nicos asked when they were in the sitting room. Terror flared around him again as he took in Eliana's wilted form. "What happened?"

"I don't want to talk about it, Nic," Eliana muttered. "You can yell at me in the morning."

"She's fine, Nicos," Jin said gently. Astrea braced herself. "Attempted robbery. They didn't realize who we were until it was too late, and they look worse than she does. It's handled."

Lies, all of it. Well, maybe not Eliana being fine; Astrea was confident in her healing. Eliana would likely have a headache for a few days, and her stomach would feel bruised, but she would be fine. But Jin was lying to one of his friends; they had to be friends if Nicos was foregoing titles and full names. He wasn't entirely reckless with protocol.

Nicos glared at Jin, but his expression softened when he looked at Eliana again. "Are you really alright?"

She nodded.

Nicos pressed his lips together. "I'll . . . I'll be outside if you need me."

Once Nicos had retreated to the hallway, Jin went into Eliana's bathroom. He returned with two fluffy white towels and followed Nicos's steps. Only instead of leaving, he locked the front door and shoved one of the towels into the opening between the floor and door. He repeated the process with the door separating the sitting room from the entry nook.

Eliana and Cressida collapsed into the armchairs, and Jin fell into the sofa. Astrea, though, couldn't make herself sit down. Instead, she moved behind Eliana.

"I need to check your head, Ellie," she said.

"Alright."

Astrea parted Eliana's hair, revealing a sliver of skin that was pinker than the rest of her scalp. Eliana's skull showed no sign of physical trauma except for the blood still caked in her hair. A shower would fix that.

"It looks good," Astrea said as she straightened. "Just take it easy for a few days."

The silence stretched on as Astrea walked on shaky legs to the chair next to Cressida. Her burns ached. So did her head. Her entire body hurt, actually, like she was coming down with the flu. *What a mess.*

"So . . . we're just not going to talk about this?" Eliana finally asked.

"What do you want me to say, Ellie?" Jin asked as he turned to look at his sister. "It's late and you're hurt. We should wait until morning."

"I'm fine," Eliana protested. "Tell him I'm fine, Az."

"She just needs a good night's sleep now," Astrea offered. "Someone needs to look at her shoulder tomorrow too, but she'll be alright."

What worried Astrea more were Eliana's volatile emotions. They jumped from sadness to anger to disbelief and back again. Not that Astrea was feeling any better.

She could barely process the fact that she'd publicly used her magic. That the shadowy man had called her 'little Lightbringer,' like in her dreams. Had she imagined it? And had none of her friends noticed the way the darkness seemed to cling to their attackers?

"I'll go to the palace healers tomorrow," Eliana said. "Which means we can talk now."

"You can't go to the palace healers." Jin crossed his arms over his chest. "Astrea needs to come back tomorrow to finish the job."

"Don't tell her what to do," Eliana fired back. "And don't tell me what to do, either!"

"You can't ask that of Az," Cressida said. "Not after the risk she already took—"

Jin shook his head. "A risk that will only spread if someone else finds out Ellie was hurt—"

"I'm *fine.*"

Jin sighed and ran a hand through his hair. "I know you're mad, but don't take it out on me. I'm not the one who attacked you. I wouldn't ask this of Astrea if it wasn't necessary."

Eliana huffed and crossed her arms, then winced.

"Cut him some slack, Ellie," Cressida said, finally raising her jade eyes to look at both Eliana and Astrea. "This is no one's fault but—"

"No one's fault?" Eliana replied dryly. "It's those . . . those stalkers' faults!"

"Those *stalkers* wouldn't have found us if we hadn't been following you!" Cressida snapped. "If we'd just waited for Nicos and the skies damned car, none of this would've happened."

Astrea forced herself off the chair, then moved across the room, away from the sitting area, and toward Eliana's desk. The paper and books were stacked neatly to one side, and as Astrea slumped into the chair, she laid her head down on the smooth wood. Any distance, however small, from Eliana's emotions would be a blessing.

Angry heat rushed over Astrea's body as Eliana said, "Oh, so now this is my fault?"

"Well, if you hadn't insisted on ditching Nicos just because you two had some stupid argument," Cressida said, "we wouldn't have been there in the first place. What do you think *that* means?"

"Both of you followed me," Eliana snapped. "No one made you come with me."

"We were trying to—"

"Will everyone be quiet for five seconds?" Astrea shouted, lifting her head and turning around to glare at her friends. "We were all wrong tonight, alright? We all made poor choices."

Cressida and Eliana stared down at their laps. Jin, however, pushed off the sofa and walked to the sideboard. He started fixing drinks, two in crystal glasses and two cups of tea.

"So what do we do now?" Eliana asked.

Astrea sighed. "I need to ask you all something."

She had no idea if she could really trust the siblings with her secret. No, that wasn't true. Even with how angry Eliana seemed to be, Astrea was sure she wouldn't tell anyone. And even as Jin remained entirely unreadable, Astrea's gut told her to trust him.

Besides, she didn't really have a choice anymore.

Gray confusion sparked to life around Cressida. "Ask us what?"

"Did you notice what those men looked like?" Astrea asked.

"Why?" Eliana frowned. "Do you want to report them to the police?"

"No police," Jin said, earning him a glare from his sister. But he didn't notice; his back was still to the group. A flame jumped to life over one palm before he brought the flame to a copper kettle.

"No police," Astrea agreed, then sucked in as deep of a breath as she could manage. "Did you notice anything strange about the Fireweaver's face? It was . . ."

"Covered in shadows?" Cressida asked. "Yes, I noticed, but I thought it was some trick of the light."

"I don't think so," Astrea muttered. She considered telling them about the nickname the man had seemingly pulled from her dream, but that had to be a coincidence. It might just make her sound like she'd lost her skies damned mind. Maybe she had.

Jin finally finished preparing the drinks, handing one of the crystal glasses to Cressida and one of the tea cups to Eliana. Then he strode toward Astrea, handed her the second tea, and returned to the sideboard to get his own drink.

"They said they were looking for you," Cressida said as Astrea took a sip of tea. Peppermint. "Why were they looking for you?"

"I don't know." Astrea couldn't think of anyone who would be looking for her. She doubted they were connected to the emperor. The situation wouldn't be unfolding like this if Emperor Aelius had sent them.

"I know I'm going to sound like an ass," Eliana said slowly, "but why were you hiding your magic? Could that have something to do with it?"

Astrea looked at Cressida. Sour regret rolled over Astrea's tongue as Cressida shrugged. She sucked in a deep breath. "When we moved here, my uncle told me I needed to hide it. He saw . . . he saw my death on the battlefield." Cold shock raced across her skin, but her friends remained silent. "I was just a child; I didn't understand the implications of this kind of lie."

She still remembered that day they'd first arrived in Kalama. She'd been just ten years old. After several very long days on the train from Novaria to Kalama, Astrea and Saros had finally arrived to start their new life. An adventure, he'd kept calling it, though even then, Astrea knew it was to get her away from the place where her mother had died.

While walking through the Kalamian train station, Saros had stopped for just a few seconds, and then his anxiety had tripled. He'd kept going like nothing had happened, and he'd taken Astrea to meet the Nikaphoroses for the very first time. She'd known something was wrong then but hadn't asked him what. The next morning, Saros had instructed Astrea to hide her magic from everyone except the Nikaphoroses, who already knew.

"That doesn't sound like a reason anyone would be looking for you," Eliana said.

"No, it doesn't." Jin set his glass down, but he didn't move from his spot by the sideboard. He leaned against it, arms crossing in front of him. "Do you have any enemies?"

Cressida laughed, a loud, ugly sound. "Jin, you have been gone for *far* too long if you think Astrea, of all people, would manage to make any enemies. I mean, she doesn't even gamble! All she does is go to work, parks, and cafés."

"You make me sound so boring," Astrea mumbled. She meant it as a joke, but she couldn't muster the energy to actually deliver it as such.

"There's nothing wrong with living a quiet life if that's what you prefer," Cressida said. "I'm just saying, out of the four of us, *you* definitely aren't the one who has to worry about enemies."

"Then why would someone be looking for me?"

"What about Saros?" Jin asked. "Could anyone be trying to get back at him?"

"Not that I'm aware of." Astrea sighed and started to lift her hands to run them through her hair but stopped as her burned skin stretched and screamed in protest.

"I don't think we're going to figure it out tonight," Cressida muttered.

"Then I'm going to take a shower and go to bed," Eliana said. "You can both stay here, if you want."

"No way I'm leaving the palace tonight," Cressida said. "Az?"

"I'll stay." Astrea couldn't bear the thought of going home to Saros like this, battered and exhausted. She needed to figure out what to tell him. She needed to figure out everything.

As Eliana went into the bathroom and started the shower, Jin excused himself, saying he'd be back in a few minutes. Cressida waited until Jin was gone before she rushed over to where Astrea was still sitting at the desk.

"Are you really alright?" she asked as she crouched in front of Astrea.

"No." Astrea huffed, tears burning her eyes and throat. "No. What the fuck am I going to do, Cress? I couldn't let Ellie—"

"I know." Cressida squeezed Astrea's knee. "Of course you couldn't. I'm not worried about these two knowing; I'm worried about those men from the alley."

The knot squeezing Astrea's stomach lessened slightly. "You think I don't need to worry about Ellie and Jin?"

"No, of course not. I mean, it's not ideal, but I really don't believe they're going to betray you. Do you think they would?"

Astrea had no idea what to think. Everything Saros had ever suggested to her was that no one could know, but Jin and Eliana had already had several opportunities to turn her in. Jin was protective of his sister; if he'd wanted to bring her to a healer tonight and expose Astrea in the process, he would have already done so.

"I guess not," Astrea finally said. "I don't know."

"Have a little faith," Cressida whispered as the door to Eliana's apartment opened again. Nicos's voice came from the hallway beyond before the door closed.

Jin poked his head into the sitting room. "Astrea, can you please come here?"

"Why?" Cressida called as she pushed herself to a stand.

"You don't have to worry, Cress," he replied. "I'm just trying to help."

Astrea sighed. As her tired magic stretched out, the only other person in their vicinity was Nicos. Somehow, Astrea forced her body to move and walk toward where Jin was waiting.

"Will you come with me?" he asked.

"Where?"

"My room."

"I'm coming to check on her in twenty minutes if she's not back!" Cressida called. "Don't push me, Auris."

"Wouldn't dream of it, Cress!" he called back, then looked down at Astrea. "I know it's a lot to ask, but trust me for a few more minutes. Please?"

Astrea nodded and followed Jin out into the hallway. Nicos said nothing as they passed him, and Jin said nothing as they headed down the corridor. He opened the door to his apartment and motioned for her to go first.

It had been years since Astrea was in Jin's apartment in the palace. Eight long years. It had actually changed. Gone were the bright Auris red and other lively colors Eliana used to decorate her living quarters, replaced by muted greens, blues, and purples. It was set up just like Eliana's room: sitting area, desk, separate bedroom and closet. Astrea took careful steps as she moved farther inside, trying not to look too closely at the art and knickknacks spread around. It felt somehow like an invasion of privacy despite having spent so much time in here over the years.

"I'm sorry we couldn't do this in Ellie's apartment," Jin said. "We need water, and I doubt she'll be out of that shower for another hour."

Astrea followed Jin into his bathroom. Rolls of gauze bandages, tubes of cream, and a glass bottle cluttered the long stretch of the bathroom counter, and two armchairs were situated nearby. Had he taken those from his sitting room? She hadn't even noticed.

"I know I may not be a healer," Jin said as he motioned for her to sit, "but it'll help you get through the night."

Astrea stared at him, looking for any sign of . . . anything. Though unreadable to her lightbringing, Jin flashed a gentle smile. She didn't know what she'd expected, but it wasn't this.

"Let's get that jacket off, shall we?" he asked.

Jin helped her out of the blazer, the movement making her nauseous. Astrea collapsed into one of the chairs. Her head swam, but she steadied herself.

"Where did you learn to do this?" Astrea asked, watching Jin dab aloe onto the burn on her wrist and forearm. The contact hurt, but she managed to stay still. "I didn't think a prince would know how to treat wounds this way."

"I didn't until I went into the military," he said as he stood and moved to the sink. He unwrapped some of the bandages and ran them under water for just a few seconds, then started wrapping them over her wrist. The cool dampness made Astrea inhale sharply, but it was also a relief. "We don't always have access to healers there, at least on my team, so we have to know how to do some things ourselves."

He started on her shoulder next, his touch so light she almost didn't realize he was doing anything.

"I'm sorry." She stared at her newly bandaged wrist.

"Sorry?" Jin asked. "Why are you sorry?"

"Because." She swallowed, tears burning her eyes again. "I'm a healer. I should've been out there . . . My uncle never should've—" Astrea sucked in a breath.

"I'm sure if most parents could predict whether their children would come home from a war, they would make the same decision," Jin said gently. Astrea's stomach tightened as his fingers brushed against her dress strap. "May I?"

She nodded but didn't look as Jin untied the bow of fabric sitting on her shoulder. The gown's bodice was stiff and wouldn't fall, but Astrea still held it up with her good hand.

"Now lift your elbow," Jin instructed. She did. "Hold it there." He picked up another roll of bandages and, after wetting them, started wrapping it around her shoulder and arm in some pattern Astrea didn't understand. "I know many people who would make the same decision as your uncle," Jin said. "I would've, too."

"Really?" Astrea asked as she looked up at him. But his gaze was focused on the dry bandages he was wrapping over the first layer.

He nodded. "Of course. Don't blame Saros. He was doing what he thought was right. And you said it yourself; you were just a child. You can't blame yourself for that. Besides," he continued as he finally met her gaze, the gentle smile returning, "I'm really glad he made that decision. I'm glad he kept you safe."

She knew it was all true, but Astrea still had to blink the tears away. She still had to swallow her fear and pride as she looked into Jin's eyes and whispered, "Thank you."

CHAPTER 19

The first thing Astrea noticed when she woke up was that she wasn't in her own bed. The silky sheets were cool against her skin, a strange sensation compared to her own cotton bedding. The second thing she noticed was the shouting in the other room.

"You thought ditching your personal guard was a good idea?"

Astrea blinked. She was in Eliana's large four-poster bed. The curtains drawn over the windows on the far side of the room kept the bedroom dark.

"I said I'm sorry, Nic."

"Sorry? You're *sorry*? What if something had gone wrong, worse than it did? You're never this reckless! Skies, I just—" Even with the door closed, ice-cold terror rolled over Astrea's skin as Nicos said something too softly for her to make out.

Astrea tried to blink the remnants of sleep away. She didn't even remember getting into bed the night before. She didn't remember getting changed into the pajamas she was now wearing or taking her hair down. She did, however, remember Jin bandaging up her injuries. Injuries she now needed to heal, along with Eliana's shoulder.

Astrea wasn't sure she had that much energy to spare, but she'd try.

The shouting in Eliana's sitting room had died down to muffled conversation, and several sets of footsteps rushed about. The bedroom door opened, and Cressida hurried in with a tray of food.

"Good," she said as she kicked the door closed, "you're awake."

Astrea forced herself to sit up. "What time is it?"

"After breakfast."

"Why didn't you wake me up? I need to check in with Saros . . ."

"I already called him for you." Cressida set the serving tray down on the small table next to the bed, then turned on the lamp. Astrea squinted. "I called last night to let him know where we were."

"Thanks." Astrea took the coffee cup Cressida offered her. "And how's Ellie? Nicos sounded upset."

"Oh, he was." Cressida sat down on the other side of the bed, her own coffee in hand. "Can you blame him? Even Ellie agreed with him . . ."

"She's tired of having routines and actions dictated by other people," Astrea said before taking a sip of coffee. "It wasn't the right choice, but I understand the—"

"Az—"

"No." Astrea shook her head. "I . . . I get why Ellie did what she did. You have no idea what it's like to not have choices."

The silence stretched on, and Cressida kept her eyes trained on the mattress. Astrea took another sip of her coffee even as her heart pounded wildly.

She was so glad Cressida *did* have choices. The Nikaphoroses had money and influence in Kalama, and they supported whatever Cressida wanted to do. But Eliana had never had very many choices despite her privileged upbringing, and Astrea had certainly never had a choice about her magic. Saros hadn't given her one. It hadn't even been a discussion. And while Jin's comment from the night before, about how any parent would do the same thing if they had the chance, was surely true, Astrea *was* mad at her uncle for taking that choice away from her.

It was a strange thing, being angry about Saros's decision while also understanding the logic behind it. Just like it was strange to understand what pushed Eliana to act so foolishly, for all three of them to act so foolishly. Astrea's head pounded in time with her heart.

"I guess you're right," Cressida finally said. "That I don't know what that's like."

"I'm really glad you don't know how it feels, Cress. Which sounds so lame, but really, I mean it."

Cressida laughed, a tired sound. "Yes, well . . . How do you feel this morning?"

"Awful."

"The burns?"

"The burns, what happened, everything. What am I going to tell Saros?"

"Do you have to tell him?" Cressida asked. "Does he need to know?"

"Of course he needs to know." As much as Astrea didn't want to have that conversation with her uncle, he had to know. He might even have answers. Jin had a point about Saros having enemies. Saros interacted with powerful people in his capacity at court; maybe that resulted in the attack somehow.

"Alright, well, I'll go with you if you want," Cressida said.

"I'll think about it." Astrea could deal with that after she had coffee and healed herself. "I need to go check on Ellie."

"Heal yourself first," Cressida said, voice low. "She's moving fine this morning. You need to take care of yourself."

Setting her cup on the bedside table, Astrea sighed and started unraveling the bandage on her injured arm. Her skin ached and stretched as she removed the last of the gauze. It didn't look much worse than it had the night before.

Astrea pulled on her magic. Starlight twinkled around her fingers, pulsing faintly. The burns on her wrist and forearm started to heal, Astrea's entire body hot and stinging as her magic did its work. But her skin turned pale and smooth again, and the pain subsided into a dull ache.

"Can you help me with my shoulder?" Astrea rasped.

Cressida helped her shrug off the shoulders of her pajama shirt, then unwrapped the bandages with slow precision. When Cressida stepped away, Astrea forced her magic to the surface again, her hand glowing as she brought it to her shoulder. The same stinging warmth returned, and Astrea gritted her teeth as her magic took hold.

She might not even have to worry about talking to Saros. She wasn't sure she'd be able to move out of Eliana's bed.

"You good?" Cressida asked, eyebrows drawing together.

"No," Astrea admitted. "Give me a few minutes."

As Cressida left the room, Astrea flopped back into the pillows. She'd need food and sleep to actually recover. She'd never used that much magic in one day before, let alone again the next day.

But Eliana couldn't go around with an injured shoulder any more than Astrea could walk around with burns. Someone would notice, and if someone noticed, they would start asking questions.

Heaving herself to the side of the bed, Astrea paused as her feet hit the plush carpet below. "Alright," she whispered. "Just a little more." Just a little more, and she could make Cressida take her home and explain everything to Saros. Then she could go back to sleep.

Astrea found her clothes from the day before laid out. She slipped on the green silk blouse first, then tucked it into her black skirt. She folded the borrowed pajamas and left them on the foot of the bed for Eliana or a maid to deal with later. Then she grabbed her coffee off the bedside table and headed out into the sitting room.

She wasn't expecting to see Jin. He sat in one of the chairs facing Eliana's bedroom door, gripping a newspaper in one hand and holding a mug in the other. How could he just be so . . . casual?

"Where's Ellie?" Astrea asked. "And Cress?"

"In the bathroom cleaning up, I believe. Why?"

"I need to heal Ellie's shoulder before I go home."

Jin's eyebrows furrowed as he finally looked up from the paper. "You don't look so good."

"Gee, thanks." Astrea set her cup down on the coffee table before falling back into the sofa. "You always did know how to make a girl feel special, Jin."

"Are we back to Jin, then?" he asked. "No more titles?"

After what had happened, Astrea didn't feel the need to antagonize him. He'd helped her. And he was still helping her; she hadn't woken up in handcuffs or at a police station. It didn't change the last eight years, but it meant something. It had to.

"Shut up," she muttered. He grinned.

The bathroom door swung open as Cressida strode out. Eliana emerged a moment later, and though she was paler than usual and moving slowly, she seemed fine.

"Come sit so I can heal your shoulder, Ellie." Astrea couldn't believe those words had come out of her mouth or that she was about to use her magic, *really* use it, for a second time in just a few minutes inside the palace walls.

Eliana joined her without saying a word. Astrea's magic faltered under her skin, faint and stubborn. Astrea pulled harder, and it surged to the surface. Light pulsed around her hands again. She gritted her teeth as her own freshly healed shoulder ached more, the mirror pain overwhelming. Eliana didn't seem that hurt.

Pulling her hands away, Astrea didn't have to wait for her magic to fade. It shut off like a light switch, and she slumped forward, resting her forehead against Eliana's shoulder. She swallowed bile as it surged up her throat.

"I'll be fine," she muttered as Eliana's worry scraped against her skin. Cressida's anxiety joined it, pulsing and bright. "Just give me a moment. This doesn't usually happen."

"I'm sorry," Eliana whispered. "This is my fault. I'm so, so sorry."

"We all made some poor decisions last night, Ellie." Forcing herself to sit up, Astrea ignored the weight of Jin's gaze on her. Instead, she looked first at Cressida, who'd sat down next to Jin, and then at Eliana. "I'm actually relieved you know the truth."

Astrea had been worried Eliana might still be angry about the whole thing. She'd been so mad the night before when she learned Astrea and Cressida had both kept her in the dark. She *should've* been mad. The attack was Astrea's fault; those men wouldn't have hurt Eliana if Astrea hadn't been with her. But now, no anger danced in Eliana's aura. No heat rolled over Astrea's skin. There were myriad other things pulsing off the princess—silver acceptance, orange anxiety, teal understanding, magenta embarrassment, and heavy fatigue—but nothing so volatile as the night before.

"What can I do to help?" Eliana asked, angling her body toward Astrea's and grabbing her hands. "Anything, you name it."

"I don't need anything—"

"You saved my life, Az. I owe you something."

"Your silence is enough."

"That's a given. You don't even have to ask. I won't consider that repayment of anything."

"Ell—"

Jin cut Astrea off this time. "Ellie's right. She owes you something. Something big." Astrea turned and glared at him, but he simply smiled. "It's only fair."

"I can't believe I'm going to say this, but I'm inclined to agree," Cressida quipped.

"Wow, the great Cressida Nikaphoros agreeing with me?" Jin teased. "This might be more of a surprise than last night."

"I don't need anything," Astrea repeated. There were, of course, many things she needed in that moment—answers, sleep, time to think—but she didn't think Eliana could give her any of those.

"Then what do you want?" Eliana asked. "There has to be something you want."

"Well . . ." There was one thing Astrea desperately wanted that Eliana could actually get her. "Can you have someone go to The White Lily and bring me back coffee? And pancakes?"

"I'll buy you the entire café if you want me to," Eliana said hurriedly. "You can be the new owner."

Astrea laughed, the tightness in her chest easing. "I don't want that. I just want breakfast."

"Consider it done." Eliana stood, then rotated her shoulder. "Consider it done for the entire week. No, not just the week, the month! I'll have Nicos go—"

"Could he bring it to me at the observatory? I need to go home," Astrea said. Eliana nodded.

"Shall we go?" Cressida asked, pushing herself up and smoothing the front of her pants. "No point putting off the inevitable."

"I'm going with you." Jin stood, too, and Astrea forced herself not to sigh.

"That's not necessary," she said. "Cress and I will be fine."

"Actually," Cressida started, "I agree with Jin again."

He smirked as he regarded Cressida. "Wow, this really is the bigger surprise. Twice in a row you've agreed with me? Maybe I should go try my luck at one of the gambling dens."

"Oh, you'll need more luck than that to win. You're a terrible card player."

Astrea rolled her eyes. It felt like they were teenagers again; Cressida and Jin had always squabbled over the silliest things. But none of them were kids anymore. They were grown, and Astrea had a very grown-up problem she needed to handle.

"Alright," she said. "Jin can come. But Saros isn't going to be happy about this."

A few seagulls squawked overhead, circling through the air over the palace gardens before gliding back toward Kalama's beaches.

They were almost back to the observatory, and Astrea still had no idea what she was going to say to her uncle. Jin's presence could either be a help or a hindrance. Saros had never liked the prince, but maybe he would listen if Jin himself vouched for his and Eliana's intent to keep their secret.

She'd deal with it when they got to the tower, its gray brick roof now visible over the treetops. Right now, she had to focus on walking. Delirious or drunk—she wasn't sure which would be the right word to describe how she felt. Whatever it was, it wasn't pleasant. Even when she'd pushed herself to the point of passing out before, it wasn't like this.

Astrea fished her keys out of her satchel as she followed Cressida up to the apartment, Jin hot on her heels. She checked the kitchen, living room, and Saros's bedroom, but he wasn't home. Even her senses were dulled now, unable to stretch as far as they usually would at her command.

"Either he's gone," Astrea said as she rejoined them in the hallway, "or he's upstairs." The telltale squeak of floorboards overhead told her everything she needed to know, but the thought of walking up more stairs made Astrea's shoulders sag.

"I'll go fetch him," Cressida volunteered, already disappearing through the apartment's front door.

Any other time, Astrea would have been embarrassed to have Jin in the apartment. Not because she was embarrassed by the space but because it was still strange to be seeing him, to be talking to him. And she might have been embarrassed when he followed her into her bedroom, but she was simply too tired to care.

"This place hasn't changed at all," Jin mused as he turned in a circle in the middle of her bedroom.

Astrea opened her wardrobe and hung her bag on the inside of the door, then closed it again. "Should it have changed?"

"No, I suppose not." Jin rolled one shoulder, then shrugged. "Will Saros kill me if he finds me in your room?"

"We're not children, Jin." She paused. "But probably."

One time, while Saros was visiting the Nikaphoroses for dinner, Astrea had snuck Jin into the observatory. Saros had caught them in the kitchen upon his return. They hadn't been doing anything other than making coffee and eating cookies Jin had swiped from the palace kitchens, but it had been enough to make Saros turn red.

Jin smirked, then turned and strode out of her room. Astrea trailed after him. Just in time, too, because frantic footsteps sounded overhead. Just what had Cressida told Saros?

The apartment's front door flew open right as Astrea joined Jin in the living room. Saros's emotions crashed against Astrea: anxiety, regret, fear, rage, shame. She shrank back, her head pounding.

"Saros—" Cressida started, but he stormed into the living room.

He looked at Astrea first, then Jin, then back at Astrea. "What have you done?" Saros whispered, his voice shaking. "Your Imperial Highness, my niece—"

"As far as I'm concerned," Jin said, "Astrea has done nothing wrong. Neither have you. She saved my sister's life last night."

Saros's jaw tightened, then relaxed. "She saved Princess Eliana's life?"

"Please, let's sit and discuss this," Jin said.

Saros stared at the three of them for a long moment before finally nodding and sitting down in one of the two dusty blue armchairs. Astrea sank onto the sofa, her body aching as it touched the soft cushions. Even her skin ached where her clothing touched it. Jin sat next to her, and Cressida took the other chair.

"You didn't think to tell me this last night when you called, Cressida?" Saros asked, pinning her with a look.

"I didn't think last night was the time," she replied simply. "Did you really want me to say that using the palace phone?"

"No, I suppose not." Saros turned to Astrea then. "Do you care to explain what happened and why I now have one of the four heirs in my living room?"

The truth was probably the best option. Astrea launched into the story, trying to downplay their ill-fated decision to walk home. She told him about how everything seemed darker, how the men seemed to know who and what she was, and how that Fireweaver's magic seemed different.

"Saros," Jin said, shifting to sit on the edge of the sofa cushion. He leaned his forearms on his knees. "I know you have no reason to believe me, but neither my sister nor I will be telling anyone about this. We are indebted to Astrea, but that's not why. I wouldn't turn in a friend for something I don't think is a crime."

"That may be, Prince Varojin," Saros said, "but that does not mean Astrea is safe. You aren't the only people who know this information. You aren't the only risk factor here."

"Then what do you see?" Jin asked. "What do you predict to be the outcome of this situation?"

"Outcome?" Saros laughed, a harsh sound, but deep blue shame pulsed around him. "I don't need my magic to know this isn't going to end well, Prince Varojin. I never should have gotten Astrea mixed up with your family."

"Uncle—" Astrea started, ready to defend both Eliana and Jin, but Jin cut her off.

"You probably shouldn't have," he agreed. "But it's too late to change that. And someone is after her."

"I'm right here," Astrea muttered.

"Someone is after *you*," he clarified, his gaze meeting hers and holding it. In the soft sunlight streaming through the windows, Jin's golden irises were almost molten. "And I want to find out who."

"And how do you plan on doing that?" Saros asked.

Jin hesitated, then turned back toward Saros and said, "I don't know yet."

"Oh, fantastic, Your Imperial Highness. Truly wonderful." Saros's wariness prickled Astrea's skin.

"Do you have any enemies who might be going after her?" Jin asked.

"Enemies?" Saros shook his head. "I work for the imperial government. There are plenty of people who would consider me an enemy."

"That may be, but if you think of someone in particular who might know about Astrea's ..." Jin paused again. "If you think of someone who might know the truth, please tell me."

Saros watched Jin for a long moment, then looked at Astrea. She'd seen that expression once before, the pain around his eyes and the slight frown. He'd looked the same way when her mother had died.

"Astrea," Saros said, "will you reconsider leaving? Surely you have the resources to get her out of the country, Prince Varojin."

Jin shifted, and Astrea swore she sensed concern from him. Cressida frowned.

"Well . . ." Astrea started, "I . . ."

"Do you not have the influence to get her out of it?" Saros challenged.

"I'm a bastard prince, Saros, not a miracle worker. My father sent me off to join the military for a reason, and he barely listens to my siblings, let alone me. You know how he is. I would call in every favor I'm owed if I thought it would work out."

The silence stretched on as Jin's words sank into Astrea's mind. *A bastard prince.* She knew his mother had been the emperor's mistress, but the woman had died a few years before Astrea and Saros had moved to the palace. It was strange to hear Jin talk about himself that way.

"I'll use what resources I can to help her leave when the opportunity presents itself," Jin said when Saros still hadn't replied. "In the meantime, I just need you to work with me on this, Saros."

Why would Jin be willing to do that? Astrea glanced at him, but his wall was steady, strong.

"I do not like this," Saros finally said. "But I will let you know if I think of anyone who may be determined to expose this, Prince Varojin. And I will let you know if the stars speak to me. But now, I think Astrea needs to rest."

"I'm fine," Astrea said. She didn't know why she lied, and even as the words left her mouth, she knew Saros didn't believe her. His expression softened.

"I need to get home anyway," Cressida said as she pushed out of her chair. "Dad's expecting a shipment at the office today that I need to help him with. Get some rest, Az."

"And I need to go check on a few things." Jin stood and offered his hand to Astrea. She hesitated, then took it. His grasp was gentle as he helped her to her feet. "Thank you again for what you did for Ellie."

"Of course."

As Jin and Cressida left the apartment, Astrea turned to her uncle. His eyebrows were drawn together, that heavy tangle of emotions bouncing around him again.

"You need to rest, my dear," Saros murmured. "You mustn't burn yourself to the ground for others."

"I couldn't let her die." Her voice cracked, those skies damned tears springing to her eyes again.

"I know."

"And I could tell you the same thing. I know how tired you are."

"Perhaps I don't have a choice either."

Astrea wanted to push him for a less cryptic answer, but the ache in her head had only worsened after the walk from the palace back home. Instead, she shuffled down the hallway to her bedroom, pulled her curtains closed, and collapsed into bed.

CHAPTER 20

Kalama was quiet. Even the palace, usually abuzz with activity, was quiet. But such was the result of a holiday weekend. Government employees all had time off for the solstice holiday, even the soldiers stationed in the barracks. They were probably drinking and fraternizing down in the city.

So when there was a knock on the apartment door, Astrea was surprised to find Nicos standing on the other side of it.

"Hi." He held up a bag, the savory smell of dinner wafting toward her. "From Eliana."

"She didn't have to do that." Even as Astrea said the words, she reached for the food. It had been a grueling two days for her body as she recovered from the massive amount of magic she'd used. It was also taking all of her mental energy to keep from panicking about this turn of events. The more distance she got from Solstice Night, the more the disturbing truth sank in: someone was hunting her.

We've been watching you all night. That was what those two men had said. Were they watching her now? Surely they knew where she lived.

"And she wanted me to bring you this, too." Nicos reached into the breast pocket of his guard's uniform and pulled out a small white envelope. "I'm not allowed to leave until you open it."

"She thinks I won't answer her if you don't babysit me?" Astrea asked, hoping it sounded like the joke it was meant to be. But her voice sounded monotone even to herself. "Alright. Come in."

Astrea opened the apartment door wider and let Nicos inside. Saros was upstairs in his observatory, more obsessed in the last two days than she'd seen him in ages. When they reached the sitting room, Astrea sank into the sofa while Nicos loitered at the edge of the room. She knew she should be more inviting, but she was too tired to care. Instead, Astrea tore open the envelope and pulled out a single slip of paper.

"Imperial dinner on Saturday. Please come keep me in check. Wear the black and silver dress. Cress will be there." *Keep her in check?* Astrea thought. In what way? Around Kaius, perhaps? Or to try to stop her from running away again? "That's what she needs an answer for?"

He shrugged. "She insisted."

"Alright, well . . ." Astrea ran a hand through her hair and sighed. She had no desire to go to any party, let alone one at the palace. But if Eliana was asking her and Cressida to go after everything that had happened, there had to be a good reason. "Sure, I'll be there."

"Really?" Nicos's eyebrows shot up. "She told me to be prepared for protests on your part."

"We both know there's no protesting when Eliana wants something."

Nicos smiled tightly. "No, there's not."

"She didn't mean any harm the other night, Nicos."

"I know." He shifted and folded his arms across his chest. "Though I can't believe you and Cressida went along with her."

"Perhaps not our brightest moment," Astrea murmured.

"What's done is done. I'm glad she wasn't alone."

If Eliana had been alone, though, she probably never would've been attacked. Those men had been following Astrea. Watching Astrea. None of that would've happened if she'd just stayed in the park.

"Are you still mad at her?" Astrea didn't actually need to ask. Nicos was an open book, a mix of annoyance, fear, relief, and shame burning through him. Of course he was still upset about what had happened—or the version of events he *thought* had happened. He'd probably lose his mind if he found out the truth.

"No."

"If you say so." Astrea grabbed the bag he'd brought. "Thanks for this."

"Why's Ellie having me bring you food, anyway?"

"She feels bad that I got sick after the festival." The lie came too easily. This was the fourth time in two days that Nicos had been by with some kind of delivery. He was the only friend she'd seen; Cressida had stayed home at Astrea's request, and Eliana was busy trying to negotiate some solution to the blockade the Delians had set up on Helosia's western coastline. Astrea hadn't heard from Jin since the morning before when he spoke with Saros.

Nicos's shoulders loosened slightly. "You're sick?"

"Starting to feel better."

"That's good." Nicos sighed and glanced down the hallway toward the apartment door. "Well, I'll leave you to rest." As Astrea started to push herself off the sofa, he shook his head. "No need to get up. I know the way out."

Once Nicos left the apartment, Astrea tilted her head back against the sofa and closed her eyes. She needed to dive back into her research. The emperor waited for no one. The books on her nightstand, the ones she'd brought home before Solstice Night, remained untouched. But research meant getting off the sofa and using her mind again. And despite what she told Nicos about feeling better, Astrea was still exhausted.

The nightmares had come back as soon as she'd fallen asleep the morning after Solstice Night. That skies damned voice whispering its threats. The other voice telling her to run. It made it so hard to sleep.

"Astrea?" Saros called as the apartment door opened again. "What was Eliana's guard doing here?"

"Bringing by some food."

"Why would her guard be bringing you food?" Saros asked as he stopped at the edge of the living room. His silver eyes were such a bright contrast to the dark circles underneath them, and his dark hair seemed almost duller than it had just days ago. Astrea's gut twisted painfully.

"Eliana's been sending him over with it. I think she feels bad about what happened."

Saros watched her for a moment, then nodded. "Then let's eat. You'll feel better."

He didn't wait for her to respond. Saros simply turned and walked down the hallway to their kitchen. Astrea pushed herself off the sofa and grabbed the bag before following him. He lifted the bag from her hands and took it to the counter, then began unbagging and plating whatever it was Nicos had brought over. Astrea slumped into a chair at the kitchen table. Saros remained silent as he set a plate in front of her, then a glass full of water. When he took his own seat, he began eating in silence.

Astrea wanted to talk to him without Jin or Cressida around, to gauge his true thoughts on the situation they now found themselves in. Why couldn't they just talk to each other like they used to? This was really the first opportunity they had to do so. Astrea had been in and out of sleep all weekend, and Saros had been up in that skies forsaken observatory of his.

Astrea couldn't forget the fatigue she'd tried to relieve him of on Solstice Night either. How it had drained her for hours and perhaps longer, considering how tired she was now. Had that impacted the fallout of overusing her magic?

Just ask him, she scolded herself. *Just try.*

"How has your work been?" Astrea asked as she cut a ravioli in half. Cheese and mushrooms spilled out. "I can heal you again if you're—"

"No more healing anyone for a while, my dear," Saros replied, his words gentle as he set down his wine glass. Astrea fought the urge to roll her eyes. "Work is as it always is. The emperor asks me to predict some great outcome for him and his armies, or his farmers, or the businesses in Kalama. And as always, it's impossible to actually give him the answer he wants."

"What is he after?" She managed to eat one bite and start on a second.

"Eager to know about this war in Corsyca."

"What do you think the outcome will be?"

"Are you asking the Stargazer or the man?" Saros asked, the corners of his lips turning up in a small smile.

She shrugged. "Both."

"It's hard to say." Saros leaned back in his chair, wiping at his mouth with a white cloth napkin. He folded it carefully and placed it back on his lap. "The Delians and Zaikudi aren't as technologically inept as the emperor would have people think. Their airships are equal to ours, as are their mages, but . . ."

"But?" Astrea prompted when he didn't continue.

"But . . ." Saros sighed and ran a hand over his face. "You asked me why I've been in my observatory so much lately. I know I haven't exactly been straightforward."

"You haven't answered me at all," Astrea mumbled as she pushed a ravioli around her plate.

Saros sighed again. "It is not easy for me to admit when I don't know things. You know people's expectations. The Stargazers are supposed to have it all figured out." Deep blue shame pulsed around him, and Astrea swallowed thickly.

"Well, I also know that's not how it works," Astrea said. "You don't have to pretend around me."

"Yes, well." Saros took a sip of water, then stared at his cup as he said, "With the war, I am only able to sense something darker on Helosia's side."

The hair on Astrea's arms prickled. Whatever Saros foresaw, nervousness and uncertainty sent shocks of orange into the air around him.

"Something darker?"

"Yes."

"But what does—" she started, only to be cut off when Saros raised his hand.

"That's what I'm trying to find out on my own time."

That certainly explained his fatigue. Doing not just his work for the emperor but also searching for . . . for whatever answers he wanted.

"Shadows stalk this city, Astrea," Saros continued. "This entire country, really. I need to figure out what they are."

She thought back to the events of Solstice Night, how the mages who attacked them seemed to be covered in perpetual darkness, their emotions unreadable. How one of them had that strange fire that wasn't quite fire.

"Do you think that's connected to the—" Astrea cut herself off when Saros shrugged.

"I don't know if what happened the other night is connected," he said, "but I'm going to try to find out. If only the stars would speak to me more, but they've been quiet."

"Is there any way I can help?" she finally asked when the silence had stretched on for a beat too long.

Saros set his fork down, his eyes searching hers as he said, "Tell Prince Varojin about this when you see him next."

"You want me to tell Jin?" An unfamiliar heaviness settled in Astrea's stomach.

"If he's not on his father's side, then he's the only one I trust with this information right now."

"But—"

"You don't want to tell him?"

"It's not that. I'm just surprised you do."

"Nothing good is coming to Kalama, Astrea. Varojin isn't my first choice, but he is someone we can apparently trust. Please, tell him."

"Alright," she said. "I'll tell him tomorrow."

"Thank you." Saros pushed his chair back, the scratch of wood on wood grating against Astrea's ears. "I'm going to eat the rest of my dinner upstairs. Do you need anything?"

Astrea needed the old Saros back, the one who didn't run away and hide in his observatory. She had so many questions about her magic and her fatigue that she hoped he could answer. Instead, she simply shook her head.

"No, I don't."

"Goodnight, Astrea." Saros picked up his plate and disappeared from the apartment, the only sound his footsteps as he retreated upstairs.

CHAPTER 21

Sunlight filtered into Astrea's bedroom, the shadows of palm fronds dancing on the walls. She sighed. After managing to get just a few hours of sleep, she wasn't looking forward to the call she had to make.

It wasn't even that she was dreading that Jin would be on the other end of the phone. Saros's warning about shadows was equally foreboding and vague. Would Jin believe her when she had so little to share?

Sitting on the edge of her bed, Astrea lifted the ear piece of the candlestick phone on her bedside table. She dialed the number for the palace operator.

"How may I direct your call?" The woman's voice on the other end of the call was light and chipper.

"Prince Varojin, please."

"May I ask who is calling for His Imperial Highness?"

"Astrea Sovna."

"Oh, hello Astrea. One moment."

There was a click, then a faint ring. The ringing continued and continued until the line finally went dead. Astrea put the phone back in its place. Where was Jin? It wasn't even the ninth morning bell yet. Could he be training with Adi again?

Astrea pushed off her bed and smoothed her skirt. She still needed to get to the library. She couldn't wait around the palace for Jin all day, and

Astrea doubted the emperor would let her have a day off just because some strangers were stalking her. Going to the library didn't seem wise if these men were indeed watching her, but what was she supposed to do?

Grabbing her satchel from the hook on the back of her door, Astrea headed out into the apartment hallway. The observatory was quiet, not even the sound of Saros's footsteps creaking upstairs. After grabbing her keys, Astrea left the apartment and headed down the circular staircase.

What was Jin even supposed to do about Saros's warning? *"Shadows stalk this city. I need to figure out what they are."* What shadows? The rebels, perhaps? Maybe the newspapers were right after all, and the rebels were more than just talk. Maybe they really were behind the recent murders.

Or could Emperor Aelius be the shadow? As Eliana had said on Solstice Night, the rebels made some good points. Emperor Aelius Auris was not the leader Helosia needed.

Or maybe it was the Corsycan war. Another conflict between three of the continent's five powers wasn't exactly a positive thing.

Astrea pushed the observatory door open and let it slam shut behind her, her brogues crunching on the gravel path outside. Warm, bright sunlight made Astrea squint, but the morning sea breeze cooled her skin as she hurried toward the gardens. A hand landed on her shoulder. She startled.

"It's just me." Jin dropped his hand back to his side as he moved next to her. "Where were you going in such a hurry? Didn't you see me?"

Astrea glanced back at the observatory, the tower looking strangely small. When she looked back at Jin, her chest tightened. She hadn't seen him since the morning after Solstice Night. She'd been worried he would act differently, but he was just . . . Jin.

Just like he had been since he'd come home. Just like he'd always been.

"Were you waiting for me?" she asked.

"I was."

"I tried calling you," she said. "You weren't there."

"Because I was here, waiting. I didn't know if I should go upstairs or if Saros would be unhappy to see me."

Astrea finally looked at Jin, really looked. His charcoal gray jacket, black slacks, and black shirt almost made up a suit. Almost. Even his wingtip shoes were out of place. Jin usually dressed as casual as he could get away with. "Why are you dressed up?"

"We need to go speak with my father."

That explained the outfit, though she was glad to see he wasn't in a waistcoat, too. She certainly wasn't wearing what she deemed appropriate for a meeting with the emperor. Her maroon skirt and silky cream blouse were only one step above casual, but it was probably too late to change.

"Does he know about—" Astrea started, but Jin cut her off.

"No, nothing like that. He wants to speak about the project. It should be quick."

"Good, because we need to talk."

The slightest hint of hesitation crept past Jin's wall. "We do?"

"Something my uncle wants me to tell you."

"Oh." Jin swallowed. "Sure. Can it wait that long?"

Astrea nodded; she didn't see why not. It wasn't like they would be able to do anything about it before this meeting with the emperor anyway. That still had to take priority.

Jin led the way to the palace in silence, offering only small nods to the handful of courtiers they passed in the gardens and the palace corridors. As they turned down the now-familiar hallway with the imperial family's offices, Jin stopped and turned to face her. She stopped short, almost slamming into him, and swore under her breath.

"He's not in a good mood this morning." Jin's voice was hardly above a whisper. "Let me hold his attention."

"Alright." As much as she didn't want to go into that office, letting Jin take the lead sounded just fine to Astrea.

Jin turned back toward the emperor's office door and knocked twice, only turning the handle when a muffled response came. Astrea followed him inside.

Emperor Aelius was definitely in a sour mood. Rusty annoyance colored the air around him, almost salty on Astrea's tongue. He leaned back in his desk chair, fingers steepled in front of his mouth. He even looked the part of an aristocrat: a well-fitted, three-piece suit in dark gray, crisp crimson shirt and matching neck tie, and plenty of gold jewelry.

"You're here," he said to Jin, all pretenses gone despite Astrea's attendance.

"You said you wanted a meeting, Father." Jin stared right at the emperor as he strode further into the room and took one of the chairs in front of the desk. Astrea followed Jin and took the seat next to him, but not before offering a small curtsy to the emperor. Emperor Aelius barely looked at her. "So yes, I'm here."

"I expected you half an hour ago."

"Which was when I received Edouard's call. Did you expect me to appear instantly, out of thin air?"

Aelius's eyes narrowed, and Astrea sucked in a shallow breath. Jin spoke with such disdain. It was a small thing, making the emperor wait, but Astrea couldn't imagine speaking to the Helosian emperor that way. She could barely raise her voice to Saros.

"Fine," Aelius snapped. "Let's get right to it since you've made me late for my next meeting, Varojin. I'd like an update."

"There's not much to update you on," Jin said.

"Have you not toured the Great Hall yet?"

"We didn't have time before the holiday."

"Is that right?" The emperor looked from Jin to Astrea, then back to his son. "I thought I asked you to view it before the festival."

Jin didn't move a muscle as he said, "Well, you didn't specify, and we didn't have time."

As father and son stared each other down, Astrea couldn't help but watch them. Whatever Jin's mother had looked like, he obviously got most of his features from his father. They shared the same strong jaw and straight nose, though Jin's cheekbones were higher.

When Aelius didn't say anything, Jin continued, "We're still trying to narrow down what the exhibit will even showcase. Five hundred years is a lot of information to look at."

"Was there not a war between a Fireweaver king and Novarian grand duchess during the Great Wars?" Emperor Aelius asked. "That's one thing I'd like you to focus on."

Astrea pushed against the urge to fidget with something. A war? *That* was what Emperor Aelius wanted to highlight?

Apparently, Jin was thinking the same thing as her because he said, "I may not be as well-versed in diplomacy as Eliana, but is highlighting bad blood and past feuds wise when we're trying to formalize an alliance with Novaria?"

"You said it yourself, my son." Poison laced the emperor's voice. "You're not as well-versed in diplomacy."

I doubt Eliana would agree with this angle either. The Great Wars were centuries past, but Novaria and Helosia hadn't been at peace for that long, either. The last emperor—Aelius's father, Serafinius—had tried to push into Novarian territory only a decade before Aelius's reign began. The campaign hadn't been successful.

"That war nearly destroyed the beginnings of Helosia," Emperor Aelius continued. "I'd like to show Grand Duchess Ysabel just how far we've come since."

Though it still seemed like a bad idea for the project, Astrea pulled her notebook out of her satchel and began taking notes.

"You'd be wise to follow Miss Sovna's lead, Varojin. She knows what loyalty and duty are."

Fabric rustled as Jin shifted in his seat. Astrea focused on her paper, on the words she was carefully scrawling across the page to avoid making eye contact with Emperor Aelius. Ice flooded her system as the emperor's tone seeped further under her skin. *She knows what loyalty and duty are.* If it weren't such a precarious position to be in, Astrea might actually laugh.

"The Great Wars it is, then," Jin finally said. "What else?"

"I already requested you look at mythology," the emperor said. "Helosia and Novaria share many myths and legends. I believe that will add some levity to the situation, which you seem keen on."

"It simply seems like good sense to not irritate our prospective allies. I couldn't care either way."

The emperor sighed as he stood. When Jin didn't stand, neither did Astrea.

"This is why I've given you this assignment, Varojin. You won't be a soldier forever. You'll have to come back to Kalama someday, and when you do, you need to be useful. You'll learn how to be a good prince eventually." Emperor Aelius motioned toward the door behind them. "I expect an update this week. Do not mess this up, Varojin. You wouldn't want your insolence to reflect poorly on Miss Sovna."

Ice pierced Astrea's senses again, but this time, as she finally glanced toward Jin, a faint trace of cobalt regret pulsed around his body. Just once, then it was gone.

Was this it, then? Was Jin going to reveal what she had done, despite his promises to her, to save his own standing? To protect himself? She tried to swallow, but her throat was too dry.

Jin stood, and Astrea forced herself to her feet.

"I'll have the update for you at the end of the week, Father."

Astrea managed to suck in one breath as she followed Jin out of the office on nothing but instinct. *I shouldn't have assumed the worst.* Hadn't Jin proven several times now that he was going to keep her secret? He'd already had a hundred small chances to reveal what he knew about her magic. He wasn't going to betray her. *Stop being paranoid,* she chided herself.

Jin stood to one side so Astrea could go into the hallway first, and she passed him quickly, eager to put that skies forsaken room behind her. As the emperor's door clicked shut, another voice made Astrea freeze.

"What were you doing in Father's office?" Prince Kaius closed his office door behind him. He had a narrow notebook tucked under one arm, his other hand still resting on the gold door handle.

"I'm not allowed to meet with my own father?" Jin retorted.

Kaius's gaze flicked to Astrea. "Ah, the pet project. How is that going?"

"It's going well, Your Imperial Highness," Astrea said, forcing the words past the dryness still lingering in her throat. "Thank you for asking."

"It doesn't look like it's going well."

"Don't you have somewhere else to be, Kaius?" Jin asked.

"Why yes, I believe I do." Kaius pulled an engraved pocket watch out of his slate blue jacket, looking at it for half a second before stashing it away again. "I have a meeting to get to. After all, some of us have real jobs around here."

As Kaius turned to walk away, Jin started forward. Astrea grabbed his elbow. "He's not worth it," she said. "Why do you still let him get to you like that?"

Kaius was only six months older than Jin, but they'd always had a strange rivalry. Astrea supposed that was inevitable when the older was born to the emperor and empress and the younger was born to the emperor and his mistress.

"He's just so fucking smug," Jin muttered. "I want to wipe that stupid look off his face."

"We have more important things to worry about right now," Astrea said. Did she really need to remind him?

"You're right." Jin ran a hand over his face, then nodded down the hallway. "Come on. Let's go to our spot."

Our spot. He said it so casually, like Astrea would automatically remember. And, of course, she did. She'd never been able to forget.

It didn't take long to weave their way through the palace gardens, nor did it take long to arrive at the gazebo in the middle of the lake near the observatory. Though she'd just met Cressida there days before, it felt like so much time had passed.

"I haven't been here in years," Jin said as he sat on the sole bench in the middle of the structure.

"Ellie, Cress, and I still come here sometimes." Astrea sat next to him. "But none of us have had much time lately."

Nervous energy buzzed under Astrea's skin. Even though she'd just sat down, she stood again and moved toward the railing where she could stare into the water. Gentle waves lapped at the gazebo's edges. The water was too opaque to see the bottom of the lake, so Astrea focused on the pink and white water lilies floating nearby.

"So . . . Saros wanted you to tell me something?" Jin asked.

"He told me shadows stalk the city. The country, actually. Something about how Helosia has something 'darker' on its side."

"Shadows?"

"He doesn't have specifics yet. That's all he's been able to glean." Astrea turned, bracing herself against the gazebo's thick railing. Something unreadable flashed across Jin's face. "Do you have any guesses?"

"I might."

"What is it?"

"Call it a hunch."

Astrea huffed. "Well, that's not very specific."

"No, it's not, but I can look into it. I'll go this morning."

"What about the museum?" When Jin's eyebrows knitted together, Astrea sighed. "Your father wants us to view the Great Hall, remember?" It was Kalama's history museum, a massive collection of art, artifacts, and relics from all over the empire. "Please don't tell me you forgot. I have to do a good job on this project, Jin."

"I didn't forget."

"That's what you said about my sixteenth birthday."

"And I swear I didn't forget that either." The corners of Jin's lips quirked up. "Your gift was delayed. It got here eventually."

Astrea rolled her eyes, and despite the situation, found herself suppressing a smile. "Yes, because every girl wants her birthday gift *eventually*."

"Maybe Kaius made me momentarily forget about the museum," Jin finally conceded, "but I swear I didn't forget about that birthday."

That year, Jin had gifted her a small telescope, one she could use on the observatory apartment's balcony. He'd had its brass exterior engraved with her birthday and her favorite constellation, the Queen. She'd used it often until he'd left for the military a few months later, finally tucking it away in a storage closet once he'd been gone for six months. She hadn't pulled it out since.

"I believe you."

"Do you really?"

"No."

"You're never going to let me forget that, are you?"

Astrea shrugged. "Maybe someday."

"Well, past birthdays aside, you should still go to the museum this morning. And I think you should take Ellie and Nicos with you."

"Ellie has better things to do."

He stood and took two steps toward her. It wasn't much, but in the small gazebo, it put them nearly toe to toe. "Did you forget that someone's hunting you?" he asked, voice low.

"No." Astrea simply didn't want to think about it. Every time she'd thought of it since Solstice Night, it had been hard for her to breathe.

"I think you need an escort around the city at all times," Jin said. "If it's not me, then Cress. And if it's not Cress, then Ellie or Nicos."

"Because that's not going to draw attention."

"Not if it's on official business when it's with Ellie."

"And when it's with you?" Astrea's tone was more accusatory than she meant. Their past was what it was; there was no changing it. "Sorry, I didn't mean—"

"I know what you meant." Jin smiled. "I have business at the library, and wherever else we might go isn't anyone's concern."

"They'll still take notice."

"Nobody notices me until they're close enough to speak with me, Astrea. I've been gone far too long."

"And the people looking for me," she said. "Seeing me with one of you four will really deter them? Because it didn't seem to last time." Guilt surged up Astrea's throat, but she shoved it deep, deep down.

"It's better than you being alone, unless you want to stay in the observatory for the foreseeable future."

Astrea's gaze flicked to the tower looming behind Jin. "No," she said. "I can't hide." Hiding was what had gotten her into this mess in the first place. As terrifying as it was, she had to try to figure this out.

Jin nodded. "Good."

"I guess I'll go call Ellie." Astrea turned, but as she took her first step toward the bridge, Jin put a hand on her shoulder.

"Before you go, I wanted to ask—"

She stifled a groan as she pivoted back toward him. Jin wasn't really trying to bring up what happened eight years ago again, was he? "As I said the other night, I don't—"

"No! No, it's not that." Jin breathed a laugh before he added, "Well, that too, but that's not what I mean. I want to talk about what Saros said the other morning."

"What?" Astrea asked.

"About how he wants me to get you out of Kalama."

"Oh. Right." Astrea had almost forgotten about that.

"I didn't want to ask in front of Saros since I know he isn't my biggest fan, but is that what you want? Would you actually want to leave if I could get you out?"

Astrea didn't know how long she gazed up at Jin. He . . . he wanted to know what she wanted? Saros never asked what Astrea wanted. Even Cressida and Eliana, whom Astrea loved dearly, didn't always ask that question. She didn't mind all that much when it came to her two best friends, but to have someone—to have Jin, of all people—ask that was almost unsettling.

"I . . ." Astrea stared back out over the lake. "He's wanted me to leave Kalama for a few months. Says it would be for the best." She shrugged. "Your father's paying me a lot for helping you with this project, and I just . . . I figured I could leave after that. But I don't really know if I want to."

"Why not?" he asked.

"Ellie's here. Cress is here. This is my home. I can't just leave, even if I don't want to hide."

Why was it so easy to admit that to Jin? Astrea finally snuck another glance at him, only to find him watching her in a way he used to all the time. Carefully. Thoughtfully. Like he was trying to read her mind.

Finally, he smiled. "Well, whether you stay or decide you want to leave, I'll help."

Astrea's throat tightened. She couldn't talk about this anymore, not right now. The shadow men, Saros's warning, the emperor's project, leaving Kalama, Jin's offer—it was all too much.

"I, uh." Astrea huffed. "I really should get started on the museum. And you'll be . . . ?"

Jin watched her for a moment longer before he said, "I'll be looking into what Saros told you. I'll meet you at the library this afternoon."

Without another word, Jin slid past her and crossed the bridge that led back into the gardens. Astrea blew out a harsh breath. She wanted to ask Jin why he was helping her. Why he would go through all the trouble when he'd abandoned her years ago. She knew she needed to talk to him about the last eight years, but that conversation felt more impossible than the mystery she now found herself at the center of.

CHAPTER 22

"Are you sure there's no way for us to speak with Lord Mattina?" Eliana asked.

Watching Eliana—and Jin, for that matter—was like watching someone slip on a mask. Eliana was kind and warm, yes, but when she had to be the imperial princess, she knew how to put on a show.

They'd just arrived at Kalama's history museum. While it had been Jin's idea for Eliana to go with Astrea, Eliana was all too happy to leave the palace behind for a couple of hours.

"I'm sorry, Your Imperial Highness." The pale woman standing behind the museum's ticket counter bobbed her head apologetically. "Lord Mattina isn't in. I can leave him a note to call you if you'd like."

Eliana smiled. "Perhaps we could take a look around and wait for him to return. My father insists we tour the space today to determine whether it would work for his event."

The woman swallowed hard, brushing her blunt brown bangs out of the way as her eyes darted from Eliana to Astrea.

"Waiting is fine, Your Imperial Highness," Astrea said. Waiting was better than going back to the library for the whole day, and besides, it was nice having Eliana with her.

Though they'd spent so much time together as children and teenagers, things hadn't been the same since they'd both graduated from university. Eliana had her council and imperial duties. Astrea had worked at Lodestar Industries doing part-time secretarial work for Balthazar for a few summers while still in school, but Astrea's library job had much longer hours. It made it hard to get together regularly. This wasn't exactly a normal day for either of them—especially not with the knowledge that someone was hunting Astrea—but she would take what she could get.

"Go ahead inside, Your Imperial Highness," the woman said. "Take your time, and please let me know if you need anything else."

"Thank you."

Eliana looped her arm through Astrea's and pulled her toward the brass turnstiles marking the true entrance to the museum. Nicos followed them through. The four-story history museum bordered the Scholar and Market districts, set apart from the university but still within walking distance. Shiny black and white tile floors spread as far as Astrea could see, and tapestries and art pieces in gilded frames covered the creamy white walls.

"Where to first?" Eliana asked.

Astrea looked around for signs. It had been a while since she'd been here, and though she was here to tour the space for the emperor, it might actually prove useful in her research too. "Let's see if we can find anything on Novaria."

Nicos trailed them at a distance, though whether that was because he was still mad at Eliana or because he was trying to give them privacy, Astrea wasn't sure. Both of their emotions were quiet this morning. Astrea couldn't remember the last time that had happened with either of them. She had questions for Eliana—was she still upset about Astrea's magic, did she blame Astrea for her near-death experience, did she realize Nicos cared deeply for her—but Astrea couldn't ask any of those now.

They left the main atrium and entered one of the exhibit rooms. It was filled with statues and busts, some cracked and some restored. Every room they wandered through had something different: ancient pottery and jewelry, old Helosian military uniforms, ornate Delian tapestries, Zaikudi weaponry, and even relics from the old Tornamian kingdom.

"Are you looking for anything specific?" Nicos asked as they passed into another room, this one housing some kind of ancient coin collection.

"Not really," Astrea said, slowing down so he could catch up with them. "The emperor is interested in the Great Wars. Oh, and Novaria and Helosia's shared mythology too."

"Hm." Nicos nodded.

"What?" Eliana asked, stooping to look at a large gold coin in a glass case.

"It seems like a strange request," Nicos said. "Fairytales?"

The museum was eerily quiet. They seemed to be the only three touring it, unusual even for a weekday. A mix of school children and older patrons usually filled these halls.

Eliana straightened, and they made their way into a wide corridor with a staircase at one end and elevator doors at the other. The princess opted for the stairs, and Astrea sighed as she climbed them.

"Really?" she asked from several paces behind Eliana. "We couldn't have taken the elevator?"

"It's not that bad."

It *was* that bad. Though she'd started to recover, Astrea was still tired after the events of Solstice Night. But she couldn't say that in front of Nicos. Instead, Astrea silently trudged up the last few stairs. The second floor was just as quiet as the first, though there was a docent at the entrance to the first exhibit room. They bowed to Eliana.

"Now *that's* interesting," Eliana said as they passed into the next room. "I don't think I've noticed this before."

She stared up at a massive painting that took up nearly a quarter of the wall. Its gold frame was ornate, designs and scrolls carved into the painted wood. The painting itself was of a volcanic eruption, a smoldering black rock sitting in the foreground. It was hard to look away from the bright oranges and reds that bled into the inky gray of clouds and smoke in the sky.

"What is it?" Nicos asked as he stopped behind Astrea and Eliana.

Eliana squinted as she read the gold plate next to the artwork. "Artist unknown."

"That's odd," Astrea murmured.

"Why?" Eliana asked.

"How would they have a piece in such pristine condition," she said, "but no information on the work itself? No title, no artist, no year?" She didn't know much about art, but based on the little she'd learned the previous month helping an art history professor dig around the Great Library's archives, the bold, hyper-saturated style was obviously from a few centuries prior. It reminded her of one that had been popular in northeastern Helosia, near both the Novarian and Tornamian borders.

"Perhaps it was donated without that information," Eliana offered. "Lots of families donate art and other possessions to the city's museums, and trust me, most of them do *not* keep detailed records. Getting old documents from any of the noble houses is like pulling teeth."

"Maybe." That didn't seem likely to Astrea, but she was a mere junior librarian, not a historian or curator. Perhaps the records *had* been lost to time even though the art itself hadn't.

"That's too bad," Nicos said. "I would've liked to know more about it. It's . . ."

"Captivating," a voice finished from behind Nicos.

Astrea turned. A short, slight man stood behind them, his wavy brown hair and round spectacles somehow familiar. His gray plaid suit made of heavy woven fabric was an odd choice given Kalama's summer heat. The color of the fabric did little to compliment his tan complexion.

"Lord Mattina," Eliana said, smiling as she walked toward him. "It's lovely to see you again."

"Your Imperial Highness." Lord Mattina bowed at the waist, glancing at Astrea and Nicos as he straightened. "And these are . . . ?"

"Nicos Masalis, my personal guard," Eliana said. "And Astrea Sovna, a librarian at the Great Library. We're actually here because she's organizing an event and needs to tour the space."

Lord Mattina's gaze swept over Nicos first, then over Astrea. She tried not to fidget, but his stare was intense, scrutinizing. She didn't know what he was looking for, but stale boredom and a hint of annoyance whispered over her skin.

"What kind of exhibition, Your Imperial Highness?" he finally asked as he faced Eliana again. "I've not been informed of anything happening here."

"I don't yet know where it will be staged. My father hasn't decided—"

"Well, whatever His Imperial Majesty decides," Lord Mattina added quickly, "my staff and I are happy to help."

Of course, Astrea thought. *My needing assistance is annoying until he finds out it's for the emperor.*

Eliana smiled and clasped her hands in front of her heart. "Wonderful. Shall we get started?"

"Actually, Your Imperial Highness, there is something I should speak with you about in private. I can send my assistant, Felipe, to help Miss Sovna with any questions she might have."

Lavender surprise colored the air around Eliana as she glanced at Astrea. "Will you be alright?"

Astrea knew what she was really asking. *Nicos and I are your secret escorts to deter any rogue mage attacks. Are you comfortable with this?*

Though the idea of splitting up made bile rise up Astrea's throat, what could she really say? Besides, would someone really try to attack her in the middle of a government institution in broad daylight?

"Thank you for your concern, Your Imperial Highness," Astrea said. "I'll be fine."

"I'll send him up shortly, Miss Sovna." With that, Mattina motioned toward the exit with a tan hand, and Eliana headed that way. Nicos shot Astrea one last look before he disappeared around the corner with the princess.

As soon as their voices were nothing but muffled sounds in the distance, Astrea turned back to the painting Eliana had been captivated by. There weren't any others like it in the room; everything else was muted, beautiful but quiet. Soft, even. Scenes of rolling countrysides, wide oceans, old sailboats, and well-manicured estates, but nothing as violent and bright as the painting of the volcano.

Astrea walked back toward it. There was no artist's signature that she could find, nor was there a date or any other identifying detail she might use. If it was from northern Helosia, it could possibly even be Novarian or Tornamian. Could this be a centerpiece for the emperor's exhibit? It was definitely something he would enjoy.

"Are you Miss Sovna?"

She jumped, pushing her magic out toward the deep voice as she turned. The man approaching her was taller than Jin—a feat in itself—and just as broad despite his wiry frame. The only thing rolling off the fair-skinned man was mild curiosity.

"I am. Are you Felipe?" she asked.

"Indeed." He pushed a few sandy blond curls from his eyes, then motioned to the painting behind her. "Stunning, isn't it?"

"It's unique."

Felipe smiled. "Is it not to your taste, Miss Sovna?"

"I was just surprised to see it in a room full of otherwise serene artwork. That's an interesting choice to make."

"That was Lord Mattina's idea," Felipe said. "He thought the contrast would be striking. But enough about art. His Lordship says you're in need of space for a special exhibition for His Imperial Majesty?"

"I am." Astrea explained what they were looking for—with the few parameters the emperor had given—and when they would need the space. "I've attended special events here before," she concluded, "but I have a few questions for you."

Felipe nodded. "Let's take a tour while I answer your questions."

"How many people can the museum hold?" Astrea asked as they started deeper into the second floor. "I'm not sure what His Imperial Majesty has in mind for a guest list, but I imagine it will be expansive."

"Oh, about five hundred just on this floor. And, of course, you would have access to the entire museum. Would that be enough space?"

"I should hope so," Astrea said, and Felipe chuckled. "And if His Imperial Majesty wants his own staff to control the catering—"

"His Imperial Majesty can do whatever he wants with the building." Though Felipe's tone was sharp, he smiled. "It is, technically, his museum."

Astrea knew that. But that didn't mean the emperor didn't want information before making his decision about what space he was going to take over completely.

"Of course," Astrea said. "Her Imperial Highness simply wanted me to check that we wouldn't be stepping on any toes."

Felipe's expression softened at the mention of Eliana. "Let her know the staff appreciates the thought but that it is no trouble. We will do what must be done. Do you have any other questions?"

Felipe had stopped, and Astrea realized they were in an empty gallery. "What's usually in here?" she asked.

"I'm not sure, actually," he admitted as he turned and surveyed the room. "I just started my job several weeks ago . . . just moved to Kalama, actually, from out west." That explained the harsh emphasis the man put on his vowels; western Helosians tended to do so. "This room has been empty since I arrived."

Astrea couldn't remember what had been in this room the last time she'd been here. It had to have been at least a full year since she was in the museum, possibly longer.

"Do you have any Novarian artifacts?" she asked. "The emperor is keen on highlighting Novarian and Helosian history. I'm sure he would appreciate anything you might be able to loan for the event."

"They are his to take, not ours to loan," Felipe said. "But I don't believe I've actually come across anything Novarian yet."

If the Great Hall didn't have Novarian artifacts, where the skies were they going to get them?

Felipe showed Astrea the rest of the second floor. They passed through more rooms with artwork, old suits of armor, statues, and jewelry. She tried to look at items as they passed the various displays, but everything seemed distinctly Helosian. As they made their way back to the first floor, Eliana's clear voice echoed through the empty halls.

"Do send my best to your family, Leopold!"

"It sounds like they're finished with their meeting," Felipe said. "Let me catch Lord Mattina before he disappears into his office again. I'm sure he'll know what we have in our collection." Without waiting for a reply from Astrea, he hurried off down the corridor Eliana and Nicos were exiting. "Lord Mattina! Can you come speak with Miss Sovna for one moment?"

As Felipe and Lord Mattina came back down the hallway, curiosity tickled Astrea's nose and green colored the air around the curator.

"How may I help you, Miss Sovna?" Mattina asked.

"I was wondering if you had any Novarian artifacts we might show-case—" she started, but he cut her off.

"Novarian artifacts? I have no such thing in the collection."

"Nothing?" Eliana asked. "You know that without checking?"

"With all due respect, Your Imperial Highness," he said slowly, "I know my collection, and I know we don't have anything from Novaria."

"You're sure you don't need to double-check your catalog?" Eliana tilted her chin up. "I wouldn't want to report the wrong information back to my father or waste my time coming back if you find you were incorrect."

"Princess Eliana," Lord Mattina said with a wry chuckle, "perhaps Miss Sovna would have better luck checking with her own institution. I do not have any such thing here."

The hairs on Astrea's arms prickled as irritation simmered around Eliana. Though Mattina's words were almost relaxed, rusty annoyance danced around the man. What could he possibly be annoyed about when he wasn't being very helpful?

"It's alright, Your Imperial Highness," Astrea said. "I know someone who can be more helpful with fulfilling the emperor's request."

Astrea smiled as cobalt regret spiked around Lord Mattina. *Good,* she thought. Not that she planned on telling the emperor about it, but Lord Mattina could sweat over the insinuation for a while.

After exchanging a few goodbyes, Eliana followed Astrea and Nicos back through the museum. She was quiet until they got out to the long stretch of stairs leading back to the street. The sidewalks, while not empty, were less crowded than usual. It was getting close to the noon bell; most people had probably gone elsewhere for lunch.

"Who do you know that might be helpful?" Eliana asked as they approached her car still idling at the curb.

"No one. I just wanted to watch him squirm," Astrea said. Eliana grinned as Nicos opened the car door for her. She slid inside, and Astrea climbed in after her. "And what did he want to talk to you about in private?"

"Oh, some nonsense about the Cultural Affairs Office. Apparently he was promised something by a clerk there and never received it. Nothing I'm going to get involved in." Eliana settled into her seat and fluffed her sage green skirt. "Where to next?"

"I told Jin I'd meet him at the library."

"Then we'll go to the library." Eliana tapped on the window separating the back of the car from the two front seats, then relayed the instructions to Nicos. As the car pulled away from the curb and into traffic, Eliana turned back to Astrea. "We'll be able to find artifacts, I'm sure. There are half a dozen other institutions in the city. Someone must have something."

"Yeah," Astrea murmured.

Though Eliana was confident, Astrea wasn't so sure. If any place in Kalama was going to have what she needed, it should've been the Great Hall. So where *was* she going to find something? Emperor Aelius obviously had high hopes for this event if he wanted to impress the Novarians.

No pressure, Astrea thought as she settled into her seat. *No pressure at all.*

The library wasn't quiet when Astrea arrived. Though Eliana had only dropped her off—she had to return to the palace for the next council meeting—the other Auris sibling in Astrea's life was in the library as promised. Jin stood with his back to the doors as Raela gestured wildly to different areas of the lobby.

"You don't think that would look good, Prince Jin?"

"It's not that I don't think it would look wonderful, but I don't think it's what my father has in mind for this gala . . . exhibition . . . whatever the skies it is."

"We've held galas here before. Just ask Astrea."

"It's true," Astrea said, and both Jin and Raela turned to face her. Lavender surprise sparked around Raela, but the only thing Astrea could read on Jin was his easy smile. She couldn't help it; she smiled back. It was impossible not to, contagious almost. "We hosted one here a couple months ago for the Tornamian ambassador."

"You're back from the museum already?" Raela asked as she followed Astrea to the circulation desk. "Prince Jin said you would be gone for at least another hour."

Jin just flashed that easy smile again. Astrea tried to ignore it as she set her bag on the desk. "Well, Lord Mattina wasn't very helpful."

"I can't say I'm surprised," Raela replied. "Leopold's never been accommodating in the past. Did you at least get the information you needed from him?"

"From his assistant, but yes."

"An assistant?" Raela's eyebrows rose. "Since when does Leopold have an assistant?"

"Since a few weeks ago, apparently," Astrea said.

"Well, lucky Leopold." Raela tucked a graying curl behind her ear. "Must be nice having that much funding."

Jin opened his mouth, but a shout from the third floor cut him off.

"Raela!" Serra called. "I have a question!"

"For skies sake," Raela muttered. "Forgive me, Prince Jin. Duty calls, and I must answer it."

Once Raela was halfway up the stairs, Jin looked at Astrea. That smile was gone, and Astrea swore a hint of anxiety pressed against her.

"Was it really that bad at the museum?" he asked.

"Everything's fine if your father wants it as his venue," Astrea said, "but Lord Mattina claims they have absolutely no Novarian artifacts, even though I swear they used to have some. How can they have absolutely nothing from Novaria when they have items from every other country on the continent?"

Maybe it was her own anxiety. She plopped on the stool behind the desk.

"What are we going to do if we can't find anything Novarian?" she asked before Jin had a chance to respond. "Oh, your father's going to be livid."

"Even if what Lord Mattina claims is true," Jin said, "I know someone who may be able to help."

"Really?"

"Yes. We can meet him tomorrow if you have time."

"I'll make time."

"Meet me at the barracks tomorrow at the tenth morning bell," Jin said. "And you might want to wear trousers."

Astrea's face and ears heated. "Excuse me?"

"Trust me."

"I don't wear trousers," she muttered. Astrea wore them on the rare occasion, but she'd never found them particularly comfortable. She liked her skirts and dresses, which were popular enough in Kalama and didn't press too tightly against her body.

The corners of Jin's mouth twitched. "I know, but I think you'll prefer them tomorrow."

What could they possibly be doing tomorrow that would require her to wear trousers? "Fine."

Jin glanced up toward the staircase, then back down at Astrea. He tapped the desk twice. "Say goodbye to Raela for me? I'm afraid it'll hurt her feelings if I don't let her know I'm leaving."

"Yes, she does seem to have taken a liking to you."

"What, like that's difficult?"

Astrea half laughed. "It's not *that* easy."

As gentle, sweet approval rolled over Astrea's tongue, she stared up at Jin. She hadn't even been thinking when she returned the joke; it reminded her of how they used to tease each other. And now he had the same look on his face as he had at the gazebo just hours before, the one when she'd accused him of forgetting her birthday.

"But yes, I'll tell her," Astrea said as the silence stretched on. "And I'll see you tomorrow."

"Make sure you have Cressida escort you home," Jin said. "If she can't make it, please call me."

"I'll be fine, Jin."

He pinned her with a look, but he didn't press the issue. Instead, Jin said, "I've got to go take care of a few things. See you tomorrow."

As the library door closed behind Jin, Astrea leaned her elbows on the desk and buried her face in her hands. Her chest tightened. Her eyes burned. *Breathe,* she reminded herself.

Where the sudden overwhelm came from, she wasn't sure. Perhaps it was finally being alone, or maybe it was just the last few days catching up with her. Astrea sucked in another deep breath, then looked at the stairs. Raela and Serra were headed toward the elevators, their loud laughter impossible to miss.

Astrea stood and straightened her skirt just as the elevator doors opened and her colleagues started toward circulation.

"Is Prince Jin gone?" Raela asked. "So soon?"

"He had some things to do and wanted me to pass along his goodbyes," Astrea said.

"Well, how thoughtful." Raela smiled. "Such a charming young man, isn't he? Is he always so kind, Astrea?"

Both Serra and Raela watched her expectantly, and Astrea shifted. He had been, at least until he'd left Kalama. And now that he was back, Astrea was having a hard time ignoring the fact that Jin wasn't so different after all.

CHAPTER 23

Astrea moved toward the barracks on the western side of the palace compound. The buildings that housed some of the city's soldiers were tall, three stories of gleaming white and gray brick. Several shorter buildings joined the area, making up what Astrea knew to be a garage, an armory, and a mess hall.

She didn't know where she was going or where exactly she was supposed to meet Jin. Astrea typically avoided the barracks, not because the people who lived there weren't kind but because she didn't like the rampant emotions. Everyone from non-mages skilled in artillery, strategy, and physical combat to some of the most powerful mages on the continent made up the emperor's army. Just as their particular talents ran the gamut, so did their feelings. Some were numb. Some were proud. Some held pain so deep that Astrea had to force herself to turn away before it overwhelmed her senses. Most were some combination, traumatized by war but still believing in what Emperor Aelius told them they needed to do.

As Astrea approached the barracks, though, it seemed quieter than usual. Nobody was in the sparring pits, nor was there a rush of soldiers moving from the barracks to someplace else in the city. A young woman scurried by Astrea, the sword sigil on her maroon uniform denoting her low rank. The only other activity was the sound of a radio coming from the garage. It sounded like a broadcast of a pro mage sports match; Balthazar and Cressida listened to them all the time.

Astrea hesitated. Was she allowed to look around? There were places she couldn't go in the palace without an escort, but she was looking for Jin. If the garage held the only sign of life, it had to be alright to investigate.

The thought of meeting Jin to work together was somehow both foreign and familiar. She appreciated that he seemed to be going out on a limb for her—working on their joint project, yes, but also protecting her secret and investigating something for her uncle, too. It was like they were still just teenagers: helping each other with school assignments, hiding from the palace guards and the siblings' governess, trying to navigate different ways through the city together.

And yet it was different now. Jin was not just a prince but a soldier. Astrea was a mage—well, she'd always been one, but now he knew. They were both getting involved in something far more dangerous than sneaking away from palace guards. And she still hadn't made peace with the unpleasant part of their past, the part where he'd hurt her. Could still hurt her, betray her for a second time.

He could've already turned me in, Astrea reminded herself. *And just because he was a bad friend back then doesn't make him my enemy now.*

"Hi!"

A tall man strode toward her as he exited the garage. When she noticed his black uniform, she realized who he was: Adi, the Earthmover Jin had been sparring with a few days prior. He had one light brown eye and one forest green eye, both friendly and warm. A small scar cut through his right eyebrow.

Pulling a cloth out of his pocket, Adi wiped his hands off before extending one toward her. A few dark spots dotted his brown skin. "I saw you here the other day with the princess's guard," he said, grinning as

Astrea shook his hand. His smile was so friendly it was almost disarming. "I'm Lieutenant Adi Kuwat."

"I'm Astrea Sovna," she said. "It's nice to meet you."

"Jin—Prince Varojin." Adi cleared his throat. "Captain Auris was telling me about you the other day."

"Oh?" She wasn't sure why, but she hadn't been expecting that, nor had she been expecting Adi to go through Jin's formal titles.

"Just that you two were friends when you were kids."

"We were."

"So what brings you here?" Adi asked.

"Your captain asked me to meet him here. He didn't say where, though."

"You're welcome to wait here until he's back," Adi offered, motioning behind them toward the garage. "I'm on duty right now, so he'll probably come looking for me if he can't find you."

Astrea nodded. It was certainly better than standing out in the open, doing nothing.

She followed Adi into the garage, the wide bay giving way to cars, trucks, and even a few motorcycles. One motorcycle, the body painted dark blue, had been separated from the others. Tools Astrea couldn't name were spread out on the floor, and she had to step over a spot of oil as she followed Adi to a workbench. On the far end of the garage, another soldier was working on a truck, but it was otherwise empty.

Cress would love this. Though Cressida, like her father, had a soft spot for experimenting with explosives, she also loved working on vehicles. One summer when they were still teenagers, Cressida had taken apart the family's car engine just for fun.

"Let me just turn this down," Adi said, reaching past Astrea to turn the knob on a small, crackling radio. The broadcast quieted, and Adi nodded. "Feel free to have a seat or look around; just don't touch anything."

"Thanks," Astrea said. "What type of motorcycle is that?"

"Oh, just whatever the military will give us." Adi picked up a wrench and went back to the motorcycle, squatting in front of what had to be the engine. "Why, are you interested in them?"

Astrea laughed. "Oh, no," she said. "But one of my best friends tried to convince me to get on one once."

"And you didn't?"

"No, I most certainly did not."

He laughed and shook his head, his short, tight curls barely bouncing. "Did Captain Auris say how long he'd be?"

"No. He just asked me to meet him here at this hour," Astrea replied as she walked the length of the work bench. Dozens of boxes were lined up underneath it, and posters and maps of the empire hung above it. Nothing seemed particularly important. "Have you worked with him long?"

"Oh, long enough," Adi said, and she detected the hint of a laugh in his voice. He turned the wrench hard before continuing. "I joined his unit about three years ago. He's the best commanding officer I've had. Got us through some really tough missions."

Astrea paused, her fingers hovering over the screwdriver she'd been about to pick up. She hadn't thought about Jin going on missions. He was, after all, one of the emperor's children. But he was a Fireweaver, and a strong one at that. He was an officer. Of course he had real assignments wherever he was stationed.

"That's good to hear," she said, then immediately felt foolish. "That he was able to get you through it, I mean."

Adi chuckled, a deep, amused sound. "I knew what you meant, Miss Sovna." He wiped his hands on the same cloth as before, then stood, wrench in hand.

"Just Astrea, please," she said, and he nodded. "How large is your unit?"

"Just four of us on his team, including him. Excuse me." Adi motioned behind Astrea, and she stepped aside as he reached for a strange tool hanging from a hook on the wall. "We've all seen things, some worse than others, but Jin—Captain Auris—got us through it. He'd do anything for us."

"Would I?"

Both Astrea and Adi turned. Jin stood near the garage's entrance, arms crossed as he leaned against the wall to his right. His outfit reminded her of the one he'd been wearing at the Whiskey Dream so many nights ago, from the black button-up shirt to the black pants. This time, though, he wore boots similar to Adi's obviously military-issued ones. Jin's gaze flicked over Astrea's body, then back up to her face. Her stomach fluttered as she resisted the urge to tug at the tapered black ankle-length trousers she'd worn. This had been his idea, not hers. She fiddled with the strap of her satchel instead.

"Hey, Captain." Adi grinned, apparently unfazed by Jin's sudden appearance. Astrea had no idea how he managed to move around so quietly. "I cleaned up your mess yet again."

"Did you?" Pushing off the wall, Jin walked toward the motorcycle.

Was he going to think Astrea had been asking about him? She had been, of course, but she didn't want him to think it was with bad intentions. The more time she spent with Jin, the more she wondered about the years they'd lost and what his life had become.

Adi motioned to the motorcycle. "It should be fixed," he said. "And just in time, apparently. Astrea was telling me that you asked her to meet you here."

She didn't miss the amusement spiking around Adi. "Oh," Astrea said quickly, cheeks burning, "no. We just need to follow-up on a lead for this project we're working on."

"Right." Adi nodded, as if her brief explanation made perfect sense. "You're a librarian, right?"

"She is," Jin said, "and thanks for fixing the bike."

"Just be nice to it and it'll work fine."

"I'm always nice," Jin said, and that warm amusement spread from Adi to Astrea again. "What do you think?"

When the silence stretched on, Astrea pulled her gaze from the motorcycle to find Jin watching her, eyebrows raised. "Oh." She looked from him to the bike. "I assumed we'd walk."

"We're going all the way to the Scholar's District," Jin said. "Walking will take forever."

"Couldn't we take a car?" she asked. "I've never been on one of those before."

A strong, muscular arm slid around Astrea's shoulders, and she peeked up at Adi as he gave her a gentle shake. "You haven't lived until you've been on one of these," he said. "*Especially* with the captain driving."

"Be quiet and give us the helmets," Jin said, but his tone was light, amused. More warmth blossomed in Astrea's chest as Adi laughed. "It's perfectly safe, and it's faster than sitting in traffic."

In a whirlwind, Astrea found herself with a helmet strapped over her head as she sat behind Jin on the motorcycle. The seat was more cushioned than she'd expected, but even with Jin balancing the bike, it didn't feel stable to her. *I can't believe I'm doing this.*

The bike angled to one side as Jin adjusted his seat. Astrea grabbed onto his wide shoulders without a second thought, her pulse thundering.

"It's okay," Jin said over his shoulder. "We're not going to fall."

"Says you," Astrea muttered.

"Wrap your arms around my waist," Jin said over his shoulder. "It's more secure."

Astrea looked at Adi, hoping he'd convince Jin at the last minute to take a car instead, but the Earthmover simply grinned and gave her a thumbs up. Sighing, Astrea slid her arms around Jin's waist. This close to him, Astrea realized he smelled like eucalyptus and sandalwood. That was new; he'd always used a particular lavender soap when they were younger. The engine roared to life, and Jin eased the motorcycle out of the garage.

"See you later, Captain!" Adi called. "Bring them both back in one piece!"

"Ignore him," Jin said over the sound of the engine. "We'll be fine. Just get closer to me."

"Closer?" Astrea asked.

"Closer."

Frowning, Astrea scooted forward on the bike's seat. Her body was pressed flush against Jin's back, and she forced herself to shove down her embarrassment as her magic fed her the sweet, fruity hints of Jin's approval.

He revved the engine once, then said, "Hold on tight."

By the time Jin stopped the motorcycle in the Scholar's District, Astrea was breathless, her pulse pounding in her ears.

"I thought you said that was safe," she said as Jin shut off the motor.

He laughed, his muscles tightening under her hold on his waist. Astrea pulled her arms back and yanked off her helmet as Jin said, "We made it here without a scratch, didn't we?"

After leaving the palace grounds, Jin had managed to get them to their destination in a quarter of the time it would take by streetcar and half the time it would've taken in Eliana's car. He'd woven in and around traffic, squeezing the motorcycle through spaces Astrea was sure were too tight.

"Admit it," he said as he turned over his shoulder. "You had fun."

"I did not."

He was always the one pushing her when they were kids, getting her to try new things that were usually more fun than she'd ever admit. And though it had been scary, rushing through the city like that had also been exhilarating.

"Liar."

"I can't believe you're even allowed to drive one of those things," she muttered as Jin helped her off the bike.

"Because I'm a bad driver?"

"Because it seems dangerous for a prince."

"So is going to the front lines, but my father let me do that, too. Well, made me."

Astrea paused. Jin hadn't said it with any malice; it was just a simple statement. But that knowledge crawled under her skin and buried itself in her heart.

"So . . . are you going to tell me where we are?" Astrea asked. A change of subject seemed best.

The street was familiar; she spent too much time in this part of the city to not know its layout well. But the homes and storefronts here were anonymous, unmarked. Jin had parked the motorcycle in front of a brown brick building, its front shutters open to reveal books and knickknacks in the window. It didn't look like anything special.

"An old friend's shop," he replied, his hand outstretched toward Astrea's helmet. She handed it to him, then followed him across the sidewalk.

A bell chimed as they entered the building, the smell of old books and dust almost making Astrea sneeze. Jin sneezed twice. Bookshelves stretched down the long, narrow length of the store. Artifacts and trinkets covered every spot not taken up by books. Music boxes, small statues and figurines, sheathed daggers, and more were scattered around the store.

"What is this place?" Astrea whispered.

"My mother's old friend," Jin said. "It's his store. He's an antiquities dealer."

"Oh."

Jin never talked about his mother; none of the Auris siblings mentioned her. Astrea didn't even know her name.

"You here, Theo?" Jin called as he scanned the store. "It's me!"

Something rustled near the staircase tucked in a dark corner, then a tan, middle-aged man came down the stairs. He had a slight build and wasn't much taller than Astrea, and his curly hair was more gray than brown. He pushed his round spectacles up his slightly crooked nose; it looked like it had been broken once and never healed. Was this the same man she'd seen with Raela at the library the week before? The one who was going to inspect that statue? He certainly seemed familiar.

"Ah, Jin!"

Jin enveloped the man in a hug, and they patted each other on the back several times. Astrea hung back, unsure what to do. This man—Theo—was hard to read, but he seemed pleased to see Jin.

"I didn't realize you were back in town," Theo said. "I can't remember the last time you were home."

"Well," Jin said, "something came up."

The man nodded, as if that explained everything in the world.

"I'd like to introduce you to someone," Jin continued. Astrea took a tentative step forward. "Astrea, this is Lord Theodore Kadis. Theo, this is Astrea Sovna."

Lord Kadis extended his hand, and Astrea shook it. "How do you do, Miss Sovna?"

"Just Astrea, please," she said.

"Then you must call me Theo." She smiled and nodded as Theo pushed up his glasses and continued, "What brings you in today, Jin? I know it wasn't just to introduce me to your pretty friend."

"No, it wasn't," Jin said, and Astrea's face warmed. "We've been tasked with putting together an exhibit on Novarian and Helosian history for my father. *By* my father, actually. It's his pet project."

Theo straightened. "An exhibit on Novaria?"

"Yes," Astrea said quickly. "His Imperial Majesty has asked us to re-search the last five hundred years of Novarian and Helosian history. We're supposed to put together an exhibit ahead of the autumn summit with Grand Duchess Ysabel."

Theo shot Jin a look, one Astrea couldn't decipher even with her lightbringing. Something passed between the two men, but Theo finally looked back to her.

"And was there something specific you were looking for?" he asked as he maneuvered past her and went behind the nearby counter. Theo stooped, then pulled out a large book littered with bookmarks and dog-eared pages.

"Nothing specific," Astrea said as she approached the counter. Jin followed her. "Though he seems particularly interested in old mythology and a battle between Helosia and Novaria during the Great Wars."

"Mythology and a *war*?" Theo arched a bushy eyebrow. "Really?"

Jin held up his hands. "I tried to tell him that, Theo. I really did."

Theo shook his head. "Typical," he muttered, turning his attention back to the book and flipping through the pages. He stopped suddenly on a page covered in tiny scrawl. "Ah!"

Jin leaned on the counter, his eyes searching the ledger despite it being upside down. "Did you find something?"

"No."

"Theo," Jin groaned. "Seriously?"

"I found *something*, but I cannot give it to you today."

"What is it?" Astrea asked.

"A book titled *Novaria: Myths and Other Legends*," Theo said. "A second edition from three hundred years ago, and it's in pristine condition."

Astrea's heart jumped. The emperor would love that. Could Theo really have something so valuable?

"And why can't you give it to us today?" Jin asked.

"Because it's not here."

"Then where is it?"

"I loaned it to the Great Hall of History."

"Wait," Astrea said, now also trying to read the ledger upside down. "Are you sure that's where you sent it?"

"I'm positive." Theo pointed to a line on the page, then turned the book around for them to read. "Three weeks ago. I delivered it to them myself."

"I thought Lord Mattina claimed he had nothing Novarian," Jin said, voice low as he peered at Astrea.

"That's what he claimed," she said.

"Perhaps he was mistaken."

"Who did you give the manuscript to?" Astrea asked Theo.

"Leopold Mattina," Theo said simply. "He's an old acquaintance of mine. Our families go back generations. Perhaps he forgot."

A sheen of gray confusion pulsed around Theo. It was possible that Lord Mattina had lost a hundreds-year-old manuscript, though Astrea wasn't so sure. People who worked with such items weren't typically careless.

"We'll go back to the museum," Jin offered. "We'll figure out what's going on. In the meantime, Theo, would you mind pulling some of the other Novarian artifacts you have lying around here?"

"I'll pull whatever I find that fits your project's parameters," Theo confirmed. "I'll have something for you in a couple of days."

They said their goodbyes, and Astrea followed Jin back out of the shop, the morning sea breeze doing nothing to cool the sun's heat. She tucked her hair behind her ears as she accepted the helmet from Jin.

"What's wrong?" he asked.

"That museum curator," Astrea said. "Why would he lie?"

Jin swung one leg over the motorcycle, then patted the seat behind him. Astrea climbed on, her arms slinking back around Jin's waist.

"I don't know what Lord Mattina is trying to hide," Jin said as he turned the engine on, "but we're going to find out."

CHAPTER 24

I'm never getting used to this, Astrea thought as Jin slowed the motorcycle to a stop behind the Great Hall of History. The bike rumbling beneath her was enough to make her nerves jump, let alone Jin's driving. He clearly knew what he was doing, but she felt every bump, turn, and change in speed in her bones.

"I can see why Adi warned me," she mumbled as she stepped onto the sidewalk.

"Again," Jin said, his voice teasing, "I got us here in one piece."

She shoved her helmet at him, which he hung off the bike's handlebars, then started down the long length of the museum. The alley was quiet and clean, and the few people they passed didn't even look at them twice. As they rounded the front of the building, the world burst to life. Students, parents, and businesspeople hurried down the sidewalk. A busker performed what sounded like an original song, and several people had gathered around to listen.

Astrea and Jin climbed the museum's stairs. A group of Tornami-ans loitered outside the museum's portico, their loose, brightly colored clothes giving them away as tourists before their sharp dialect could. Kalamians didn't shy away from colors, but jewel tones and pastels were in fashion in the Helosian capital, not the intensely saturated colors worn by many from southern Tornama. Inside, a group of Kalamian students in drab school uniforms clamored for tickets to enter the exhibits.

Astrea hung back as Jin approached the ticket counter, visitors moving out of the way when they realized he was being serious about cutting the line. Annoyance and confusion arced out in a mix of rust red and gray. A few of them whispered in hushed Tornamian, and another signed something in quick, angry motions.

Though the crowd wasn't hiding their feelings, Jin still was. What, exactly, had he gone through with Adi? Was that why he was so hard to read now? Jin's emotions had been easy to identify when they were younger, intense feelings he didn't shy away from.

"The ticketer claims Mattina isn't here," Jin said as he joined Astrea at the back of the line.

"And you don't believe her."

Jin shrugged. "I have no reason not to believe her."

"But?" Astrea prompted. She knew that look. She'd seen it on him many times over the years.

"But," Jin continued, jaw muscle flexing, "I had no reason to believe her, either."

"So . . . what do we do? Just wait for him to show his face?"

"No," Jin said. "He won't be coming out if he knows we're here."

"Why?"

"Because he obviously didn't want you or my father to have the manuscript in the first place. Why else would he lie about it?"

"Maybe we don't even need it." Astrea didn't want to cause trouble, but she also didn't want to disappoint the emperor. He'd made it plenty clear that any missteps on either her or Jin's part would lead to unpleasant consequences. "Maybe we don't even need to tell your father about it. Theo must have other artifacts we can borrow."

"No." Jin turned, searching the crowd. "There's a reason Mattina is doing this."

She sighed. "How can you know that?"

"I just know."

Of course he just knows, she thought. What was he going to do, cause a scene to force the curator to come out?

"Let's just look around," Jin finally suggested. "We're already here. Maybe I'll be wrong and he'll show up soon."

After passing through the entry turnstiles, they moved through the space unnoticed, everyone absorbed in their own conversations. They circled the main atrium first, then moved into one of the large exhibit rooms. It was a similar path to what Astrea, Eliana, and Nicos had taken the day before, and it yielded nothing new. It was the same mix of art and artifacts, no books or manuscripts in sight.

"What are we supposed to be looking for?" Astrea finally asked, cringing as a toddler screeched. Two men chased after her, trying to wrangle the child as she waddled into the atrium. The little girl squealed as she ran toward an elderly woman with outstretched arms. Both the woman and child giggled, and warm delight washed over Astrea.

"I know Lord Mattina wouldn't have put the book on display," Jin said, his hand brushing the small of Astrea's back as he guided them into a different room. She tried not to stiffen. "But maybe we can find the entrance to his office or the man himself."

"We can just come back tomorrow," Astrea tried again. "I don't want to be a burden."

"Astrea." Jin stopped, pulling her toward an empty bench in the art room they'd just entered. "Sit and listen to your gut."

"My gut?" she asked as she dropped down next to Jin. Her gut was confused these days.

"How does this situation feel to you?"

"Frustrating."

"No." Jin shook his head, voice low. "What does your intuition say?"

Sighing, Astrea pushed against the feeling that she was causing trouble and tried to look at the situation again. Jin saw something here. A manuscript his father would probably want. A museum curator who had apparently stolen the thing from another collector and was now blocking Eliana from finding it. Which meant he was trying to stop the emperor from getting it for some reason.

"What could be so important about an old book that someone is trying to prevent your father from getting it?" Astrea asked, finally meeting Jin's gaze again.

His lips pulled up into a smile. "*That's* why I don't want to just come back tomorrow. People play enough games in Kalama without adding this into the mix. Let's just see what we can find while we're here."

"That's absolutely not what happened!" Astrea exclaimed, her voice echoing through the empty exhibit room. It was filled with marble statues from the Rebuilding, the time just after the Great Wars.

"I'm fairly certain that's exactly what happened," Jin said. "You and Cressida had the brilliant idea to see what would happen if you each drank an entire pot of coffee in the twenty minutes before our Novarian language lessons started."

"First of all," Astrea said as they passed a bust of a woman wearing an ornate crown, "it was Ellie's idea. Second of all, *you* dared us to."

"Hm." Jin hummed the word, lips pursing. "Doesn't sound like me."

Giggling, Astrea nudged his arm with her shoulder. "You're such a skies damned liar."

He laughed, too, the sound like a hug. "You're right. I am a liar. I definitely dared you to do that."

When Astrea had been just fifteen, Eliana had thought it would be hilarious to see what would happen if Astrea and Cressida ingested that much caffeine before a lesson with Saros. After a bit of encouragement from Jin, Astrea and Cressida had both followed through, and the results had been less than pleasant. She'd never felt her heart race so quickly, and her hands had shaken so much she could barely write out answers to whatever assignment Saros had given them.

"At least you're finally admitting it," she said as they entered a familiar room. That painting with the volcano, the one Eliana had been captivated by, hung nearby.

They'd spent hours in the museum, scouring the building from top to bottom. They read every plaque and examined every door and hallway they found. They'd found several locked doors, and Astrea had wished more than once that they'd brought Cressida with them. She could break any lock with her Metalli magic as long as it wasn't platinum.

Though they'd searched all four floors of the museum, there was no indication of where Lord Mattina might have gone, nor was there any indication the book was in the building. Felipe wasn't even around.

"I suppose we should go," Jin said as he looked at the watch on his wrist. Astrea's stomach growled loudly, and she ducked her head. "It's getting late."

They retraced their steps all the way to the front of the building, exiting through another turnstile and stopping near the ticketing counter.

"Excuse me," Jin said as he veered toward the counter. The same woman from before was behind the desk, packing several folders into a large canvas tote.

"May I help you, Your Imperial Highness?" she asked. If she was surprised to see Jin, the woman didn't reveal it. Astrea's magic found nothing but cool curiosity.

"Lord Mattina doesn't happen to be in now, does he?" Jin asked.

"No, Your Imperial Highness. He hasn't been in at all today." The woman glanced over her shoulder to a clock hanging on the wall. "I do apologize, but I need to close down the museum for the night. You're welcome to check back tomorrow."

"Thank you," Jin said.

Jin was silent as they stopped under the museum's portico. It was the quietest he'd been since they entered the building. He'd been surprisingly talkative all afternoon, explaining different artifacts and bits of history he knew about. Astrea had to correct him more than once, which just made him laugh. It had made her laugh, too. He'd even called forth memories of their younger years: time spent both studying and running away from tutors—even Saros and the coffee incident.

Perhaps more surprisingly, Astrea had enjoyed his company. Despite their true reason for being there, it felt familiar. Normal, even. Good. Astrea couldn't help but wonder if the last eight years would've been filled with more days like that had Jin not left for the army.

"Maybe, if you're not busy," Astrea said as they loitered near the museum's front doors, "we could stop for dinner on the way home." She wasn't sure where the idea had come from; it just felt right to suggest it. Besides, going back to the observatory didn't appeal to her. Saros had been a little more talkative the last couple of days, but he was still spending almost all of his time in his office.

"Dinner?" Jin asked, a hint of his surprise tickling her nose. He smiled. "I'd love to get dinner. Where do you want to go?"

"Anywhere is fine. Nothing too loud."

"You mean you *don't* want to go to the Whiskey Dream again?"

"No, thank you."

"Then we'll find someplace quiet, maybe down near the water."

They started down the museum stairs, heading into the dusky night. Hints of purple and dark blue still clung to the horizon, and the first stars weren't even out yet.

"Could Mattina actually be a rebel?" Astrea asked as they reached the sidewalk. It was a thought she'd had hours before but one she didn't want to mention until they were alone. "Maybe he simply wants to make this project difficult for your father."

"Well, I suppose he could be sympathetic," Jin said, "but this would be a silly thing for him to do. It doesn't really accomplish much."

There were plenty of Helosians who were sympathetic to the rebel cause even if they wouldn't get involved. It wasn't hard to wish for change when you and your children were being sent off to another war.

Astrea sighed and stared out at the darkening sky. "Now what?" she asked. "I just hate that we couldn't find it."

Jin blew out a heavy breath and ran his hand through his hair. "I don't like unanswered questions either, but Theo said he's pulling together some other artifacts. We'll have something to present to my father if that's what you're worried—"

An ear-piercing scream cut off Jin's words. Astrea spun. The streets were nearly empty, no surprise, considering the museum had just closed. There weren't any restaurants or bars around here; everyone would've gone back toward the Market District for dinner.

"What was that?" Astrea asked. Another scream echoed through the area, followed by fear pushing against Astrea's chest. So much fear. It bubbled up her throat and suffocated her, somehow both familiar and foreign as it overwhelmed the rest of her senses. Astrea doubled over.

"What's wrong?" he asked, his hand landing on her shoulders.

"Something's . . ." Astrea tried, but her skull ached to the point that she couldn't think. "I don't understand." There was still no one in sight; she could sometimes feel emotions or pain through walls, but not like this. Never like this. She searched for the edge of her lightbringing senses, but pain clouded her mind.

Jin frantically searched her face, as if it would hold the answers Astrea couldn't voice. "Come on." He took Astrea's hand in his. His skin was warm and rough, a tether to the real world. Astrea gritted her teeth as they hurried down the length of the museum toward where he'd parked the motorcycle. "Stay close to me," he whispered, "and do not use your magic."

Astrea wasn't sure she could manage to use it even if she wanted to.

They crept down the alley. It was dark here, much darker than on the main street out front. Tall buildings rose up on both sides of them, their windows shut for the night. Jin's steps were careful, calculated as they moved through the dark. Astrea tried her best to mimic him.

"Wait here," Jin whispered.

Jin dropped her hand and inched toward the end of the alley. He was silent, stone-still as he peered around the corner. A flash of gray confusion colored the air around him. The fear burning in Astrea's veins grew stronger, and despite Jin's orders to wait, she followed him.

Her breath caught in her chest. A woman was lying on the cobble-stone street, her body prone unnaturally but her eyes wide. Undulating shadow and bright white panic danced in the air. A tall, hunched figure loomed over her. Shadows dripped off the attacker despite a nearby streetlight.

She'd seen that before. Their attackers on Solstice Night.

Astrea had tried to convince herself it was a trick of the light or even a trick of her own mind, but no. Those men had been cloaked in shadow, and now this person was, too. Astrea's magic zipped past the shadow man, almost like he wasn't even there.

Astrea tugged on Jin's sleeve, trying to push away the woman's pain as they retreated back into the alley. But she couldn't. Her body throbbed with every beat of her heart.

"I think that's him."

"Who?" Jin asked.

"Solstice Night." She hoped her short words were clear enough that she wouldn't have to explain much past the pain. "It hurts . . ."

"Stay here."

Jin raced back down the alley, the heat of his fire strong. Astrea clenched her jaw and followed him as he disappeared around the corner. *Foolish,* she thought, though whether it was about herself or Jin, she wasn't sure. Astrea just knew they needed to save that poor woman.

Jin sprinted down the pedestrian street, chasing the shadow man. The attacker was moving faster than a person should be able to, faster than Jin. Who would be able to outrun a trained Helosian soldier?

Foolish, Astrea thought again, skidding to a stop near the woman and dropping to her knees.

The woman pointed in the direction Jin had run. "Help . . ." The word was barely more than a whisper of breath, her hand shaking as she tried to point. "Help . . ."

"Yes," Astrea said quickly. "Yes. It's alright. You'll be alright."

But she didn't know where to touch the woman to heal her. Her entire body was covered in inky shadows, the marks flickering like a flame. Where there should've been veins under the woman's pale skin, there was just more darkness. Her hands, forearms, and neck were all being consumed by an invisible cold fire Astrea could feel in her own body. She could barely think straight as she burned.

Astrea had never experienced pain this intense without healing the other person. What was wrong? Astrea searched for anything on the woman's body besides those shadows. A wound near her heart gushed black, the liquid spreading over her crisp shirt.

"It's alright," Astrea said again, her voice shaking. "It's alright. I'm going to help."

There had to be something she could do. There had to be some way to help this woman. Jin had told her not to use her magic, but Astrea couldn't just let this woman die. She tried pushing her magic out, but it couldn't find anything without some kind of physical contact. No place on this woman's body was untouched by shadow, and Astrea wasn't sure she should touch it.

It was too late anyway. The woman's hand fell limp against her abdomen. The burning in Astrea's veins stopped, like someone had flipped a switch and simply turned it off. The overwhelming fear and panic were gone, too, replaced by a deafening silence.

The woman's eyes had glazed over, the inky shadows continuing their dance. Astrea didn't need to feel for a pulse. She was dead.

Astrea stared down in horror. Just seconds before, she'd felt this woman's complete agony, the gut-wrenching fear as something killed her.

And I couldn't save her.

She was half tempted to check for a pulse on the off chance she was missing something. It was hard to tell who she was by her face, distorted as it was with the shadows. But as Astrea looked down at the woman's clothes, tote bag, and blunt brown bangs, recognition struck her. The ticketer from the museum, whom they'd spoken to just minutes before.

Astrea pushed herself off the ground, looking one direction down the street, then the other. Jin was nowhere in sight. There was *nobody* in sight. It was just Astrea and this dead woman, surrounded by the low light of the streetlamp buzzing nearby.

What if someone thought she did this? Her breath came faster. What if a city police officer came down the street on patrol and found Astrea hovering over the body of a dead woman? Then what? Would they think Astrea had killed her?

Astrea sucked in a breath, ready to call for someone, anyone, to come help, but a warm hand covered her mouth before she could speak.

"It's just me," Jin whispered in her ear. He lowered his hand and guided her back toward the alley.

"What the skies was that?" Astrea hissed, peering over her shoulder and trying to see the dead woman around the corner. "Why is she covered in . . . covered in . . ."

The words wouldn't come. Her mind grew fuzzy, distant, the sound swimming in her ears as she met Jin's golden gaze.

"That was the same man who . . ." she started, but those words wouldn't come, either. Her breath was coming too fast now, her heart beating so wildly in her chest, Astrea was sure she was about to explode.

She looked down at her hands, trying to see if those same inky shadows covered her skin. Had she contaminated herself? Accidentally touched the dying woman? But she couldn't see past the darkness clouding her vision. She couldn't see anything past the tears, hear anything past the roar in her ears.

Jin's hands settled on her shoulders. They were walking. Astrea didn't know where they were going, but Jin had tucked her against his side. Her legs each weighed a ton, every step as impossible as each breath she tried to take in. They stopped moving, and Astrea swore she heard glass shatter. Jin ushered her along again.

"Come, sit."

She sat.

"Hey, there she is." Jin's smile was the first thing Astrea saw as the fuzziness receded to just the edge of her vision. It was gentle, warm, a lifeline when she felt like she was drowning. "Can you take a deep breath? Like this."

Jin breathed in deeply through his nose, then blew out through his mouth as he pulled his hands away from her shoulders. But Astrea shook her head, the movement forced. She was suffocating. She couldn't breathe at all.

"I know it's hard," he said softly. "Just try it a few times, however much you can. I'll do it with you."

Astrea tried following his lead, each breath loosening the rope tied around her heart.

"Keep doing that," Jin said. "Can you keep doing that while I go right over there?"

She nodded.

"I'll be right back."

She nodded again.

As Jin retreated, Astrea took in her surroundings. They were back inside the museum—somehow—and she was sitting on a bench just inside the front door. Shards of glass near the handle explained that; Jin had broken in. The only light came from the flame hovering over Jin's palm as he used the phone behind the ticket counter.

Astrea's cheeks burned as she blew out one more harsh breath. Her head was starting to clear, her heartbeat and tears slowing. *Why did I react like that?* Yes, the woman had died, but Astrea was safe. Jin was safe. *Aren't we?*

And Jin had seen her freeze. What would he think of her now?

You're just a weak little Lightbringer, hiding from the world for her whole life, she thought as she watched Jin put the phone receiver down. He ran his hand through his hair, his back heaving with a heavy breath.

Because you are weak and scared and pathetic. The thoughts came fast and unbidden, like water rushing out from a broken dam. *And you'll never be a help to anyone if you can't hold it together.*

Astrea wiped furiously at her wet cheeks. She needed to dry them before he came back. This wasn't supposed to be happening. She'd stayed in control on Solstice Night. She'd been able to save Eliana. She hadn't broken down. Why couldn't she stay in control now?

Jin turned around, unreadable as he made his way back to her bench. He squatted in front of her, his face expressionless despite the warmth burning in his eyes.

"I called the police," he said. "They'll be here soon."

Astrea nodded.

"I didn't tell them who we were. We won't have to talk to them."

Astrea focused on her lap, her fingers playing with a crease on the top of her trousers. "Alright," she said. But still, her mind whispered, *Weak.*

Jin stood, offering her his hand. Astrea didn't take it. She pushed herself off the bench and shouldered past him. Outside, the night air was cool, a balm against her burning skin. The city was quiet, not even the sound of police cars whining in the distance, though she was sure they would be coming soon. It was like the night knew what she'd done, how small she was.

They said nothing as they walked back to the motorcycle. Skies, it was so close to that poor woman's body. Astrea almost closed her eyes, but Jin blocked her line of sight with his body.

"It's alright, you know," Jin said as he handed her one of the helmets. "You've been through a lot in the last few days. Some of my teammates have—"

Astrea grabbed the helmet from him, turning around as she settled it on her head and buckled the strap under her chin. "I'm fine."

"But it's alright if you're—" Jin cut himself off when Astrea glared at him. He said nothing else. Instead, he strapped on his helmet and climbed onto the bike.

Astrea sat behind him and wrapped her arms around his waist. She didn't want to be weak. She wished she could have saved that woman, and even though she was sure the stars weren't listening to her, Astrea sent up a plea for forgiveness anyway.

Jin revved the engine once, and then they were off, racing through the city's darkening streets. Back toward home, toward safety.

Maybe someday she wouldn't have to hide. Maybe someday she wouldn't be so reluctant when someone needed her help. Maybe someday she would be strong.

Not today, little Lightbringer.

CHAPTER 25

The night had finally turned to day, but Astrea was exhausted.

It was that woman who kept Astrea up all night. Her hand outstretched, pointing, as she pleaded for help. The shadows, dancing over her skin and jumping to Astrea's, consuming her. The way she was too weak, unable to hold it together.

And it wasn't just her. Saros's warning about the city being stalked by shadows had run in circles in Astrea's head all night, and it continued its endless race now.

"Hey." Cressida snapped her fingers in front of Astrea's face, making her blink. "You sure you're alright?"

They were on a streetcar in the middle of the Scholar's District on the way to the library. Astrea had filled Cressida in on the details of the previous day much earlier in their journey.

"I'm fine," Astrea said, giving herself a mental shake.

"You don't seem fine. You've been quiet for the last half hour."

A white car raced by, horn honking. The streetcar driver raised her hand in a rude gesture, then eased the vehicle toward the curb. As it finally stopped, Astrea stood and disembarked from the rear exit, Cressida not far behind. They were some of the last passengers to get off, though a few people climbed on board at the front entrance.

"I'm fine," Astrea repeated when they were far from the streetcar and any pedestrians. It was just a short walk to the library from here, and most of the stores bordering this side of the street still had their shutters closed.

Cressida clicked her tongue. They both knew she wasn't fine.

"You saw someone die," Cressida said, her voice low as she took Astrea's hand and squeezed it. "You don't have to be fine. I'd be more worried if you *were* fine."

"There's something I didn't tell you earlier." Astrea couldn't look up as she admitted it. "I had . . . some kind of breakdown after everything."

"After seeing that, I would've too."

"No." Astrea shook her head. "Like the kind I used to have."

It had taken her a while to make the connection, but in the middle of the night, she'd realized why the panic felt so familiar. She'd had similar attacks when she'd first moved to Kalama, but that hadn't happened in years. Cressida had seen it, once, before they stopped.

Cressida squeezed her hand again, and Astrea finally tore her gaze away from the sidewalk.

"Like I said, you don't have to be okay right now." Cressida smiled tiredly. "Do you want to talk about it or something else?"

This was part of why Astrea loved Cressida so much. She knew when to push her and when to back off, like right now. Astrea was just proud of herself for admitting as much as she had.

"I don't understand any of it," Astrea said slowly. "Why did Mattina try to hide the book from us?"

Cressida was quiet for a moment. They passed another store, and the front door eased open as an elderly man stepped onto the sidewalk. He smiled at them, placed an "Open" sign on the door, and disappeared back inside.

"I don't know," Cressida said.

"And if the shadow man was there looking for me, why would he kill that employee?" Astrea couldn't see a reason for such violence, though she also couldn't see a reason for why the shadow man was looking for her in the first place.

"Maybe he was trying to get information from her," Cressida said. "Obviously, he wants something with you. He's tracked you down twice."

Astrea scrubbed at her face, her eyes burning and mind slow as molasses. Even the air seemed hard to move through this morning, the humidity thick and heavy. The sky was already turning gray, a promise of the rain to come.

Was this Astrea's fault? Had she brought this on herself somehow, been caught using her magic in public? She didn't think so. She never took that risk. But how else would those men know about her magic? And even if they did know, why would they want her? Why would they be willing to kill someone to find her?

They were the same questions she'd been asking herself—and trying to ignore—since Solstice Night. And they still led to the same dead-end.

"My head hurts," Astrea muttered.

"I can't tell you to ignore it," Cressida said, "but I'd really like to help figure out what's going on, if you'll let me."

"I'd love your help, but don't you have your own work to do for the emperor?"

Cressida stopped at the bottom of the library stairs. "When I have spare time, I can at least try to help you solve the mystery of where Theo's book went. *And* I can do your hair before that palace dinner this weekend since I know you hate that part."

"Skies." She'd almost forgotten about that damn dinner. That seemed like the least of her worries now. "If this shadow man is that intent on finding me, is the library safe? Or the observatory?" Jin had said it wasn't safe for Astrea to be alone, but what if her mere presence put everyone else in danger? She couldn't just go into the library and endanger the patrons. She couldn't put Raela, Lena, Serra, and Felix in that kind of danger. She couldn't put anyone in danger. Maybe she needed to find a way to leave Kalama immediately.

"No shadow man is getting into the palace compound," Cressida said. "And so far, you've only run into him at night. I think you'll be alright at work."

Astrea hated this. She hated not knowing who this man was or what he wanted. She hated not knowing why Mattina was hiding the manuscript from Theo and the emperor. Most of all, she hated that she couldn't shake the deep ache building in her bones.

"Alright." Astrea sighed. "I would love if you could help with the Mattina problem."

"Perfect. Where shall we start? I have all of today off."

"I need to check in with Raela first."

Cressida started up the stairs, and Astrea joined her a few heartbeats later. *You can do this,* Astrea told herself as she followed Cressida through the doors. *It's just another work day.*

Raucous laughter greeted her first, and Astrea spotted three figures at the circulation desk. Raela was perched on her stool behind the desk, and Jin was leaning on the counter. Felix, unmissable with his red hair, was moving books from the counter to a cart.

"Oh, Astrea!" Raela waved her over, and Astrea's brogues clicked on the marble floor as she walked toward the desk. "Good morning. Cressida, good to see you."

"Hi, Raela." Cressida was no stranger to the library or Astrea's coworkers; they met frequently enough for lunch or coffee breaks over the years that Cressida had earned a spot in Raela's good graces.

"Would you like some coffee?" Felix asked. "I just made a fresh pot."

"No, thank you," Astrea said.

Jin hadn't said anything to her yet, but she couldn't ignore the weight of his stare. If anyone noticed, they didn't address it, and she didn't want to either. She had barely been able to meet her own eyes in the mirror that morning, and Astrea had no idea how she'd be able to face Jin. He must have thought she was such a fool after all that had happened. Her entire face burned just at the thought of it.

"Astrea, are you feeling alright?" Raela leaned across the desk, pressing her wrist against Astrea's forehead. "Declining coffee? Do I need to call a healer?"

When were people going to stop asking her that? No, Raela had no idea what was actually going on, but skies, Astrea just wanted to be left alone.

"I'm *fine*." Astrea pulled away sharply.

"Well, Felix will take over reshelving duties," Raela said, cautiousness dancing over Astrea's skin. She'd never snapped at Raela before. "Perhaps you should work on that special project today."

Astrea finally glanced at Jin, who was holding a newspaper in one hand. She grabbed it from him, ignoring his startled cry as she read over the headlines. *Push on Western Front Leads to Two Hundred Helosian Casualties.* She bit the inside of her cheek. Bad news but not what she was looking for. Below the fold was a smaller headline. *Another Murder in Kalama; Rebels Deny Link.* There, in black and white, was a photo of the museum. The paper, thankfully, hadn't printed any other images.

"You know what," Astrea said, anger bubbling in her veins, "I think I'll go start on that right now. I have a few things I need to look into."

Maybe, she thought, *I should find Theo and see why he sent us to that skies forsaken place.* Because maybe, Astrea reasoned, if she hadn't gone there with some murderous shadow man stalking her, that poor woman would still be alive and there wouldn't be a family grieving their loss.

Maybe, if Theo Kadis hadn't asked them to do his dirty work, Astrea wouldn't be responsible for that death. Maybe there would have been no need to heal the woman, and she would be at her job this morning, handing out tickets to schoolchildren and tourists.

Astrea was halfway out the door, newspaper tight in her grasp, when she realized Jin was behind her, calling for her. She kept going, but he grabbed her arm.

"Astrea."

She pulled away from him and marched down the stairs. Part of Astrea's mind, a far-off part that seemed to be watching her from above as she started down the sidewalk, knew this didn't make any sense.

That wasn't going to stop her. She wanted to *do* something, try to figure out what was going on. Lord Theo Kadis was her only link between the missing book and what happened at the museum, so that had to be her first stop.

"Astrea!"

Jin grabbed her arm again, the feeling of his hands familiar and warm. She stopped, her breathing labored. When Astrea looked back, she realized she'd gotten nearly a half block away from the library. In the distance, she could make out Cressida standing at the top of the library stairs, orange anxiety and gray confusion bursting bright in the air.

"What's wrong with you?" Jin asked. "Where are you going? You shouldn't be out here by yourself."

Astrea shoved the crumbled newspaper toward him, some of the ink stuck on her hand from sweating in the morning heat. "I'm going to talk to your friend who sent us to the museum in the first place," she snapped. "Unlike some people, I care about figuring out what happened to that woman."

"You think I don't care?" Jin asked, his jaw set in a hard line. "Why do you think I don't care?"

"Are you out there looking for her killer?" Astrea asked, ignoring the man walking past them. Jin, still holding onto her arm, pulled her toward the building to their left. "Are you doing anything to help her family?"

"She had no family," Jin muttered. "After I took you home, I was out all night trying to find answers. I only went home a few hours ago."

Astrea finally looked up at Jin. His sun-kissed skin lacked its usual glow. He'd changed clothes at some point, his all-black ensemble from the night before replaced by a loose button-down shirt and gray slacks. That damn wall of his, though, was firmly in place, blocking her out once again.

"I didn't know," she finally managed to say. "I couldn't stop thinking about her all night."

"I couldn't either."

The fight had gone out of Astrea's heart just as quickly as it had taken over her. Her shoulders dropped. If Jin had no luck finding the shadow man, then what was there to be done? *Why couldn't I have saved her last night?*

"And what does any of this have to do with Theo?" Jin asked. "You said that's where you were going?"

Astrea scrubbed at her face. "I don't know. He sends us to the museum on an errand for him, and then the shadow man tracks me down . . ."

"Astrea," Jin said gently, "Theo isn't involved."

"How do you know?"

"Besides the fact I've known him my whole life?" When she shrugged, he said, "Because it wouldn't make sense for Theo to ask for our help, then send someone to kill us. What would that possibly accomplish?"

She stared out across the street, toward the piazza and vehicles circling it. Jin was right, of course. That wouldn't make any sense.

"Well, what do we do now?" she asked.

"We need to find that book."

"What about the shadow man?"

"We need to find him, too." Jin looked back toward the library. "If Cress can stay with you today, I can go look into something. Just . . . focus on being careful, alright? Keep your head down and focus on the project for my father."

Astrea's fingers twitched. "You want me to focus on being careful?"

Jin frowned. "Well, I certainly don't want you to get hurt."

"Is this because of what happened last night?"

"What?" The faintest hint of lavender surprise pulsed around Jin.

"Do you think I'm too weak and scared to be involved?"

The purple pulsed brighter, but it disappeared just as quickly as it had come. "That's not what this is about." Jin lowered his voice as he added, "Someone's hunting you, Astrea. How and why, I don't know, but even just standing here right now is a risk. I can't let you take any more risk than you absolutely have to. You need to stay at the library until you go home for the day."

When were people going to let her make her own decisions? It felt like every time Astrea took one step forward, someone else pushed her two steps back. Just a few nights before, Astrea had finally gotten to make decisions for herself. To save Eliana. To use her magic for something good. She could do that again if she had the chance. She could prove she wasn't weak.

But now Jin wanted to take it all away again.

Astrea crossed her arms over her chest. "No."

His eyebrows rose. "What do you mean *no*?"

"I mean no. I'm not just going to sit around and hide."

How many times had they stood in the palace gardens like this, arguing over something silly like who was going to get the last slice of cake or last bit of coffee? Who was going to distract the guards so Eliana could sneak away from her lessons and join them. Who was going to lie to Saros about where they were going.

Except this was bigger than teenage shenanigans. This was life and death.

"Astrea." Jin peered over her shoulder, eyes darting as someone walked past them. "I know you're upset. I *know*. But it's not safe."

"I don't care."

Part of Astrea didn't care. After all, no place in the city would be safe until they found the shadow man. Part of her was terrified of everything: the emperor, the shadow man, those horrendous inky flames that seemed to eat the woman from the museum. Even now, in the light of day, Astrea couldn't help but imagine her friends being eaten by those very same flames.

All Astrea knew for certain was that she couldn't let that fear dictate her next steps. She just couldn't. She had to figure this out.

"I don't care," she repeated, and Jin sighed.

"Tomorrow," he said after a heartbeat. "Will you come with me tomorrow?"

"Where?"

"Just be ready by the ninth bell," Jin said. "I'll meet you at the observatory."

Chapter 26

"Hand me that book, will you?"

Astrea looked over at Felix, standing on the middle rung of a ladder and wedging a novel back in its place on a high shelf. She passed the last book on their cart to him.

He smiled toothily as he took it. "Thanks."

All afternoon, Astrea had been helping Felix reshelve books. Though she needed to work on her research, this was the only task that helped her mind stray away from the image of the dying woman for more than a few moments.

Of course, now she was thinking about it. Jin may have had a good point about Theo not being connected to the murder, but he was one of the few leads they really had for Novarian artifacts. Maybe it would be worth paying him a visit now that she'd regained some of her composure.

"Felix," Astrea said as his feet hit the floor. "Can I ask a couple favors of you?"

Groaning, Felix asked, "It's not desk duty, is it?"

"No, not that." Astrea smiled. "I need your help finding a few books on Novaria for that exhibition I'm helping Prince Varojin put together. I found some, but this place is too large for me to go through by myself, and His Imperial Highness doesn't need to be climbing ladders and sifting through the collection."

"Sure, I can do that."

"And can you cover for me this afternoon while I go check out a lead?"

He groaned again. "But it's just going to be me and Raela!"

"I promise, it's just for this afternoon. I'll even cover one of your other shifts for you. You have that exam you need to study for next week, right? I'll come in on Saturday morning."

"Fine," Felix said, "but you'd better have a list of books you've already reviewed. I don't want to be doing more work than needed."

She grinned. "Thanks, Felix."

After going through her notes and copying the books she'd already sorted through onto a new list for Felix, Astrea went back to the lobby. Neither Cressida nor Raela were around, but Cressida wouldn't have ventured far. Astrea headed toward Raela's office. Muffled voices echoed down the narrow hall, followed by Cressida's laugh.

"Excuse me," Astrea said as she poked her head into Raela's office. Sure enough, Cressida was lounging in the chair opposite Raela's desk, and the librarian was perched in her seat. "I hope I'm not interrupting."

"Not at all, Astrea," Raela said. "Come in, come in."

Astrea pushed the door open wider but didn't enter. "Actually, I need to go check on something for Prince Varojin, and I was thinking Cressida might like to go with me."

"By all means!" Raela waved her hand toward the door. "I have no authority to keep her here, though I do need to get that strawberry cake recipe you were telling me about, Cressida."

"I'll bring it tomorrow," Cressida said as she stood.

"Perhaps you could also help me move a new piece for our collection?" Raela asked. "A statue. It's been sitting in the basement for far too long."

"Oh, don't put her to work, Raela," Astrea muttered.

"I don't mind," Cressida said quickly. "Whatever you need."

"Then I'll see you both tomorrow?" Raela asked. "I assume you won't be back this afternoon, Astrea."

"Probably not." Astrea actually had no idea how long this would take. "I'll see you tomorrow."

After saying their goodbyes, Astrea grabbed her satchel from the second staff office, slung it over her shoulders, and followed Cressida outside. Though the air was warm, the afternoon sea breeze rolling through the city pushed some of the humidity away. Dark storm clouds loomed beyond Tinale Bay, just at the horizon.

"You really don't have to help with the statue if you don't have time, Cress," Astrea said as they went down the stairs. "Raela can hire movers."

"Oh, I don't mind. It's not like it'll take me long." Cressida's magical talents went beyond controlling metal; she could also work with dirt and stone, just like Earthmovers. "So, where are we going?"

"To Lord Theodore Kadis's shop."

"I thought Jin told you to stay in the library."

"That's supposed to stop me?"

Cressida grinned. "Look at you, breaking the rules."

Finding her way back to Theo's shop wasn't going to be difficult. Despite Jin speeding through the city on his motorcycle, Astrea had made a mental note of the address. It was only a fifteen-minute walk from the library, down a few pedestrian streets and past one of the large public gardens in the district.

With any luck, Theo would be able to offer Astrea some kind of insight into Novaria, or the manuscript, or the emperor. *Or maybe all three,* she thought hopefully. Theo had promised to round up some artifacts for the emperor's project, but even if he didn't have those ready, Astrea hoped he'd have a list prepared. Anything to narrow down her and Jin's focus.

As they arrived at the store and Cressida reached for the brass door-knob, a man pushed the door open first and brushed past them. He was familiar somehow, but with his tan skin, salt-and-pepper hair, deep frown, and linen suit, he looked like half of the businessmen in Kalama. Whoever he was, he didn't acknowledge Astrea or Cressida as he passed. It was like they weren't even there.

"Excuse you," Cressida muttered. If the man heard her, he didn't stop. "That was rude."

"Forget him," Astrea said. "Let's just go in."

The store was just as crowded with artifacts, paintings, and tiny treasures as it had been the day before. It was also just as empty of customers. Lord Theo Kadis was alone behind the counter, his head barely visible around the wide bookshelves and stacks of objects.

"Lord Kadis," Astrea said as she approached the counter, "do you remember me from yesterday?"

"Ah! Astrea." He looked up from a notebook and pushed his spectacles up his nose. "Of course I remember. It's not every day Jin brings pretty girls here. In fact, I don't think he ever has in all the years I've known him. Please, call me Theo." She didn't know whether to laugh or roll her eyes—Theo had used the same line the day before—but Astrea's cheeks warmed nonetheless. "And who is your friend?"

Cressida stuck her hand out to him. "Cressida Nikaphoros, my lord. How do you do?"

"Nikaphoros?" Theo asked as he shook Cressida's outstretched hand. "Are you connected to the Lodestar—"

She nodded. "That's my family, yes." Cressida's family had earned a reputation thanks to the success of Lodestar Industries. Their company was responsible for bringing a lot of new technology to Kalama and had a hand in a variety of projects around the capital.

"Your parents are delightful. I met them at a gala several months ago for . . . oh, what was it? A charity of some kind."

When Cressida only offered a tight-lipped smile, Astrea asked, "Do you remember the manuscript you asked Jin and me to find?"

"Did you find it?" Theo closed the notebook and set it aside. "Please, tell me you found it."

"No, unfortunately," Astrea said. "The curator wasn't there, and after what happened last night . . ."

"Nasty business, isn't it?" Orange anxiety and tangerine fear tangled together in a tight knot around him. "You'd think the police would be able to do something about all this crime. In all my years living in Kalama, I've never felt unsafe."

"You think it's that bad?" Cressida asked.

"Of course!" Theo exclaimed. "What are the police even doing? I blame the tourists. All kinds of . . . *rapscallions* . . . are allowed in the city these days. Anyway . . ." He shook his head and sighed. "Let me stop before I get started. You said Leopold wasn't there, Astrea?"

Theo wasn't the first Kalamian Astrea had heard blaming tourists for any number of things. She certainly couldn't correct him about this particular situation. Instead, she said, "No, we never got to speak to Lord Mattina."

"Typical," Theo muttered.

"What do you mean?"

Theo eyed Astrea through his glasses. He wasn't much taller than her, their gazes almost level. "Please, come with me," Theo said as he moved out from behind the counter.

Astrea glanced at Cressida, who simply shrugged. They followed him up and down the aisles of his shop, past shelves filled with marble busts, tattered books, coins, jewelry, and more. It looked more like a haphazard museum than a store.

"Do you see all of this? These are mere trinkets," Theo said. He paused and picked up a long golden necklace, then put it back down again before moving on. "Items bought and sold in any market in the countries and cities I've been to. Easily sold to Kalamians as unique or interesting, significant in some way despite their . . . *common* . . . origins."

Astrea wasn't sure where he was going with this. Was he admitting to some kind of scam operation? And why would Jin be friends with someone like that? He'd told Astrea that Theo had been his mother's friend; maybe he was just holding onto that connection.

"I don't know what Jin has told you about my business—my *real* business. I'm an antiquities dealer. I don't deal in the ordinary. I find very rare items, either thought stolen or lost to time."

"As in you discover them?" Cressida asked.

"Sometimes they're in private collections," Theo explained as they turned down another long aisle. When he stopped again, he picked up a long dagger in a leather sheath. "Sometimes they're in small museums. Sometimes they're simply at their original resting place."

"And you sell these items to new owners?" Cressida asked.

"I do."

Was that any better than them being in private collections in other places, though? Astrea didn't ask. Even though Theo seemed kind, she doubted he'd appreciate criticism of his profession.

"And when I find these items," Theo continued, "I'm not usually the only one searching for them. Nor am I the only dealer in the city, nor are all of my buyers trustworthy."

What was she supposed to do about that?

"I believe Lord Mattina may have stolen the manuscript from me," he continued, "rather than simply borrowing it for research as he claimed he intended to do."

"What was he researching?" Astrea asked.

"I'm not sure." Theo shrugged. "All he said was that he was researching something and it would help. I'm not even sure it matters. He's taken what's mine and something the emperor may be interested in as well."

"I thought you said your families go back generations," Astrea said. "Why would he steal from you?"

"They do, but that doesn't mean we're always on friendly terms. I hadn't expected this from Leopold, otherwise I never would have loaned the manuscript to him. I thought he respected the sort of unspoken agreement those in our profession have."

Astrea blew out a breath. It felt like a win in a way, that she had this new information about Lord Mattina. But that didn't help her in this moment. It didn't explain where the manuscript was, nor did it give her anything concrete to present to the emperor.

"Do you know where we might find Lord Mattina if not at the museum?" Cressida asked. "I know Jin would love to see that book."

"Perhaps his vacation home in Sezia," Theo offered. They'd circled back to the counter, where Theo opened his notebook again. "Perhaps at his townhome here in the city."

Astrea swallowed, watching as Theo jotted something down on a blank page. She couldn't read his handwriting upside down; it was too messy, the letters too close together.

"You mentioned you were going to pull together some other artifacts from Novaria for us to borrow," Astrea said. "Do you have the names and descriptions of even a few of those things? I'd love to be able to present them to Emperor Auris this week."

"Indeed I do." Theo pulled out another sheet of paper, one with at least a dozen separate items written on it. He started making another note at the bottom of the sheet.

"Do you serve many buyers, Theo?" Cressida asked as she bent down to examine a small statue sitting on the counter.

"Oh, plenty," he said, spreading his arms out to gesture at the store. "It takes all kinds to keep my business running. Just before you came in, I was speaking with an old friend about a dagger he's interested in procuring."

"A dagger?" Astrea asked, the image of the rude man flashing in her mind's eye.

"Indeed," Theo said, flipping through his notebook again. "The emperor isn't the only one interested in Novarian artifacts these days, it seems. Now, if you ladies would like to come with me, I have something more . . . interesting to show you than those little trinkets."

Again, they followed Theo, this time toward the stairs. The steps squeaked as they ascended into the darker second floor of the shop.

"I believe I can help you with this project, Astrea," Theo said as they walked down a narrow hallway. He stopped in front of another door. As he turned the knob, the door swung open slowly. "I've found plenty to share."

Though the downstairs of Theo's store was messy, this room was messier. No shelves lined the walls, but rectangles covered in drop cloths—paintings, Astrea assumed—small statues and marble busts, narrow crates, and more filled the space in no particular pattern.

"All Novarian," Theo said. "All available for your exhibit." The rustling of paper made Astrea turn back to Theo just in time to accept two folded up sheets of paper from him. "Mattina's addresses and the list of items I was thinking would be suitable for you and Jin."

"Thank you," Astrea said. "Really, Theo, thank you. This is amazing."

Finally, Astrea had something real she could offer the emperor. Next time he wanted an update, she'd actually have something useful to share.

Theo smiled. "Anything for Jin and his friends."

CHAPTER 27

Fire burning. Shadows dancing. A bright, brilliant light. Gentle hands and a soothing voice.

Astrea woke with a start, heart pounding and skin slick with sweat. She looked around. She was in her room in the observatory, the early morning sunrise filtering in through the gauzy curtains hanging over her window.

She leaned back into her pillows, willing her heart to calm. *Just a dream,* she reminded herself. "Just a dream."

Rolling toward her nightstand, Astrea checked the clock. It was just after the sixth hour; she still had plenty of time before she needed to meet Jin. Her head was pounding. She'd spent so much time crying before falling asleep that her mouth and skin were dry.

Another breakdown. Two breakdowns in two days.

Astrea threw the blankets off herself and climbed out of bed. As she sat in front of her vanity, Astrea sighed. She looked as awful as she felt. Dark circles under her eyes, saggy skin, frizzy hair. She needed a shower if she was leaving the apartment.

After taking her robe from its hook near her wardrobe, Astrea crept toward her bedroom door and opened it slowly. The apartment was silent, the observatory above her quiet. Instead of going to check on Saros, she tiptoed down the hallway to the small bathroom near her room. It wasn't as fancy as what Eliana or even Cressida had, but it was hers, and it had everything she needed: a clawfoot tub with a shower installed above it, a sink and mirror, and even a narrow window near the ceiling to let in the sunlight.

Astrea turned the shower on. When the water was warm, she stepped in and breathed in the steam. She took her time washing her hair and even used the special peony and lavender soap Sarsali had given her the month before.

After toweling off and pulling on her robe, Astrea made her way back to her room, closing the door behind her as quietly as she could. She wanted coffee, but she really needed to talk to Saros. She hadn't told him about what happened at the museum, unable to make herself speak the truth.

Just go check for him in a few minutes, Astrea told herself. *Finish getting ready.*

She opted for a white blouse with billowy sleeves, pairing it with a plum skirt and flat brown brogues. Too impatient for her hair to finish drying, she toweled it off as much as she could, then braided it down her back and tied it off with a lavender ribbon.

She felt partly human again, refreshed, except for her desperate need for caffeine.

"Pull yourself together," she scolded her reflection in the mirror. It seemed to mock her, its dead stare painful to look at.

Astrea gathered the papers from Theo, tucked them into her satchel, slung the bag across her body, and left her bedroom. The apartment was still quiet, but a floorboard overhead squeaked. Astrea grabbed her keys and headed out the door.

She didn't make the climb to Saros's observatory as often as she used to. Part of that was because of his gloom the last few months, but another part of it was just life getting in the way. The last few years, she'd been busy finishing her second university degree, then adjusting to her job at the library, and trying to balance a small social life amid all of it. She simply didn't see Saros as much as she used to.

When she got to the third-floor landing, Astrea reached for the doorknob, then paused. She used to barge in all the time when she was younger, but now, that felt like an invasion. So she knocked instead.

Through the door, Astrea sensed Saros's surprise, electric and strong. Moments later, the door swung open.

"Astrea?" Saros asked. His hair was pulled up into a disheveled bun, and his black linen shirt was a wrinkled mess. Had he stayed up all night again? "What's wrong?"

"Nothing's wrong," she said. "We just need to talk."

"I don't like the sound of that," Saros muttered. Still, he moved to the side and motioned her in. "You don't have to knock, you know."

"Just wasn't sure if you were busy," Astrea lied as she walked past him. Lying was easier than explaining how disconnected everything felt.

Saros's observatory was as messy as it always was. It was just one big room—almost the same size as their whole apartment—filled with furniture. Bookshelves lined two walls, their contents haphazardly displayed. Astrea had tried to organize the books for him once, but Saros had eventually returned them to their original chaos. Papers and old coffee cups littered the worn mahogany desk tucked away in one corner.

And, of course, there was his large telescope sitting in the middle of the room. Despite the name of his magic, Saros didn't actually need a telescope to stargaze. Still, Stargazers always claimed it was easier to connect with their celestial magic if they could see the void and stars. The dome roof was closed this morning, though Saros could open it whenever he needed.

"So, what did you want to talk about?" Saros asked, orange anxiety vibrating around him. "Does Varojin have news?"

"He might," Astrea said. "I'm going to speak with him shortly. It's actually about what happened at the history museum."

Saros frowned. "The latest murder?"

"Jin and I were there."

Saros's anxiety spiked, harsh and grating. "You were what?"

Astrea explained exactly how they'd found themselves in that situation: the meeting with the emperor, the dodgy museum curator, Theo Kadis, the book, the shadow man. Saros paled, his eyes wide by the time she finished the story. Explaining everything had been easier than she'd anticipated, though her stomach was in knots. She did, however, leave out the part about Jin's motorcycle. That might just send Saros over the edge.

"Anyway," Astrea said, "Jin's been looking into what you said about the shadows. I just thought you should know what's been going on in case it can help you in some way."

"I see." Saros swallowed hard, cobalt regret and deep blue shame joining the anxiety still pulsing around him.

"Uncle—" Astrea started, but he shook his head.

"The new information may be helpful, thank you, my dear." He turned and stalked toward his desk, leaving Astrea standing alone near the door. She huffed. "I'm glad to see you're alright, though I wish you'd told me sooner."

"Sorry, I'll get other information to you—"

Again, he cut her off. "Not that, Astrea. That you were in danger."

"Oh." Why was it such a surprise that Saros was worried about her? "Sorry, I just . . . Trying to focus on the emperor's project and sort out the rest has been hard, and I didn't want to bother you."

Saros's face softened. "It's not a bother."

"Do you have anything you want me to pass on to Jin when I see him?" Astrea asked.

More blue sparked around Saros as he said, "Nothing yet."

"Really?" Astrea didn't want to call her uncle a liar, but what was he feeling so bad about now?

"Really," he said. "I will tell you when I have something."

Just when she'd thought Saros would be able to have a real conversation about all of the problems staring them in the face, he did this. He hid something again. Astrea ground her teeth together, then forced her jaw to loosen. *Not now.* Trying to force him into conversations had not worked in the past, and Astrea doubted blowing up at him now would be helpful.

"Alright." Astrea hoped her voice sounded as steady as she wanted it to. "Well, I'm going to meet Jin, then go to work. I'll be home tonight."

Astrea hurried out of Saros's office without waiting for him to reply. Now she really wanted nothing more than to get out of the tower, to get away from him and the returning gloom. She descended the stairs as fast as her tired legs would carry her.

It was still too early to meet with Jin, but Astrea knew she shouldn't go into the city alone to get breakfast. She could kill time in the gardens, then maybe convince Jin to make a stop for coffee along the way to wherever he wanted to take her.

The walk from the observatory to the gardens was quiet, not even the wildlife humming their morning songs. It was like they could read her mood, like they knew how she felt deep in her bones.

Despite the early hour, the gardens buzzed with activity. A few Tornamian ambassadors Astrea recognized, thanks to Eliana, were wandering about, servants trailing at some distance behind them. She also spotted a familiar imperial guard.

"I feel like I haven't seen you in forever," Nicos said as he walked toward her. "Where have you been?"

Astrea shrugged. "Busy."

"I'd say, by the looks of it. No offense," he quickly added. "You just look tired, is all."

"It's alright," she said, laughing despite herself. She'd seen her reflection. She couldn't be upset with him for pointing out the obvious. "I just haven't been sleeping well."

"Do you want to talk about it?" he offered as they walked.

They were well away from the other people in the gardens, and it would have been so easy to have a private conversation with Nicos here. But she didn't want to talk about it, especially with someone who didn't have even half of the information they'd need to truly understand.

"No. Thank you, though."

As the silence stretched on, Astrea looked up at Nicos. He was staring straight ahead, but his shoulders were pushed back too far for him to be relaxed. After the morning at the museum, she'd thought everything between him and Eliana had been resolved, but now Astrea wasn't so sure.

"Do *you* want to talk about something?" she asked.

"Just trying to kill some time before my shift starts." They walked for another few moments, and as they turned a corner, Nicos blurted out, "I take my job very seriously, you know."

"I know," Astrea said. Nicos had always been protective of Eliana. Such young guards weren't usually assigned to the imperial siblings, and Astrea had always assumed that the emperor saw how devoted Nicos was.

"I just keep replaying everything over and over in my mind. Trying to figure out where I went wrong. Why I wasn't there. I can't stand the thought of something happening to her."

Astrea's face burned. What kind of friend was she to Nicos? Here he was, feeling guilty over something that wasn't his fault. Not really. He would be so angry if he knew what had really happened. If he knew that Eliana had only gotten hurt because of Astrea.

Astrea forced herself to smile as she placed a hand on his forearm and squeezed once. "I know, Nicos." When he said nothing, she added, "And I think Ellie knows that, too."

Nicos breathed out, a harsh sound. "I really hope so."

"I didn't expect to see you two here." Jin sat on a bench tucked away between two hedges, one leg crossed over the other as he leaned back and watched them carefully.

Nicos nodded. "Hello, Your Imperial Highness."

"Nicos."

"I better go see if your sister is ready. Her schedule is packed today," Nicos said. Then, turning to Astrea, he added, "I hope you get some sleep soon."

She waved at him as he turned and left, his footsteps crunching over the gravel until he turned out of sight and earshot.

"Get some sleep?" Jin asked, eyebrows raised. He was still on the bench, like he didn't have a care in the world.

"It's nothing," she said. "I just haven't been sleeping well."

"Do you want to talk about it?"

"Why does everyone keep asking me that?"

Jin raised his hands in surrender. "I didn't realize that question was off-limits."

"You're early," she said, hoping he'd get the hint and change the subject.

"So are you. You look nice, though."

"So do you." And he did. Jin must have just showered, as his curly hair was still damp, glistening in the morning sun. He wore simple chinos and a black shirt, the first three buttons undone.

"Oh, this old thing?" he said, voice light, and Astrea laughed despite herself. He smiled. "It's nice to see you laugh."

"Shut up."

He'd always been able to make her laugh, even when she was in a bad mood. His jokes didn't even have to be funny; they often weren't. But there was just something about him trying that she'd never been able to resist.

"Are you ready to get started?" he asked as he finally stood. "I thought we'd start in my room."

Astrea glanced at the palace. "In your room?"

"There are some things I didn't want to work on at the library." Jin smiled again, motioning for her to go first. "That's the first stop, then coffee. You look like you could use it."

Returning to Jin's room was not what Astrea had expected. Without the fear and fatigue of Solstice Night clouding her mind—with Jin finally knowing who she really was—it almost felt like it used to. It almost felt like home again.

She'd spent so much time in Jin's apartment over the years, often studying but sometimes just enjoying his company when he'd still been her best friend. Despite the color scheme change, his sofa and armchairs were the same ones they'd sat in for years, and the art on the walls was the same as she remembered. If Astrea ignored their obvious problems, she could almost pretend she was just there for a visit.

"This is what I wanted to show you," Jin said as he strode across the sitting room.

Astrea followed him to his desk, a thick, mahogany thing. The top of it was nearly empty except for a few folders stacked in one corner. Jin unlocked a drawer with a small brass key, then pulled out a rolled-up paper. When he set it on his desk and unrolled it, Astrea's eyebrows furrowed. It was a map of Kalama, small circles drawn in various places.

Some were black while others were blue, and a variety of colored lines crisscrossed the map to connect the dots.

"What is this?" she asked.

"My theory," Jin said.

"This?" She didn't understand what it even was.

"After what happened on Solstice Night, and after Saros had you pass on that message to me, I told you I had a hunch," Jin started. Astrea nodded. "I started digging. What happened at the museum confirms what I feared."

Jin's wall was steady. Unmovable. If he really was scared, Astrea couldn't tell. She looked at the map again. "Alright," she said, "but I don't understand what any of this is."

"I don't think you're going to like it."

"I already don't like any of this, Jin. Whatever you're thinking can't make it worse."

"Over the last year, there have been other murders in the city. I've mapped them out with these circles, the ones connected by the red lines." Astrea's eyes traced the red lines, no pattern jumping out at her. "And then I've marked witnesses with the blue circles."

There were fewer of those than the actual murders, and Astrea frowned. "What about the green lines?" she asked. They connected four spots on the map: one near Sunrise Way, one at the museum, one on the border of Nobleman's Hill and the Market District, and one further south.

"That," Jin said, the word heavy in the air, "is my theory. I don't think what's happened to you—to us—is separate from the other attacks."

Astrea's blood chilled. She hadn't thought the shadow man might be the one committing all of the other murders. What could make him murder random Kalamians when he seemed to be searching for her? Besides, none of the newspapers had mentioned anything about shadowy men.

"What makes you think that?" she asked.

"I was able to get the police files for the different cases," he said, leaning over his desk and lifting up that stack of thin folders.

"That doesn't look like a lot of research on their part," Astrea murmured.

"Exactly."

"You think the police are behind it?"

"No, but I don't think they're trying very hard either. There was a note in one of these files," Jin said, his long fingers flipping through the folders. "This one, here." He handed one to her. "Go ahead, read it."

The file was light in her hand. Astrea opened it. The pages seemed to be out of order, but the note Jin wanted her to see was obvious. In neat, typed font, Astrea read the word "shadow." That was all she needed to see. She snapped the folder shut and shoved it back at Jin.

"On Solstice Night . . ." The words caught in her throat, and she swallowed. This shouldn't be so hard to talk about. But if Jin was right and the shadow man was committing *all* of these murders, then . . .

Then it was her fault. Just like Eliana getting hurt. Just like the museum employee dying. *My fault, my fault.*

She blew out a harsh breath. How could she tell him? How could she tell him that every time she closed her eyes, she saw those damn shadows? Shadows consuming the museum employee, consuming her friends, consuming everything.

"Before you got there on Solstice Night . . ." Astrea started again. "The shadow man said he'd been . . ." She swallowed and focused on the map. "I don't know why this is so hard for me."

"Because it was terrifying. I think most people would find it hard to talk about."

"I really need some coffee," she muttered.

"Do you want me to call down to the kitchen for some?"

"No." She shook her head, finally turning to look at him. "It's fine."

"Why do you always say that?" he asked. "Why do you always say it's fine?"

The gentleness of his words caught her off guard. How was she supposed to explain it to him? That if she acted like everything was fine, then maybe it would be? Maybe she could force everything to just be calm. Maybe she could go ignored again, overlooked. Maybe everything could just go back to the way it was before.

But that wasn't what she got to do anymore. She was smack in the middle of something, though she didn't know what, and she had to figure it out. She had to. Astrea's skin crawled.

"Can I tell you something?" Jin asked, finally breaking the silence.

"You don't have to ask," she said.

He took her hand, tugging gently as he led her over to the sofa. Her palm burned, but she fought the instinct to shake him off. Instead, Astrea sat down next to him, her back painfully straight.

"I don't know what Ellie's told you about my time with the army," he started slowly. "But it's not what people think. No sitting around in a fort all day, shielded by other mages. I was eventually selected for a . . . specialized team."

"A specialized team?" she asked, curiosity getting the best of her. She didn't know anything about Helosia's military aside from how important it was to the emperor.

"This team was made up of some of the strongest mages in the army, and we were sent on more . . . complex missions. Even with the extensive training I went through, they never taught me how to deal with the fallout. I was young, far from my home and family, and being forced to . . ." He shook his head. "Zephyrine, my commanding officer, was the one who eventually taught me how to cope with the stress. You may have seen her with me on Solstice Night? The tall woman with the white hair."

So that was who Jin had been with. Had Astrea seen her around the palace before? She supposed it didn't really matter. What Astrea really wanted was to ask what Jin had been forced to do, what he'd had to learn to cope with. Adi had alluded to something similar. Her mind ran a million directions, but Jin's hand on her shoulder brought her back to reality.

"Talking about it is hard, but it helps. And you don't have to confide in me, but I hope you talk to someone. Maybe Cress or Ellie?"

Astrea blew out a shuddering breath and stared at her hands. "The shadow man said he'd been watching me."

"Yes," Jin said. "You mentioned that a few days ago."

"He said that he'd been looking for me for a long time. Or his boss has been, I guess." She risked a glance up at him. "Is that why all of those people are dead, Jin? Because of me?"

"No." His answer was immediate, strong. "No, it's not because of you. Even if all of this is somehow connected, it's not your fault."

"Ellie wouldn't have gotten hurt if I hadn't been with her." The words sounded so small, even to her. "They wouldn't have bothered her if I hadn't been there."

"And how were you supposed to know that would happen?" Jin asked. His voice was so soft, just like it used to be when she went to him with her worries. "The way I see it, you were just trying to keep her safe while she did something foolish."

Could Jin be right? He often was right about these things, or at least, he had been in the past. Astrea's chest heaved as she willed her tears away. Jin couldn't see her cry. Not again. Not after what happened at the museum.

"Well." She looked toward his desk, where the map still was, then back at him. "How do we figure out if your theory is right?"

"That one file I showed you is the only one that mentions anything about shadows," Jin said. "Only one witness claims to have seen anything like that. I think we need to go speak with them." Standing, Jin offered his hand to Astrea. She took it. "It's time to really figure out what we're dealing with."

Chapter 28

The White Lily was as busy as it was any other day. Jin was at the counter, paying for their order, while Astrea waited at a far corner table. The breakfast crowd was in full swing, a line of people complaining about everything under the sun: the war, the wait, the weather.

But this controlled chaos felt like home. The cool table top under Astrea's fingers, the worn wooden chair, the clink of ceramic cups, even the competing emotions—it was all familiar.

Jin carried two to-go cups to the table, setting one down in front of Astrea. "One latte," he said, "with extra brown sugar. Shall we?"

Their walk through the city was leisurely at first. People rushed past them, some on their way to work, others on their way to school or meetings or whatever else they had going on that day. Now that Solstice Night festivities were done, Kalama was back to business as usual.

Astrea filled Jin in on her trip back to Theo's; he needed to know. At first, he'd seemed frustrated that she went at all, then as she provided more details, he'd become equal parts curious and confused.

"He gave me Lord Mattina's addresses here and in Sezia."

"Do you have them now?" Jin asked.

"They're in my bag." Her fingers hovered over the buckles holding it closed, then moved away again. "I can give them to you later."

"What I can't understand is why Mattina would steal something from Theo," Jin said.

"Do you know Lord Mattina well?" Astrea asked. The side street they turned down was quiet, the homes smaller here. They were in the southern part of the city, closer to the Warehouse District than the palace.

"Not particularly," Jin said. "He's a younger son in his family. He has fewer responsibilities than many in the peerage."

"Is that a good thing?"

"Good, bad—everyone has their own goals in that circle of society. He may very well enjoy just working at the museum and not worrying about whatever his siblings are up to. His brother is a marquis in a province in central Helosia."

Astrea tipped back the last of her coffee. She was glad she wasn't part of that world, not entrenched in the strange politics of it all.

"Speaking of *that* social circle," Jin continued, voice low despite nobody being around. "Are you still comfortable attending my father's dinner? Ellie told me she invited you."

"Why would I be uncomfortable?" Astrea asked. She knew exactly why she was nervous about going, but Astrea wanted to know what Jin was worried about.

"These things get . . ." Jin trailed off as he looked away from her. "The dinners are usually boring, but the after parties are . . ."

"Extravagant?" she suggested. "Opulent? Ridiculous?"

He chuckled. "It's like the Whiskey Dream," he said, "only more room for the gossip mill to get stories moving. These parties rarely end without some kind of scandal."

"I can't say that surprises me that much, honestly."

"Oh?" he challenged. "Is the palace that predictable?"

Shrugging one shoulder, Astrea snuck a glance up at him. He wasn't looking at her but rather their surroundings, his gaze darting from the street to the rooftops and back again.

"I think I'll be fine," she said. "Ellie wants me there, right?"

"Right." Jin nodded. "I just don't want you to feel like you're out of your depth."

Astrea was already far out of her depth, alternating between drowning and swimming with every new situation she found herself in. There was too much to think about, too many pieces on the board. But admitting that would mean admitting she wasn't cut out for any of this, and that thought hurt too much.

"I'm sure it'll be alright. Ellie will tell me anything I need to know."

They passed the next few blocks in silence as Jin led them down several different streets. A few people were sweeping their front stoops, working in the flowerbeds lining the homes, or taking laundry off the line, but Astrea assumed most other people were at work for the day.

"There's something I should warn you about before the dinner," Jin said as they passed a barking dog. The animal ran to the fence, its bark following them as they turned down another street.

"You already warned me it's going to be scandalous. What more could I possibly need to know?"

"My father decided my siblings and I were only allowed one guest each."

Where was he going with this?

"And because Ellie also wants Cress to be there," Jin continued, "I . . . may have put you down as my guest instead."

Astrea's feet stopped moving. Jin stopped and half turned to look at her.

"Sorry," she mumbled as she started again.

"I can switch your name with Cressida's," he offered, "if that makes you more comfortable."

"It's not that." Astrea wasn't even sure why she was surprised. The last couple of weeks had somehow brought them back to their old friendship, especially the last few days. Years ago, she never would have been surprised by Jin inviting her as *his* guest. "I was just surprised your father is placing that kind of a limitation on you."

"You are such a bad liar, Sovna," he teased.

Astrea swallowed thickly. "There wasn't someone else you wanted to invite?"

"Well, Adi might like the food, but I don't think he'd enjoy wearing a gown for the evening," Jin said, and Astrea laughed. A hint of sweet amusement drifted past Jin's wall before he added, "But no, there's nobody else I'd rather invite."

Astrea's heart jumped, and she shoved the feeling down. "Are we there yet?"

"Almost. Can you read this witness's emotions when we get there? Let me know what they're feeling?"

"I'll try."

"What do you mean you'll try?"

Though she'd never told him or Eliana about her magic, Lightbringers weren't total mysteries, even if they were rarer types of mages. There were plenty of them in the army, and she knew there were others in the city, even if she'd never been able to seek them out.

"I can't just tell what anyone is feeling."

"You can't?"

"No," she said with a laugh. "People's walls have to be down."

"Their walls?"

Astrea looked up at him. Jin was watching her in that guarded way he had. "You keep yours up most of the time now," she said. His eyebrows furrowed. "I can't read whatever it is you're feeling, not really. But many other people are the opposite. If your witness is like that, I'll be able to know how they feel."

"And you can tell when someone has those walls up?"

"Yes. It's like they're wearing a mask or like there's something made of stone, blocking me out. Actually," she said, "this shadow man. I tried to read him both times, but he was different."

"Different how? Like he had walls up?"

"Sort of," Astrea said. "It was like he was invisible."

"What do you mean invisible?"

"Like he wasn't there," she said. "Like the space was empty."

"That's odd."

"People feel all different ways to me." She wished she knew another Lightbringer she could ask; there was so much she didn't understand about her magic.

They skirted to opposite sides of the sidewalk, narrowly avoiding a group of kids running and shouting about ice cream. She glanced over her shoulder to see a vendor opening a cart for the day. As much as she liked sweets, it still seemed far too early for ice cream.

"Just one more block," Jin said, ushering Astrea down another pedestrian street. It was narrower than she expected, the tan walls of the homes and storefronts covered in vines and other flora. Above them, fragrant lilies and tulips lined window boxes. Jin sneezed.

Pausing in front of the white door of a home marked fourteen, Jin smoothed his hair and straightened his cuffs. "Ready?" he asked, and Astrea nodded.

Jin knocked on the door. No response. Jin knocked again.

This time, footsteps shuffled behind the door. Though Astrea looked up and down the street, it remained empty. It felt somehow wrong to be here, but Jin seemed relaxed enough.

Finally, the door cracked open. A blue iris peered out at them.

"Hello," Jin said, putting on that damn smile that could charm anyone in the city. "I was just hoping to—"

"Oh, oh my!" the person exclaimed, surprise slamming into Astrea so hard that she almost stumbled backward. They shut the door, and just when Astrea thought they weren't going to open it again, the door opened wide. A woman, maybe sixty years old, stared out at them. Her blonde hair was mostly white, and she had the most striking blue eyes, the same color as Tinale Bay. "Prince Varojin! What . . . what an honor! I'm sorry, I wasn't expecting guests, Your Imperial Highness."

"Oh, that's quite alright," Jin said with a practiced chuckle. His shoulders tightened. "Are you Miss Nora?"

Her already pink cheeks flushed. "Indeed, I am, Your Imperial Highness."

"I'm so sorry to bother you, ma'am, but I was hoping to ask you a few questions about something." Jin motioned to Astrea. "This is my friend, Astrea. May we come in?"

Though she looked far less impressed by Astrea, Nora motioned for them to go inside. It was a quaint home, solidly middle class with its sturdy furniture, brightly painted walls, and white trim. The blues and greens of her decor reminded Astrea of the ocean. Nora locked the deadbolt on her front door.

"Please, Your Imperial Highness, sit, sit," she said, motioning for Jin to sit on a small floral-patterned settee in the front sitting room. "I'll get a chair for your friend. Can I get you anything to drink or eat?"

"Oh, no, that's quite alright," Jin replied as he perched on the sofa. Astrea could've fit on it with him, but she stayed standing. Nora didn't leave to get that spare chair. "We'll be out of your hair in just a few minutes anyway."

"I'm sorry, Prince Varojin," the woman said, glancing at Astrea for only a second. "I don't understand how I can be of help to you."

Astrea had no idea how Jin was going to explain the situation to the woman. Judging by the notes she'd seen that morning, the police had already questioned Nora, and Jin wasn't exactly a detective. Would the woman think this was strange? Astrea sure would.

"I wanted to ask you about what happened to your neighbor, Mister Ozols, a couple of months ago," Jin said.

Nora slowly lowered herself into one of the armchairs opposite him. Her back was to the window that overlooked the alley, and her curtains were drawn. A framed photo of the imperial family sat on one of the shelves of the armoire to Nora's left. It was an old photo from nearly a decade prior and even included the now-deceased empress.

"Oh, dear," she said. "Salvo was such a kind man, always helping any of us on the street who needed it. He was older, older than me. He moved to Kalama from the Novarian mountains so many years ago. We bonded over that, you know, as my father was Novarian." She shook her head. "It was such a shock, what happened to him. He never bothered anyone."

"I understand you're one of the people who went to his aid when you heard the attack," Jin said. "Can you tell me anything about what you saw that night?"

Nora's hands folded together in her lap. This woman had no walls around herself; she was an open book for Astrea to read. Her emotions were a mess: confused, sad, and deeply, deeply scared.

"Prince Varojin," Nora said, "I don't understand why you're here asking me these things. I already told the police what I know."

"I understand," Jin said. "I was hoping you might be able to go over it again with me. I just returned from the front and found out what's happening in the city. I'd like to help solve these crimes."

Nora sat up a little straighter, her shoulders pushed back as she looked at that framed picture of Jin's family before looking back at him. Jin's features tightened.

"I really admire that about you, Your Imperial Highness," Nora said. "You and your siblings all really seem to care about this city and this country."

Jin's honeyed voice faltered as he said, "It's hard to see something I care about under attack."

Nora nodded, then sucked in a deep breath. "Well, that night, I was in the kitchen making tea when I heard a scream outside." Nora's pain penetrated deep into Astrea's bones, and she had to put a hand on the back of the sofa to steady herself. "I didn't know exactly who it was, but I went to the window, this window"—she motioned behind them—"and saw Salvo. A very tall man was standing over him, or at least I think they were a man."

"Did you get a good look at him?" Jin asked.

"Yes," Nora said. "His face . . ."

"Yes?" he asked when she didn't continue.

Nora twisted her hands together in her lap. "His face was covered in shadows."

Astrea's heart nearly stopped beating, but Jin remained steadfast in his questioning. "As in it was too dark to see him?"

"No. I've never seen anything like it," Nora said, her voice low, like someone might be listening to them. "Shadows crawled up his face, Prince Varojin. Like . . . like bugs or flames or something."

Jin shifted in his seat slightly, the only sign of his discomfort. His walls were still up, still solid. Astrea blew out a breath as quietly as she could and fought back the images of the museum attack that trickled into her mind.

"What about his eye color?" he asked. "Did you see his eyes?"

"They were as black as the void itself," Nora whispered.

An icy shock penetrated Astrea's gut, but she wasn't sure if it was her own, Nora's, or Jin's. She hadn't noticed the man's eyes. Eye color across the continent varied from purples and blues to browns, grays, and greens. Even silver and gold, like Astrea and Jin. But void-like eyes? She hadn't noticed that on Solstice Night or at the museum.

"And you're sure?" Jin asked. Nora nodded. "Was Salvo a mage? Did you see him try to fight back?"

"No, no," Nora said quickly. "No, Salvo had no magic of his own. Loved listening to the sports matches, though. He used to play that thing so loud . . ."

"What else can you tell me?" he asked. "Your description was very good."

"It's what I told the police, Prince Varojin." Nora's pain dissipated slightly as gray confusion took over her aura.

Jin paused and looked up at Astrea. It was the first time he'd looked at her since they sat down. Astrea hadn't read all the police files; she'd barely gotten through the one note. But judging by Jin's furrowed eyebrows, he didn't have whatever else Nora told the police.

"Oh, I shouldn't have said anything . . ." the woman whispered.

"No!" Jin exclaimed. "No, it's alright. Please, tell me what you know. I must have forgotten what was in their notes."

Sucking in a breath, Nora wrung her wrinkled hands together. "The same shadows I saw on the man's face . . . they were on Salvo's body."

"On his body?"

"Up his arms and face," Nora clarified. "Like he'd . . . like he'd infected Salvo with something, and he was so pale. I knew right away he was dead."

Astrea hated asking this poor woman to relive that night. Tears clouded her eyes, her aura wavering blue with shock and sadness.

"I know this is hard, Nora," Jin said gently, "but were there any wounds you could see?"

"One," she said. "A knife in the heart."

Chapter 29

Astrea felt like all she did now was go to the library or the observatory. Not that she'd ever really gone elsewhere, but she hadn't even been going to the park or meeting Cressida at restaurants. Not since before Solstice Night.

Cressida had walked with her again to work that morning and was now downstairs, keeping good on her promise to help Raela move that statue still sitting in the basement. Raela wanted it displayed on a stand near the library's main staircase, ready to attract the attention of visitors.

Astrea had also filled Cressida in on the conversation with Nora on their walk to the library. Whoever these shadow men were, one thing was clear: they were looking for Astrea, and they had murdered at least two civilians. Jin was confident they were responsible for more than two, and Astrea was inclined to agree.

The question that remained was why? Why would they be murdering seemingly random Kalamians? The victims Jin had files on were not connected to Astrea in any way. And why would anyone want to bother her? Astrea had no idea. She kept her head down. She minded her own business. Yes, she was friends with Eliana, but there were better ways to hurt the princess if that was what the shadow men wanted. So was it about her Lightbringer magic? There were plenty of Lightbringers in the city, so why would they target her specifically? Neither of the two victims had been Lightbringers. And her stalkers obviously weren't going to turn her in for lying to the emperor; they could've already done that if they wanted to.

Every clue they uncovered just seemed to highlight the fact that they were still missing so many pieces of the larger puzzle.

"Astrea? Did you hear me?"

A hand landed on her shoulder, and Astrea jumped, willing her magic to stop its humming when she saw a bespectacled face staring at her. Felix frowned, his ginger eyebrows drawing together.

"Are you alright?" he asked. "I didn't mean to scare you."

Astrea swallowed. "Yes, sorry. I guess I didn't hear you."

She was sitting at one of the long tables on the second floor. Each floor of the library had an open area with tables and chairs, some cozier and some more practical. Astrea had chosen one of the hard-backed chairs, thinking it would keep her focused, but it hadn't.

"Are you done with those?" Felix asked, motioning to a stack of books sitting in front of Astrea. She'd been separating them by category to go back to their proper homes up here, but she'd only gotten two books in before getting distracted.

"No, sorry." Astrea straightened, pretending to go back to what she was doing. Felix wouldn't really care, nor would he tell Raela, but she didn't want any more questions.

"Oh, that's alright," he said, pulling out the chair next to her. "I have something more interesting for you anyway." Felix pushed aside the other stack of books, dropping three more in front of her. "I found one book on Novarian mythology, plus two on Helosian, Delian, and Zaikudi mythology. Is that helpful?"

Astrea perked up. "Which one has the Novarian myths?" she asked. Maybe this would give her some clue as to what was in Theo's missing manuscript that everyone seemed to want.

"This one." Felix pulled out the bottom book, its black binding dim in the library's light. It looked like it had been passed through a thousand hands, the edges of the cloth cover fraying. "Is this what you were looking for?"

Taking the book from him, Astrea opened the front cover. *Myth and Magic: Novarian Legends* was stamped on the title page, and under that, an illustration of mountains. The title wasn't what she'd hoped; Theo's book was called *Novaria: Myths and Other Legends*. Still, Astrea thumbed through the pages. She'd need a little time to figure out if this was useful, but it was certainly a start. She felt so behind in her project after spending part of the week running around the city with Jin.

"I think this gets me on the right track, at least," Astrea said. "Thanks, Felix."

He grinned. Felix was just a few years younger than Astrea, but the roundness of his face and toothy smile made him seem more like a child than a young adult.

"Anything to help," he said. "Let me know if you need anything else."

"Could you sort these books for me?" Astrea asked.

Felix rolled his eyes as he picked up the books, but his smile remained. "See ya later, Astrea," he called over his shoulder. "Don't forget you're covering my shift tomorrow morning!"

Astrea hadn't forgotten that. She'd need to head straight home from the library if she was going to also have time to get ready for that damn imperial dinner. Her only consolation was that at the palace, there would be no shadow men, just a ton of courtiers and politicians.

Astrea ran her hand over the cover of the book, then glanced at the other two. Both had faded red covers; they didn't look to be in much better shape than the one in her hands. Scooping them up, Astrea hurried down the stairs to the lobby. Jin would want to know about this. He'd met her that morning by the observatory to let her know he was going to try to help Eliana at that morning's council meeting and couldn't make it to the library. *But he might be done by now,* Astrea thought.

"Oh, Astrea!" Raela waved Astrea over toward the circulation desk. "Look who's here to see you."

Theo Kadis stood opposite Raela, pushing his glasses up his nose. He gave a little wave, which Astrea returned. Behind him was a short, muscular woman. An Earthmover, Astrea assumed, based on her dark brown eyes and the impossibly large crate sitting next to her. Cressida was nowhere in sight, and there was no way Theo and one other person had carried a crate that size.

"What's all this?" Astrea asked.

"Theo here was just telling me that he's brought over a gift," Raela said. "For your project. Artifacts, right, Theo?"

Theo. That was awfully familiar; did Raela and Theo know each other after all? She'd forgotten to ask.

"Indeed," he said as he smoothed the front of his white linen suit jacket. "I thought they might be helpful. Whatever you don't need can be returned to my shop."

Astrea wasn't sure what to say. It was kind of him to go through the trouble to bring them here, but she still didn't know what the emperor wanted. Maybe having a wide selection for him to choose from would keep him satisfied with their progress. It would be nice if Jin were there to sort through things with her.

"Thank you, Lord Kadis," Astrea said.

"It's no trouble. I'm happy to help you and Prince Varojin with whatever you need."

Astrea looked down at the books cradled in her arms, eyeing the black cover of the *Myth and Magic* book. "I actually have something I'd like to show you. Do you have time to look at it?"

"I'd be delighted," Theo said. "Raela, handle the crate, will you?"

"Already on it!" Raela called over her shoulder, motioning for the woman to follow her toward the basement. The crate lifted in the air as the Earthmover balled her hands into fists.

"So, what would you like to show me?" Theo asked as both Raela and the woman disappeared downstairs.

"Let's go to one of the private meeting rooms," Astrea suggested.

She took one of the keys from behind the circulation desk, then led Theo down the same hall she'd led Jin down nearly a fortnight before. So much had changed since then. Astrea pushed the thought from her head, focusing on unlocking the meeting room door. It was next to the room Jin hadn't used in days, the only other one in the library.

"This is all quite mysterious," Theo said with a laugh. He sat in one of the chairs surrounding the long table in the middle of the room. "I must say, you've piqued my curiosity, Astrea."

"Lord Kadis—Theo," she corrected when he pinned her with a look, "I know your manuscript on Novarian mythology is missing, but one of the library pages found this book."

She passed it to him, and Theo set the book down on the table so gently it was as if he were setting down a newborn baby. "Fascinating," he murmured as he opened the cover and flipped through the pages. "You found it here?"

"Yes," Astrea said. "I haven't had a chance to look through it yet, but is this at all similar to the one you lent Lord Mattina? I know Jin is eager to find the one stolen from you; perhaps knowing what he's looking for will help him."

"Give me a moment." Theo smoothed each page as he turned them. Green curiosity and teal approval danced in the air. "Interesting."

"What?" Astrea asked, peering over his shoulder. Each page he turned was filled with a mix of words and images Astrea couldn't name. There were two-legged creatures with horns and wings, animals that looked like two different species morphed together, cityscapes, and fires. "What is all of this?"

"I hate to ask," Theo said, closing the book, "but do you need this?"

"I'm sorry?"

"I would love to have a closer look at this, but I simply don't have time to look through it all today. I can give you a better answer if I have a few days to look it over."

Astrea hesitated. She didn't want to offend Theo after the help he'd offered her and Jin, but she couldn't let the book go. He'd lost the other manuscript; what if he lost this one, too? Or worse, what if he "found" the book and passed it on to one of his customers?

"I'd really like to look at it myself ahead of my next meeting with the emperor, and Jin hasn't seen it yet. Perhaps, if I look over it this weekend, I can bring it to your shop next week."

Theo's gaze met hers, surprisingly steady despite him pushing up his glasses again. The colors dancing around him faded, the scrape of annoyance grating on Astrea's skin. "Of course," he said finally, smiling as he handed the book back to her. His sleeve moved up with the motion, revealing a small tattoo on the inside of his wrist, a four-point star surrounded by two concentric circles. Astrea hadn't taken him for the type to get tattoos, but Theo Kadis seemed to be full of surprises today. "I didn't consider that Emperor Auris might be calling on you soon."

Hugging the book to her chest, she returned his smile. "He likes frequent status updates."

"Very well," Theo said, standing and moving toward the door. "Before I forget," he continued as he looked at her over his shoulder, "please send my regards to Jin when you see him next."

"I will."

"And do let me know what you find out about that book, yes? I look forward to any insights you may have."

"See you next week!" Astrea called as he hurried into the hallway. Once she was sure he was gone, she closed the meeting room door and sank into the nearest chair.

There was only one person she wanted to show this to besides Jin.

Astrea opened the door to the observatory apartment and hurried to her bedroom. On the last stretch of her commute home, it had started pouring. Thunder cracked overhead now, so loud even the observatory walls seemed to shake with the force. *Hopefully Cress got inside.* Cressida had dropped her off just outside the palace gates; it was still a long walk from the palace to the Nikaphoroses' home.

The front door closed. That had to be Saros coming downstairs for a break. Astrea knew almost nothing about Novarian mythology—or any mythology—but her uncle might.

After changing into a dry set of clothes, Astrea grabbed the *Myth and Magic* book and headed back into the living room. A rustle came from the kitchen, and she found Saros pouring a glass of wine.

"Uncle?" she asked as she turned into the kitchen.

"Astrea? I didn't realize you were home."

"I just got back." The book under her arm grew heavier by the second. "I'm glad you're down here, actually. I have something I really need your help with."

Dark green concern burst to life around Saros as he crossed the short distance to their kitchen table and sat down in his usual chair. "What is it?" he asked. "I need to get back upstairs soon."

Astrea took the chair opposite her uncle and set the book in front of him. "You know the emperor wants to include Novarian mythology as part of this exhibition, right?"

"Yes, you mentioned something about it the other morning," Saros said. "Why?"

"Well, we found this book at the library today. It's probably a long shot that it's even related to the one we're looking for, but I was hoping you might look at it. It's not really what I was expecting."

Saros didn't say a word as he opened the book's fraying cover. Curiosity rolled over Astrea's senses, so light compared to the regret she could feel lingering in the background of her uncle's mind.

She'd flipped through the book a dozen times at work. Stories of ancient mages, battles against monsters and men alike, and tales of all kinds of heroes filled the pages. She recalled a few of the stories from her own childhood, but most of them were unfamiliar to her. Though she still needed to compare it to Helosian mythology to find some overlap for the emperor, part of Astrea kept going back to the drawings of the monsters. Some of them were covered in shadows, much like the dead woman at the museum.

"Before the Great Wars, people held different beliefs about magic and the way the world worked," Saros said slowly. "Every region seemed to have its own variation on the stories, but at their cores, they were the same. The elements and the void, all balanced together. While life existed on the planet, the void held the souls of those lost. And while the planet contained the energy for the earthly magics—water, air, fire, and earth—the void held our magic, the magic of the stars. Only those chosen by forces outside of humanity would be granted any such magic."

"That doesn't sound all that different from now," Astrea said.

"Well, maybe not," Saros conceded. "But I don't know anyone who still thinks they're chosen to bear magic. We know it passes through family lines, and not everyone believes the dead return to the stars."

Astrea could think of just a few people who held any of those old beliefs about the souls of the dead. She wasn't sure what she believed, and she didn't think it mattered. She'd find out someday if those old beliefs were true or not.

"What about these monsters?" Astrea flipped through the pages until she found one of the horned creatures. "They're covered in shadows like the men from Solstice Night and the museum."

Saros hesitated as he looked down at the image. "I don't know much about the old beliefs," he said. "You'd be better off reading the stories."

Astrea sighed as thunder rumbled again. The storm was quieting, though rain still smacked against the kitchen window. "Do you know who might be familiar with them?" she asked. "Would someone at the university know?"

Though this wasn't the same book Theo had lost, it was strange. Monsters that happened to be covered in shadows like the men hunting Astrea? That couldn't be a coincidence. But the shadow men clearly weren't monsters, even if their actions were awful. They were human. She wasn't sure of much, but she was sure of that.

Saros was silent for a long moment. He leaned forward, elbows on the table as he ran his hands through his hair. "I've messed up so much for you, Astrea," he whispered, that familiar regret and shame exploding around him.

"Uncle—"

"No." He shook his head. "Every choice I've made for the last fourteen years has been the wrong one. *Every* choice, Astrea. What would your mother think of me? Her own brother, screwing things up so badly for her only child."

Astrea stared at her uncle, unsure what this had to do with the book or her unanswered question. To say that every choice he'd made was wrong seemed dramatic. But Saros seemed to believe what he was saying, his aura spiking with deep blue sadness, gray confusion, orange fear.

"Not every choice was so bad," Astrea offered. "I love the friends I've made here, and we have the Nikaphoroses. I went to a good university—"

"What would Roxana think?" Saros continued, cutting her off again. "To know what I've done now."

Astrea didn't remember much about her mother. That part of her childhood was a blur, just glimpses of her mother's smile and laugh, her kindness, the Novarian countryside and mountains. Still, Astrea was sure her mother would've had something to say to comfort both her and Saros, something to give them clarity.

"What have you done?" she asked.

"I have failed to protect you, Astrea," he said, those silver Sovna eyes meeting hers. "Everything that's happened is my fault."

"Uncle." Astrea sighed as she pulled the book toward herself and closed it. "You keep saying the same thing. What have you failed to protect me from?"

"The emperor, these men—" Saros cleared his throat. "There's something I've been keeping from you."

More secrets. Astrea wasn't even surprised. She'd had an inkling that Saros was keeping his work from her, as he often did. There was much he couldn't tell her, much that was just for the emperor and the council to know. But this felt different. It felt wrong.

"I've got my own special assignment from the emperor," Saros continued.

That didn't actually surprise Astrea either. Saros was, after all, the court's Stargazer. A diviner, a seer of potential futures. It was an imprecise branch of magic, nearly impossible to control and predict. Special projects were basically Saros's entire job description.

"I've been working on something even his council is unaware of," Saros continued. "About six months ago, the emperor found a meteorite in the Badlands."

The Badlands were a barren region to the northeast, bordered on the south by the Ring of Fire. The volcanic landscape and lack of resources meant little attention was typically devoted to that area of the empire. The fight Eliana had with her father and Kaius in front of Astrea flashed through her mind. "You may not think this is important," Prince Kaius had said that morning, "but it is."

"How did Emperor Aelius find it?" Astrea asked.

"Me," Saros said. "The meteorite and its location came to me in a vision."

"And what does he want with a meteorite?"

"At first, he thought it might be interesting to study," Saros said. "But there's something wrong with this meteorite, Astrea. There's something unnatural about it." He shifted in his chair, the wood creaking with his movement. "I believe it's from the void."

"Of course it's from the void," Astrea said. "It's a space rock."

Everyone knew the void was what the night sky was made of, that emptiness between the stars, the moons, and the planets. Meteorites had fallen to the earth before. This was not the first, nor would it be the last.

"No." Saros shook his head. "I mean, yes, of course it's from the void, but . . ." He shook his head again. "I know you must think I'm a fool."

"No," she said quickly. "No, I just don't understand what any of this has to do with the void, or me, or even Mom."

Maybe Saros really was losing his mind, overworked by an emperor trying to find any advantage he could over the other powers on the continent. Exhaustion did strange things to people. Saros wasn't making any sense.

He stood and retrieved his forgotten wine glass from the counter. "I am responsible for what's been happening in Kalama. Putting you—and your friends—in danger."

"But you're not the shadow man," Astrea said.

"I may as well be," Saros retorted. "After I told the emperor about the meteorite and he brought it to the city, the murders started. It's my fault."

"Uncle." Astrea paused. She didn't know what to tell him, what to say to convince him that he wasn't at fault. *Just like maybe the murders aren't my fault, either,* Astrea's mind whispered. Jin had said the same. Still, steely determination rolled off Saros in waves; he truly believed what he was saying. "It sounds more like a coincidence than a cause. How can a space rock be responsible for the crimes of a man?"

Saros shook his head again. "Mark my words, Astrea. The shadows are coming, and I need to find out what they are before it's too late."

CHAPTER 30

Thunder clapped overhead. Astrea's bed and floorboards rumbled. Another evening thunderstorm, just like every other summer she'd lived in this apartment.

After Saros's warning—which Astrea still didn't understand—they'd talked more, with Saros apologizing over and over for everything he'd put them through. Eventually, Astrea had gotten him into bed, where he'd fallen asleep only after a little encouragement from her magic.

Now she was exhausted and didn't know what to do. Part of her still thought that Saros might be having a nervous breakdown, but there was something about the way he pleaded for her forgiveness that felt all too real.

Astrea leaned back into her pillows, then picked up the book. After running a finger along the book's cover, she finally flipped it open. The paper gave away its age, delicate but not so much that she would rip it. It had to be a century old, perhaps a little more. Faded gold lined the pages, each one catching the lamplight as she turned them.

Thunder rumbled overhead again, but it grew distant as the storm moved deeper into the city. More might come later, but for now, it was quiet.

Astrea was too tired to give the book a thorough read, but the images were extraordinary. Monsters and animals, their snarling faces faded through the years. Shadows like those at the museum. The longer she examined the book, the more she wondered if they'd only been partially right about the shadow man showing up that night. What if he'd been at the museum for Theo's book, too? It couldn't be a coincidence that these images were so similar to what Astrea and her friends had been seeing.

The phone on Astrea's bedside table rang, an annoying, tinny sound. She picked it up. "Hello?"

"Astrea?"

Who else would it be? she thought wryly. But instead, she replied, "Hi, Jin." She'd know his voice anywhere, even over a crackling phone line.

"I know it's late," he said, "but I was hoping you'd be able to take a drive."

The clock next to the phone said it was almost the ninth evening bell already. Tired as she was, there had to be a reason for his call, and she wanted to tell him about the meteorite Saros had mentioned. Maybe he would know something about it.

"Sure," Astrea said. "I'll get dressed."

The night air had turned humid after the storm, and Astrea wished she'd braided her hair. It was impossibly sticky out, and for a moment, she regretted agreeing to go with Jin.

He'd told her to wait outside the observatory, and so she was. She'd opted for trousers again, pairing them with a loose linen blouse. Before leaving, Astrea had also left a note for Saros. They'd been keeping enough from each other; if he woke up while she was gone, she wanted him to know who she was with.

Two headlights appeared on the wide gravel road leading from the observatory back to the palace. Had Jin brought a car all the way back here? She stuck close to the tower. The car rolled to a stop, and the driver's door opened. A tall form got out, then a bright flame sparked to life, illuminating Jin's face.

"You ready to go?" he asked as she walked toward him, careful to avoid the puddles marring the path.

"Ready," Astrea said.

Jin hustled to the passenger door and opened it for her. Astrea's cheeks burned. What was he doing that for? The last time someone had opened a door for her like that was when she'd gone on a date over a year before, and that definitely wasn't what this was.

He climbed back into the driver's seat, but before he could put the car in gear, she said, "Are you even allowed to drive back here?"

"Well." He laughed. "What are my father's rules if not polite suggestions?"

Astrea rolled her eyes. "And is it safe?"

"Nobody's out, and besides, I'm a great driver."

"Not if your motorcycle skills are anything to go off of."

Jin whistled, the sound low, as he put the car in gear. The faintest wisp of amusement tickled Astrea's nose. "Damn. You've got me rethinking everything, Sovna."

Her face burned brighter, and Astrea was grateful for the darkness around them. "Just drive."

Butterflies danced in her stomach as he laughed again and said, "Yes, ma'am."

Jin somehow managed to turn the car around without hitting any of the trees lining the path to the observatory. He took them down a series of narrow roads on the palace grounds before they got back to the main driveway. They made it through the gates in one piece, and the guards there waved Jin through without a second glance.

"Where are we going, anyway?" Astrea asked. They'd turned down one of the main roads in Nobleman's Hill and now headed east toward Tinale Bay. There were no stores or restaurants in this part of the district, just rows of large townhomes that belonged to noble families and a few hotels for the wealthier visitors of the city.

"We're going to Mattina's townhouse," Jin said.

"Now?"

"I didn't want to be seen."

Between the storms and late hour, Astrea doubted many people would be out. "Do you think he's home?" she asked.

"Doubtful," Jin muttered. "He knows we're looking for him. He'd be a fool to stay in Kalama, but I'd rather know for certain if he's still in town."

"Couldn't we just tell your father about this?" she asked as Jin navigated down an empty street. "If he decides he wants the manuscript for his exhibit and Mattina has it, he could do something about it. Better than us sneaking around."

"I'd rather not bring my father's wrath down on anyone unless we really need to."

That actually probably was for the best. Emperor Aelius didn't even know about this manuscript yet, but he would probably severely punish Mattina just the same.

"Well, regardless," Astrea said, and Jin glanced briefly at her, "I'm glad you called me."

Jin paused. "You are?"

"Yes. Felix found a book that might help us with the project, and I need to tell you something about Saros."

"Oh." Jin nodded, though his eyes were glued to the road. "Alright, let's save that for after we deal with Mattina."

"Alright," she agreed. Astrea needed time to explain what had happened with Saros and the book, more time than a short drive through the district could provide.

Jin pulled the car over and parked near the curb. The homes in this part of Nobleman's Hill were smaller than Astrea had imagined they'd be, the street populated by at least a dozen parked cars, probably more. But it was quiet, no people in sight. It was dark, too, with only a few streetlamps lighting the way.

Jin was already opening his car door as he said, "We'll walk from here. Let me get your door."

"You don't need to—" Astrea started, but Jin was already on her side of the car. He opened Astrea's door from the outside, motioning for her to climb out. She did, watching for puddles as she stepped on the street. It was drier here than at the observatory.

Jin moved down the sidewalk without saying a word, as if Astrea was just supposed to know where they were going. She bit back her questions and hurried after him.

"It's just up here," Jin said, voice low as his steps slowed.

They stopped in front of a townhouse that looked like any of the others on the street. It had the same wrought iron gate, the same pastel stucco exterior, the same overabundant garden. Jin walked up to the gate, and just when Astrea was about to ask if it was locked, he pushed on it. The gate swung open on silent hinges.

Of course, Astrea had known they were going to do this. But as Jin started through the gate, her stomach dropped. "Have you lost your mind?" she whispered as she hurried after him. "What if he's in there?"

Or what if the shadow man is waiting for us? Astrea didn't voice that concern aloud. Jin knew exactly what was going on. There was no way he hadn't considered that.

"The house is dark," Jin replied as he closed the gate behind her. "All of the neighbors' homes are dark too. Can you sense anyone nearby?"

Astrea pushed her magic out as far as she could manage, extending through the front garden toward the back of the property and across the house. It came up empty; she sensed nothing other than Jin's heavy wall. "I think we're alone."

"Then let's check it out."

They crept down the right side of the house, Astrea's breath catching as they entered the shadows cloaking that side of the yard. The house was tall despite being only two stories, as were the shrubs growing in the front garden. They blocked out most of the little streetlight there was, and the moon was absent tonight, hidden behind the thick storm clouds.

It felt too much like that night in the alley by the museum, like they were going to get to the backyard and find the shadow man shoving a knife into someone else's heart.

"What are we looking for?" Astrea whispered.

"The back door." Jin slipped his hand into hers, pulling her along, and she tried to ignore how her pulse skittered. "Careful," he whispered, a small flame jumping to life over his other palm. He nodded at a root from the nearby orange tree sticking out of the ground.

They continued down the length of the house until, finally, the rear garden came into view. This was neither a large house nor a large garden, but Astrea felt like they were going too slowly. They were too exposed, being out here in the dark. She gripped his hand tighter.

"Anyone?" Jin whispered.

"No." Being this close to the house, Astrea would surely be able to feel *something* if someone were in there, whether that was emotions or someone's wall. "Just us, I think."

That seemed to be good enough for Jin. He nodded, then tugged on her hand as he started moving. They entered the back garden, which was more overgrown than Astrea expected. The tall, leafy trees would've provided plenty of shade had it been a sunny afternoon.

Steps led up to a narrow back porch. Jin climbed them first, and Astrea stayed as close to him as she could.

"Does Ellie know we're here?" Astrea asked as Jin pulled something out of his pocket.

"She doesn't need to know." He slid two thin pieces of metal into the door's lock. After a moment of fiddling, the lock tumbled free. "There."

Astrea stared at Jin. "Just what have they been teaching you in the army?"

"All kinds of things."

Without another word, Jin opened the door to Mattina's house. They were really doing this, breaking into a Helosian noble's home late at night. Doing this while some shadowy murderer roamed the streets looking for Astrea. If it wasn't dangerous, she might laugh. *Ridiculous,* she thought as she crept after Jin. *Absolutely ridiculous.*

Still, Astrea forced herself to focus on her senses as they moved into the pitch-dark interior. She let them push out as far as they could in every direction, but the house still felt empty.

"Nobody's home," she whispered.

A flame popped to life over Jin's hand. The space around them lit up just enough to reveal the setup of a kitchen. A refrigerator hummed in one corner, and the counters were clean except for a few canisters tucked near the stove. "Then let's get to work," he said. "Look for the book or anything that might prove he stole it."

As they moved through the kitchen and then a hallway on the first floor, Astrea was sure of two things. The first was that dark and silent homes were even more eerie than she'd ever thought. The second was that Mattina liked to keep things tidy. As they crept through a dining room, a sitting room, and an office, not one book or accent pillow was out of place. None of those rooms yielded anything of interest, though Astrea had been unfortunate enough to find an old letter Mattina had saved from a lover.

"You don't think Mattina's the shadow man, do you?" Astrea asked as they started down the second floor's hallway.

"Mattina? No," Jin said. "He's not a mage, and this shadow man obviously is."

That made Astrea feel marginally better, though when a floorboard squeaked loudly, she grabbed for Jin's hand. When he turned to her, he was smiling.

"That was just me."

"I know." She pulled her hand away quickly and pushed at the spot between his shoulders. "Keep going. We shouldn't be in here too long."

They checked two bedrooms and both bathrooms. Still, there was nothing. No diaries spilling Mattina's secrets. No mythology books of any kind. No letters to co-conspirators. *That would've been too easy,* Astrea thought ruefully.

"Last room," Jin said as they approached another door, "and then we'll go."

The door opened with a creak. Jin's fire illuminated the space, long shadows stretching over the walls. With the large size, ornate bedroom furniture, and obviously expensive linens, Astrea was sure it was the owner's bedroom. As Jin began rummaging through a chest of drawers, Astrea headed for the wardrobe. When she opened its double doors, all she found was a set of mostly empty hangers. Just a couple of shirts haphazardly arranged remained. That did not fit with Mattina's tidiness. It was rushed. Sloppy.

"Jin," she whispered. "I don't think Mattina's in Kalama anymore. I think he left in a hurry."

"I think you're right." He joined her, then handed her a single sheet of paper. "A note for his housekeeper." Astrea skimmed the neat handwriting; it was just instructions for while Mattina was 'out of town.' "We should get going," Jin said.

They made their way back through the house, Astrea's heart pounding in her chest and up her throat as they snuck out the back door again. The garden was just as quiet as it was before except for the distant rumble of thunder over Tinale Bay.

They'd actually broken into Lord Mattina's townhouse. No, they hadn't found Theo's book, but they knew Mattina wasn't in the city. It was disappointing, but Astrea wasn't actually surprised. If Mattina was trying to keep the manuscript away from the imperial family, he wouldn't stay so close to their home.

"Do you think he went to his Sezian house?" Astrea asked as she followed Jin a few houses down, away from Mattina's home and back toward their car. "Theo did say Mattina owns property there."

"It's probably a good idea to check," Jin said as they passed a flickering streetlamp. "He might've gone there if it was too hard to leave Helosia. But I think that's a problem we'll have to solve tomor—"

"Hello?" The voice was unfamiliar, husky and low like someone who had smoked far too much blue lotus. "Who's there?"

"Fuck," Jin muttered.

Astrea froze. She hadn't seen lights on in the house behind them, nor had she sensed anyone. But there. Someone's harsh, grating annoyance scraped over Astrea's skin. They stalked closer. Had this person overheard their conversation? Heard them sneaking around? Would they have called the police? Astrea looked back at Jin only to find him watching her, a strange expression on his face.

"Don't hate me," he whispered as a gate squeaked.

Astrea didn't have time to think. She could barely react as Jin whirled on her, his body covering hers as he pressed her against the garden wall. He buried one hand in her hair at the nape of her neck, the other cupping her cheek as he leaned his forehead against hers.

"What are you—" she whispered, but he shushed her quietly, his gaze full of warning.

"Hello?" the voice came again.

Astrea tried to slow her breathing. Jin was so close to her, his breath hot on her cheek. She didn't dare look away, didn't dare move a muscle, as Jin pressed in closer.

"Oh, for skies sake! Can't I have my evening tea in peace?"

Jin closed his eyes, his lips parting. Astrea steeled herself. Her stomach curled. But he didn't move. There was no way he was really going to—

"This isn't the Warehouse District!" the stranger called. "I know you can hear me. Get a room!"

The gate squeaked again, then slammed shut. A lock clicked, followed by shuffling feet and a front door closing as the stranger, whoever they were, went back into their house. That annoyance disappeared, too, as it moved farther away. The only thing Astrea could feel now was Jin's wall—and his skin on hers.

Skies, he was warm. Her face burned under his touch. She couldn't believe she was this close to Jin. She couldn't believe he was still standing there, frozen, as he cozied up to her like they were lovers.

"I think they're gone," Astrea whispered when Jin still hadn't moved.

Jin's eyes popped open. He remained unmoving as he gazed down at her, and Astrea's breath hitched.

"Sorry," he said, finally pulling away. "Anyone who lives here would probably know me on sight, and that was all I could think to do."

"Oh. Right." Astrea swallowed. It *was* Nobleman's Hill. Everyone around here was connected to the palace and imperial family in some way. "Well, I doubt they could see anything. It's dark, and with you . . ."

"Right." Jin nodded, pulling at the sleeves of his black shirt. "We should go back to the car."

As they started down the wide sidewalk in silence, heavy rain began to fall and thunder clapped. They broke into a sprint. As soon as they reached the car, Jin opened the passenger door and pushed Astrea inside. He scrambled in behind her, shutting the door with a thud.

They were squished between the passenger door and the driver's seat, the space barely big enough for the two of them. Astrea could've moved over, but she stayed put. She stared at him in the shadows of the car, only truly taking him in as lightning cracked overhead. Jin's usual self-assurance disappeared as he looked toward the spot they'd just been standing in. Astrea looked at it, too, a mix of disappointment and laughter bubbling within her. When her first giggle escaped, she couldn't stop herself.

"What?" Jin asked. His eyebrows drew together, but that only made her laugh more. And then Jin's mask cracked, his lips quirking up as he, too, began laughing. "What's so funny?"

"I don't know," Astrea muttered. She sucked in a deep breath, steadying herself as she wiped at the tears and rain stuck in her lashes. "That . . . that was ridiculous. I mean, sneaking around some nobleman's fucking townhouse?"

"I don't know about *ridiculous*." Jin leaned back, and Astrea swore he inched closer to her as he propped his arm on the back of the seat. A few raindrops clung to his hair and beard, glistening as lightning flashed outside.

"We almost got caught," she said.

A hint of that sweet amusement whispered past his wall. "But we didn't, did we?"

"Skies." Astrea leaned back into the seat, too. "I need a drink."

"We can go get one if you want."

"Should we really be out like this? With the shadow man running around, I mean."

"So far, we've only run into him in secluded places," Jin said. "We should be alright if we go someplace a bit more crowded."

"You really think it'd be safe?"

"It certainly can't be any riskier than what we just did."

The rain started hitting the windshield even harder. Another flash of lightning illuminated Jin's face. "We could go for just one drink," Astrea whispered.

"Just one," he agreed. "Then I'll take you home."

Jin opened the passenger door, then ran through the rain as he circled the car. And when he climbed back into the driver's seat and put the car in gear, Astrea couldn't help but focus on the satisfaction radiating off Jin as they sped away into the night.

They'd agreed that going to a place not too close to the palace would be best; Jin didn't want any questions from courtiers. So Astrea had suggested a small restaurant called Ravintola. It was near the Nikaphoroses' home, one she went to with Cressida all the time.

Two weeks prior, Astrea had received that skies forsaken letter from the emperor while at work. And now, here she was, sitting across from Jin at a small table in the back corner of a restaurant. Astrea never could've imagined everything would lead to this moment. She never could've imagined that despite how much he'd hurt her years before, she'd actually *want* to be sitting at this small table with him.

The restaurant wasn't empty, but the only other patrons were seated closer to the front. And though Astrea couldn't always tolerate the clinking of utensils on plates, she was glad for that small bit of extra noise. That and the radio playing behind the bar would be helpful for what came next.

"Can we talk here?" Astrea asked as she picked up the wine glass in front of her.

"I think it'll be alright," Jin said. His whiskey sat untouched.

"I asked for Felix's help finding some mythology books at the library," Astrea started, her voice low. She explained the *Myth and Magic* book's contents—including the shadowy pictures—how Theo had come by the library earlier in the afternoon, and even how he'd asked to keep the book.

"I assume you didn't let him keep it," Jin said.

"No. It's at home."

Jin glanced toward the bar. "And you said there was something about Saros, too?"

"Yes, actually, I showed him the book when I got home. And then he—"

Lavender flashed to Astrea's right, followed by bright green curiosity. "Az?"

Cressida walking into this restaurant wouldn't be a surprise on any other evening. It was, after all, one of her favorites. But it was late—well past the tenth evening bell—and she looked exhausted. She'd pulled her thick curls away from her face with an embroidered bandanna, like she always did when she spent time in her workshop.

"Cress." Astrea was sure her aura was lighting up the very same colors. "What are you doing here?"

Grinning, Cressida crossed the rest of the short distance to their table. "I could say the same about you two. What are *you* doing out this late?"

Her gaze flicked to Jin, then back to Astrea. Her eyebrows lifted with a silent question.

"Why don't you join us?" Jin offered, and uncomfortable jealousy surged through Astrea's body. What did she have to be jealous about?

Cressida pulled a chair over from an empty table, then dropped into it. Fatigue pressed against Astrea's mind, mingling with the curiosity still skittering over her skin.

"Long day?" Astrea asked.

"Incredibly. I just got done at the palace," Cressida said. "I was just going to get a drink before going home."

"I thought you had the day off?" Astrea asked. Cressida hadn't mentioned her own imperial project in days, but that would be the only explanation for why she was at the palace.

"Well, I did, but after I walked you home, I got a call asking me to go over."

Jin's eyebrows raised, but he looked back at Astrea. "We can finish talking later."

"Don't stop on my account," Cressida said. "Unless . . . it's something I shouldn't be here for?"

"It's fine, Cress," Astrea said. "I was just going to tell Jin something that Saros said to me."

"Then let me get that drink first." Cressida popped out of her chair and hurried to the bar. Once she was out of earshot, Jin leaned across the table.

"Really, sorry if I overstepped," he said. "I just assumed Cress could—"

"It's fine," Astrea said. When he still didn't look convinced, she smiled. "I promise." Getting Cressida's take on the situation might actually be good. She knew Saros far better than Jin did.

Cressida returned not long after, a glass of clear liquor in her hand. She dropped back into her seat, then motioned for Astrea to continue.

After catching Cressida up on what she'd told Jin, Astrea said, "I showed the book to Saros. He didn't really know what those shadowy pictures were and . . . I don't know. It triggered something in him. He just kept going on about how he'd made so many wrong choices and failed me."

"Oh, shit," Cressida whispered. Jin's eyebrows just furrowed.

"And then Saros told me about his own special assignment." The other patrons in the restaurant were absorbed in their conversations. Another couple had come in, and they were laughing loudly at the bar. "He had a vision of a meteorite in the Badlands," Astrea continued, lowering her voice even more. "I guess your father went to find it, Jin, and he brought it back to Kalama. Saros thinks the timing of everything is connected to it."

"A meteorite?" Jin asked as Cressida mumbled a string of curses. Teal understanding bubbled around her.

"Cress?" Astrea asked.

Cressida shook her head. "I should've fucking known."

"Known what?"

Sinking back into her chair, Cressida took a quick sip of her drink. "Do you remember when you told me about the fight Ellie and her father had about the Badlands?"

Astrea nodded. Nearly two weeks prior, Astrea had witnessed Eliana arguing about that very location with Kaius and their father. When she'd told Cressida about it, Cressida had mentioned her special assignment was related to that location. Astrea hadn't even considered the connection, thanks to Saros's chaotic reaction, but now it all clicked.

"I told you he'd already been there—" Cressida started, but Astrea cut her off.

"Your project. Is that . . ."

"I assume so."

"But what does he want with it?"

"I've been trying to—"

"May I ask," Jin finally said, "what you two are talking about?"

Cressida sighed and scrubbed at her face with her free hand. Her copper complexion was usually bright, but her entire appearance was dull, tired. It had been a long two weeks. "You two aren't the only ones with special projects this summer, Jin. Your father assigned me one the same morning Astrea got hers—yours."

Jin's jaw tightened. "Oh?"

"He told me it was classified. With everything else going on, I thought it best to just keep my head down and work on it . . ." Cressida sighed again, orange anxiety sparking around her. "He wants me to fuse the meteorite's iron with existing weaponry. He's convinced it's stronger than normal metal, that it will yield something . . . greater."

"And will it?" Jin asked.

"I don't think so," Cressida said. "At least, not that I've been able to figure out yet. It seems like any other metal to me."

"My uncle says it's from the void," Astrea murmured.

"Well, it *is* a space rock," Cressida said. "It's from the void."

"I know, but . . ." How did Astrea explain this? "He thinks that makes it important for some reason. Or different, I guess? He couldn't explain why; he was too broken up about all of it."

Gray confusion flickered around Cressida, but Jin's wall was tight. Tighter, perhaps, if that were even possible. Astrea reached for her wine again and took a long sip.

"Can you get a piece of it for me?" Jin finally asked Cressida. "Do you think my father would notice?"

"I can probably take something small," she said. "And I do mean small. He's got it under tight surveillance."

"Can you get it before the party tomorrow night?"

"I'll do my best."

Astrea blew out a harsh breath. This was not what she'd imagined when she'd planned on telling Jin about the meteorite. She supposed it was best that they knew this so they could work with the new information, but where did it fit in with the rest? She needed Saros to sit down and explain everything clearly, but the odds of that happening seemed low.

CHAPTER 31

Astrea stepped into the library elevator, sighing as she pushed the button for the lobby. She was dreading tonight. She had just a couple more hours before she needed to go back to the observatory to get ready for dinner at the palace.

After learning the details of Cressida's project and how it was tied to Saros's vision and concerns, Cressida had gone home, and Jin had driven Astrea back to the observatory. Saros had still been asleep when Astrea returned, and she'd been torn between waking him to ask him for clarification and letting him sleep. She'd ultimately decided to leave him to rest, and he'd been back up in his observatory that morning. Why couldn't he just talk to her? She'd thought they were making progress, even if their timing was a little off.

The elevator descended several floors, and the doors chimed as they opened. Astrea stepped back out, heading for the circulation desk. That was her work duty for the rest of the day since Raela was out for another meeting.

She sat down in Raela's usual spot, setting her notebook and the *Myth and Magic* book on the desk with a thunk. Astrea needed to double-check the list of Theo's recent delivery against her own list, but she hadn't had time yet.

And now, she was too distracted. Why had Jin almost kissed her the night before? She could understand his reasoning to an extent, but wouldn't simply turning around and walking the other way have been enough?

Astrea played with the edge of a blank page in her notebook, rolling the corner back and forth until it tore off. Despite everything, the last couple of weeks had been good with Jin. It felt like they were friends again, even if they had never spoken about why he left without telling her. That was her fault; he'd tried to bring it up several times.

Maybe I'm more like Saros than I've ever realized. Avoiding the problem didn't solve it. It was just so long ago. Did it matter? It bothered Astrea, but she also desperately wanted to just move on from it. She wanted one less thing to worry about, and besides, she wanted to be friends with Jin again. Things might never be the same as they once were, but she'd missed him—

"Oh, Astrea! Hello!"

The words echoed through the empty lobby. Theo Kadis waved as he strode toward her.

She sat up straighter. "What are you doing here?" The words were harsher than she meant, but she hadn't expected to see the antiquities dealer until the next week, when she was supposed to give him the book.

"Ah." He pushed his glasses up his nose as he set a folio on the desk. "I'm actually here to see Raela."

"She's out for a meeting," Astrea said. "She should be back tomorrow, though. Would you like me to pass on your message?"

"That's quite alright; I can come back tomorrow." Theo pushed his glasses up again, his gaze darting over her shoulder. Astrea turned, finding the stone bust Raela had unboxed weeks earlier now on display near the stairs. "I'm glad to see you, actually," he continued. "I want to apologize if I overstepped yesterday. You must understand," he said with a chuckle, "I sometimes get overly excited about books." Amusement reached for Astrea's magic, followed by the heat of embarrassment.

"Oh, you don't have to explain it to me," she said. "I understand." She did, but she mostly also wanted to save the man his embarrassment. Getting excited about books wasn't exactly a faux pas.

"Well, my excitement means I don't always think things through," he said. "So I do apologize. While I have you here, though, have you had a chance to look through it?"

In the little time she'd spent with the book the night before, Astrea hadn't just focused on those shadowy images. She'd skimmed over it all in an attempt to find something relevant to the emperor's project. There were stories about ghosts and vengeful spirits, about fate, about creatures that would come for children in the night. There were even a few tales of monarchs who were victorious in battle. The stories covered a spectrum of tales and lessons, and the drawings were even more elaborate than she'd first realized.

"I have," Astrea said. She slid the book toward herself and opened it. "May I ask you a question?"

"Of course." Theo leaned against the desk and smiled. "A friend of Jin's is a friend of mine."

"Why is your book so important to you?" That same embarrassment as before rushed toward Astrea, flashing magenta in the air around him. "Is some old book of fairytales really so valuable?"

"Ah." Theo pressed his lips together, nodding just once. "Mine is valuable, of course," he said after a moment, and the bright embarrassment around him dissipated. "Quite valuable financially. But more than that, it's a record of the old philosophies and beliefs which, despite being ancient, also hold value."

"In what way?" Astrea pushed. The way Theo now focused on the book in her hands made Astrea shift in her seat. "Surely there are other books"—she nodded to *Myth and Magic*—"that explore the same topics."

"May I?" Theo motioned toward the tome.

Reluctantly, Astrea slid it to him. She doubted he'd try to run off with the book, but she still felt oddly possessive over it. Theo flipped through a few of the stories, seemingly disinterested in them as he scanned more pages. He paused occasionally, perusing the text on the page before moving on. Finally, though, he turned the book around so she could see it properly.

"I'm not a historian," he said, "but I know enough thanks to my work. Are you familiar with the Great Wars?"

"A bit, just what my tutors went over." Astrea loved reading about all kinds of things, but war had never been something she cared about.

"My missing book contains information on them, firsthand accounts," he said. "Very valuable information. Interesting stories, too. Are you familiar with void demons?" He'd flipped to another page and pointed at it.

"What?" Astrea looked up at him.

When Theo nodded for her to look at the book, Astrea let her gaze drift down. On the left-hand page was a story in faded ink, the corresponding image on the right. It showed an oblong prison cell with blue circles on the bars, a red-eyed monster locked inside.

"Just one example," Theo said, chuckling. "My book may have real history in it, but the stories, too, are fun. Stories just like this one."

What that had to do with why the book was so valuable, Astrea didn't know.

"Perhaps what you should be asking yourself instead," Theo said as he closed the book and slid it back toward her, "is why Emperor Aelius is so interested in stories about ancient monarchs and monsters. What use would a leader have for such tales?"

"For an exhibit showcasing shared Novarian and Helosian history," Astrea said. "He's trying to solidify an alliance with Grand Duchess Ysabel and thinks this will be a gesture of good will."

Theo paused, his emotions calm and unremarkable. "Is that what he wants? Or what he wants you to think?"

"What else would he want with old stories?" Astrea asked. Even as the words left her mouth, ice penetrated her gut. The emperor's request had been a bit strange, but she had never considered he might lie to her and Jin both. And why lie about it?

"He could truly want that, of course." Theo straightened and tugged at his shirt cuffs. "Even old history is worth studying. Perhaps Emperor Aelius really does want to show the Novarians he understands our shared histories and cultures."

"I should think that is the case," Astrea said with a nod. But even as she said the words, the very core of her bones chilled.

"Well," Theo said, "good luck with your studies. I'll be back in search of Raela tomorrow morning. Have a lovely rest of your day, Astrea."

As Theo left the library, Astrea stared down at the book's fraying cover. Could Theo really be right that the emperor might have ulterior motives for researching those very same tales?

Smoothing the bodice of her gown, Astrea examined her reflection in the mirror. As instructed by Eliana's original note, Astrea had chosen the gown she'd worn for the previous year's Solstice Night festival. It was a floor-length gown of black silk and silver tulle that almost perfectly matched her eyes. The fabric flowed smoothly over her round, wide hips. Tiny, beaded stars embroidered on the dress glinted as she turned. The neckline dipped low between the small swell of her breasts, and the back was cut in a mirror image.

It looked great, but it felt all wrong. This wasn't her, this blend of formal and sultry. *Ellie knows what to suggest,* Astrea reminded herself. This was a different affair than what Astrea usually attended; this was probably exactly how courtiers dressed for such dinners. If Astrea didn't try to blend in, people would question her.

Astrea slipped on her flat shoes, then reached for the same crescent moon clips she'd worn to Solstice Night the past weekend. She pulled her dark hair back in a half-updo, letting most of the large curls flow over her shoulders and down her back. Astrea had even done her makeup for the occasion, her lashes darkened and pale cheeks brightened with blush. Cressida was *supposed* to help with this part, but she'd called from the palace and said she needed to check on something for one of her father's palace contracts. Astrea assumed that was code for stealing that piece of meteorite Jin had requested.

Just get going, Astrea silently told her reflection. *You look fine.*

As she slipped out of her bedroom, Saros was nowhere to be found. She'd tried to tell him about the dinner that morning before she left for work, but he'd only grunted a response from his office. Now, Astrea left him another note, just in case he'd forgotten.

Maybe Sarsali and Balthazar can speak with him, she thought as she made her way through the gardens. She needed to talk with them as soon as possible. Saros always took their counsel into consideration. Maybe they'd get him to finally, truly explain everything.

The sun hadn't quite set yet, but in the distance, beyond the gardens, cars with bright headlights were pulling up the palace driveway. The dinner didn't start for a while, but Astrea wanted to check in with Eliana. They hadn't seen each other all week. She hurried up the steps to the palace's eastern entrance and slipped inside the empty corridor.

She'd just started up the side stairway that would take her toward Eliana's apartment when a throat cleared behind her. Prince Kaius stood there, watching her.

"Miss Sovna." His golden gaze traveled down her form slowly, then back up. Astrea's skin crawled. "My father wants to speak with you."

"Now?" she managed to ask past the dryness in her mouth. She mentally scolded herself. Of course the emperor wanted to know what she'd found, and of course he'd ask tonight. *Maybe I could go get my notes . . .*

"Now."

Hesitating, Astrea descended the stairs, then followed Kaius. He led her through the main atrium, where the night's guests had started to arrive. To Astrea's relief, everyone was wearing similarly styled outfits, though some of the attendees had chosen brighter makeup.

"I see you're my brother's guest tonight," Prince Kaius said as they turned down a now-familiar hallway. The gold embroidery on his maroon suit caught the overhead lights as they walked.

"What?" Astrea asked.

"You're Varojin's guest," Kaius repeated. "He listed you as his guest tonight."

"Oh, right." She fiddled with the tulle of her skirt. "Yes, he invited me."

"You've never attended one of these dinners before."

"He thought it would be good for me to get out for once. He says I spend too much time in my books and not enough time having fun."

The lie came easily, comfortably. It was actually something Jin had said to her once, years ago. Astrea could feel the weight of Kaius's gaze on her, his emotions pounding in time with her heart. Whatever the prince was feeling, she couldn't name it; it was too messy.

"Well," he finally said as they approached the emperor's office door, "here we are."

"Thank you, Prince Kaius."

He started to walk away but turned back toward her, thin lips pursing. "May I offer you a piece of advice for tonight, Astrea?"

No, thank you. She smiled and nodded, hoping she looked equal parts innocent and confused.

"You might look the part"—his eyes traveled up and down her body again—"but there's a reason you're my half brother's guest. Remember your place tonight."

As Kaius turned and walked away, Astrea sucked in a deep breath, then blew it out slowly. Kaius couldn't be counted on for much, but he was always an asshole.

Which also spoke to her next problem: the emperor. Kaius had delivered her to the lion's den, but he hadn't bothered to let his father know the task was complete. Did she knock? Wait for him to come out? Was Caliban going to appear? The hallway was empty.

After a few minutes passed with no activity, Astrea faced the door. She needed to get this over with. She knocked three times.

"Come in."

The gold door knob was cold under Astrea's hand as she turned it, opening the door just wide enough to fit through. She closed it behind her, focusing on her breathing as she finally turned around and approached the emperor's desk.

"It's good to see you again, Miss Sovna," Emperor Aelius said, smiling. The air around him remained light, unmarred by the annoyance and anger that had been there last time they'd spoken. "Please, sit."

Astrea gathered her skirts and sat down.

"All dressed up for our dinner tonight, I see," Emperor Aelius said as he leaned back in his chair. He wore an extravagant outfit of his own, a three-piece suit of gold brocade. A golden crown was nestled in his dark brown hair, something he hadn't worn in their past meetings. "Are you looking forward to it?"

She was actually dreading it, unsure how to handle herself in such a situation. She didn't dine with aristocrats. Eliana may have been a princess, but any meals they had together were private, comfortable.

"Yes, Your Imperial Majesty."

"And you are the guest of which of my children?"

"Prince Varojin invited me."

Emperor Auris nodded. "Has he been getting you into any trouble?"

"No, no trouble." She swallowed. "Was there anything . . . in particular you wanted to discuss with me this evening, Your Imperial Majesty? I'm afraid I didn't think to bring my notes with me."

"Straight to business. That's why I appreciate you, Miss Sovna. You don't beat around the bush, as they say."

She smiled, but it felt hollow.

"A little birdie told me you and my son have been trying to track down a Novarian manuscript." Emperor Aelius leaned back in his chair, so casual despite his literally golden appearance. "I'm so curious to learn what's in it."

How did Aelius know about Theo's book? Jin definitely hadn't told him. Astrea's hands began to sweat. What was she supposed to tell the emperor? She cursed herself for not thinking to ask one of her friends about what she should do in this situation. The longer he stared at her, the tighter her chest grew. *Why didn't you see this coming?*

A lump formed in her throat, but she couldn't cry, not right now. Sucking in a breath, Astrea shoved her emotions into a little corner of her mind, willing them to stay there until she was alone at the end of the night.

"Well, Your Imperial Majesty," she started, "about that . . ."

"You haven't found it?" he asked, one eyebrow arching.

"No," she said. The air around him crackled, almost electric. Was that her magic or his? The truth was the only option she saw—part of the truth, anyway. "We've been looking for it. But I found something else that may be a suitable alternative, at least until we can find the other one."

"I see. And what might that be?"

"It's another Novarian mythology book." The air around the emperor cooled. "I don't believe it's as old, but it covers many different myths and stories." She explained what she'd found in it, including some of the illustrations and the names of two myths she could remember.

"Interesting." Emperor Aelius smiled then, standing and walking to the front of his desk. He pushed back some of the knickknacks he had there, then leaned back on the surface, arms crossed loosely over his chest. "Do you think these stories will be of interest to the Novarian delegation in the autumn?"

". . . Your Imperial Majesty?" Was he really asking her opinion?

"Honestly, Astrea, it's a simple question," he snapped as he turned and picked up one of the objects. "Surely you can answer a simple question."

She opted for the truth again. "I don't know what they'd enjoy, Your Imperial Majesty."

He frowned, turning the item around in his palms. It was that strange egg she'd seen the last time she was here.

"I think they would enjoy it," he said after a moment. "Tell me, do you think we could incorporate some of these stories into the exhibit?"

"Of course." Despite the fact that this was supposed to be Jin's project, whatever the emperor wanted was the direction Astrea was going to take it. "Whatever you want to do, we can make it happen."

"Good." He smiled. "Perhaps you and my son can also visit the theater. I was thinking we'd hire some of the stage designers to create something for the space. Do make it a priority in the coming week."

"Of course, Your Imperial Majesty."

"And I'd still like you and Varojin to find that older manuscript. Make that a priority, too."

"Of course, Your Imperial Majesty," she said again.

"I won't keep you any longer. Enjoy your evening, and don't let my son forget to take you to the afterparty. That's where the fun truly begins."

Astrea hurried out as soon as she was dismissed, grateful to find the hallway empty. She didn't know how Emperor Aelius had heard about Theo's manuscript, but it didn't matter. He knew. Somehow, he knew.

As Astrea approached the main atrium, the world burst into life again, voices and music reaching her. It was like someone had turned the volume on a gramophone all the way up, too loud to be enjoyable.

The crowd was dressed in outfits of every color. Though she recognized a few faces in the crowd, there had to be at least three dozen people Astrea didn't know. Everyone seemed to be in good moods, at least.

She moved through the crowd in search of her friends, sidestepping someone who almost backed into her. A server walked by, his black and white suit a sharp contrast to the multitude of colors surrounding her. Astrea was nearing the edge of the gathering, but a soft hand grabbed her forearm.

"Az!" Eliana grinned at her. "I can't believe I haven't seen you all week."

"I've been busy," Astrea said, but there was no malice in Eliana's voice or aura. It was a simple observation. They hadn't seen each other since that day at the museum; Astrea had been running around Kalama with Jin, and Eliana had been in countless meetings.

"So I've heard," Eliana said as peach amusement danced around her.

"Are you good?" Astrea asked, lowering her voice. "Your note . . ."

"I'll be fine," Eliana said. "Things are better. Much better."

That was both as cryptic and as specific as Eliana could be given the people surrounding them. Her note had requested Astrea attend to 'keep her in check,' whatever that meant. But Eliana's emotions were steady, unlike the disaster that had been Solstice Night. Astrea nodded.

"Will you go find Jin?" Eliana asked. "He's missing out."

Astrea looked around. Sure enough, she spotted Cressida talking to a man with a very large mustache. She pretended to laugh as displeasure prickled Astrea's skin. Kaius was nowhere in sight, nor was Jin.

"Sure," Astrea said. "Is he upstairs?"

"Yes, he should be. Thank you!" Eliana called over her shoulder, already disappearing back into the crowd.

The walk upstairs and through the empty halls of the royal residence was blissfully quiet again. The bottom of Astrea's skirt rustled on the marble floors as she walked, the only sound aside from the faint music downstairs. She didn't even see any of the palace staff, an odd but welcome respite. She hadn't realized the party would be so large.

Astrea paused outside of Jin's door, hand raised to knock. The door opened before she had a chance, and she found herself staring up into golden eyes.

"Oh." Jin smiled. "I thought I heard something. I thought it was going to be Ellie."

"Just me," Astrea said.

"Even better." Jin stepped to one side of the door, motioning for her to enter. "Come in. I'm almost ready."

Astrea moved past him, hyperaware of her movements and the way her cheeks burned. "May I sit down?" she asked as she followed him into his living area.

"Why are you asking permission?" He chuckled. "Please, sit. Relax."

She plopped down onto his settee, looking up when Jin offered her a glass of water.

"I just spoke to your father." The words came out of her mouth before she even knew what she was saying. "And your brother."

Jin sighed as he walked around the little sofa toward the large, gilded mirror leaning against the far wall. "I hope Kaius didn't bother you too much."

"No, just bothered me enough."

"What did he say?" Jin's voice had gone cold, sharp.

Hesitating, Astrea turned and said, "He warned me not to forget who I really am tonight and not to forget which brother I'm attending with."

"Fuck." Jin's nostrils flared, the muscle in his jaw tightening. "He's lucky I don't find him right now."

Astrea suppressed a shiver and shrugged. Kaius was always an ass.

"What did my father want?" Jin asked as he fiddled with the cuffs of his deep blue shirt. On top of that, he wore a black waistcoat that matched his fitted black trousers. A black suit jacket with silver embroidery was slung over his nearby desk chair.

"He wanted an update," she said. "He knows about Theo's manuscript."

Jin's eyebrows rose in his reflection. "You told him?"

"No, he just knows about it. I don't know how."

Jin sighed. "Wonderful."

"I told him about the book Felix found, and now your father seems keen on focusing solely on the mythology aspect. Oh, and he wants us to go to the theater."

"The theater?"

"To hire the set designers. Apparently, he wants them to decorate the place." As Astrea said it, Jin's eyebrows furrowed. "He wants us to do that next week," she continued. "And he wants us to find Theo's manuscript. He wants it done as soon as possible."

"Did you tell him Mattina stole the book?"

"No."

"Probably for the best," Jin admitted with a sigh, meeting her gaze in the mirror as he fastened a gold chain around his neck. "Is he angry with you?"

"Yes and no." She finally took a sip of the water, steadying herself as she focused on its weight in her hands. "He's very hard to read. He's so hot and cold."

"He's been that way my entire life." Jin finally moved from the mirror, disappearing into his walk-in closet before coming back out. He had something in his hand, another necklace. "We're going to break into his office later."

Astrea nearly choked on her water. She coughed once, then again. "I'm sorry, we're what?"

"We're breaking into his office tonight. I already told Ellie, and she's going to keep everyone busy later, but I'm going to need your help."

"You want my help . . . breaking into your father's office?" Astrea couldn't believe the words coming out of her mouth. This night was not going according to plan, not at all. "You want me to break into the most powerful man in the empire's office? The most powerful man on the continent?"

"Yes," Jin said. "And if anyone finds us, it will all fall back on me."

Astrea stood and turned to look at him. "You cannot be serious."

"Something's going on with my father, Astrea. I've been trying to get information from Eliana and the council, but they don't seem to have any idea what he's doing in the Ring of Fire, why he's pulling money from his own war, or what he wants with this meteorite Saros found, or even why he's become obsessed with mythology."

"But—"

"*And*," Jin continued, "if we can get into his office while everyone is entertained, we might be able to finally find the information we need."

"Why do you need my help?" she asked.

"Because you can tell far better than I can if someone is lurking around or not."

"But you're a soldier," she protested. "Don't they teach you how to do that in training?"

"They do, but I'm not a Lightbringer."

Astrea twisted her hands together. Breaking into the emperor's office was a big request. It was a ridiculous plan, a massive risk. But Jin was right. Something was going on, and they needed real answers. Maybe this was how they got them.

"Fine," she said. "But I don't like it."

Jin smiled. "Noted." Then his tone softened as he asked, "Will you please come here?"

Astrea eyed Jin even as she walked toward him. "Why?"

"Because," he said, holding up the silver necklace dangling from his fingers, "I want to give you something."

Her stomach flipped, but Astrea met Jin in front of the mirror. "What for?"

"You ask too many questions sometimes. Turn around."

She turned.

Astrea watched in the mirror as Jin laid her hair over one of her shoulders. Then he slipped the necklace around her neck, his fingers brushing her collarbone as he brought the clasp around to secure it. Astrea touched the delicate sapphire hanging from the chain.

"What is this?" she asked. But their reflections in the mirror explained everything.

Her black and silver dress. Jin's black and silver suit jacket. His blue shirt. Her necklace.

"If I'm taking you as my guest tonight," Jin explained from behind her, his body so close she could feel the warmth radiating off him, "we may as well look the part."

"Ellie's the one who told me to wear this dress."

"And she's also the one who told me to wear this suit. I just thought this would be the finishing touch."

Astrea stared at Jin in the mirror again, trying to take in the image. It still felt like they were teenagers sometimes, but it was clear that wasn't the case. Jin's taller, harder body. Her softer one that had filled out over the years. They really were grown, really were dressed up to go to some ridiculous party. How had they come from not speaking in years to this moment?

"We may as well look the part." Was that what this was, then? A part? Another role to play, just like what happened near Mattina's townhouse? She'd known attending as Jin's official guest would come with whispers among the other attendees, but this was . . . this was different. Astrea wasn't sure she could do it. She wasn't sure she could really help Jin break into his father's office, either, but she had to try.

"Well," she whispered, "it's a beautiful necklace."

Jin was silent for a moment as he watched her in the mirror, but after a few heartbeats, his lips quirked up in a smile. "Are you ready?"

"I'm ready."

Jin slipped his suit jacket from the back of the chair, shrugged it on, then offered Astrea his arm. "Shall we?"

CHAPTER 32

Walking into a party full of courtiers on Jin's arm was not Astrea's idea of a good time. As they descended the grand staircase that led to the main hall, a hush fell over the space. At least a dozen more people had joined the mingling crowd in the time Astrea had been gone, and now, they all watched as Jin and Astrea made their way down the last few stairs.

This was going to give them something to gossip about for *weeks.* The often-absent Prince Varojin returning to court with a woman on his arm. And the Stargazer's niece, of all people. Saros was respected enough at court, but Astrea had no rank here. She hadn't considered the optics of the situation. She'd never had to in the past.

"This was a bad idea," Astrea whispered, but she didn't drop her death grip on Jin's forearm. He placed his hand on top of hers, warm and steady.

"I thought they'd all be on their way to the dining room." Jin's words were barely audible, even to her.

"There you are!" Eliana exclaimed as she met them at the bottom of the staircase. With her word—and apparent acceptance of the sight—the crowd all turned back to their conversations. "We're just waiting on Father now."

"Any sign of him?" Jin asked.

"None." Eliana smiled, but anxiety rolled off her. She looped her arm through Astrea's free one and started pulling her and Jin toward the crowd. "Nice entrance. Dramatic much?"

"I learned it from you, Ellie," Jin quipped.

Eliana leaned toward them. "Just try to keep people talking for now, alright? They're getting a bit antsy." And with that, Eliana stepped away from Astrea to speak with an elderly gentleman dressed in burgundy.

"Right." Surveying the crowd around them, Jin rolled his shoulders. "Keep people talking. My favorite."

"You're good enough at it," Astrea said, offering a small smile at a middle-aged woman who passed them, eyebrows tilted up in curiosity.

"Just because I'm good at it doesn't mean I enjoy it." Jin's muscles flexed under Astrea's hand, then he whispered, "Oh, here we go."

"Prince Varojin!" a husky voice exclaimed. A plump, pale older woman emerged from the crowd, both gloved arms lifted into the air. The cocktail in her hand sloshed slightly as she brought her arms back down. "Now *that* was an entrance. Haven't seen the crowd quiet like that at one of these parties in *years*!"

"Madam Larousse," Jin said, that honeyed voice of his back. "Why am I not surprised to see you tonight?"

She laughed, then brought her glass to her pink-painted lips. "I simply can't stay away." Lowering her voice, she added, "You know how these things are." Madam Larousse fixed her gray eyes on Astrea. "You two make quite the pair. You're the Stargazer's girl, right?"

"Saros is my uncle, madam," Astrea said.

"Right . . ."

"Astrea," she said. "Astrea Sovna."

Madam Larousse extended a gloved hand, and Astrea shook it. "Madam Larousse. My husband is a senator." She pulled her hand away and switched her cocktail to it, green curiosity bubbling around her perfectly styled salt-and-pepper hair. "Prince Varojin, I'm surprised to see you here at all tonight, let alone with such a lovely girl on your arm. Last time you were at one of these parties, what . . . three years ago? Four? You were alone."

"You know as well as anyone that I serve at my father's pleasure, madam." Jin smiled, a hint of annoyance escaping his wall. "If he wants me on the front, that's where I go. If he wants me back here, at home, then I return home."

Before Madam Larousse could reply, the wide double doors behind them opened with a groan. Astrea turned first, Jin forced to follow her movement thanks to their still-looped arms. Caliban strode into the atrium, his white hair blinding under the chandeliers.

"His Imperial Majesty Emperor Aelius Auris is ready to receive you. You may enter the throne room."

A few whispers of confusion danced over Astrea's exposed arms, including from Jin. The room was mostly filled with a mix of excitement and heady anticipation, though. When Astrea glanced back over her shoulder, Madam Larousse was disappearing back into the crowd.

"What's going on?" Astrea whispered.

Jin frowned. "He wasn't supposed to do this tonight."

Eliana emerged from the crowd, her crimson gown a stark contrast to Cressida's chic violet one. Astrea hadn't noticed before, but a petite gold tiara encrusted with diamonds and rubies spiked up from Eliana's hair. The shape reminded Astrea of the rising sun.

"Did you know he was going to—" Eliana started, but Jin shook his head.

"No, I didn't."

Pursing her lips, Eliana motioned for the doors behind Jin. "Well, let's go. I can't believe he didn't tell us."

Cressida shot Astrea a look, but she just shrugged. Astrea had thought they were going to dinner. Dinner, then the afterparty. But apparently, the emperor had other plans. The courtiers had already started filing through the throne room doors, and Jin's muscles flexed under Astrea's hand again as he guided her inside.

She'd only been in the emperor's throne room a handful of times in all her years living at the palace compound, and it took Astrea's breath away every time. Gleaming white stone walls and floors, a line of arched windows on the back wall, thick columns lining the center aisle, an array of floral arrangements and tapestries, and a dais at the far end of the room that was home to not one but several thrones tonight. Emperor Aelius was already seated on the throne in the middle, the largest one by far. Sitting there in his golden suit, he seemed more like a painting than a man. To his right was Kaius. There was still one empty chair to the emperor's left.

"Why are we here?" Astrea whispered as Jin pulled her off to one side of the room. A throng of nobles passed them, their eagerness suffocating her. "Are you alright?"

"I just hate these kinds of nights." Jin's lips pressed together as he watched the crowd moving in behind her, then he looked at the dais.

Astrea followed his gaze only to find Kaius watching them. Now he, too, wore a crown, one much smaller than his father's. "Why is he looking at us like that?"

"Because he's a fucking busybody." Jin flashed a too-smooth smile down at her. "Hopefully this doesn't take too long."

"What—" Astrea started, but Jin was already guiding her farther into the throne room, past the crowd of guests toward where Cressida stood near the front. *Just great.*

Eliana climbed the dais, taking the empty seat to the left of her father. Eliana, Kaius, Emperor Aelius—with dawning horror, Astrea realized there wasn't space up there for Jin. Nor was there room for Apelo or his wife, Thana—not that they were in attendance. But purposefully excluding Jin while he was home? While all of the party guests knew he was home? That was quite the message to send.

"Jin," she whispered.

He smiled down at her, but it was tight. "It's alright."

It wasn't alright. Even if Jin didn't like court life and didn't live in Kalama, it was cruel of his father.

"Welcome!" Emperor Aelius called over the noise, and the crowd silenced. "Before we enjoy our meal and our evening, it is time to continue a tradition once established by the Auris dynasty many, many generations ago."

"This ought to be good," Cressida whispered as she leaned toward Astrea.

Though she had relaxed into her throne, Eliana radiated rusty annoyance. Kaius's emotions were steady and light, a satisfied smile on his face as he looked toward their father. And next to Astrea, Jin had gone entirely still.

"When my forebears first founded the Helosian Empire, they agreed the countries they absorbed could retain certain control over their lands in exchange for tribute. And though our system has since been refined, and though we do not usually use such dinners for this purpose, not accepting tribute from you tonight would be a disservice to Helosia's long-held values of tradition, respect, and loyalty."

Tribute? This was about tribute?

Helosian states and smaller territories paid tribute to the imperial government—to the emperor and his family—several times a year. Payments ranged from actual lire to artwork to public projects. It didn't really matter *what* was paid as long as it held a certain monetary value. On top of that, states and territories still had to pay taxes.

Eliana had criticized the practice for years in private, saying it was pointless and only about upholding status and image. Astrea had never actually seen tribute be paid. She'd thought it was just something regional leaders would send to the palace rather than such a . . . show.

At least that explained why both Jin and Eliana appeared uncomfortable. But why hadn't their father told them about this? And why hadn't he invited them to be in the throne room ahead of the guests?

"When your name is called, step forward and present your gift," Aelius called over the crowd.

Count Lorenzi, a tall, fair-skinned man with a receding hairline, was up first, though Astrea was surprised to see the man there despite his apparent rebel sympathies. Just the week before, Eliana had been sent to speak with him about such rumors. He presented the emperor with a small trunk full of gold coins first, then turned to Eliana.

"Your Imperial Highness," he said, bowing low to her. "Though my wife could not make it tonight, she wanted me to present you with an additional gift."

A servant standing to the count's left stepped forward and opened a box. Astrea couldn't see what it was, but lavender surprise bubbled around Eliana.

"Jewels from her collection to add to the dynasty's," Count Lorenzi said.

More reactions from the crowd pushed in against Astrea—surprise, delight, irritation, anger. She pulled magic in as close to her body as she could, but even that didn't spare her. She nearly reached for Cressida's hand, a reflex when her magic overwhelmed her, but stopped herself. That might seem strange if she was supposed to be playing the role of Jin's guest. Instead, Astrea clasped her hands tightly in front of herself.

Though Eliana's smiled was relaxed, orange anxiety sparked once around her. "Thank you, Count Lorenzi. Please pass my thanks on to your wife. This won't be forgotten."

No, it certainly won't be. Kaius stared daggers at the man, though Emperor Aelius didn't seem particularly bothered. Was it wise for Eliana to accept the gift considering the rumors about Lorenzi and the ones that the rebels supported her?

Next was Lady Hale, a timid woman with warm ocher skin and the softest voice Astrea had ever heard. She presented an enormous painting in a gold frame, though what the art was, Astrea couldn't see. The palace staff didn't even turn it around to show the crowd as they carried it out of a side door.

More names were called. Count Magjan, a noble who ruled over a small territory near the Zaikudi border, offered a new piazza in his city that would be named after Emperor Aelius, complete with a statue of the emperor. He also gifted a sword to Kaius. Duke Diallo was there, too, and paid in not just a chest full of lire but a donation of food and supplies to the armies on the Corsycan front lines. Astrea didn't see his son, the one who had been speaking to Eliana at the Whiskey Dream, anywhere in the crowd.

Some, like Lorenzi and Magjan, gave gifts to either Eliana or Kaius, while others stayed focused on the emperor. Though Astrea didn't know much about the aristocrats and politicians in attendance, it was clear the guests were split on which sibling they supported.

The event dragged on until the only people who hadn't been called were the handful of senators in attendance as well as Cressida and Astrea.

And the entire time, Kaius's attention kept drawing back to Astrea. She tried not to look at Kaius, but something about the way he watched her was unsettling.

When the last gift was passed on to palace staff to be removed from the throne room, Emperor Aelius stood and smiled at the crowd. "We thank you for your tribute," he said. "Now it is my turn to thank you for your continued loyalty. Let the evening begin."

Emperor Aelius turned first toward his children, that golden suit of his catching the light from the ornate chandeliers hanging overhead. Kaius bowed while Eliana curtsied. The emperor didn't even glance in Jin's direction.

Without another word, Emperor Aelius descended from the dais and strode back up the center aisle. Everyone in the crowd hurried to pay their respects, and Astrea dipped into the quickest curtsy she could manage as Emperor Aelius brushed past. Kaius followed behind, then Eliana moved into place, Cressida by her side.

Jin offered Astrea his arm again. "You ready?"

"Absolutely not," Astrea whispered, linking her arm with his. More curiosity and disgust and frustration pushed in against her, but Astrea tried to block it out.

The politics were concerning, but she wasn't here for that tonight. She and Jin had a mission of their own, and if they were going to succeed, she'd need to stay focused.

Dinner was no less of a show than the tribute payments had been. As soon as they'd entered the enormous dining room, staff had guided everyone to their seats at the main dining table, which was large enough to seat nearly two dozen. The imperial siblings were seated there, of course, though Jin and Astrea were seated at the far end of the table from the emperor. Anyone not lucky enough to earn a spot there was shown to one of several smaller tables placed in the room. Bottles and bottles of wine were served, followed by multiple courses of rich food.

Astrea hadn't had much of a stomach for any of it, but she'd forced herself to eat as much as she could and drink two glasses of wine in between listening to innocuous conversations happening around her. Jin had chimed in when asked questions by the other guests, but he'd spent a good deal of the dinner trying to make Astrea laugh. Now, the palace staff were setting dessert out in front of the guests, miniature cakes made with Taipoli rum and topped with tropical fruit and powdered sugar.

"So," Jin murmured as he leaned toward her, "is this what you imagined it would be?"

Well aware of the partygoers' curiosity pressing in around her, Astrea smiled up at Jin. "Dessert? Well, I'd been hoping it would be chocolate—"

"No." He chuckled, bumping his knee into hers under the table. Her stomach flipped. "I meant the party."

Astrea bit her lower lip, then shrugged and picked up her fork. "It's a bit boring, honestly." She supposed if they didn't have half a dozen courtiers trying to listen in on their conversation, this might be a little more fun. "Now I understand why you used to barge into the observatory to complain about them."

That made him laugh again, genuine amusement reaching out to her. She took a bite of cake, and Astrea swore he watched her mouth as she pulled her fork away.

"I don't think I *barged*—"

"Oh, you definitely did." Astrea took another bite of her cake, savoring the sweet fruit and sugar. "Though I didn't mind as long as you brought those cookies. What were they?"

"Those cookies . . ." Jin's voice trailed off, and he turned back to his dessert. "The ones with the caramel were your favorite."

"And the ones with the white chocolate were yours."

Several moments passed, and Jin still hadn't said anything. If anyone was listening to the conversation, they didn't show it. Instead, Astrea focused her attention on Jin. He looked sad as he murmured, "You remembered that?"

"Of course." Astrea swallowed hard. "Of course I did." She'd remembered all the little details: his favorite cookie, how he took his coffee, his favorite spots in the gardens. She'd never been able to forget, even as much as she'd wanted to at one point. Now, Astrea was glad she hadn't.

As Jin opened his mouth to reply, the emperor stood and began speaking. He was saying something about enjoying the afterparty. The excitement flooding the room made it hard for Astrea to concentrate on the emperor's exact words.

Two guards opened up a set of wide double doors into an adjoining ballroom, and another pair of guards opened doors onto a long veranda that led to the gardens.

"Come on," Jin said, offering her his arm again. "I could use some fresh air."

As Astrea stood and took Jin's arm, she looked over her shoulder for Eliana and Cressida. They were absorbed in their own conversations; Eliana's annoyance clung to her like a wet blanket as Kaius chuckled. Cressida placed a hand on her arm.

"Where's your father going?" Astrea asked, watching as Emperor Aelius left the dining room with Caliban.

"He always retires to his rooms after these things."

Jin led her away from the table toward the veranda doors. When they stepped into the balmy night air, Jin pulled her toward the darkest corner. He angled his body so that it blocked Astrea from anyone who might be exiting the palace behind them, and by the sound of it, several couples had also gone outside for fresh air.

"So, what do we do now?" Astrea whispered. Talking about the old days at dinner was one thing, but they needed to focus. They were here with a mission: break into the emperor's office. Astrea had no idea how they were going to sneak away to do so, though. She really hoped Jin had a plan. "How long should we—"

"A while," Jin said, voice so low she almost didn't hear him. "Give him time to get settled in upstairs and for us to make it believable."

A raucous laugh further out in the gardens made Astrea turn, but whoever it was, they weren't close enough to hear their conversation. "Make what believable?"

He sighed and took her hands in his, the faintest dusting of blue regret pulsing around him. Jin's mask slipped back into place as he murmured, "Make leaving together believable."

"Oh." Her heart sped up as she repeated, "Oh."

"I assumed you understood—"

"I get it."

And she did. The coordinating outfits, the grand entrance, being invited specifically as his guest—it all made sense. The looks people gave them at dinner suggested they were already believing the ruse. Besides, Astrea wasn't a prude, nor were Kalamians. But being *such* gossip mill fodder was . . . well, she didn't love the idea of Saros potentially hearing those rumors.

Still, untangling the web around them seemed more significant than her feelings on court gossip.

"I don't want to make you uncomfortable—" Jin started again, but she cut him off.

"It's not uncomfortable," she said, heat crawling up the back of her neck. "We need answers, right? We'll do what we have to."

Jin's face was unreadable in the darkness. "Right. Then . . . I suppose we should go back inside."

Without another word, Astrea fell into step beside Jin, her arm looped through his again. He pulled her close as they moved into the ballroom. Though large, it was one of the smaller ballrooms of the palace, and the staff had somehow made the setup seem cozy. Multiple seating areas, all capable of holding just a handful of people, were already filling up. Refreshment and dessert tables lined one wall, and Astrea didn't miss the couples moving off to solo settees overlooking the gardens.

"Where do we start?" Astrea whispered.

"Wherever you want." That honeyed voice of his was back, his entire body relaxed as they moved to the middle of the room. "There's just one rule."

"And what's that?"

"We let people come to us. When you're a member of the Auris family or with a member of the Auris family, you don't seek others out. Even the bastard prince is worth finding on a night like this."

There he went again, calling himself a bastard. "Jin—" she started, but he cut her off.

"Wine first? A different dessert? We can find you that chocolate." He motioned to the room with his free hand. "I think Lord Ruthien is bringing out the blue lotus soon."

Astrea sighed. "This is no better than the Whiskey Dream."

He chuckled, that same throaty, deep sound she was beginning to recognize. It was a very specific, very practiced laugh. "I know. How about I just go get us some wine?"

She didn't want to drink more, but at least it would give her something to hold besides Jin's arm. "Sure."

"I'll be right back."

Jin started toward the refreshment table on the far side of the room, the hand that had been holding hers flexing once as he strode away. Astrea swallowed. Hadn't pretending to be here together been his idea?

Turning in a circle and shoving down whatever the knot was in her belly, Astrea searched the room for Eliana and Cressida. They were on the opposite side of the room, speaking with a woman wearing an old-fashioned gown with a large bustle. The style hadn't been popular in Kalama for decades and looked particularly out of place next to the sleek, slinky dresses Cressida and Eliana wore.

She considered going to join them, but she was supposed to be there as Jin's date. Leaning on Eliana and Cressida wouldn't give that impression. Sighing, Astrea turned toward one of the sitting areas in clear view of the whole room. The back of the sofa faced the windows, and two armchairs and a few floor pillows were scattered around. A group of palace staff started setting up a table a couple dozen feet away, and a nobleman dressed in a persimmon-colored suit shuffled cards in his hand as he oversaw their work. She could at least sit while she waited for Jin to return.

Halfway to that part of the ballroom, Astrea suddenly found herself staring up into golden eyes. But they weren't Jin's, nor were they Eliana's. Prince Kaius peered down at her, a too-nice smile spreading across his face.

"Enjoying the party?" Kaius asked.

"It's lovely, Your Imperial Highness," Astrea said. "The dinner was especially good."

Kaius's expression was unreadable for a moment before he smiled again. "Where's my brother? Abandoned you already?"

Astrea glanced in the direction Jin had stalked off earlier, finally finding his tall form among the crowd. There, near the dessert tables, he was speaking with a tall man in a green suit.

"He's just getting us something to drink."

"Hm." Kaius followed Astrea's gaze for half a heartbeat, then turned back to her. "Varojin hasn't been getting you into any trouble, has he?"

"Trouble?" Though dark gray hate pulsed around the man Jin was talking to, Astrea forced herself to look at Kaius again. The emperor had asked her that same question earlier in the night. "What trouble could Jin possibly get me into?"

Kaius shrugged, the rich fabric of his suit barely wrinkling with the movement. "Jin always was one for finding trouble. He's been dragging you around Kalama, hasn't he?"

"We've been working together on your father's project," Astrea said. Had Kaius been following them? Did he know something? His emotions remained steady, calm. Curious, maybe, but with so much going on around them, it was hard for Astrea to focus.

"And how has that been?" Kaius asked. There it was, a hint of . . . jealousy? That didn't seem right. "I didn't think you two were exactly friends anymore."

"What makes you say that?" Astrea heard herself ask over the pounding of her heart. Did everyone know Jin had abandoned her?

He sniffed. "Just my impression."

"Well, impressions can be wrong, Your Imperial Highness. Jin always was my favorite Auris sibling. Enjoy your evening."

She pushed past Kaius, and just in time. Jin was headed her way, his jaw tight. Astrea made her way right to him, plastering on the biggest smile she could muster.

"Kaius has been watching us," she whispered once Jin was close enough to hear. "I think he still is."

Jin immediately wrapped an arm around her waist and tugged her closer. She held back a squeak and instead tilted her head up toward him.

"Sorry that took so long, darling," he said, voice loud enough that anyone nearby would definitely hear. Her entire body heated with the false pet name. "I was trying to find your favorite raspberry wine, but someone has to go fetch it."

A nearby shout made Astrea jump, drunken . . . something sliding over her magic. She risked a look to her right and was rewarded with the sight of an older gentleman kissing a much younger woman on the mouth. Astrea's nose wrinkled, but both guests pulled away from each other and laughed.

"Raspberry," Astrea mused. "You remembered."

"How could I ever forget?"

It wasn't actually her favorite—peach was—but Jin wouldn't know that. They'd never drank together. It didn't matter, though. They angled toward Kaius just in time to see him roll his eyes and head the other way.

Astrea steered Jin toward the sitting area she'd wanted to go to in the first place. He dropped onto the settee first, and when she hesitated, he offered her his hand.

This was it. Believable. They had to sell it to everyone in this room. Astrea was hopeful they'd at least sold it to Kaius.

Astrea gathered her skirts, then sat. Believable. She moved closer to Jin, and his arm circled her shoulders, pulling her into his side. Despite his muscular body, leaning against Jin was comfortable. Familiar, almost. He used to pull her in like that for hugs all the time when they were younger.

"Who was that man who was speaking with you?" Astrea asked after a moment. "He didn't seem to like you."

"Yes, well, Lord Hale has never liked me."

"Why not?"

"Astrea." She tilted her head up to look at him. "Surely you've noticed the way some of the groups in this court treat me," he said. "The problem child, the bastard, the son of the mistress. They see me as a threat to my father's 'true' line regardless of where they fall on the heir issue."

Astrea hadn't noticed until tonight. But she'd also never seen Jin interact with the court as an adult, and Astrea doubted she would've ever picked up such cues as a child. Would people even have made such passes at Jin when he was so young?

"You've been gone," she said, hating how small she sounded. "I haven't exactly seen you speaking with the aristocracy, Jin."

A waiter approached them, lowering a golden tray with two wine glasses situated in the middle. Jin took one and handed it to Astrea, then took the other, and the woman disappeared back into the growing crowd.

Astrea took a sip of the heavy, sweet raspberry wine Jin had promised as her gut twisted. His fingers brushed the top of Astrea's arm, tracing the same path up and down. His touch was so light it almost tickled. It was a small thing, but it helped Astrea relax.

"I've been home for two weeks and already I'm sick of their bullshit." He sighed and sank deeper into the sofa, his fingers continuing to draw that line on Astrea's arm. "I'm sorry it has to be like this. I'm sorry for a lot of things."

"We can't have that conversation right now." Getting teary-eyed over the past wouldn't make anyone believe . . . this.

"You're right." Sighing again, Jin took Astrea's half-empty wine glass from her and set it on the floor. "Sorry, you're right. We need to focus."

"Don't apologize. I'm the one avoiding it."

If they were supposed to keep working together, they needed to have that conversation. When Jin had first arrived in Kalama, Astrea had been sure it would be simple: he would stay until the autumn equinox, then he would be gone, and she wouldn't have to see him again.

But Astrea didn't want that. She didn't want things to go back to the way they were. She wanted her friend back, whatever that looked like considering the circumstances. Would he still have to go back to the front when this was all over? Would she possibly leave Kalama and start over somewhere else? Then what?

Astrea leaned into Jin, tucking herself further under his arm and pressing the side of her body against his. He settled in next to her, pulling her close.

Good, Astrea thought. The more convincing they were, the sooner they could leave, and the sooner they could leave, the sooner she could go home and take off this dress. It suddenly felt too tight, the room too loud, everyone's inebriated emotions too big. She just needed to keep pretending for a little longer.

CHAPTER 33

Being curled up against Jin on that small sofa was almost comfortable. Could've been comfortable had they not been surrounded by drunken aristocrats and politicians, all of them shouting about card games and imperial policy.

After the first hour, the steady stream of visitors to Jin and Astrea's little corner of the party had slowed. Senators' spouses making the rounds for gossip—including Madam Larousse again—nobles interested in whatever shred of influence Jin might hold in court, a few young men looking for Eliana—they'd talked to all sorts. Their emotions had been all over the place, ranging from enthusiasm to excitement to curiosity and embarrassment. There was even more of that gray hate on occasion, but that, at least, seemed rare.

Astrea had even gotten used to the foreign coziness of Jin's heart beating steadily under her ear. Surely they were being convincing, right? She settled further against him, his warm, steady presence an anchor amid the chaos of the night.

The party was in full swing now. The band had finally set up, and the slow melody of their current song shifted to something faster. Someone started clapping with the beat. A couple got up to dance, then two more couples joined. The people playing cards were shouting about something, but judging by the strained excitement in the air, it was all in good fun. Even Eliana and Cressida were laughing and talking among some of the other guests a few dozen feet away. Kaius, thankfully, was nowhere to be found.

"You good?" Jin whispered.

Astrea glanced up at him. They'd somehow tangled their bodies together in the last hour, as much as they could with Astrea's full skirts getting in the way. Jin's face was impossibly close now, and Astrea searched it, though she wasn't sure what she was hoping to find.

"The crowd is a lot," she finally said, hoping he understood the hidden meaning there. She was trying to keep her magic pulled in as close as she could, but it seemed to be slipping further and further out of her control.

"I can only imagine."

Astrea stared down at his free hand, tracing the shapes of his simple gold rings with her eyes. "Can I tell you something?"

"You can tell me anything."

She smiled up at him as she said, "Peach wine is actually my favorite."

Jin's eyebrows furrowed, then he laughed. It was his real laugh, almost disarming after a night of so much being done just for show. "Peach," he finally said. "Not raspberry. I'll remember that."

"I just wanted to set the record straight."

He reached out with his free hand, brushing a few hairs from her face. The tips of his fingers whispered over her skin, first tracing over her cheek and then down her jaw. Jin lingered there for a moment before pulling his hand away.

Astrea's heart pounded, almost mimicking the beat of the band's song. She swallowed. *Believable.* That was all this was.

"Do you remember on Solstice Night," Jin murmured, "when I offered to tell you a secret?"

When Jin had found Astrea alone in the park that night, she'd confided in him about Saros not being well. It was all she'd felt she could tell him when he didn't know about her magic. When she still wasn't quite sure if he was who she remembered from all those years before.

"Yes," she whispered. "Ellie interrupted us."

"Do you want me to tell you now?"

Earlier in the week, Astrea had been happy to forget all about that supposed secret with so much else going on. It was just one more thing for her overwhelmed mind to contend with.

"Yes," she whispered again. Astrea wanted to know. Desperately.

"I—" he started, but a high, crisp voice cut him off.

"Prince Varojin!"

Disappointment flooded Astrea as, once again, they were interrupted. Would she ever get to know that secret?

Jin, however, barely moved as that sharp voice called out his name again. A pale blonde woman around their age floated their way, her updo still perfect despite the hours it had been since the night had started. Her gown, a pink, low-cut thing, glittered as she stopped in front of them.

"I didn't realize you were still in town until I saw you in the throne room," the woman said. "You look great tonight."

Astrea stiffened, but Jin's free hand slid toward her knee, squeezing once. What did that mean?

"Still here, Lady Hiflow," Jin said. "Enjoying the party?"

"Oh, yes." Lady Hiflow smiled, revealing perfectly straight, perfectly white teeth. "You know," she practically purred, "it's almost as fun as our night at the Whiskey Dream."

Jealousy surged through Astrea, but Jin chuckled that very specific chuckle of his. The fingers that had been trailing her arm found their way to Astrea's hair, and Jin twirled a few strands around. She forced herself to relax.

"Really?" he asked. "Poor comparison if you ask me."

"Varojin?" Lady Hiflow's smile faltered, one of her hands resting at the base of her throat while the other crossed over her chest. A ring with a large stone winked on her left ring finger. On her right was a coordinating silver band. Who was she married to? "I thought we had quite the connection that night."

Astrea's heart sank, but what for? *Don't be foolish.* Who Jin spent his time with—and how he spent it with them—wasn't her business. They'd just become friends again.

"Connection . . ." Jin mused. "I watched you play a single round of cards, and then you chased after me when I left to find my friend." As Jin said it, his fingers continued playing with the ends of Astrea's hair. She didn't dare breathe as Lady Hiflow glared at her. "Doesn't sound like much of a connection to me. Kaius might be up for a party, though. Perhaps you should check in with him instead."

Lady Hiflow's jaw tightened. "Perhaps I will." She stormed off, heeled shoes clicking on the floor as she melted back into the crowd. Madam Larousse—who'd been hovering nearby all night—glanced at Jin and Astrea for a few moments, then went back to her conversation with Lord Ruthien, the man largely responsible for the blue lotus smoke drifting in the air.

"What was that?" Astrea asked, smiling as Madam Larousse and Lord Ruthien looked their way again. How did Eliana and Jin do this, forcing themselves to act a certain way around these people? How had Eliana, especially, managed to do this for so many years?

"Lady Ilara Hiflow," Jin muttered. He stopped playing with Astrea's hair, instead shifting so their bodies were even closer. "She's been trying to get into my bed for, skies, the last nine years? It started before I left Kalama and has continued any time she's found me on the rare occasion I'm home."

Astrea swallowed that unwelcome jealousy again. "And you're not interested?" she heard herself ask.

"No."

"Is it because she's married?"

"What?" Jin's wall slipped for just a moment as he peered down at her. Confusion, surprise, worry. But then the emotions disappeared again, there one heartbeat and gone the next. "No. I mean, I wouldn't be regardless. Never have been. But it seems she can't take a fucking hint even after all this time."

"Oh." She nodded once. "Good."

And there it was again, the brief slip in his wall. Minty relief coated her tongue.

As Astrea breathed in deeply, she realized just how heavy the scent of blue lotus was. She looked down to where her leg was twined with Jin's. The hand that wasn't playing with her hair or brushing her arm was dangerously close to her thigh. Astrea took a shallow breath, then grabbed his hand.

"I need some fresh air," she whispered.

He nodded. "I think I do too, actually."

Jin stood first, then helped Astrea to her feet. Curiosity spiked around the card table as they passed it, but Astrea didn't look back. She focused on the door to the veranda, on the fresh air blowing into the room. She focused on the way Jin's hand tightened around hers, even when they were alone outside.

"I didn't expect Ruthien to keep at it so incessantly," Jin muttered. He finally dropped Astrea's hand, but he stayed close to her as she walked toward the veranda's thick stone railing.

Astrea breathed deep, letting the fresh air soak into the very core of her bones. She hadn't realized while sitting down, but as she looked back, the haze of smoke in the ballroom was obvious. "I'm already starting to feel better." Simply being around blue lotus smoke wasn't enough to cause a strong high, but it could still make your head swim.

"Are you enjoying the party?" Jin asked.

"Enjoy might be a strong word."

He laughed. "It's not all bad."

Astrea couldn't believe she was even going to think it, but no, the night wasn't *all* bad. Despite how overwhelming it was to be in that room, having Jin next to her was . . . nice. "Maybe not."

They had to have been at the afterparty for close to an hour and a half by now. Astrea stared up at the stars, picking out the handful of constellations she could see without the palace's looming structure blocking some of the sky. The Queen, the Serpent, the Dove.

Astrea turned to Jin. He was watching her, and her entire body heated. This wasn't the way Kaius had sized her up earlier, nor was it the way the courtiers had watched them walk down the staircase together. If she didn't know better, it was almost . . . intimate. Appreciative.

Believable.

"Do you think we can get out of here now?" she asked.

"I thought you'd never ask."

The playfulness in his voice made Astrea roll her eyes. Jin grabbed her hand again, this time threading his fingers through hers. She hated the way her stomach curled so pleasantly with his touch. Maybe her head hadn't cleared from the blue lotus yet after all.

"Straight through the party would be best," Jin said. "Let them see us leave."

"Whatever we need to do."

It wasn't just the people at the card table who watched as they passed back through the ballroom. Eliana and Cressida were at a nearby seating area, and Astrea dared a look in their direction. The courtiers with them were all curious, but Eliana smiled, teal approval exploding around her.

Cressida simply nodded; did she know where they were going? Astrea assumed Eliana had filled her in about the plan to break into the emperor's office.

Saros wouldn't love the rumors if he heard them, but it would be worth it if they figured out what the emperor knew. It would be worth it if they found even a single answer to their many questions.

"I think it's time we start a new game!" Eliana called above the noise. "Large bets only to make the night more interesting!" Hoots and hollers met Eliana's announcement before she added, "I'll have the staff get more cards."

Jin tightened his grip on Astrea's hand as he led them toward the door. But a man stepped in Jin's path. They were so close, just a few feet from escaping.

"Off for the night, Your Imperial Highness?" he asked, upper lip curling as he looked toward Astrea. His copper eyes were bright despite the low light in the room, and Astrea swallowed. She knew him. The man from the Whiskey Dream.

What was he doing here? She hadn't noticed him all evening.

"Get out of my way, Nazarov," Jin growled. A scrape of annoyance made it past his wall. Behind them, the party grew louder, excitement pressing so forcefully against Astrea that it was painful. "I thought I told you to get lost weeks ago."

"I was just asking," the nobleman spat, hands raising in surrender. As he did, his jacket sleeve moved up his arm, revealing something else familiar. A tattoo on his tanned wrist, a four-point star in the middle of two concentric circles. The same tattoo Astrea had seen on Theo's wrist. "I thought your . . . *date* might like to know what all her options are."

"Her options?" Jin laughed. "You wouldn't make the cut, Nazarov."

"You're really going to take the bastard's offer over mine?" Nazarov asked, glaring at Astrea. "Do you remember what I told you at the Whiskey Dream?"

"I—" she started, but another voice interrupted her.

"Is there a problem here, Your Imperial Highness?" Nicos walked over; Astrea hadn't noticed him before, either.

"No problem at all." Jin hadn't taken his eyes off Nazarov. "Miss Sovna and I were just leaving for the night."

Jin shoved past the nobleman, his grip still tight on Astrea's hand. She hurried after him, past Nicos and through the double doors. As they left the room, Nazarov's voice rang out over the rest of the chaos.

"I told you the shadows had plenty to offer, Miss Sovna! I won't make this offer again!"

Astrea didn't dare speak until they'd passed the main atrium. Jin led her down the now-familiar halls that led to the emperor's office, but she needed to stop.

She'd almost forgotten about Victor Nazarov. She'd actually forgotten what he said to her that night at the Whiskey Dream. But those words. *I told you the shadows had plenty to offer.* She'd chalked it up to a strange young man trying to be poetic that night, but now . . .

"Jin—"

"Come on." He tugged her along, the sound of their steps muffled by the ornate carpet lining the hall.

The man had the same tattoo as Theo. Plenty of people in Kalama had tattoos. Could it be a coincidence that they had the same one, tattooed on the same spot on the same arm?

Hypothetically, Astrea thought as they crept through the halls. She needed to ask Jin about it—all of it—later when they were somewhere private. Somewhere that wasn't the emperor's office.

"Jin, slow down," Astrea whispered. "Wait."

That careful wall he kept around himself was weakening, and she didn't know why. But Astrea could feel it, like wind whispering across her skin.

Jin didn't stop until they were standing in front of his father's office door.

"How are we going to get in?" she asked, voice low. Though her magic sensed nothing other than Jin, she wasn't willing to risk Kaius or the emperor himself being behind one of these doors.

Jin untangled his fingers from hers, then reached into his jacket pocket and pulled out a delicate gold key.

"Where did you get that?" Astrea asked.

"I have my ways. Is it clear?"

"Clear."

Was breaking into the emperor's office really that easy? Pretend to be the prince's date, act flirtatious, and sneak off after a few glances and whispers from the partygoers? If that were the case, they should've done this days ago.

The door was opening before Astrea had time to ask any more questions. She followed him into the dark office, closing the door behind her. Shadows danced around them as Jin's summoned flame lit up the space.

"Are you alright?" he asked.

"*Me?*" She almost laughed. "What about you?"

He pressed his lips together, turning away to go deeper into the office, but she grabbed his free hand. Swallowing past the butterflies in her stomach, Astrea forced herself to look in Jin's eyes as she said, "You're the one that told me talking about it helps."

"It's hard to be met with your own mistakes," he said. "Let's look around."

Was he upset that she hadn't wanted to talk about their history earlier in the night? She assumed that was what was bothering him; what other mistakes he might be referencing, she didn't know.

"Jin." Astrea pulled on his hand again, forcing him to stay in his spot. He sighed, waiting. Except Astrea wasn't really sure what to say. "Maybe we can talk about it later," she offered. "You know. Everything."

"You mean all of the things I'm sorry for?"

Astrea shrugged one shoulder. "You wanted to earlier."

"I did." Running a hand through his chestnut curls, Jin sighed again. "Alright, let's get to work. We're not going to have much time once Kaius notices we're gone."

"Right. What are we looking for?"

"Anything on Mattina," Jin said as he stalked toward the desk. "Anything on the rebels, the murders, the Badlands, or the meteorite."

Because that's a short list. Astrea hurried over to the desk, her skirts swishing against the floor. Jin pulled files out of his father's desk one at a time, flipping through them carefully before putting them back in their place.

Astrea began skimming through the files in the other drawers. There were all kinds of things here, from budget reports to what seemed to be intelligence reports about the Delians and Zaikudi. There was a file on Tornama despite the emperor's supposedly friendly attitude toward the eastern republic. She even found a folder containing two identical proclamations—one for Eliana and one for Kaius—about the official heir. They were undated and unsigned; it made Astrea's stomach sink, but she shoved the folder back in its place.

As her fingers skimmed the next file, Astrea paused. *Badlands.*

The file was thin, just a few pages of typewriter paper tucked inside. Most of it was correspondence with a commander at Blackrock Garrison, dated for the winter prior. No mention of a meteorite or Saros. No mention of another planned expedition. Just messages about provisions and training regiments. Astrea slipped it back in place.

"Nothing over here," she said.

Jin nodded. "I'm almost done."

"It'll be faster if you use both hands," she said. He looked up at her, brows furrowed, and she motioned toward the fire still burning over one palm. "I can do it."

"You're not using your magic in my father's office," Jin hissed. "Have you lost your mind?"

"Aren't you the one who said Kaius will be looking for us soon?" The thought of using her magic *here*, in the emperor's office, made Astrea's pulse jump, but getting caught red-handed by Kaius would have worse and immediate consequences.

"Fine." The fire in his hand disappeared and plunged them back into darkness.

A tiny ball of light formed over Astrea's left hand. She leaned close to Jin, unwilling to make the light any brighter in case anyone could see under the office door.

He searched through two more files before finally pausing. Jin's eyebrows furrowed, then he shook his head.

"What is it?" Astrea whispered.

"His directive for cutting off military pay for a while."

"He's still going to do that?"

"Apparently, and it's a deeper cut than he originally said. It's dated for tomorrow." Jin closed the folder and set it back into its proper place. "Ellie really thought the council might be able to convince him not to do this."

"So, even with the council against it, he's still going back to the Badlands to . . . look for what?" Astrea asked. "More meteorite?"

"I would assume so. Hopefully Cress was able to get that piece for me. I didn't get a chance to see her before the party."

Astrea huffed. It wasn't exactly what she'd hoped to find, but obviously the emperor had plans. Had Saros had another vision that was leading the emperor to do this? Or was Emperor Aelius simply hopeful he'd find more if he went looking?

"Come on," Jin said. "Let's get out of here."

Astrea let the light in her hand filter away, the last remnants of stardust disappearing into the air around them. Somehow, they made their way back to the door in complete darkness.

"Still clear?" Jin whispered as he stopped in front of her.

"Yes."

The door cracked open. A sliver of light illuminated the office. As they slipped into the hallway, Astrea sighed in relief despite her magic already confirming that yes, they were alone. Jin locked the door again, then slipped the key back into his pocket.

They'd made it into the office and back undetected. Astrea's heart thrummed in her chest, but it was almost pleasant. They'd done it. It hadn't exactly been productive, but they'd done it.

Astrea trailed after Jin as they moved back down the long corridor. As they neared the junction, voices came from somewhere around the corner, both deep and familiar. They'd made it away from the offices, but they were still out in plain sight.

"Well, fuck," Jin muttered.

Heat crept over Astrea's skin, her heart pounding in her ears. Now what? They were *so* close, so close to being done with this.

Just like they had been the night before when they broke into Mattina's house.

That was already the pretense of them leaving the party, wasn't it? Everyone thought they were there together.

"Last night," she whispered as the voices got closer. "Outside of—"

Jin pushed her to the wall, his body nearly flush with hers as cool stone pressed against the exposed part of Astrea's back.

Maybe it was the wine, or the adrenaline, or just the simple fact that she didn't want to get caught, because Astrea whispered, "At least pretend like you want to be doing this."

"What makes you think I don't?" Jin asked as he brought his hands to her waist. That same hint of approval she'd felt just the night before slipped past his walls, and Astrea suppressed a shudder. "Do you promise not to kill me if I kiss you?"

"No."

He laughed loudly, the sound both smooth and false, so unlike the way he'd laughed in his room just hours before. "Well, I guess I better have a healer on standby, just in case."

Astrea's breath caught in her chest when he dipped his mouth toward hers. Jin pushed in closer. His hands tangled in her hair as he pressed her even further back against the cold wall. He searched her face, one thumb running over the apple of her right cheek.

The voices were getting closer. They'd literally be there any moment. What was Jin waiting for?

"What—" she started, only for Jin to press his lips against hers.

Jin was *kissing* her.

And she was kissing him back.

His lips were soft and sweet, so much softer than she'd ever imagined. Was that a hint of raspberry wine she tasted? Astrea wrapped her arms around his neck, trying not to give into the nerves pulsing through her as she managed to somehow pull him even closer.

Jin's tongue teased the seam of her lips, and she opened her mouth just enough for his tongue to barely slip inside. Astrea couldn't stop the soft moan that left her, nor could she ignore the way Jin's entire body pressed into hers. Her head tilted back, deepening the kiss. One of Jin's hands brushed the side of her neck while his thumb traced her jaw. She moaned again, trembling under his delicate touch.

Astrea couldn't believe they were doing this. She couldn't believe—

"Oh." Kaius scoffed. "Why am I not surprised?"

Jin pulled away, but he didn't disentangle himself from Astrea. He sucked in a shuddering breath, and she swore a hint of cobalt regret danced around his head.

"What do you want, Kaius?" he snapped.

Believable. Astrea peeked around Jin's shoulders, the rest of her confidence melting away as she found Kaius's glare and Caliban's empty expression. *Foolish.*

"I certainly didn't want to find you with your new"—Kaius sniffed—"plaything."

"Then mind your own business," Jin snapped again.

"Don't get mad at me, brother," Kaius said. "If you wanted privacy, maybe you should have brought her to your room."

"Maybe that's where we're going."

Kaius folded his arms over his chest. "Really? Because you're nowhere near the stairs."

"We're not?" Astrea heard herself saying. She giggled. Hopefully it sounded a little bit drunk, enough to convince Kaius. She even looked around the hallway dramatically before saying, "Oops."

"Typical," Kaius muttered, rolling his eyes. "Just get out of my way, would you?"

"Whatever you say, *brother*." Jin swept Astrea up into his arms, somehow managing to gather her ridiculous skirts up with her. She squeaked;

she didn't have to fake that. "Just do me a favor, Kaius!" he called over his shoulder as he started down the hallway. "Don't bother us until the morning."

CHAPTER 34

Jin didn't put Astrea back on her feet until they were in his apartment and the door was locked behind them.

"Told you he wouldn't mind his fucking business tonight," Jin muttered, ushering Astrea into his sitting room. "I think he bought it, though."

"Yeah," Astrea mumbled, resisting the urge to put her fingers to her lips.

They'd *kissed*. For show, to be *convincing*, but the way Jin had spoken just before that, the way he'd cradled her to his chest on their way upstairs, the whole skies damned night of . . . No. No, Astrea couldn't go there. Even when her mind tried to stray that way, she forced it back.

"Do you want a drink?" he asked.

"You wouldn't happen to have coffee up here, would you?" she asked as she sat on the settee and kicked her flats off. Astrea needed something to make her focus, to stop replaying that stupid kiss in her mind. When he shook his head, she sighed. "Water?"

"Water for you, whiskey for me."

Jin moved to the credenza, grabbing two decanters and two of the crystal glasses lined up in a neat row. Once he'd brought the drinks over, he sat on the chair adjacent to her. He seemed so far away now after they'd spent so much of the night in each other's space.

"I'm sorry." He huffed a sigh. "I shouldn't have dragged you into that down there."

"I agreed to help you," she said. "I'm glad we did it." They had new information about the emperor's plans, even if that information was vague. That was worth it.

"I put you in Kaius's line of fire, and now I . . ." He set his now-empty glass on the coffee table and scrubbed at his face. "And now I have to ask you to stay in my fucking room tonight because of what I said to my brother downstairs."

Right. "*Don't bother us until the morning.*" That, of all things, was not something she was particularly worried about. Not even after that kiss. Astrea's cheeks were ablaze, but she shrugged. "It doesn't really bother me."

"Well, it bothers *me*."

"I've slept in Ellie's room plenty of times." Jin pinned her with a look. "Not the same, I know, but it's alright. Really." Weeks ago, maybe even days ago, Astrea never would've imagined that to be true. But it really would be fine, even if it was awkward.

"Alright, well . . ." Jin stood and walked back to the credenza, his back to her as he started fixing a second drink. "Do you think Saros would be willing to speak with me about this meteorite? I meant to ask you last night."

Good. Talking about anything else than what had happened downstairs was good.

"Oh. Well . . ." How did she put it diplomatically? "I don't think Saros is your biggest fan."

Jin snorted. "I don't really care if he likes me. I care what he knows about my father's plans in the Badlands."

Astrea twisted the water glass in her hands, watching as the liquid swirled. "I just don't know that he'll want to speak with you. He barely speaks with me these days."

"Could you at least try to get him to agree?"

Maybe Jin knocking on the observatory door would elicit some kind of response. "I'll try talking to him," Astrea said.

"Thank you."

Astrea hated the growing silence and the way Jin wouldn't look her in the eye. Had she taken the kiss too far? Maybe she shouldn't have goaded him like that in the first place. Astrea wished she could read him, figure out why he was acting so odd. Was he simply consumed in his own thoughts?

Other topics seemed like a safer bet than that line of questioning.

"I . . ." she started, then shook her head. "The other day, when Theo came into the library, I noticed he had a tattoo. I saw it again this morning when he came in looking for Raela."

That got his attention. Jin turned, one eyebrow arched. "Theo?" he repeated. "*Theo* has a tattoo?"

"Yes, a four-point star with two circles around it. Nazarov has the same one."

"Fuck," Jin muttered before tipping back a mouthful of whiskey. "I doubt it's a coincidence."

Astrea's heart sank. She'd known that was improbable, but still, some tiny part of her had hoped it *was* a coincidence.

Jin set his drink down and walked to his desk, retrieving a pencil and pad of paper before he sat down again. "Can you draw it for me?"

Astrea sketched out the design as best she could. It wasn't perfect, but it was close enough. "Why do you need this?" she asked as she slid it toward him.

"I want to ask Zephyrine about it. Maybe she'll know what it means. I don't think either Theo or Nazarov have served in the military, but some units get specific tattoos. Maybe it's just one I don't know."

Astrea nodded. A military unit, perhaps another organization or club. There were lots of reasons they might share a tattoo like that, even if Nazarov seemed like a sleazeball.

"What do you think about what he said to me?" Astrea asked.

"What who said to you?"

"What Nazarov said to me, as we were leaving." When Jin still didn't seem to understand, Astrea repeated the words. "'I told you the shadows had plenty to offer.'"

"What the fuck does that mean?"

"I don't know. He said that to me at the Whiskey Dream, before you came over . . ."

"The night he grabbed your arm?" Jin's voice was steely as he picked up the drawing and carried it back to his desk.

"Yes."

"Maybe it's what your uncle was talking about," he said. "Shadows and all that."

"That's what I was afraid of." Weeks ago, when Lord Victor Nazarov had first said those words to Astrea, she'd assumed he was just flirting in a very strange, very aggressive way. But shadows? What were the odds that Nazarov would use that phrase and act so strangely with everything else going on? And if he shared a tattoo with Theo . . . She didn't like that implication. "I'll talk to Saros as soon as I can," Astrea said. "Maybe I should go now."

"Don't go." Jin spent a few heartbeats at his desk, his back to her as he fiddled with something. "There's no way Kaius isn't sniffing around. We can talk to Saros in the morning."

Right. Of course Kaius was going to be looking for them. He'd gone looking for them just minutes before. Had been watching them, apparently, for the last couple of weeks. The only consolation Astrea had was that he couldn't have known about her magic. Kaius would never keep that a secret.

Jin retrieved his whiskey and sat in one of the armchairs again. Tense silence followed, and Jin wouldn't look away from the coffee table separating them. Skies, she just wanted him to look her in the eye. Was the kiss really that bad? Was it really so awful that she had to sleep in his room for the night?

"Jin," Astrea whispered. "What were you going to tell me before Lady Hiflow came over?" Now certainly wasn't the right time to ask, but Astrea wanted to know. Needed to know. What was this secret he'd planned on telling her, and why hadn't he brought it up since?

He blew out a breath, harsh and shuddering, before he finally looked up at her. "Obviously you see why I feel so out of place here." Astrea didn't trust herself to speak, so she nodded. That much had been made crystal clear in the last few hours. "Even as a kid, I knew none of this was right for me. But you . . ."

"What about me?" she asked when he hesitated.

"You," he said, those golden eyes locked on hers, "were the only thing here that ever felt right."

Astrea's breath hitched. She didn't know where the pain or anger came from, why they surged up so violently in her body as she stared at her old friend. Eight years. Eight years she'd kept it under control, and with one sentence, she was about to break.

"No." Astrea slammed her glass on the table, then pushed to her feet, heart thundering so fast it felt like she'd just run across the city. "No, that can't be what you were going to tell me."

"I know I don't have a right—"

"No right?" Astrea half laughed as she circled behind the settee. She gripped the back, welcoming the pain of the wood pressing into her palms. "Of course you have no fucking right."

"I didn't mean it like that." Jin blew out another heavy breath as he focused on the whiskey glass still cupped in his hands. "You were always my one true friend. The one person who really saw me. Ellie never fully did, but you *always* did, Astrea."

"If that's true," Astrea whispered, hating the way her voice cracked, "then why did you leave?"

"It wasn't my choice."

"And not saying goodbye? Was that not your choice either?"

Tears clouded Astrea's vision. Maybe they shouldn't be having this conversation now. Maybe that blue lotus smoke had been too thick. Maybe she'd had too much wine after all. Eight years of hurt was too much for her to sort through tonight.

Jin abandoned his whiskey before pushing himself to his feet. He didn't move, though. The settee separated them, a shield for Astrea against whatever she was sure he would say next.

"Do you remember my eighteenth birthday party?" he asked.

She nodded. The emperor had hosted a party in the palace gardens, something fancy but still far less of a to-do than Eliana's birthdays. Both Astrea and Cressida had been on the guest list, as had Saros.

"Moments before he sent me out into the gardens to greet everyone, my father told me he was sending me off to join the military, and that was that. Off to fight in his wars, no time, no choice. I didn't know when I was going to come back, or if I was going to come back in one piece. I just . . . I couldn't bear to say goodbye to you after all the years we'd been friends. That would have made it too real, made the possibility that I wasn't coming home too real."

Jin had seemed down that night, but he'd told her it was just that he'd received poor scores on an exam that morning. Now it all made sense. Eliana had told Astrea that their father was the one ultimately responsible for Jin leaving the capital. Jin hadn't even been old enough to join the military; conscripts had to be twenty. The realization that Jin didn't have *any* choice in it cut deep. But so, too, did the way he'd avoided her for years.

"I—" Astrea started, then pressed her lips together. She didn't think she could say the words.

"What, Astrea? What?" Jin pleaded. "I can take it. I deserve it, honestly. Whatever you need to say, say it. Please."

"I'm sorry he did that to you." One tear, then two, then three, slipped down her cheeks. Astrea blinked, trying to force the rest away. They didn't stop coming. "I really am. But I wrote to you for six months, Jin, and you didn't think you should reply to even one letter?"

"I know you have no reason to believe me, but I tried." Jin's voice strained as he said, "I wrote you back between every training session and every mission. But all I could think was that losing me that way—the way you did—would hurt you less than losing me to one of my father's wars. Selfishly, I thought it would hurt me less, too. That maybe I wouldn't be so scared of dying if you were at least able to move on. And so, I never sent those letters. I couldn't."

"I thought I'd done something wrong."

For the first few years after Jin left, she'd thought she'd done something to offend him. Breached a boundary, crossed the line too far past protocol, *something*. She'd eventually realized that wasn't the case, but even admitting it now, Astrea felt so badly for her younger self.

Why had she blamed herself for this when it was Jin's decision? Even if his father hadn't given him a choice about leaving, Jin simply disappearing on her without a single word *had* been his decision. Not sending those letters back to her had been his decision, too. And maybe he'd made those choices out of a very realistic fear, but that didn't make it hurt less. It didn't make it right or okay, even if she could empathize with it.

It was just like what Saros had done years ago when he'd forced Astrea to keep her magic hidden. He'd made that choice out of fear for her, fear of the potential future he foresaw, fear that her mother would be disappointed with how things were turning out.

It was what Astrea herself had been doing for years, choosing again and again to play it safe, to make herself small, to ignore what she wanted, to go unnoticed by just about everyone.

Wasn't that why she had even been tiptoeing around Saros the last couple of weeks? Because even though she needed answers, she was afraid he would just shut down and retreat more?

Fear was a powerful thing.

How many times had she and Jin been in this very room before, complaining about studies or guardians or even the summer heat? How many times had Astrea come to find Jin when she was sad and needed cheering up? Or after she'd gotten frustrated with Eliana for something? How many times had they been here, in similar positions but with so much less hurt between them?

"Of course you didn't do anything wrong," Jin said, his voice cracking on the last word. "Of course you didn't. You were my best friend. You were only ever good to me, and I did the worst imaginable thing because I was a coward."

"You broke my heart." Astrea didn't know how she managed to say those words without bursting into tears. His leaving had hurt more than the two romantic breakups she'd been through. Nothing had ever compared to that feeling of waking up and realizing he was gone. That he hadn't said goodbye.

"I know. I broke mine, too, and I don't think I'll ever forgive myself for any of it. I'm so, so sorry."

Astrea hated this stupid sofa between them. She hated that Jin seemed so far away from her right now. She hated that any of this had happened. How it had all happened.

Fear was a powerful thing, yes, but Jin had just been a kid stuck in an impossible situation. So had she. And while one conversation couldn't repair everything, it was a start.

The fact that Jin had been by her side every step of the way since he came home was a start, too. He'd protected her secret from his father. He'd been trying to find whoever was hunting her. The last few weeks, while a whirlwind, had proven that in a place where she could trust few people, she could trust Jin.

He may have broken her heart years ago, but Jin was here now. Owning up to it. Apologizing for it. Trying to make it right. Even without her magic, Astrea could see how bad he felt about all of it. How much he must've tortured himself over it. The pained look on his face said everything.

"I should've had a choice," Astrea said quietly. "You should've given me a choice. Talked to me and had a conversation about what you being sent away meant."

"I know." His voice shook. "I know I should have."

"You could've told me what you were scared of. We could've figured it out together."

"I know that, too."

Astrea breathed in, slow and deep. Maybe some people would think she was a fool, but she had a choice to make now. And though almost everything in her life had been turned upside down, Astrea knew one thing she wanted. She wanted to be friends with Jin again. She wanted to forgive Jin. Not just wanted—she was *ready* to forgive him. And she was ready to forgive herself for all the times she had hidden herself away, all the times she had acted only out of fear.

"A couple of weeks ago," Astrea said slowly, her death grip on the back of the sofa loosening, "Sarsali told me that I have to be brave and stand up for what I want. That I have to stop letting other people make decisions for me."

Jin said nothing as he watched her.

"I know there's a lot of bad going on in Kalama, but . . ." She swallowed. "But it's felt like we're friends again."

"I know," he said. "I know. It's been the best kind of torture."

The only way they could move forward was if they both started letting go of all their hurt and anger and blame from the last eight years. Tonight had to be the first step.

Astrea sucked in a breath. On surprisingly steady legs, she circled around the sofa, stopping only when she was wedged between it and where Jin stood. He looked down at her, his eyes cloudy. "That's what I want," she said. "To be friends again. I'm tired of living in the past."

"Astrea—" he started, but she cut him off.

"And I want you to try to forgive yourself," she said, "because I forgive you, Jin."

CHAPTER 35

"You . . . forgive me?" The full force of Jin's surprise crashing into Astrea's body, electric and strong, made her stumble back half a step. Next came the regret, the bone-deep pain she was all too familiar with. And finally, minty cool relief, a balm to it all.

Jin closed what little distance remained between them and pulled her to him. One of his hands cradled the back of her head as the other wrapped tightly around her body. Astrea let her arms snake around his waist and buried her face in the crook of his neck. This wasn't like downstairs. There was no trying to fool anyone here.

"I'm sorry, Az," he whispered into her hair.

Az. Jin hadn't called her that in years. But it felt so right, as did holding onto him so tightly she thought she might crush his ribs.

"I'm so sorry," he said. "For all of it. The last eight years. The last few weeks. Whatever my father's doing. Everything."

"I know." Her voice was muffled against his chest. "I'm a Lightbringer, remember?"

A startled laugh rumbled under Astrea's ear, and Jin finally loosened his grip. He nudged her toward the sofa, and only when they were both sitting down did he ask, "Do you really mean it?"

"You've seen me use my magic, Jin."

He laughed again. "No. That you forgive me."

"I do."

Relief. Relief. Relief. Bright, minty waves pulsed off Jin, coloring the air and cooling Astrea's skin. Something else tangled with the feeling, though she wasn't quite sure what. Joy? Gratitude?

When Jin reached for her to pull her into another hug, Astrea didn't hesitate. Crammed together on the small settee, the hug was more laying half on top of him. She didn't care. Astrea focused on the relief still flowing off him, the way his chest rose and fell under her cheek. She focused on the way her own body relaxed, how she didn't have to force it like she'd been forcing it for most of the night.

Astrea didn't know how long they sat in silence like that, but she was the first to speak. "Remember how after Solstice Night, you told me that Ellie owed me something big for saving her life?"

"Did you actually take her up on it?"

Astrea pushed up slightly so she could look at him. "No, I didn't. But in the spirit of forgiveness and fresh starts, I think you owe me something big, too." She couldn't help teasing him despite how tired they both were.

"I couldn't agree more," he said quickly. Earnestly. "What do you want? Just name it, and I'll find a way to make it happen."

"Well . . ." She smiled. "You did miss eight birthdays. And you still haven't admitted you forgot my sixteenth, so I guess that makes nine."

His head tipped back, exposing his throat as he laughed. "Oh, not this again." Jin's arms wrapped around her shoulders, keeping her close. "Let's see. Nine birthdays. That's quite the task, you know."

"And two graduations. Don't forget those, too."

As Jin gazed up at her, his eyes bright and clear, Astrea suddenly became all too aware of their bodies touching. How she *was* practically on top of him. But she didn't move, nor did he.

"Nine birthdays and two graduations. I really do have a lot to make up for." Astrea was sure she imagined his quick glance at her mouth. "I know one way I can start."

She steeled herself as Jin gently sat them both up. And then his arms dropped from around her shoulders. As he picked up his whiskey glass and stood, Astrea shoved away the disappointment growing in her belly.

"And how's that?" she managed to ask.

"You can take the bed tonight. I'll stay out here."

"What?" she asked. That was . . . unexpected. "Where are you going to sleep?"

When he nodded at the settee, Astrea scoffed. It was barely large enough for two adults to sit on, let alone sleep on it. Jin would have to curl up in a ball, and even then, she wasn't sure he would fit. She could make it work for herself, though.

"It's fine, Az," he insisted. "I've slept on mountaintops and in the desert with nothing more than a military-issue blanket. Anywhere I sleep in this room will be far more comfortable."

"But—"

"Please."

There was no point in arguing. Jin's jaw was set the same way Eliana's did when she had made up her mind about something.

"Alright," Astrea said quietly. "If you're sure."

"I'm sure." Jin went to his closet. When he returned, he slung a black silk shirt over the back of the settee. "For you to sleep in tonight. I doubt that dress will be comfortable."

"Oh. Thanks." Astrea grabbed the shirt and went into the bathroom. She took her time taking her hair down out of its clips and cleaning off her makeup. After splashing more cool water on her face, Astrea looked at Jin's shirt.

If she left tonight, would Kaius know? Did she really need to stay to convince him of the ruse? Probably. What was all of this for if he got suspicious because she was being shy? Friends could have sleepovers, even if this was all in the name of keeping it believable.

Astrea wiggled out of her gown, then slipped the shirt over her head, the material cool against her skin. It was long on her, the fabric ending several inches below the ample curve of her bum. Even the lace of her bloomers was covered by the shirt. Though she hated the thought of not sleeping in her favorite pajamas, for tonight, she would make it work.

Astrea gathered her discarded dress in her arms and opened the bathroom door. Jin's sitting room was dark except for one lamp in the corner. He was sitting on the settee, his back to her.

"I won't look," he said.

"I wasn't worried about that."

"Then why are you just standing there?"

Huffing, Astrea scurried by the sofa, indeed worried about him looking. But Jin didn't turn around. He only moved to reach for his refilled glass of whiskey. Astrea shook her head as she entered the bedroom.

She hadn't actually been in Jin's bedroom in years. It had changed, the wallpaper no longer bright red but light gray. The rug was still the same blue one he'd had when they were kids, but the bed had also been exchanged for something much larger. It was bigger than even Eliana's bed, the four posters holding up a gauzy curtain. It could easily fit three people in it.

Astrea peeked back into the sitting room. He still hadn't moved.

"Goodnight, Jin."

"Goodnight, Az."

Az. Her heart danced.

Astrea closed the door just enough to block out the light from the sitting room, then tossed her dress on an armchair in the corner. Summoning a ball of light in her hand, Astrea tiptoed toward the bed, then pulled back the blankets and sheets and climbed in.

The night hadn't gone the way she'd expected. She hadn't had to keep Eliana 'in check.' She'd helped Jin break into his father's office. They'd had to convince Kaius of something more illicit between them. Astrea hadn't even gotten to spend much time with Cressida. And skies, did she need to go talk with Saros.

But she and Jin were in a better place. Her chest wasn't so tight anymore. There was a lot they still needed to talk about, she was sure, but they would. Given time, they would.

Flames burned. A woman screamed. Shadows danced, skittering along pale skin.

"Shadows, little Lightbringer," that voice said as she emerged in the alley behind the museum. "Don't you want to know what they can give you?"

Soul-deep terror filled her. But was it hers, or did it belong to the other woman, the one dying on the ground?

"Don't you want to see how the shadows burn? Don't you want to know what happens when light meets dark?"

A laughing face appeared, eyes alight with the reddest flames. A dagger plunged into her heart, pain searing her as her skin melted from her bones.

"Don't you want to know, little Lightbringer?"

"Az!"

Astrea tried to look around for the source of that voice, for whoever was calling her name, but the darkness was suffocating, burning her from the inside out. She lashed out, trying, *trying* to find some way through, but strong arms pinned her down.

"Az, hey!"

She knew that voice, but it sounded far away.

"Wake up!"

Astrea pushed back against the weight holding her down. She clawed at her shirt, but as she popped the first button open, then the second and third, and reached for her burning skin, she found nothing. There was no dagger. There wasn't even a scratch. It was just her smooth, unmarked skin.

She looked up. It wasn't red eyes that she found staring at her but familiar golden ones, concern etched into the fine lines around them. Something gray, then mint, then blue, danced in the air around that face, only to disappear just as quickly. She knew those colors, but Astrea's mind couldn't find the words for them.

"Jin?" she whispered.

She couldn't see Jin's face through her tears, but he pulled her close, and she let him, curling into his body.

"It's okay," he said. "It was just a dream."

But it *wasn't* just a dream. She was reliving the moment that poor woman died in that skies forsaken alley, reliving the pain she felt as the shadow man murdered her, as he stole her life. Night after night, Astrea had some version of this dream. Night after night, that same voice came to her, taunting her.

"He was speaking to me," she croaked.

"Who?"

"The shadow man." The words made her cry harder, her heart squeezing so tight that Astrea thought she might simply die in Jin's bed. What a story *that* would be for the newspapers. Madam Larousse would have tales to tell for weeks. "He knows. He knows, and he's trying to find me. He's going to—"

Jin shifted so he could hold her upright. "Az, look at me."

She looked. His face was blurry, cloudy in the darkness of the room and through her tears.

"What are three things you can see right now?" he asked.

"W-what?" Astrea asked, wiping at her eyes with the back of her hand as another sob tore from her throat.

"Name three things you can see in my room right now." His voice was tight. "Please."

"Your bed," she managed, eyes darting to one of the bed's tall posters. "That chair. The curtains."

"Good." He smiled. "What three things can you hear?"

"My breathing," she choked out. "The clock ticking." Astrea focused, trying to hear a third sound, but the room was quiet. "Your breathing."

Jin squeezed her shoulders. "And three things you can smell?"

"Whiskey. Laundry soap. Sandalwood." Jin always smelled faintly of sandalwood and eucalyptus lately; even his shirt she was wearing carried the scent.

"Do you feel better?" he asked after a heartbeat.

The overwhelming feeling that she was about to die had drifted away, replaced by a throbbing ache in her head and chest.

"It felt so real."

"I know. I know it did."

Reality crashed over Astrea like a wave crashing onto the beaches of Tinale Bay. She was in Jin's bed, and he was there, holding her, calming her.

And he wasn't wearing a shirt.

Astrea tried not to look, but she couldn't help her eyes flicking down his torso. Jin was lean, all muscle and smooth skin except for the light trail of hair dipping from his belly button and disappearing under the band of his pajama pants. Heat engulfed her entire body.

"I am *so* sorry," she whispered. "I'm so sorry for waking you up." Embarrassment rolled through her again and again. Maybe dying right here would be better, newspapers and gossiping courtiers be damned.

He laughed, and she glared at him.

"What's so funny?" she asked.

"I wasn't asleep."

"Isn't it the middle of the night?"

"It is."

Astrea sighed. She was so tired, the adrenaline of the nightmare fading just as quickly as it had come on. Her bones were like jelly, though that spot on her chest—the very top of her sternum—still hurt.

"It won't happen again," she finally said. "I'm sorry."

"Do you want to go back to sleep?" he asked.

"Not really."

"Do you want me to stay?"

There was no point in lying. She was too tired, and besides, she'd probably just wake him up again in an hour or two. The shadow man never visited her dreams just once a night.

"Yes."

"Then scoot over. You're hogging the middle of the bed," he said. Astrea shifted to one side, and Jin moved to the other, his back to the window as he lay down. "Lie down, Az."

Some distant part of her mind wanted to sass him, to say something witty or even harsh. Anything to replace the dread building deep within her again. But something in Jin's voice was giving her permission to rest, to simply be there in that moment, to breathe. She laid down on her back and closed her eyes.

"Not like that," Jin whispered as he leaned over her. "Come here."

She was going to regret it in the morning. She was so going to regret this. But Astrea rolled onto her side.

Jin's arms circled her waist again; how many times he'd touched her that night, she wasn't sure. But as he pulled her back against his chest, his skin warm even through her shirt, Astrea relaxed.

"Is this alright?" he whispered, his breath tickling her cheek.

"It's fine."

"Fine?" He pushed up on one arm, the mattress dipping behind her. "What was it you said earlier? 'At least pretend like you want to be doing this.'"

Astrea buried her face in her hands and laughed. She laughed despite the ache burning through her body, despite the anxiety coursing through her veins, despite the absolute shamelessness she'd had when she said that very phrase earlier. The last of her tears rolled down her cheeks, and Astrea wiped them away.

"What a ridiculous night," she murmured as Jin lay back down behind her.

"Ridiculous," he parroted. "I don't think all of it was ridiculous."

"Well, whatever it was." Astrea sighed. "I don't think I want to repeat any of it."

"Oh, it wasn't that bad." Jin's arm, the one draped over her waist, tightened. "There are a few parts I'd repeat."

Astrea suddenly became aware of every inch of her body. Her bare legs. The tiny, silky bloomers she'd chosen much earlier in the day. Jin's body heat burning into her back.

She swallowed. "Like what?"

She almost didn't want to hear what he had to say. Was this actually a dream? Her head was still fuzzy, fatigue trying to pull her back down into the realm of sleep. It was the kind of tiredness that left her feeling drunk, almost giddy. *Ridiculous.*

"Well . . ." He paused. "The food was good, among other things."

Another giggle traveled up Astrea's throat before she could stop it, and that sweet approval of Jin's coated her tongue. Why did it have to feel so good to get even a glimpse of how he felt?

When Jin's arm tightened around her waist again, Astrea leaned back into him as much as she could. She stopped fighting back against the night. What was the point when she was so, so tired?

She focused on the warmth of Jin's body curled around hers, on his steady breaths behind her before finally, blissfully, she let sleep take over again.

CHAPTER 36

Muffled giggles forced Astrea's eyes open. Rolling over, she found the bed cold and empty. She pushed up onto her elbows. Jin's bedroom door was closed, and a faint trace of light trickled in behind the thick curtains.

"Oh, fuck," she whispered as everything came back to her.

The kiss. Kaius. The nightmare. The *spooning*.

She'd spent the *night* with Jin.

"I know you're awake in there!" Cressida sounded beyond giddy.

"Shut up or I'm not coming out!" Astrea called back, and Eliana cackled with glee. Where was Jin? Had he given Cressida and Eliana permission to be there?

Throwing the blankets off herself, Astrea realized she was only wearing Jin's shirt and her bloomers. Her friends were never going to let go of this.

Stalking to the door, Astrea swung it open to find Cressida right there, grinning, and Eliana perched on one of the sitting room chairs, also grinning.

"I knew you had it in you," Cressida said.

"Had what in me?" Astrea asked.

"My brother," Eliana deadpanned, sending both herself and Cressida into a fit of laughter.

Astrea's cheeks heated, but she stifled a laugh. It was a little funny. "I did not," she said. "Nothing happened."

"Nothing happened," Cressida repeated as Astrea pushed past her. "Then why are you wearing nothing but his shirt?"

"Do you always crash your grown friends' sleepovers?" Astrea asked, her voice coated with false sweetness.

"Oh, we're just teasing," Eliana said, pointing at a pile of fabric on the coffee table. "Jin called me earlier and asked me to bring you a change of my clothes. He already told us what happened."

How much had he told them? Had he told them about the kiss? The nightmare? Those were both topics she'd rather avoid altogether.

"Then I don't need to fill you in," Astrea said simply, taking the clothes as Eliana passed them to her. "I'll be right back."

Once in the bedroom, Astrea traded Jin's black silk shirt for the brassiere and sage green blouse Eliana had given her. Though Astrea didn't mind the blouse being boxy, she had to tighten the brassiere's straps as much as possible. Even then, it was too large, but it would do until Astrea returned home. After slipping on a tea-length black skirt, Astrea looked to Jin's bedside table. The sapphire pendant sat there, untouched. It had been meant for her to wear so they could match, so they could make the whole thing believable. What about now? She almost reached for it, then shook her head.

After re-braiding her hair, Astrea went back into the sitting room. Jin had returned, too, his hair wet like he'd just showered. He was, mercifully, wearing a shirt this morning.

"Good morning," he said as he settled into the seat across from his sister.

"Morning." Astrea remained standing, loitering a few paces away from the settee.

"I've already given you our update," Jin said, directing the comment to Eliana and Cressida. "Nazarov, the tattoos, the Badlands, Kaius."

"Anything about the budget changes?" Eliana asked.

"He's moving forward with cutting military pay for that expedition, but he's cutting more than we thought. Should be announcing it today."

"Damn it," Eliana muttered, bright red anger flaring around her. "Lady Demaria and Lord Asiter kept asking me about it last night. They're very upset about his little . . . excursion."

"His own council turning against him?" Cressida asked. "Sounds like the rebels may be getting more support soon."

"Saros said Father brought some meteorite back from the Badlands months ago." Jin looked toward Astrea, but she kept her focus on Eliana. She didn't know why she felt so shy now. "Do you know what that's about, Ellie?"

Cressida reached into her pocket and placed a small rock on the coffee table. No, Astrea realized as she inched closer. It was metallic, its edges rough and sharp.

"This is part of it," Cressida said. "Just as you requested, Jin."

Eliana frowned. "What meteorite?"

"My uncle didn't tell me much," Astrea said. "Just that he'd somehow connected with a meteorite and that he thinks it's from the void."

"The void?" Eliana's perfectly shaped eyebrows shot up. "I mean, it is a space rock. Why is that such a jarring conclusion?"

Astrea shrugged. "That's all he would tell me, but he seems to think there's more to it than that. He swears something bad is coming to the city."

Light gray confusion danced around Eliana. "Something bad? Like what?"

"I don't know. I don't think he does, either."

"And," Cressida said, "your father gave me my own special project a couple of weeks ago. I mentioned it to you." Eliana nodded. "This is it. Working with this space rock."

To Astrea's surprise, Eliana simply nodded again and reached for the chunk of meteorite. Astrea would've expected annoyance or anger or something from Eliana, but she was calm. Focused.

"What does he want you to do with it?" she asked Cressida.

"Turn it into stronger weapons, but I don't know if that's possible."

"Have you worked with something like this before?" Eliana lifted the meteorite up, turning it this way and that as she examined its rough edges.

"No, but other Metalli have," Cressida said. "As far as I can tell, this is just like any other metal."

"I want to speak with Saros," Jin said. "Today. Can you make that happen, Az?"

"I don't know." And Astrea really didn't know. Was Saros in meetings today? Would he even come out of his office? Had he remembered to eat dinner while she was gone?

"Maybe we can get him to go to my parents' house," Cressida suggested. She nodded at Astrea, a silent signal. She'd heard Astrea and Saros's arguments often enough; she knew Saros wasn't Jin's biggest supporter. "I hate to ambush him, but I think it's the only way."

Astrea's stomach sank. She, too, hated the thought of ambushing Saros with a meeting again—just like they'd done after Solstice Night—but if it would get them answers, answers so they could help him and Helosia, then maybe it was worth it. The more they learned, the more it looked like the emperor was at the center of this web.

"Alright," Astrea said. She finally glanced at Jin, unsure what she expected to see after what had happened the night before. One corner of his mouth quirked up. "I'll call you soon to let you know what time."

"I might be out," Jin said. "I need to take care of a few things, but I'll come by no later than the noon bell. Can you keep him there for that long?"

"I don't know—" Astrea started again, but Cressida waved a hand.

"See you at noon."

"Will you be there, Ellie?" Astrea asked. She hoped so; they were falling back into their old pattern of not seeing each other often due to other obligations. And if Saros was right—if something dark was coming for Kalama—then Eliana really needed to know about it as soon as possible.

"I'll try," she said, "but I need to speak with the Delians again. I was going to go after this."

"Again?" Jin asked. "That's, what, the fourth meeting this week?"

Eliana shrugged. "Father and Kaius won't talk to them. Someone has to, unless you want to take that job, Jin?"

"No, I'll leave diplomacy to you."

"Smart man."

"You say that like you're surprised."

"Maybe I am."

"If you two have no more insults to trade," Cressida said, "Az and I should be going. I have a feeling it's going to take us a little while to convince Saros to leave that tower."

Getting Saros to agree to a lunch at the Nikaphoroses' home had been surprisingly painless. As soon as Cressida and Astrea had returned to the observatory and knocked on his office door, he'd agreed to go. The trickier part had been buying Cressida enough time alone with her parents to tell them the plan.

But they'd even managed to pull that off. Now, Saros was in the kitchen chatting with Sarsali while everyone else waited for Jin to arrive.

"You know we were just teasing you this morning, right?" Cressida asked, startling Astrea.

They were in the back garden, sitting at a café-style table near Cressida and Balthazar's backyard workshop. Though Lodestar Industries had a separate office building downtown, both father and daughter liked having a place to work at home. The one-story building offered some shade from the early afternoon heat. Cressida twisted the chunk of meteorite over and over between her fingers, its dull shine occasionally catching the sun.

"Sure." Astrea nodded.

"And you also know it'd be fine—great, even—if you decided to—"

"Cress, we're repairing our friendship. Things just got out of hand with Kaius. We did the only thing we could think of to get him off our backs."

Astrea wanted to tell Cressida that Jin had kissed her. That she'd basically dared him to do it. She wanted to tell Cressida about the way he'd held her all night. She wanted Cressida to help her figure out what she was feeling.

But what good would come of that? What good would come out of admitting that maybe some tiny, foolish part of Astrea's heart hoped Jin hadn't just been trying to be convincing after all? That was very different than simply being friends again. It was very different from how she'd expected to feel. She probably shouldn't even be getting attached to the idea of him being around this much; it was just until the autumn equinox. He'd likely head back to the war front after that.

"Alright." Cressida crossed her arms. "If you say so. But I just want you to know, I would be really happy for you if—"

"Cress."

"Fine, fine. We don't have to talk about it."

"Thank you."

They sat in silence, the only sounds those of the occasional car driving by or seagulls squawking overhead. Just how angry was Saros going to be when he realized the real purpose behind this little outing? Astrea supposed he might welcome a visit with Jin. After all, Saros had said that if Jin was their only available ally, they'd have to work with him. Maybe it wouldn't be so bad after all.

"Oh, girls!" Sarsali called from the back porch. "Lunch is ready!"

Cressida stood. "Let's get this over with."

Inside, Saros, Balthazar, and Sarsali were bringing the last of the serving dishes to the table.

"Please, sit," Sarsali said. "Balthazar is just going to grab the last thing from the kitchen."

Saros sat down in the chair opposite Astrea. He'd cleaned up before they left the observatory, but the dark circles under his eyes and his sallow skin were still noticeable. Had he not slept at all the night before?

The thought of forcing Saros into a conversation with Jin was suddenly even less palatable, as was the lunch the Nikaphoroses had generously prepared. It was a smaller selection than their usual meals, but there was pasta, vegetables both raw and roasted, and bread so fresh Astrea could still see the steam rising up from it. She swallowed.

Saros, though, seemed to be ready to eat. He filled his plate as Sarsali passed him various serving dishes. He didn't say much as they waited. On their way over, he'd asked Astrea if she had a 'nice' time the night before. He hadn't even seemed to notice she'd come home in someone else's clothes.

Balthazar returned with two glass pitchers, one filled with ice water and one with iced tea. He offered Astrea her choice of drink, and she picked tea; Balthazar Nikaphoros made the best iced tea in the city. It was just sweet enough and never bitter.

When Cressida bumped Astrea's knee under the table, she realized Sarsali had been trying to ask her a question.

"How are you feeling, my dear?" Sarsali repeated, her smile gentle.

"Oh, I'm fine," Astrea lied. "I guess I'm just tired."

"Perhaps I can make you some coffee after we eat. Cressida made those delightful little turnovers you like yesterday . . . the guava ones."

"When did you have time to do that?" Astrea asked.

Cressida grinned. "You know me."

"Can't keep her away from the kitchen for long," Balthazar said.

"Oh, surely that's no surprise," Sarsali murmured, a hint of a smile on her lips. "She takes after you, darling."

The pet name Sarsali always called her husband made Jin's voice echo in Astrea's head. *Sorry that took so long, darling.* She sank deeper into her chair and stabbed a piece of roasted potato with her fork.

Balthazar and Sarsali filled the silence as the noon hour approached, speaking of new recipes, a contract Balthazar hoped to win for Lodestar, the Greenkeeper work Sarsali was doing in the public park near the train station, and plans to try a new restaurant for dinner. Saros even chimed in occasionally, but Cressida and Astrea stayed quiet.

They were halfway through their meal when there was a knock on the front door. Astrea's heart nearly jumped out of her chest.

"Allow me." Balthazar folded his napkin and set it next to his plate before disappearing into the hallway.

Astrea glanced at Sarsali, who simply smiled. They were so calm. They knew what they were doing here, and yet, all three of them were so calm.

"It seems we may need to set a sixth place at the table, dear!" Balthazar called from the front hall. Astrea tensed as two sets of footsteps neared the dining room. "We have a guest."

Balthazar appeared first, and Jin came in behind him. Balthazar was no small man, but even he didn't seem as large with Jin hovering behind him. He was now the perfectly styled prince: sculpted curls, white linen pants, and a dark blue shirt. He was even wearing the long, loose summer jacket popular in Kalama.

"Oh my, Jin!" Sarsali exclaimed as she popped out of her seat, golden joy flashing twice around her. How long had it been since Sarsali had last seen him? He used to come around often when they were kids.

"I'm sorry to drop in, Sarsali," he said, returning her hug.

"Nonsense." She waved him to the seat next to Saros. "Please, sit and help yourself."

Jin glanced at Astrea, his eyebrows furrowing with a silent question. She lifted one shoulder.

Saros made no move to stand. "Your Imperial Highness," he said, voice sharp. "Good afternoon."

Jin returned the greeting as he sat. The group's pleasantries continued for a few minutes—how Jin was adjusting to being home, how good it was for him to see the Nikaphoroses, how the weather was so different than what he was used to now—but Astrea's mind was working overtime. How were they going to transition from lunch to . . . well, everything else?

Saros set down his fork and knife, then sighed. "This is no coincidence, is it?"

"What do you mean?" Sarsali asked.

"That Prince Varojin shows up at our lunch, which we never have together."

"Saros," Balthazar tried, "why would we—"

"It's alright," Jin said, turning to Saros. "I asked them to host us," he explained. "I have questions I thought best answered off palace grounds, and I'm hoping you can shed some light on the situation."

"Shed some light?" Saros chuckled, a dark sound. "What an interesting phrase, Your Imperial Highness."

Jin sighed. "You've known me since I was twelve years old, Saros. You don't have to use formalities with me."

"Don't I, though? I'd hate to get my niece in trouble with your father by disrespecting his bastard son."

"Uncle!" Astrea exclaimed. This was not off to a good start.

"You think I'm going to run to my father to cry about titles and protocol?" Jin asked.

"With all due respect, Prince Varojin," Saros spat, his anger heating Astrea's skin, "I don't know the slightest thing about you. I haven't had a real conversation with you since you were eighteen years old—aside from when you told me you'd learned all about Astrea's magic."

Astrea felt that pain deep in her bones. But Jin was kind and good and careful, just like he'd always been. He'd proven that time and again in the last few weeks.

"Fair enough," Jin said. "Cards on the table, then. I know you don't like me, Saros. I wouldn't either if I were you, not after everything I've managed to drag Astrea into in just a few weeks' time. Especially not after realizing one of the emperor's children knows her secret. No, I'd hate me too."

Saros's rigid posture softened slightly, and the heat pulsing through the room lessened. "Well," he said, "I suppose I can at least be grateful that you aren't a complete fool."

"How do you think I've finally managed to avoid my father's attention? I've learned my lessons."

Saros shifted in his seat. "What do you want, Varojin?"

"I want to know about the Badlands."

Saros's gaze jumped to Astrea. "You wanted to share information with him before," she said.

Saros ran a hand over his face, and a flash of silver acceptance lit up the air around him. "Fine," he said to Jin. "Ask me your questions."

"What, exactly, did you tell my father about the Badlands, and why do you think it's connected to the murders in the city?" Jin asked. "Anything that can help me keep the city safe, keep all of *you* safe, is important."

"What do you know of Stargazing magic?" Saros asked after a few moments of silence.

"Almost nothing, honestly," Jin said.

"People, your father included, always want guarantees, but it doesn't work that way," Saros said. "The energy I tap into grants me some ability to see glimpses of events. A few images, a few moments, with little context. It's up to me to try to figure out what they mean. I sometimes get another vision that provides clarity, but it's not as powerful a magic as most think."

Jin nodded. "And you had one of these visions about the Badlands?"

"Yes," Saros replied. "About six months ago. It came to me suddenly, aggressively." Astrea swallowed. "It was of a meteorite crashing in the Badlands, close to the Ring of Fire. That much I knew."

"And you told my father about it?"

"I tell him almost everything. How can I not when he controls my livelihood, my niece's security? Though I am the only Stargazer at the palace, I am not the only one in the world. There is only so much I can keep from him, and at the time, this particular vision seemed inconsequential."

"Why?" Jin asked.

"Many are. These things I see are not set in stone, nor does everything come to pass. The future changes every day based on decisions people make in the present."

"This meteorite," Jin said. "Astrea told me you think there's something different about it? That it might be connected to the void in some . . . new . . . way?"

"I know that tone," Saros snapped. "You think I'm losing my mind."

"No, I don't. But I don't understand why it's so strange or why it has you so worried."

Cressida cleared her throat. That small chunk of meteorite, the one she'd stolen, hovered in the air in front of her. With a gentle flick of her wrist, she pushed it toward Saros.

"Where did you get this?" Saros asked as he grabbed it out of the air.

"I was given my own project by our esteemed emperor," Cressida said. Sarsali started to protest, but Cressida shook her head. "There was no stopping it, Ma."

"And what did he ask you to do?" Balthazar asked.

"To fuse this metal with what he uses to create weapons."

"It looks like any other rock," Jin said.

Saros set the chunk of metal on the table and sighed. "Much like Astrea can perceive the energy of people's emotions, I can access a more . . . universal energy. It's in everything, exists everywhere. But when your father brought the meteorite back to Kalama, he had me examine it. I could sense nothing."

Astrea's blood chilled, realization pulsing through her. *That* was how the shadow man felt, how the emperor's guard felt, to her magic. Not invisible but empty. *Void.*

"The shadow man," Astrea whispered. "He didn't feel like anything to me. Neither does that guard your father has, Caliban."

"He's only been at the palace for less than a year," Balthazar said.

Jin searched Astrea's face. She was sure she knew what he was thinking. The strange magic. The meteorite. These hollow people. The mythology the emperor was so interested in that just happened to show monsters covered in shadow.

"Could void magic exist?" Astrea asked. "Could this shadow man have harnessed the meteorite's power somehow?"

"There are things in this world that cannot be explained," Saros said. He motioned to that tiny chunk of stolen meteorite. "But I can feel it here, now. This is not a normal meteorite, and those are not normal people hunting you, Astrea."

"I have one more question," Jin said slowly, "if you're alright with my asking."

Saros nodded. Jin reached into his pocket, pulling out a folded piece of paper. He pushed his plate back, then spread out the sketch of Theo and Nazarov's tattoo that Astrea had made for him the night before.

"I asked an old mentor about this before coming here," Jin said. "It's a tattoo Astrea noticed on both Theo, an old friend of my mother's, and on a nobleman."

Saros took the paper in one hand. He remained silent as he stared at it, icy fear piercing Astrea's gut.

"Uncle?" she asked. "What's wrong?"

He shuddered. "I've seen this."

"On a person?" Jin asked.

"No. In a vision."

"Have you told the emperor about it?" Balthazar asked.

"No, it seemed unimportant at the time. It was graffitied on a wall, then washed away."

Astrea swallowed. *But that was weeks ago.* Weeks before, she'd been walking through Nobleman's Hill with Eliana and Nicos and had seen a Tidebacker washing graffiti off a wall. Graffiti that, if it had been completed, could've made the same image as the tattoo. The crowd had been so upset, accusing the Delians and the Zaikudi and the rebels of defacing the building. How had she not put this together sooner?

"I saw it," Astrea said. "I saw that graffiti, days before Solstice Night. I was in Nobleman's Hill with Ellie and Nicos, and we thought it was just some prank—"

"Something is not right," Saros said as he handed the paper back to Jin. "Something is very, very wrong."

That was what he'd warned her of just a couple of nights before, wasn't it? That something was wrong, that something was coming to the city. Something dangerous. Something connected to the void.

"Would anyone like some coffee?" Sarsali asked. "I'm getting a headache from all of this."

"I'll help," Cressida offered, her chair legs already scraping against the floor.

As they disappeared into the hallway beyond the dining room, Astrea fiddled with the end of her braid. Could void magic actually be real? Could Theo, Nazarov, Mattina, and the emperor all somehow be connected to it?

Perhaps most importantly, what would void mages want with her? Astrea couldn't forget that they were, for some reason, looking for her. She knew nothing about the void. She barely even knew anything about her own magic.

"Varojin," Saros said slowly. "May I speak with you alone?"

"Uncle . . ." Astrea started, but he shook his head.

"It will only take a moment, I promise."

Jin stood. "Of course."

"You two can speak in my office upstairs," Balthazar said, gaze darting between the three of them. "Take your time."

Astrea sighed and leaned back in her chair. Saros and Jin's footsteps echoed as they went upstairs. A few floorboards above the dining room creaked.

"Here we are," Sarsali said, bringing in a tray of coffee cups already filled. Cressida followed after, the promised guava turnovers on a second tray. "Where did they go?"

Balthazar shrugged and reached for one of the cups. "Saros wanted to talk to Jin. Alone."

"Why didn't you tell me about what you felt from those men?" Cressida sat next to Astrea and placed the tart tray between them.

"You know people can be closed off from my magic. I thought it was just another version of that."

"A reasonable assumption," Sarsali said. "I know Roxana taught you some things, but you need someone to teach you the nuances of light-bringing."

"Technically speaking, we don't even know if it's true," Balthazar said. "All we have right now is a theory."

A theory. One more clue in a spiderweb of clues. If void magic was real, where had it been for . . . well, forever? Had it somehow disappeared and had now returned? Was it entirely new? Only connected to this meteorite for some reason? And why did the emperor have such an interest in it?

They drank their coffees in silence, Astrea managing to eat just one of the small pastries. Guava turnovers were one of her favorite treats Cressida made, but it may as well have been ash in her mouth thanks to the anxiety crashing into her from every part of the room. The clock on the wall behind Balthazar suggested that fifteen minutes had passed already. What could Saros and Jin be talking about that was taking so long?

Floorboards creaked above them again, and Sarsali stood as both Saros and Jin returned.

"It might be a bit cold now," she said as she smoothed the front of her long purple skirt, "but I brought coffee."

"Thank you, Sarsali," Jin said, arms crossed as he took up a spot near the windows overlooking the rear garden. "I don't think I'll be staying much longer."

Astrea wanted to accuse Saros of saying something rude to Jin, but her uncle was calm. Reserved. Understanding. Even the tension in his shoulders and around his eyes had lessened greatly. Jin didn't seem particularly upset, either.

"Anything you'd like to fill the rest of us in on?" Balthazar asked, his thick eyebrows raised as he brought his coffee cup to his lips.

"I want to go to Sezia," Jin said. "To find Mattina and this missing manuscript that both Theo and my father want. That's the only place I can think to look in Helosia. If he's not there, then he's left the empire. But it's going to narrow down what we need to focus on."

"You're going with him, Astrea," Saros said.

Her stomach dropped. She wanted to argue out of principle, that he couldn't just tell her what to do, but no words came out when she opened her mouth.

"It's to keep you safe," her uncle continued, the words pleading. "Something is coming to Kalama."

"And you think it won't reach Sezia?" Astrea asked. The seaside town was just a few hours' drive from Kalama.

"Not at the same time, no."

"I'd like Cressida to join us," Jin said. "We could use her help."

Cressida nodded. "Of course. Tell me when to start packing."

"Excuse me." Balthazar sat up straighter. "What, exactly, is this threat to our city? Should I be sending Sarsali with you?"

Sarsali scoffed. "Yes, because your wife can't protect herself."

"I know you can," Balthazar replied. Affection and pride rolled off him in waves, the air around him tinged pink. "But I would feel better if one of us were there to watch over our daughter—both of our daughters." His gaze flitted to Cressida, then Astrea, and he smiled.

Tears pricked the back of Astrea's eyes. She knew the Nikaphoroses considered her part of the family, but it felt so good to hear Balthazar say it.

"I don't want to seem insensitive to your concerns, Balthazar," Jin said slowly, "but the fewer people who go south, the better. This is already going to draw my father's attention. We need to find that book before he does. That seems to be the key to all of this."

When Balthazar hesitated, Sarsali put a slender hand on his forearm. "They'll be fine." Then she looked at Cressida. "Go to the holiday house. You'll be safe there."

"I'd like to leave within the next couple of hours," Jin said. "I just need to speak with my sister first. Should I pick you up here, Cress?"

"I'll be ready."

He nodded. "We should only be gone for a couple of days, so pack light."

Everyone around Astrea jumped to action. Saros was speaking with Balthazar about something, and Sarsali and Cressida were shouting about packing and supplies. All Astrea could do was stare at Jin, the only one left in the dining room with her.

"I'll walk you out," she said, standing. Activity still hummed around them, the house loud as the Nikaphoroses rushed around to prepare. Astrea supposed she should be rushing to get back to the observatory, too. She needed to call Raela and tell her she was going out of town for a few days and would miss her next shift.

"Are you alright with this?" Jin asked, staring down at her as they stopped near the front door.

"I want answers as much as you do," she said. "It just feels sudden."

"I know. Saros is just worried about you." Jin's hand dipped into his pocket, and metal flashed as he pulled something out. "You forgot this."

Astrea stuck her hand out, watching as Jin dropped the silver necklace with the sapphire into her palm.

"I thought I didn't need it," she said. "The dinner—"

"It was a gift, Az," he said. "A practical one, yes, but still a gift."

Astrea's fingers closed over the necklace, the metal cool to the touch. She didn't know what to say. Eliana had gifted her jewelry before, for birthdays and the winter solstice festival, but this felt . . . different.

"Thank you."

Jin opened the front door, glancing over his shoulder as he stepped outside. "I'll see you soon?"

Astrea nodded. "We'll be ready."

CHAPTER 37

Though Astrea had never been to Sezia before, she immediately saw the appeal. The city was beautiful, the buildings a mix of tan, white, blue, and pink stucco and brick. It was a smaller, less flashy version of Kalama, and the mountains rising behind the city were a welcome change. Lush green landscape went on as far as Astrea could see to the west, the sea sparkling and dazzling to the east.

Too bad they weren't there for a real holiday.

"Is this the right place, Cressida?" Adi called over his shoulder as they pulled up to a home on the outskirts of town. It was a good twenty-minute walk from the small downtown they'd just driven through.

Astrea had been surprised to see Adi earlier in the day when he'd shown up at the Nikaphoroses' home with Jin. How much did Adi actually know about the situation? Neither he nor Jin had specified. In fact, Jin hadn't said much at all on the drive down from Kalama, nor had Astrea. Cressida and Adi had been happy to make small talk, though.

"That's it," Cressida replied. "Let me get the gate."

Cressida climbed out to open the black gate blocking the driveway. Once it was moved, Adi drove the car the rest of the way to the house. Cressida, however, stayed behind to lock the gate once more.

Astrea had only seen the house in pictures; Saros had never let her go on trips with the Nikaphoroses. It was two stories, the front architecture symmetrical. A wide double-front door marked the entrance. Two thick columns held up a porch roof, and arched windows lined both the first and second floors. Green vines with purple flowers crawled up one corner of the white stucco home. It was beautiful, almost cozy despite its large size.

"Well, let's go," Cressida said as she rejoined them.

She unlocked and opened the front door, revealing a wide foyer and staircase. Cressida gave them a tour of the kitchen, parlor, dining and sitting rooms first. Dark wood floors ran through the house, matching the wainscotting that lined every wall. Unlike the deep, rich colors of the Nikaphoroses' Kalamian home, their Sezian one was decorated in muted neutrals, blues, and greens. Next, Cressida showed them the back terrace and garden, which faced east toward the ocean.

The sun had started sinking below the horizon. The Sezian air was cooler than that of Kalama. Astrea sucked in a deep breath. *It's just for a few days,* she reminded herself as she gazed up at the pink and orange sky. The whole drive down from the capital, she'd been sick with worry about her family staying in the city. If it really was that dangerous, shouldn't they all be trying to leave while they had the chance?

"I'll make dinner," Cressida called as they headed back into the house. "But let me show you to your rooms first."

The others debated what to have for dinner as Cressida led them up the wide staircase. Five bedrooms occupied the second story, each with their own bathroom attached. Cressida suggested she and Adi take the rooms to the left of the stairs. Astrea and Jin would take the two to the right. Astrea almost rolled her eyes.

After unpacking, Astrea didn't know what to do with herself. She wasn't great in the kitchen, so she'd just get in Cressida's way. Adi and Jin were in the garden, talking about security for the perimeter of the house. A high wall surrounded the yard, and the house's locks were all platinum, but the two men seemed convinced they could do more.

Astrea stared out the parlor window into the back garden, watching Jin and Adi as they paced the yard. What if Saros got found out by the emperor? What if something happened in Kalama and Eliana was stuck there? What if one of the shadow men found his way to the observatory? What if he visited her again in her sleep? Astrea hadn't forgotten that skies damned nightmare, the way she could feel the dead woman's emotions just like she had that night in the alley.

"You look pensive," Cressida said as she walked into the parlor. "Help me set the table? Dinner's almost ready."

"Sure." Astrea followed Cressida into the kitchen, then grabbed a stack of blue and white patterned plates off the counter. "Where do I put these?"

"We'll eat on the terrace."

Eight chairs surrounded the long oak dining table on the terrace. Astrea set half of the table as Cressida brought more tableware outside, trying to focus on doing something rather than thinking about everything that might go wrong while they were away from the capital.

Sarsali and Balthazar had sent them off with a bag of supplies, and Cressida had made mushroom and aubergine risotto, as well as a salad of mixed greens and red cabbage. There was even fresh bread, the kind Balthazar usually made that was covered in a variety of seeds. Jin even brought out two bottles of peach wine, and Astrea took a glass when it was offered to her. He smiled as he sat down across from her.

Astrea ate instinctively, barely tasting the food even though, in some distant part of her mind, she knew it was good. Cressida's cooking was always good.

"So, Astrea," Adi said, breaking her trance. She looked across the table. Adi's dual-colored eyes scrunched up with his wide grin, a dimple forming in the cheek under his green eye. "I never did get a chance to speak with you after we met at the garage. What did you think of Jin's driving?"

Jin's driving? she wondered. "Oh, the motorcycle?"

Adi laughed, a warm sound. "Yes, the motorcycle. He brought it back to me in one piece," he said, gaze dragging over her form dramatically, "and *you* seem to be in one piece, so it couldn't have been awful."

"It was a bit scary, I'll admit," she replied, trying to infuse energy she didn't have into her voice.

"You'd get on a motorcycle with *him*?" Cressida asked, gesturing across the table to Jin. "But you wouldn't get on one with *me*?"

"In all fairness to Astrea," Jin said, "I didn't give her much of a choice."

"I'm certainly not a convert," Astrea muttered. "I'll stick with cars."

The conversation moved on to Sezia itself and the times Cressida had visited for family trips. There was apparently a boardwalk Cressida wanted to show Astrea some time, and Jin had a coffee shop he insisted they try if they had the opportunity.

"So," Adi said, voice low, "when are we going to look for Mattina?"

"I filled him in before we met you all," Jin explained. "He knows about my father, the tattoos, the murders, the meteorite, the void, everything."

"Everything?" Astrea asked.

"Yes," Jin said, "unless you think I've forgotten something important."

Did that mean he hadn't told Adi about her being a Lightbringer? Astrea didn't think Jin would reveal that information without her approval.

"I think that covers it." Astrea wasn't even opposed to Adi—or Nicos, for that matter—knowing about her magic anymore. If Saros was right, they had much bigger problems than the emperor finding out she was a Lightbringer. She just wanted to tell them on her own terms.

"Do we go tonight?" Cressida asked.

Jin leaned forward, grabbing the half-empty wine bottle and pouring the last of it into their glasses. "I think we should go into town tomorrow morning, scope out the house, and see if there's any activity there."

"You don't want to go now?" Astrea asked.

"Well, we've been drinking," Jin said, "but even beyond that, no. We need to go when we're well-rested. It's been a very long day."

"That it has," Cressida said.

"And Ellie is safe?" Astrea asked. "You made sure she's filled in too?"

"Eliana and Nicos both know what's going on," Jin said. "So does a friend of mine and Adi's." When Astrea opened her mouth to protest, he raised a hand. "Zephyrine knows just enough. She's offered us resources if we need them. She has connections."

That made Astrea feel marginally better. If Saros, Balthazar, Sarsali, Eliana, Nicos, and Jin's old mentor all knew that something was coming, they would surely be able to stay safe.

"Alright." Astrea reached for her wine glass and drank what was left in it, willing herself to relax.

"Cressida," Adi said, "would you help me with some of the changes I want to make around the garden walls?"

"Changes?" Cressida asked. "What's wrong with my house?"

"Security," Jin cut in, gesturing vaguely toward the garden. "We were thinking about ways to add a bit more protection."

Cressida's brows drew together, but she got up and followed Adi down the terrace steps and into the darkness beyond. After a moment, they were laughing about something, like they'd been friends for years. Warm amusement spread over Astrea's skin and settled in her chest.

"I think I'll go to bed," Astrea said as she stood and slid her empty glass toward Jin.

A low rumble sounded behind them, followed by more laughter from Adi and Cressida. Whatever they were doing, they seemed to be having fun.

"Will you be alright tonight?" Jin asked. "After last night—"

"I'll be fine."

He watched her, unmoving even as Adi called for him.

"I'll be fine, Jin."

"You're sure?"

Adi called out for Jin again. Rusty annoyance flared brightly in the dark yard.

"Adi's mad at you," Astrea said. "You should go see what he wants."

Jin sighed, but he stood and started toward the veranda's stairs that led into the garden. "Goodnight," he called over his shoulder.

"Night."

She didn't wait for anything else. Astrea wound her way through the home's first floor, climbed the stairs, and went straight into her bedroom. She even locked the door. It wouldn't stop Cressida from coming in if she needed to, but it would stop anyone else. Astrea needed time, time to think, time to figure everything out.

Fifty-two tiles. There were fifty-two bronze tiles on the bedroom ceiling, alternating with decorations of stars, flowers, and suns.

Astrea had already counted them at least a dozen times as she tried to get her mind to quiet down. It was well past midnight, and if she didn't get to sleep soon, she'd be in no shape to look for Mattina.

The details they had—the answers, the questions, the hints—almost made up a full picture in her mind's eye. But there were too many holes, too many other questions they still had no answers to. *I told you the shadows had so much to offer.*

Thinking of Nazarov's strange words only confused her more. What did he want? How was he connected to the void? And why was he so interested in her?

Astrea twisted a lock of hair around and around her fingers. What was it that Saros always did for her when she couldn't sleep as a child? She couldn't remember. If she called the observatory, would he be awake?

Pushing herself out of bed, Astrea slipped into her robe and crept toward her bedroom door. Staring at the ceiling wasn't helping. Maybe a cup of water would, or tea if there was any in the kitchen. Maybe the act of simply doing something would get her mind and body to quiet down.

The hallway beyond was silent. No snoring, no voices, not even footsteps. Astrea opened her door, mindful of the slight squeak in the hinge, and padded down the stairs. The front hall was dark, the curtains and shutters drawn tight. Faint white light twinkled over Astrea's hand, illuminating enough of the hall that she didn't trip on anything. Falling and breaking her nose in the middle of the night was the last thing she needed.

She made her way toward the back of the house, but Astrea paused as she neared the kitchen. Someone had left a light on in the dining room. Astrea hesitated, then headed that way. Balthazar would hate the waste of electricity. But when she entered the room, she stopped short.

"Oh, sorry."

Jin sat at the dining room table, a book open in front of him and a whiskey glass in one hand. He glanced up at her, eyes flicking once over her robed form, and smiled. "Why are you apologizing?"

"I thought someone left the light on . . ." Astrea crossed her arms over her chest, the cool night air prickling against her bare legs. "I just came downstairs for some water."

He regarded her for a moment. "Can't sleep?"

"No."

"Me either."

"Obviously."

That smile returned. "I thought a little reading would help."

"Did it?

"No. As it turns out, children's bedtime tales don't actually help a grown man sleep, nor do they answer my thousand questions about what my father's up to. I was honestly surprised that the Nikaphoroses even had such a book here." He took a sip of whiskey, then set his glass down. "Sit with me."

She only hesitated for a moment. Astrea slipped into the room and took the seat directly across from him.

Jin closed the book and slid it toward the middle of the wide table. "Do you want a drink?"

"No, thank you."

"I thought you came down for water."

"I guess I did."

"You guess?" Jin shook his head and stood. "Hold on."

"I—" she started, but he was already disappearing into the darkness of the hallway.

He returned a moment later, two glasses of ice water in hand. Jin set one in front of her, then sat down again. "So, why can't you sleep?" Jin asked. "Was it—"

"No." She knew what he was going to ask. "No, I never even fell asleep. No nightmares."

"I don't know which is preferable."

Astrea shrugged. Neither were preferable, but at least being awake didn't make her body burn like that dream had.

Jin flashed a lazy half smile and pushed a loose curl from his eyes. "If it makes you feel any better, this is how I spend most of my nights."

"Drinking alone and reading children's bedtime stories?"

The quip earned Astrea another smile, and her heart fluttered.

"No, not exactly." Jin gestured to the empty room. "Awake. Alone. Sitting in a poorly lit room."

"Even on the front?" Astrea asked. She'd wanted to ask him about his time away for weeks but hadn't worked up the courage. She didn't know what she was afraid of him telling her.

"Even on the front." Jin took another sip of whiskey, staring down at his glass when he was done. "It's funny, actually. I slept better out there than I have since I've been home."

"How is that funny?"

"I sleep better near a warzone but can't in the impenetrable walls of my father's palace. How is that not at least a bit ironic?"

"Why do you think that is?" Astrea asked. "That you slept better while you were away."

"I don't know. I have all the distractions in the world in Kalama. You'd think it would keep my mind off things."

"Things?"

Jin's jaw tightened. "Many things."

Astrea knew the stories. Soldiers coming home from the front so traumatized they couldn't function in regular society anymore. Soldiers who couldn't eat, couldn't sleep. Soldiers whose injuries were beyond what healing could easily treat, whose lives were turned upside down one way or another. It seemed everyone in Kalama knew someone who had been to the front. Lena's older sister had been deployed as a Purifier, and Lena always said she hadn't come back the same person.

Was that what had happened to Jin? He'd been gone for years. Not always on the war front. No, the Corsyca issue had only really flared a year earlier. But one year—even one week or one day—was a long time to be participating in something so dangerous. And not long before that, there'd been a war with the Delians alone, and countless other skirmishes before that still. How many more wars would there be during Emperor Aelius's reign?

"I'm sorry," Astrea whispered.

"Why do you keep apologizing?" Jin's body relaxed, his voice just as soft as hers.

"I doubt you want to be talking about this right now. I shouldn't have asked."

"I wouldn't have answered if I wasn't comfortable with it." He sighed, shifting in his seat and crossing his arms over his chest. "I slept enough last night, and I usually manage to sleep a few hours other nights. I should be fine for tomorrow if that's what you're worried about."

"I never said I was worried about that."

"But it's something you *would* worry about."

"And how can you be so confident in that assessment?"

"Because you've always worried about Ellie, Cress, and me."

Astrea blushed as she watched him watching her. That stupid smile of his was back, the one he always wore when he knew he'd won an argument before it had even begun. She'd seen that smile countless times when they were teens, and she'd always hated it. Mostly because it meant she was wrong about something. Astrea hated being wrong.

And Jin *was* right. Hearing that he barely slept instilled no confidence in her, but it also wasn't healthy for him. Saros had barely been sleeping, and he was falling apart before Astrea's very eyes. When was that going to happen to Jin?

She turned her forgotten water glass between her palms. "Maybe I do worry a bit."

"A bit?" he challenged. "You worry more than a bit."

"And how do you know? Are you a secret Lightbringer, too?"

"I don't need to be a Lightbringer to know that."

"Then please, enlighten me."

Jin leaned forward, that smug smile back. "You always fretted over Ellie's antics as kids in the gardens because you worried about her getting hurt."

"That hardly counts as 'more than a bit.'"

"You didn't let me finish." Astrea rolled her eyes, but Jin continued anyway. "You always warned Cress not to eat too much sugar because you knew it would lead to her inevitable crashes during her afternoon mage training. You would ask after Ellie's sparring injuries for several days after they'd been tended to by palace healers . . . which I suppose makes sense now, given, well . . ." He shrugged. "And you helped me study because you were worried about what would happen if I didn't get high marks."

"I still don't think it's that much," Astrea muttered, but she blushed again as Jin's smile softened.

"Maybe not to you, but most people don't try to take care of their friends that way. At least, none of my other friends cared that much."

Despite the shadows in the room, Jin looked so warm and open sitting across from her. His walls were solid tonight, and Astrea was sure she imagined his quick glance at her mouth.

"You can tell me what you're worried about, you know," he said.

"I know."

After their talk the night before, after everything these last few weeks, Astrea was sure she could confide in Jin. But rehashing everything she was worried about and everything they were trying to figure out didn't seem useful.

"I should go back to bed," she murmured.

He nodded. "Try to get some sleep."

"You should come upstairs, too." Astrea pushed up out of her chair, hesitating. "With me, if you wanted."

Her heart pounded against her ribs as the words hung in the air between them. He was going to think she was a fool, but Astrea couldn't help it. She needed some sleep, and so did he. "*I slept enough last night.*" Jin's words echoed in her mind. And as much as she knew this could only end in disaster, Astrea had slept better than she had in weeks after he'd joined her in bed at the palace.

"With you?" Jin finally asked, a hint of surprise tickling the end of Astrea's nose. It almost made her sneeze.

"Yeah . . ." Astrea picked at the front of her robe. "Like last night."

"Like last night," he echoed. "You're sure?"

"I wouldn't be inviting you if I wasn't sure."

He smiled, but it wasn't smug this time. It was soft, gentle. The one she didn't get to see often. The one she missed.

"Go on up," he said. "Let me just clean up, then I'll join you."

Astrea's heart skittered as Jin stood and picked up the three glasses still sitting on the table. She couldn't believe he'd agreed. She couldn't believe that she was actually looking forward to sharing a bed with him—twice in two nights.

"Sure." She swallowed and started toward the hallway. "Just come up when you're ready." And then she slipped back into the darkness, trying to slow her pace as she made her way to the stairs.

Jin was coming to her bed.

And she'd invited him.

CHAPTER 38

Astrea noticed two things when she woke up: the sun was barely filtering through the gauzy curtains, and something very warm and hard was pressed against her back.

Jin put off ridiculous amounts of heat in his sleep. She'd been exhausted the night before, dozing as soon as she lay down. Jin had come up some time after, waking her enough to say goodnight. He'd held her close just as he had at the palace, and it had been nice. Comfortable. Familiar somehow.

It wasn't nice anymore. Astrea tried to move out from under him, but his grip on her was tight. "See if this happens again," she whispered as she pushed on his forearm. "Skies, you weigh a ton."

"And there's a problem with that?" he asked, his voice raspy. "Stop wiggling unless you want to make things awkward."

"What—" Astrea clamped her mouth shut as realization washed over her. "Shut up."

"Just relax," Jin whispered. "For a few more moments. Please."

His grip loosened, the heat decreasing as Jin put a few inches of space between their bodies. Astrea pushed up on her elbows, and Jin groaned.

"What happened to lying still?" he asked.

"I just want to know what time it is." The clock on the table accenting his side of the bed indicated it was barely the seventh hour.

Jin rolled over to look at the clock and groaned again. "Seriously? Come on, let's go back to sleep."

But Astrea wasn't looking at the clock. His back was on full display to her, the muscles flexing as he ran a hand through his hair. A series of pale, raised scars that reminded Astrea of lightning ran down the left side of his back. Where had he gotten those? Her mind called back to that conversation with Adi, the one about how Jin would do anything for his team. And there was more. A knotted round scar on his left shoulder and a thin, narrow scar on his right.

If he noticed her staring, though, Jin didn't show it. He lay back down and gazed up at her, eyes half closed and hair messy. Something tugged at Astrea's heart. She swallowed hard.

"I'm going to get up," she whispered. "You should get cleaned up in your room."

After a heavy sigh, Jin pushed himself up, those scars on full display again. She was so tempted to reach out, to touch them, to ask what had happened, but Jin tugged his shirt on and got out of the bed. He scooped up the rest of his clothes from the day before as he went, and without another word, he slipped out the door and into the hallway.

Astrea jumped up as soon as the door closed behind him. She stalked into the bathroom and started the shower. The water was barely tepid, but she stepped under it anyway, the heat stuck to her skin melting away.

She needed to stay focused on their task here in Sezia: track down Mattina, figure out what the emperor wanted with the stolen manuscript, and discover how this was all connected. *No distractions*, Astrea thought as she rinsed the soap from her body.

After braiding her wet hair, Astrea slipped on a simple lavender dress. She hesitated as she reached into her bag and pulled out the sapphire necklace. She turned it over in her hands once, then fastened it around her neck.

When Astrea finally went downstairs, she found Cressida in the kitchen, humming to herself as she flipped something in a pan. The whole room smelled like cinnamon and coffee.

"Is that what I think it is?" Astrea asked.

"Oh, skies!" Cressida put one hand to her chest, the spatula still gripped tightly in the other. Lavender surprise lit up the kitchen for half a heartbeat. "You scared me, Az. I didn't even hear you get up."

"Sorry. Do you need help?"

Cressida's loose blue blouse rippled in the breeze blowing in through the open kitchen window. "Just bring the coffee and plates to the table. Pancakes will be done soon."

Astrea gathered the coffee and plates and took them into the dining room. Its windows faced the house next door, which was nearly half a city block away. In the dark the night before, Astrea hadn't realized how much space this property actually had.

Adi came downstairs first, dressed in gray pants and a green shirt. His drooping eyes suggested he didn't want to be awake yet. Jin came downstairs next. He looked good. His hair was wet from a shower of his own. He'd also changed his clothes, opting for black slacks and a white shirt. He smiled at Astrea as he sat down at the head of the table, his gaze flicking to her neck. She reached up, touching the necklace, but Jin had already turned his attention elsewhere.

Astrea served the coffee, and once Cressida brought in their breakfast, they ate in silence. Adi woke up with each bite, and he drank an extra cup of coffee, adding what Astrea thought was far too much sugar to each cup.

"Alright," Jin said as soon as everyone had finished eating. "Ideally, we'll find Mattina today and get some answers."

"Should we split up into pairs?" Cressida asked.

"I want to stick together," Jin said. "We'll take a look around town first, and if we don't see him, we'll check out his house."

"Wouldn't it be better to split up, though?" she pressed. "One group can check out his house, and the other can check town."

"I'm not willing to take any chances of us being overpowered."

"Not to sound overconfident," Adi started, "but don't we have three of the strongest mages in Helosia here? How would he overpower any of us?"

Jin glanced at Astrea. "This man we've come up against twice now," he said carefully. "He's powerful. A different kind of powerful."

"This shadow man?" Adi asked.

Astrea nodded. "Yes."

Despite seeing it for herself, she still couldn't wrap her mind around the idea of void magic. What *was* it? What could it do? Were they even correct in their guess, or was this something else?

"Do you think Mattina is one of them?" Adi asked.

"No, I know he's not a mage." Jin sighed. "But I'm still not willing to take a chance."

The first and only time Astrea had met Lord Mattina, his emotions had been there, open for her to read. That didn't line up with the shadow men, either.

Jin looked around the table. "Any other questions?"

"About a thousand," Adi said, "but I don't think they're relevant right now."

"Then let's go."

Sezia may have been smaller than Kalama, but that didn't slow the people down. Pedestrians hurried around them, shoving past their group as they loitered on the corner of a sidewalk near the town's main plaza.

"This is going to be impossible," Adi muttered.

A half dozen restaurants surrounded them, patrons spilling out into the square and filling up the metal bistro tables. Could Mattina be here? There had to be hundreds of people in the area.

Was being in downtown Sezia just after the breakfast hour really the best idea? Perhaps that had been Jin's reasoning. With the throng of people leaving restaurants and going to shops and other businesses for the day, it gave their group a way to blend in.

"We'll split up," Cressida said. "You two take that half"—she pointed to the left—"and Az and I will take this side."

"And do what?" Astrea asked. "Ask every waiter if they've seen a man who fits Mattina's description?"

Rusty annoyance danced around Cressida. "I'll tear this town apart to find him if I have to."

"We're not splitting up," Jin said. He turned his back toward the plaza. Adi, though, kept his gaze on the square, intense concentration rolling off him.

"But we can cover more ground if we split up. You know what Mattina looks like; so does Az," Cressida argued. "Split into two teams and meet back here in twenty minutes. It's efficient."

Astrea didn't like the idea of splitting up either. She could do something her friends couldn't. She knew what to look for with her magic, the signature of the shadow man. The onslaught of emotion from the crowd was almost painful. But that was good; there were no voids she could feel. None nearby, anyway. "I think it's alright," Astrea said slowly. "If we don't go too far."

Cressida grinned, but Jin met Astrea with that unreadable expression he sometimes had. The one when he was thinking, analyzing. Did he know what she was saying? She just needed to tell Adi about her magic, but this didn't seem like the time or place.

"Fine." Jin nodded. "Twenty minutes. If you two aren't back on this street corner in twenty minutes, I'm burning the town to the ground."

"Wow, Captain," Adi said. "What did Sezia do to you and Cressida? You two are determined to take the city down."

"Twenty minutes," Astrea agreed. "We'll meet you back here."

She didn't wait for Jin to change his mind. Instead, she looped her arm through Cressida's and started pulling her away.

"You do know what Mattina looks like, right?" Cressida asked as they skirted the northern edge of the plaza.

"Yes, but that doesn't mean spotting him will be easy." Astrea focused on the crowds, straining to pick out the museum curator she'd met just once. "He looks like half the men in Helosia. There's nothing remarkable about him."

"Well, tell me what I'm looking for anyway."

"Tan skin, a bit paler than Ellie. Curly brown hair. Glasses. He's somewhere between our two heights."

"Shorter than the average Helosian man," Cressida said. "That's something."

They finished their circle of the plaza easily, but Astrea didn't see anyone who resembled the museum curator. She also didn't see Jin or Adi anywhere in the crowd. Where had they gone?

"Let's try to find an antiquities store," Cressida suggested as she led them onto a side street. "Maybe he pawned off the manuscript when he realized someone was after it."

It wasn't the kind of thing a man like Mattina would just pawn off. He knew he had something valuable; he wouldn't have stolen it from Theo if he thought it was just any old book.

"Maybe," Astrea said. It was worth checking, just in case.

After another city block, past colorful row homes and closed storefronts, they finally found another pedestrian. An elderly woman waddled toward them, her cool brown skin and beaded white dress glowing in the morning sun.

"Void?" Cressida whispered.

The woman was readable, her emotions neutral but accessible. "Go ahead," Astrea said.

"Excuse me, ma'am," Cressida said as they approached. "I was hoping you might be able to give my friend and me some directions."

The woman stopped, green curiosity bubbling up around her. "Directions?" She shifted the large purse clasped in her hands. "To where?"

"We were hoping to find an antiquities store," Cressida said. "Or perhaps a bookstore that sells rare books? I'm a collector, but it's my first time in the city."

The elderly woman's thin eyebrows raised as she sized up both Cressida and Astrea. Whatever she was thinking, she kept to herself. "There is an antiquities store up the street." She turned and gestured the way she'd just come from. "Go three blocks in the direction you're headed, then take a left. Go another block, and the store will be on your right. It's the closest one."

"Thank you!" Cressida called as the woman waddled away. "Have a wonderful day!"

"Four blocks," Astrea said. "Do we have time?"

"We'll make time."

"Cress . . ." Jin's warning to burn down the city wiggled its way back into Astrea's mind. She didn't think he'd actually do it, but he wouldn't be happy if they were late.

"Come on." Cressida grabbed Astrea's hand, and they hurried up the street. "Just a quick look around. We're already here. We need to look."

Astrea kept pace with Cressida as she practically jogged up the street. They went three blocks, made a left, and continued down the final block. Sure enough, on their right was a storefront advertising antiquities and rare books. There was also a large 'closed' sign on the door.

"Damn," Cressida muttered.

"Now we know where it is," Astrea said. "We can come back later when they're open."

"It's damn near the tenth morning bell." Cressida pressed her face against the glass as she tried to look inside. "Why aren't they open yet?"

"We can just come back." Astrea hadn't brought her pocket watch, but they surely only had a few minutes before they needed to be back at the plaza. "Jin and Adi might even want to be here for this."

Cressida pulled her face away from the glass and sighed. "Fine. Let's go. I think I know a shortcut to get back anyway."

"You do?" Astrea asked as they headed back down the street.

"It's been a year since I was at the holiday house, but yes, I think so."

"Because that makes me feel confident."

Cressida grinned as they turned down a side road Astrea hadn't noticed before. Flower boxes filled with colorful blooms lined the windows of the homes, a few laundry lines crisscrossing between the windows above them. "When have I ever led you astray?"

"Well, there was the time at the winter festival two years ago, and—"

Astrea stopped. She simply stopped talking, stopped walking.

On their left. A door leading into a gray row home. Painted in its top right corner was a familiar symbol: a four-point star in the middle of two concentric circles.

"What's wrong?" Cressida asked.

"There, on the door. The gray house."

Lavender surprise exploded around Cressida. "Well, fuck."

She'd seen the drawing the afternoon before, at the lunch with Saros. She knew what it was.

What did this mean? Saros had a vision of the symbol; weren't they supposed to be safe leaving Kalama? *Or*, some quiet part of Astrea's mind whispered, *maybe this is exactly where I'm supposed to be.* Maybe she was supposed to be here to figure out what the symbol meant and how it was connected to everything else.

"Come on." Cressida slung her arm around Astrea's shoulders and steered her down the road. "We'll come back. I know how to get back here."

"We can't just leave—"

"Let's tell Jin, see what he wants to do," Cressida said, voice low as they turned right down another street. "Unless you're trying to break into some . . . some void house."

"Jin's not going to want to do anything about it right now," Astrea muttered. She understood why Jin was trying to be careful, but this was an opportunity. The house had looked deserted.

Another left turn, then straight for a city block, and they were back at the plaza. It was a different road than the one they'd left on, but there, across the expanse of half-empty tables, were Jin and Adi. Orange anxiety pulsed around the Earthmover, and when Astrea locked eyes with him, the orange faded. Adi grabbed Jin's shoulders, much as Cressida still held onto Astrea's, and steered the prince toward them. They met at the fountain in the middle of the plaza.

"That was more than twenty minutes," Jin hissed.

"And I'm very glad to see you didn't burn the town to the ground." Cressida smiled. "Relax. We found something."

"You did?" Jin looked to Astrea, and she nodded. "What?"

"The tattoo," she whispered despite the fact that nobody was close enough to hear them, especially not over the splashing of the fountain.

"On someone?"

"Painted on a door."

Jin scanned the storefronts behind Astrea as he asked, "Where?"

"A house a few blocks away," Cressida said. "The place was deserted."

"Could that be where Mattina went?" Adi asked. "Maybe he's connected to Theo and Nazarov and this tattoo."

"Why would he steal something that belongs to a comrade?" Cressida asked.

"Perhaps they had a disagreement?" Astrea suggested. "Maybe they were working together but he saw a better opportunity." Based on what Theo had told her and Cressida about his profession, that could very well be possible. A lucrative payday might tempt Mattina into trying to outrun lots of people, including the emperor.

"Do we go back?" Adi asked. "Maybe we should go check it out."

Jin surveyed the plaza, his expression hard. "No. We stick to the plan. We'll go to Mattina's home first, and depending on what we find there, revisit whatever you two found."

"But the tattoo," Astrea started. "My uncle—"

"I know it's important," Jin said, "but I don't like Mattina having something my father wants. Whatever it is isn't going to be good."

"You're sure?" Cressida asked.

"When has my father ever done something out of diplomacy or pure interest with no other motivations, Cress?" Jin asked.

"Never."

"Never," Jin agreed. "Let's go find Mattina."

CHAPTER 39

Lord Mattina's house was just a few minutes outside of Sezia proper, nestled in a neighborhood filled with modest homes and well-kept gardens. Midmorning sun glared off the white brick structure. Two tall fruit trees stood just inside the front garden wall, the sickly, too-sweet smell of rotting fruit hanging on the breeze.

"Should we come back tonight?" Cressida asked.

The house was silent, unmoving. They'd been studying the residence for five minutes, and though the road was quiet, one car pulled out of a long driveway a few houses down.

"The windows are open," Jin said. "Unless he forgot to close them before leaving, someone's in there."

Astrea hadn't noticed that. Two of the windows on the second story were open, the white curtains inside fluttering with the sea breeze.

Jin moved without saying anything. He started across the street, ignoring the honk of a driver who had to slam on the brakes to avoid hitting him. He simply waved a hand at them and kept going.

"Oh, for skies' sake," Cressida muttered as they rushed after him.

The front gate was unlocked, squeaking on its unoiled hinges as Jin pushed it open. If Mattina was indeed home, there was no way he wouldn't know they were coming now. Jin took the terrace steps two at a time, his fist pounding on the door as soon as he was within reach.

"Is anyone home?" Jin asked, looking over his shoulder at Astrea.

Mattina had been an open book at the library. Even with her senses pushed out wide, Astrea couldn't find a hint of emotion inside. There were no walls other than Jin's steady one, nor were there any voids.

"I don't think he's in there," Astrea said. "I don't think anyone is."

"No void?" Jin asked.

"No," Astrea said as green curiosity sparked around Adi.

Jin turned to Cressida. "Can you—"

"I'm way ahead of you." Cressida stooped and placed her hand on the doorknob and lock plate. A soft *click* sounded as the locks tumbled out of the way.

"So cool," Adi murmured as Jin opened the front door.

Jin stood to one side as he held the door open, ushering the rest of them inside. As soon as Astrea crossed the threshold last, Jin closed the door again and locked it.

"Be quiet," he whispered, "and be quick. Split up. Check every book you can, any files you find, anything. I want proof of whatever it is he's done or planning to do."

The hard edge to Jin's voice made a shiver crawl up Astrea's spine.

"Theo's book is called *Novaria: Myths and Other Legends,*" Astrea reminded them. They nodded.

As everyone went in separate directions, Astrea decided to check the parlor first. It was a relatively bare room. The light green walls were the only color; almost everything else was shades of cream and beige, except for a few darker wood accents in the room. It was unlike typical Kalamian styles, which were far more colorful. Two bookcases sat on the wall opposite the door, only a few dozen books lined up. She checked the spines first, but most of the books were unmarked, so she started flipping through them.

Each book she examined and replaced made her heart fall. Some of the books were novels, a few were about Helosian history, and some were yet-to-be-filled journals. None of them were Novarian or about mythology.

Astrea returned to the foyer. In the kitchen, Adi was busy searching cupboards and drawers. In the study near the front of the house, Cressida was searching through files laid out on a petite writing desk. There wasn't much else to see on the first floor: the powder room, which had no books, and a couple of narrow closets, but those, too, were empty.

Floorboards creaked above Astrea. She could help Jin while Cressida and Adi finished searching the first floor. Bedrooms had lots of places to hide books.

The stairs turned twice before landing on the second floor. A narrow hallway stretched before Astrea, three doors already pushed open. Jin muttered something to himself from the room closest to the stairs. One door at the far end of the hall remained unopened.

Astrea crept toward it, pushing her magic out as her hand landed on the doorknob. Still nothing that she could sense other than her friends. She twisted the knob. The door creaked open. As she poked her head inside, it looked like a normal bedroom. A large bed sat against one wall, several windows adjacent to it.

"Oh," she whispered. It was the room they'd seen from the street, the one with its windows open. Should she close them and draw the curtains in case someone was watching the house from across the road? *Should we have thought of that before breaking in?* Astrea almost laughed at the thought.

But the laugh caught in her throat. She took a few steps into the room.

An open book laid on the floor nearby, just out of reach of an open hand.

Not just a hand. An arm, a *body,* covered in faded black marks.

Faded shadows, Astrea realized, the image of the woman from the museum jumping into her mind unbidden.

She crouched, slow and controlled, as she put her hand over her mouth. That man had to be Mattina. He was wearing the same wire-frame glasses she'd seen him wearing at the museum, and the jacket of the wool plaid suit he'd been wearing that day was thrown over a chair in the corner.

But something new caught her attention. The wrist of his outstretched hand.

The tattoo.

It was there in simple black ink, a four-point star within two concentric circles. Shadowy magic sinking into his skin nearly obscured it. But these shadows were different. Where they'd been almost alive on that woman behind the museum, these were dried up, lifeless, just like Mattina.

Why did she feel bad for this man? Hadn't he tried to take something important? He was obviously connected to this conspiracy. How had the shadow man found him first . . . and why?

She knew the pain Mattina must have felt before he died. How much had that poor woman at the museum suffered? Whoever Mattina was, whatever he was involved in, he didn't deserve a death like that. Nobody did. The burning veins, the dagger to the heart, that gut-wrenching fear . . . Even now, Astrea's entire body ached with the memory, so real she thought she might vomit.

"Az?"

Jin's voice was soft as he crouched next to her. She hadn't even heard him come in. In fact, she hadn't realized she was crying, but her cheeks were wet.

"It's him," she rasped. "He's dead."

"I can see that."

Astrea pointed at the open book on the floor. "Is that it?" As Jin reached for it, she whispered, "Be careful."

He slid the book over, leaving it on the floor in front of her. It was open to a page marked with someone's handwriting. No images, no drawings.

"It's some kind of journal," Jin said.

"Not Theo's book?"

"I don't think so."

The tears continued trailing down her face despite the unfamiliar calm settling over her like a blanket. "That's unfortunate."

Jin was silent for a long moment, then he stood. "Alright," he said. "Come on. You don't need to see this."

"I'm fine," Astrea muttered, pulling away as he tried to help her stand.

"Nobody's fine seeing a dead body, Az. Especially not when you know exactly how he suffered. Come on."

Astrea picked up the book, keeping it open on the page Mattina had possibly last been looking at. "He has the tattoo," she said as Jin led her from the room, his hands on her shoulders. "The same one as the others."

"I'll go back and look."

"I'm fine," she repeated. "I can handle it."

"I never said you couldn't handle it. But I think you should go back to Cress's house, and you should take the journal with you."

Astrea wiped at her eyes as they walked downstairs, trying to rid her face of the proof that she couldn't handle any of this. Adi surely could, given his life in the army, and Astrea was willing to bet Cressida could also handle it.

"Everything alright?" Cressida asked as Jin steered Astrea to the front door.

"Mattina's dead," Jin said simply, and Cressida swore under her breath.

"He had some kind of journal with him." Astrea held it out for Cressida to see. "I need a bookmark."

"Stay here," Jin said as Cressida went in search of something. "I'll be right back."

Jin disappeared into the kitchen, and the soft thunk of cabinets stopped. Cressida came back with a blank sheet of paper, folding it twice before setting it in the journal's crease.

"Az?" she asked.

"I'm fine. I already told Jin that."

Cressida pressed her lips together. "I think we need to go back to the house. I don't like this one bit."

"Actually, I'm going to have Adi go back with her," Jin said as both he and the Earthmover left the kitchen. "I need you to do something here for me."

Cressida sighed, not breaking eye contact with Astrea. "You good with that?"

"Go, Cress," Astrea said. Why did her entire body feel like it was filled with radio static?

Cressida took two backward steps toward the stairs, but she said nothing.

"No detours," Jin warned. "Right back to the house."

"No detours." Adi nodded. "That's the plan."

"Get that book back to the house," Jin said, his hands on Astrea's shoulders again. She nodded. "We won't be long."

The sea breeze cooled Astrea's hot cheeks, a welcome distraction from what they'd found at Mattina's house.

After getting back to Cressida's family home, Astrea had set Mattina's journal in the dining room for safekeeping. She didn't want to touch it, half convinced the magic that had burned Mattina's skin was going to jump out of the book itself. They could all look at it when Jin and Cressida returned.

"Did Jin ever tell you about the time he saved my life behind enemy lines?" Adi asked. He was seated next to Astrea on the back terrace steps. He'd been there for the last twenty minutes, apparently comfortable with the silence between them.

"No," Astrea said, glancing over at him. "I don't really know anything about that time of his life."

"It was over two years ago." Adi scratched at his round chin and the fresh beard growing there. "I was still new to his team. We were sent into Posan."

"I thought Posan was a Zaikudi-Delian dispute," Astrea said. Like Corsyca, Posan was another province being fought over all the time, but it was farther north and shared no boundary with Helosia.

Adi shrugged one broad shoulder. "Tell that to the emperor."

Emperor Aelius was determined to gain control of any territory he could, no matter how small of a victory and no matter the cost. How much had he sunk into the military in recent years? Eliana had told her the number once, but Astrea couldn't think of it, her mind foggy.

"What happened?" Astrea asked.

"Things went wrong early on in the mission. We were supposed to be doing reconnaissance, nothing more. Get in, figure out what the two armies were doing, and get out. It was my first mission on his team, four of us, including him. I fucked up, got caught within a few hours of reaching our target."

"I'm guessing you made it out okay," Astrea said, "since you're sitting here."

Adi sighed, squinting as he leaned further into the sun. "Jin did things he swore he'd never do to get me back. He didn't even really know me yet. But as he said, we were partners. We were a team."

"Did you complete the mission?" Astrea asked.

"Wiped out the entire camp and staged it to look like the Delians did it," Adi said. Deep blue shame pulsed around him. "Rule number one: Leave no teammate behind. Rule number two: Leave no witnesses. That's why you always have to stick to the plan."

Astrea's breath shuddered. Even with her limited military knowledge, a camp like that in a war zone wouldn't be small. "I didn't know Helosia had the resources to get involved in Posan."

"Jin's team, well, we weren't—*aren't*—exactly . . ." He sighed. "We were a finite resource for a long time."

"Why?"

"The best of the best, ordered to do things no one should be asked to do."

Just what had Jin's life been like those eight long years he was gone? What had he seen, and what had he done?

"There's a reason Jin hates his father so much," Adi said. "But those aren't my stories to tell. What I can tell you is that Jin took me under his wing, just like our old commander, Zephyrine, took Jin under hers. That's why I'm here today. Because Jin did everything he could to make sure I came home."

"That sounds like him." Even when they were growing up at the palace, Jin had kept a watchful eye over her, Cressida, and Eliana. He didn't have to; there were plenty of guards and governesses and attendants around for Eliana's sake. But he always had.

"Just remember that not all scars are physical, Astrea," Adi said, steel pain flashing bright and cold in the air. "Not mine and definitely not his."

She turned the words over in her mind. Was that why Jin was so closed off to her magic most of the time? He'd shown up in Kalama that way, long before he knew she was a Lightbringer. Was he just trying to hide that pain away from the world?

"Why does everything feel like it's out of control?" Astrea didn't know why she asked Adi. It just felt easier than talking to Cressida or Jin, like he had less to judge her for.

"Because that's what happens when everything starts to change," Adi said. "I know I don't know you that well, but think about everything that's happened. A big change at your job, whatever mess this is . . . Jin coming back. Anyone would feel that pressure."

Astrea groaned. "You know about all that?"

"Jin talks about you a lot." Adi grinned. "He always has."

"Always has what?" Cressida asked from behind Astrea. She turned just in time to see Jin approaching too.

"I'm sure Adi's just trying to embarrass me somehow," Jin said as he stepped onto the terrace. "Glad you two made it back safely."

"You too, Captain." Standing, Adi offered Astrea his hand. She took it and let him pull her up. "Find anything else?"

"I managed to get into a safe Jin found in one of the closets," Cressida said. "Although it wasn't my most subtle work. Had to rip the damn thing open. It had a platinum lock."

"But the rest wasn't platinum?" Astrea asked.

"Painted to look like it, but no. It was steel," Cressida said. "But I got in, then put it back together."

Astrea's eyebrows shot up. That explained why they'd been gone longer than anticipated.

"Was there anything important in it?" Adi asked.

"A letter." Jin held up an envelope, the top of it jagged where it had been opened.

Adi nodded. "And the body?"

"I couldn't report this one," Jin said slowly. "Word would get back to my father too quickly."

Astrea didn't need to ask any clarifying questions. Based on Cressida's ashen face and Jin's tight hold on his own wall, she didn't want to know the answer.

"The journal's inside," Astrea said instead.

"Then let's go take a look, shall we?" Adi asked.

Cressida shot Astrea a questioning look. Astrea nodded; she was okay. She was for now, anyway. Then she gave Cressida the same look. Cressida nodded, then tilted her head in Jin's direction. Astrea rolled her eyes, only for Cressida to smile.

"Do you want to hear about how I forced the safe open?" she asked Adi.

"I would love that," he said. "I've always been jealous of Metalli . . ."

Their conversation drifted into the house as they headed toward the dining room, leaving Jin on the terrace with Astrea.

"I'm alright," she said before he could speak. That was what Cressida had meant, right? To reassure Jin? "Are you?"

"I'm fine."

"I think that's my line," she joked half-heartedly.

Jin stepped toward her, and her foolish heart skittered as he slung his arm around her shoulders and pulled her into his side. "Come on. Let's go see what Mattina was up to."

Cressida and Adi were already in the dining room, the cracked curtains offering an obscured view of the side garden and its abundant flowers. Astrea dropped into the chair next to Cressida.

"Well, it's definitely not Theo's manuscript," Cressida said as she pulled the book toward herself and opened it. "He's got addresses written down."

"Addresses?" Pushing down her fear of the shadows, Astrea pulled the book away from Cressida. Magic couldn't live on this page, and besides, this was the best lead they had on that skies damned book. "One in Sezia," she said, "and one in Talmaris."

The first, in Sezia, was for a 22 Opal Street. The second, in Talmaris, was for 564 Juniper Way.

"Talmaris, as in the capital of Novaria?" Cressida asked.

Leaning back in his chair, Adi crossed his arms over his chest and frowned. "Why would Mattina have a Novarian address?"

Jin had opened the envelope and pulled out a single sheet of paper, his eyebrows knitting together. "You said Talmaris? The letter mentions a meeting in Novaria, with 'the true leader.'"

"The true leader?" Adi echoed. "That's it?"

"That's it." Jin looked up. "Where was the house with the symbol painted on it?"

Astrea slid the book toward Cressida, who read over the page twice. "I didn't get the house number," she said, "but it's near here. Could be this one."

"Maybe Mattina was working with Theo and Nazarov," Adi said, "then betrayed them for a payday. Maybe he had a buyer—this so-called leader—in Talmaris and was trying to get out of the country."

"But did they send the shadow man after him to get their book back," Cressida asked, "or does he just happen to have an interest in it?"

Astrea chewed on her lower lip. Images of the monsters and shadows from the *Myth and Magic* book flashed in her mind's eye. If Theo's book held some valuable information—maybe even about void magic itself—was the shadow man trying to keep it out of the emperor's hands? Had Mattina had plans with Theo and Nazarov, then had a change of heart that led him to flee Kalama? And what did any of this have to do with Astrea herself?

"I think the only thing we know for sure is that this isn't a coincidence," Jin said. "Is there anything else in Mattina's journal that can tell us more?" As Cressida flipped through, revealing blank page after blank page, Jin muttered a curse.

"So what do you want to do, Captain?" Adi asked.

Jin crossed his arms over his chest and sighed. "We'll take you two back to Kalama first thing in the morning," he said, nodding to Cressida and Astrea. "Then Adi and I will come back and investigate further."

"What do you mean you and Adi will investigate?" Astrea glared at Jin. "Cress and I are the ones who found the damn house. We can show you where it is. We should be there."

"Do you not understand what this is?" Jin asked. "One man with this tattoo is deeply connected to me and my family. Another is interested in you and keeps talking about shadows. A third took something my father wanted and is now dead."

"So?"

"So it's some kind of conspiracy and a dangerous one at that!" Jin exclaimed. "I'm not leading you and Cress into the lion's den. You'll be safer in Kalama with my sister."

"But—"

"You two have been more than helpful, but you don't have our training. I can't be a good team leader if I'm trying to watch your backs the entire time."

Astrea's entire body burned. Nobody else said a word. *A good team leader?* What, were she and Cressida just some half-assed replacement for his old elite team Adi had been telling her about? Was that what all of this was?

"Fine," Astrea snapped, jumping to her feet. "Do whatever you want."

Blissfully, nobody tried to stop her, and she couldn't see past her own anger to read any of their emotions. Astrea stormed back through the house, not stopping until she reached the far end of the rear garden. She dropped into the grass and leaned her forehead on her knees.

Where did Jin get off? Why couldn't he let her help? Was she really that worthless, that fragile? She shouldn't have cried when she found Mattina's body. It was the third time Jin had seen her upset in just a few weeks. *No wonder he thinks you can't handle it.*

"Hey, you alright?" Cressida asked as she plopped down next to Astrea in the grass.

"Why does he have to be like that? Why can't he see that we can help?"

"I think he's just doing what he thinks is best," Cressida said. "Can't blame him for that."

Astrea's jaw tightened. "He's not going to know what he's walking into if I'm not there. I have my talents to contribute."

"I know you do, but it's dangerous. You have to see that."

"Come on, Cress." Turning toward her, Astrea grabbed both of Cressida's hands. "They can't just walk in there without knowing who's around. I'm the only one who can tell them that. Who can warn them about the void. And you can kick anyone's ass. And break locks. They need us."

Cressida's lips pressed together, but her aura slowly lit up with teal approval.

"We can just check it out before they go," Astrea continued. "Make sure it's actually abandoned like we thought. I'm the only one who can determine that without going inside."

"Fine," Cressida said, "but we're going when it's dark."

"Of course."

"And we'll wait until they go to bed."

"Completely reasonable."

"And if it looks like it's going to be dangerous, we're turning around and coming back here."

Astrea nodded. "Thank you, Cress."

She grinned. "Well, I can't let you have all the fun by yourself."

CHAPTER 40

Astrea's entire body tensed as she approached her bedroom door. The hallway beyond was silent. She forced her magic out, reaching until she brushed against Jin's mental wall. He was in the room next door. The other two were to her right, both calm.

Astrea slipped into the hallway. She even managed to close her bedroom door without a sound and avoided the squeakiest of stairs. When she reached the ground floor, Astrea loitered near the front door. Cressida finally appeared at the top of the stairs, and she, too, avoided the loud spots on the old staircase.

Wordlessly, they left the house. The front yard was impossibly dark, the moon and stars invisible behind the thick clouds.

"You're sure you want to do this?" Cressida asked as she unlocked the front gate at the end of the driveway.

"Don't back out now, Cress."

"Me, backing out? Never."

Once they were past the gate, Cressida locked it again, then they were off. Astrea tried to focus on her magic, on whatever she could feel around them. There wasn't much other than the occasional whisper of emotion from inside the houses they passed, as well as a handful of drunk but friendly pedestrians on their returns home. When they got to the same plaza from that morning, Cressida turned down a dark side street. Astrea had no idea where they were going, but all around them, Sezia slept.

It was a good thing Cressida was with her, because after turning down street after street, Astrea was completely lost. The town looked so different after dark.

"It's coming up," Cressida whispered. "Careful."

Heart thundering in her chest, Astrea followed Cressida to the next corner. To their right was the side street with their destination. She remembered this one, its quaint window boxes and hanging planters sticking out in her mind's eye.

"Wait." Cressida put her arm out, stopping Astrea's advance. "Look."

Activity buzzed around the corner, voices low and unintelligible. Astrea pushed her magic out wider, gripping Cressida's forearm as she did. Why did it hurt so much? But there, at the edge of her senses, was what she was looking for.

The line of people waiting outside the house were a mix of void and emotion. There had to be at least fifteen people, maybe more. Those Astrea could see were all obscured by the shadow of the building, and masks covered their faces.

"Void," Astrea whispered. "Some of them."

"Fuck. How many?"

"I can't tell." The ones she could sense, though, were giddy with excitement. A flash of peach amusement. A glow of golden joy. As one man summoned a black flame in his hand, and then another joined in, someone's orange fear jumped to life.

"We should leave," Cressida whispered, tugging on Astrea's forearm. "Come on."

"Not yet."

"You promised we'd leave if it looked bad."

"Not yet."

Obscured in shadows of her own, Astrea watched the small group from around the corner. Who were these people? And what did they have to do with Theo, Nazarov, Mattina, and the emperor? Were they the ones who wanted her?

"Az—"

"Hold on."

The front door opened, and a tall, thin man stepped onto the front porch. As he started waving people up the stairs, they either showed him pieces of paper or flashed that dark fire. Was it some kind of club? A meeting? There had to be at least two dozen people trying to get into that house.

Astrea couldn't leave now. They'd agreed to just check it out, but something was happening. If they tried to go back for Jin and Adi, they'd probably miss out on something important. She needed to do this.

"Let's wait until they all go inside," Astrea whispered. "Then we can try to look in the window."

"You've gone from bold to reckless," Cressida shot back. "Do you have a death wish?"

"Do you want to figure out what's going on or not?"

Hesitation brushed across Astrea's senses, aching. She hadn't realized there was such a physical cost to that side of her magic, but she didn't regret it. She'd just found a whole group of people with that same void as the shadow man.

"Fine," Cressida whispered. "But if this gets us killed, I'm going to come back as a ghost and tell everyone that it was *your* bright idea."

"Deal."

It didn't take long for the last of the people in line to file into the house. The man acting as the bouncer took one last look around the now-empty street before he, too, disappeared inside.

Astrea was already moving, and Cressida hissed a curse behind her. The home's windows were almost too high for Astrea to reach, but if she positioned herself just right, she could see inside. The people were still wearing their masks, some of them black trimmed with red, others red trimmed with white, and a half dozen other combinations. They milled about the interior, drinks in hand. Was it some kind of party?

A large form moved past the window, and Astrea ducked deeper into the shadows. Cressida grabbed her hand as she followed.

"Who is that?" Cressida whispered.

"I don't know."

Astrea peered back up at the window. Whoever it was, they lifted something over their head.

A book. They had a book, and inside, hints of focus, relief, surprise, and approval burst to life around the cold, unmistakable voids of some of those people.

Was that it? Was that Theo's missing book?

"Cress—" Astrea turned to face her friend, but it wasn't jade eyes she found staring at her. Rather, a pair of very angry golden eyes burned in the darkness. "Shit."

Astrea sank back into the soft sofa cushions. The walls of the sitting room in Cressida's family home felt like they were closing in on her, especially with Jin looming like an angry parent in the middle of the room.

"What the fuck were you two thinking?" Jin asked.

"Now, hold on," Cressida said, leaning forward in her seat next to Astrea. "We learned something very valuable tonight."

Jin's black shirt strained as he crossed his arms over his chest. "Valuable?" he repeated. "You think what you did was valuable?"

"Did you not see the same things we did?"

At least half the people approaching that door had been impossible to read, cold and empty like the shadow man. Like the emperor's guard. And the magic they'd been happy to show off under the cover of night . . . The knot around Astrea's heart tightened.

"What you did or didn't learn isn't the point, Cress!" Jin turned his back to them, pausing only for a moment before facing them again. "The point is you two could've gotten yourselves fucking killed! I ordered you to stay here!"

Adi loitered near the doorway, gray fear and confusion coloring the air around him. The shades were so similar they were almost impossible for Astrea to distinguish. She was sure her aura would reflect the same. She had *never* heard Jin raise his voice before. Even when he was annoyed with his siblings—the only people she'd seen him get genuinely upset with—he never yelled.

"You ordered us?" Cressida shouted. "We aren't your fucking soldiers to command!"

"If we're on a mission—" he started, but Astrea cut him off.

"Oh, please," she muttered. Who did he think he was? This wasn't like Jin.

He glared at her. "I haven't even gotten to how this was apparently *your* brilliant idea. You should know better than anyone here—"

Astrea pushed off the sofa. Jin was only a couple of paces away, towering over her, but she wouldn't be intimidated. "You don't get to insist on foregoing titles and rank only to pull them back out when it's convenient for you."

"Convenient for me?" One of his eyebrows quirked up. His jaw tightened. "You think it's convenient for me? You think any of this is convenient?"

"Well it certainly makes your life easier being able to play both sides, doesn't it? You just get to slip into the role whenever it suits you best." She scoffed. "Must be nice."

"You think I want to be in this position? Do you even know me?" Jin seethed. As Astrea stared at him, a mix of cold fear, hot anger, and something she couldn't name slammed into her, forcing her back half a step. "I'm just trying to make sure you two don't fucking die—"

"Well excuse me," Astrea snapped. "Neither of us asked you to do that."

Even as Jin opened his mouth to respond, Astrea stormed out of the room. She ignored the concern rolling off Cressida and the confusion sparking around Adi as she pushed past him and into the hallway beyond.

None of this was supposed to happen. Mattina wasn't supposed to be dead. They weren't supposed to find some . . . some clandestine meeting of void mages marked with the same symbol as Nazarov and Theo. She wasn't supposed to be friends with Jin again, and she was never meant to get involved in some kind of mystery.

She wasn't strong enough for this. She wasn't brave enough or smart enough. That foolish attempt at gathering information was proof enough. Because as much as she didn't want to admit it to Jin, going out there had been a terrible idea. Catching the wrong person's attention would've had her and Cressida in the same position as that poor woman from the museum. She was just so tired of not finding real answers, of making no progress.

Suppressing a violent shiver, Astrea climbed the last few stairs leading up to the second floor. The hallway was dark, but she didn't need light to find her way to her bedroom door. As she pushed it open, a hand landed on her shoulder.

"Leave me alone," she muttered, shrugging the hand away and moving toward her bed.

"This conversation isn't over." Jin's voice was low, and his words held the same sharp edge as before.

Astrea just wanted to go to bed and pretend none of this was happening. Anger pulsed bright and hot under her skin as she whirled on him. "You don't get to come back into my life after eight years and tell me what to do, Jin! Everything's just become one giant mess since you've been back."

His face fell as the words crossed the distance between them. Astrea knew it wasn't fair to blame this on him. None of this was actually his fault. Her chest heaved.

Jin waited at the doorway's threshold for a long moment before finally closing the door with a gentle click. He took several measured steps toward her, stopping just an arm's length away. "I'm sorry."

"For what?"

"For everything." Jin shrugged, a tight half laugh leaving him. "You're right. I don't get to insist on foregoing rank only when it suits me, and I certainly don't get to come back into your life and tell you what to do. And for that foolish fucking mistake I made years ago . . ." He sighed. "I will try to make it up to you every day for the rest of my life."

Astrea pressed her lips together. He was saying everything she wanted to hear. He was saying everything right. But she couldn't read him, couldn't get past that wall of his. Why wouldn't he just let her in?

"I've missed you every skies damned day for the last eight years, Az. And I shouldn't have yelled at you, but just the thought of you dying because you did something so reckless—"

"I know it was a bad choice"—she huffed—"but I'm not dead."

"No." The ghost of a smile flickered across his lips. "I can see that."

The heat from before lingered around Astrea, smoldering and growing.

"You may not have been hurt tonight, but you could have been," he continued. "And just the thought of it is enough to drive me mad. To make me react in ways I don't like."

"You've never yelled at me before."

"I know. And I'm sorry. I shouldn't have yelled."

Astrea glanced at the door, then back at Jin.

"Moving forward, though, I would really appreciate you listening to my advice in these situations," he said gently. "Cress was right that you're not soldiers for me to command. But I know what I'm talking about, Az. I know danger. I know risk. I know we haven't talked about it, but that's all my life has been for the last eight years. And what you two did tonight was incredibly reckless."

Wasn't that what Adi had been hinting at just hours before? That Jin had seen and done—been forced to do—some terrible things? What Jin himself had hinted at the night before when he admitted he had trouble sleeping. He'd just been stationed near the Corsycan front lines. He'd been in the army during the Delian-Helosian war.

Foolish didn't begin to describe her choices. But skies, Astrea just had to do *something*. She had to. She just needed answers. It didn't make it right, but couldn't he see that?

Astrea swallowed. "I'm sorry."

"I know."

"How can you know?" she asked. "I haven't even told you what for."

"Because I know you, even after all this time. Even if I have no right to. Skies, Az . . . I just . . . ." He ran a hand through his hair. "I missed you so fucking much."

Astrea swallowed again.

Everything she wanted to say seemed to get stuck in her throat, the words burning and impossibly heavy to speak. How sorry she was for trying to figure this out on her own. How she understood that his life in the military must've been hard. How he was right, that he still knew her. Had always known her.

Why did this have to be so hard? Why couldn't she just say what she wanted to say?

Astrea's lungs tightened as Jin closed the space between them. He reached for her cheek, swiping at a rogue tear with his thumb.

"I've missed you, too," she finally whispered. Those four words were the closest she could get to telling him everything she wanted to. She just hoped he could feel everything behind them, the way they'd been weighing her down for years. "I missed you."

Jin gazed down at her, his golden eyes molten in the low light of the bedroom. "I fear I'm being selfish," he murmured, "because I should be satisfied with that. But I'm tempted to push my luck and kiss you again."

Had it really only been two days since they'd kissed? That dinner party felt like a lifetime ago. But that had been to convince Kaius, hadn't it? Neither one of them had brought it up again, even if she'd imagined that moment a dozen times in her head since.

Awareness pulsed through Astrea's body as she studied his face. Jin was so close to her now.

"Maybe you should push your luck," she whispered, one of her hands brushing his. "It's worked for you so far."

He smiled again, then gently took her face in his hands. Astrea's blood sang as Jin's lips neared hers, all of the nervous energy melting away as he kissed her.

Her arms threaded behind his neck, pulling him closer until there was nowhere else for them to go. Jin's arms wrapped around her waist as his tongue swiped her lower lip, and Astrea groaned.

This was what she wanted. Never mind that it could very well wreak havoc on the fragile repairs they'd made to their friendship. Never mind that she would certainly get more attached to the idea of having Jin around. Kissing him felt right. It made sense somehow. And now Astrea couldn't help but wonder if every other part of him would feel this right, too.

Jin started backing her toward the bed. Astrea was tempted to pull away and get them there faster, but Jin's slow, burning kiss kept her pulled in. He picked her up, his lips traveling down her jaw and neck before he laid her down on the bed.

He hovered above her, almost like he was going to say something, but Astrea pulled him back down. Jin moaned against her mouth, tart lust exploding across her tongue. Every inch of her body came alive, hyperaware of his skin on hers.

Jin broke the kiss again, this time leaning his forehead against hers. "I can't believe I'm going to say this," he murmured, his breath coming in heavy gasps, "but we can't do this."

The sting of rejection was quick, sharp, biting as Jin pulled away from her.

"We can't?" she asked, hating how her voice cracked, but this was worse than she—

"Skies, no, Az . . ." He sighed. "Can't do this *tonight*. I want this more than anything, but there are things we still need to talk about before that happens."

"Oh."

"Besides, I can't make love to you with Cress and Adi downstairs." His voice trailed off as his eyes scanned her face. "The walls are too thin, and I want to take my time with you."

Heat crept up Astrea's body until her entire face was flushed. Kalamians—even the imperial family—weren't shy about sex. Prince Kaius was always flaunting his partners around Kalama's nightclubs. Astrea knew of at least two partners Eliana had been with, and Cressida had explored several relationships over the years, both serious and casual. Even Astrea, with her secrets to keep, had enough experience to know what she liked.

But that wasn't why she was blushing now. Astrea had never thought of Jin that way before, certainly not before he left Kalama. She rarely thought of anyone that way at all. Now, though? Now she couldn't stop thinking about it. Something in her had awoken, and if she was honest, it had started before this moment.

"I want to do this the right way." He helped her sit up, the distance between them nonexistent again as Jin kissed her forehead. "And if you're open to that possibility, we should talk when we get back to Kalama."

"Not tonight?" she asked, not quite sure how she wanted him to answer.

"No, not tonight." His thumb dragged over the apple of her cheek. "It's been a long day."

"Yeah."

This wasn't something to rush into. Astrea needed a clear head, and her head was anything but clear right now. But there was hope. There was a chance this wasn't just a fling for him. If he was insistent on talking, on doing it the 'right' way, that had to mean something.

Astrea didn't know whether she was thrilled or terrified by that prospect.

"We should go downstairs," he said after a moment. "We still need to talk about what happened tonight."

"You're not going to scold me like I'm a child again, are you?" she asked, hoping he could hear the joke in her voice.

"No." He smiled. "But I really want to hear about what you and Cress saw."

Astrea nodded. "You can go down now if you want. I just need a moment."

"A moment for what?" he asked as he helped her off the bed.

Astrea pushed past him and opened the door to her small bathroom. As the lights flickered to life, she was glad she'd thought to check her appearance. Her hair was a mess, her lips swollen. Faint red marks on her neck betrayed where Jin's mouth had been.

Jin's reflection appeared behind hers, a mirror image with his own messy hair and dazed look in his eye.

"Well that's a dead giveaway," he muttered, fussing with his hair until it fell in its natural way. "Do you need help?"

"No, I'm fine. It's probably better you go down first."

"Is it?" he asked, his gaze meeting hers in the mirror.

"Yes."

Cressida would lose her mind when she found out Astrea had been keeping this from her, but Astrea also wasn't ready to tell her anything. What would she say? She had no answers about where this was going. Not yet.

Jin lingered for another moment before nodding. "Will you be long?"

"No." She forced herself to smile. "I just need a minute."

As Jin left, Astrea looked back in the mirror. Without Jin on top of her, kissing her, she couldn't believe what they'd almost done.

But she still wished he hadn't stopped it.

Pull it together. We have a mission. Until she was out from under the emperor's thumb and figured out why someone was hunting her, she needed to stay focused.

By the time Astrea forced herself back downstairs, Cressida, Jin, and Adi were in the front sitting room, Mattina's journal sitting open on the coffee table. The clock hanging on the far wall indicated it was almost two in the morning.

Jin was the first to look her way, his expression unreadable. "Let's get started," he said, standing and motioning for Astrea to take his seat next to Adi. When she was seated, Jin reached for the journal and held it up. "So. I owe you two an apology."

"Yes, you do," Cressida said.

"I shouldn't have yelled at you, and for that, I'm sorry," Jin said. "Truly. You two deserve more respect than that."

"Yes, we do." Cressida nodded. "Thank you."

"But . . ."

"Wonderful. There's a 'but.'"

"While you were right, Cress, that you aren't soldiers," Jin continued, "and while Az was right that I don't get to pick and choose when my rank counts for something, I want you to know I'm being serious when I say you need to be careful. We're dealing with an unknown enemy—one we don't know how to fight—and I hope you can see why I didn't want you two out there alone."

"We fought them on Solstice Night," Cressida muttered.

"Az scared two of them off. There's a difference. We don't know what the outcome would've been had she not been there."

Adi shifted next to Astrea, the fabric of his pants rustling in the silence of the room. He was the only one who didn't know. *You trust Jin,* Astrea reminded herself, *and Jin trusts him.* If Adi was there to help them, he would need the full picture.

Astrea looked at Jin. He was watching her, still silent. She looked at Cressida, who was also watching.

"Adi," Astrea said, angling on their shared sofa to face him. "There's something I haven't told you."

"Gee, I don't like the sound of that," he said with a tight laugh.

"I'm . . ." She didn't know why this was so hard. She just needed to say it. "Well, I'm a Lightbringer."

Adi watched her, those two-tone eyes assessing as they scanned her face. His gaze flicked over her shoulder—to Jin, she guessed—then back to her. "I see." Teal approval and understanding mingled around his body. "I have so many questions."

"That's privileged information," Jin said.

"Already figured that was the case." Then, Adi whispered to Astrea, "But seriously, I'd love to talk to you sometime."

Astrea nodded, breathing out a single laugh as she smiled. "Sure."

Not so bad. Adi was going to keep her secret too. She didn't know what questions he might have, but this was good.

"Getting back on track," Jin said, and both Adi and Astrea focused on him. "What did you two see at that house?"

Astrea explained everything. She explained the mark on the door, the line of people waiting outside like it was some Kalamian nightclub, the bouncer. She explained the masks, the party, the shadows, the mix of emotions and void. She also had to fill Adi in on how she could sense these strange gaps in certain people, that cold emptiness.

"How many people were there?" Jin asked.

"Twenty? I didn't get an exact count."

"And how many had this void?"

"Half?"

Jin ran a hand over his face. Indecision warred on his features, and he looked down at the journal he'd long since placed back on the table. "And someone had a book?" Jin asked Astrea. When she nodded, he sighed. "Adi . . ."

Adi was already pushing himself off the sofa. "Way ahead of you." Without another word, he left the room, his footsteps light as he headed upstairs.

"Where's he going?" Cressida asked.

"To get our gear. Adi and I are going back to the house—"

"You cannot be serious," Cressida challenged. "Skies knows what's going on in there."

"That's what we're going to find out."

"How? By knocking on the front door?"

"Cress—" Jin started, but Astrea cut him off.

"Jin." Astrea said his name so softly she wasn't sure he would hear, but his gaze tracked straight to hers. She knew he wasn't going to like what she proposed, but it was their only option. "I need to go with you."

"Absolutely not."

"I know it's dangerous, and I know I don't have your training, but you just said it yourself. I scared them off on Solstice Night." When he started to speak again, she added, "And I'm the only one who can tell you if anyone is in that house."

"But—"

Cressida was the one to cut him off this time. "Jin," she said gently. "Let her join you."

Jin's eyes fluttered closed, his jaw tightening. Astrea had no idea what it would actually be like going with Jin and Adi back to that house. She had no idea what she would see or what she might be asked to do. But they needed answers. This was the only way to get them safely—as safely as they could, anyway. She should've asked Jin and Adi to go with her in the first place.

"Fine." Jin turned to Astrea, his back entirely to Cressida as his eyes roamed over her body once. Her stomach tightened, the memory of his lips on her throat burning her skin again. "But you cannot wear that."

Astrea smoothed the front of her lavender dress. The loose bodice, the flowing skirt . . . it certainly wasn't practical for this kind of mission.

"I'll find her something else," Cressida said quickly. "I'm sure there's something upstairs. Give me five minutes."

As Cressida hurried out of the sitting room and up the stairs, Jin offered a hand to Astrea. He pulled her off the sofa and said, "And you're following my orders."

She nodded.

"Stay near one of us at all times."

She nodded again.

Adi returned, dropping two knapsacks on the coffee table. "You ready, Jin?"

"Five minutes," Jin said. "Astrea's joining us."

Even though Adi's eyebrows shot up, a faint hint of minty cool relief whispered off him. "Good choice."

Astrea really hoped it was.

CHAPTER 41

On the dark streets of Sezia, it was almost impossible to tell Jin and Adi apart. Nevermind their similarly tall and muscular builds. While Astrea had changed into the dark leggings and a tunic Cressida had found somewhere in the house, Jin and Adi had transformed completely.

Gone were Adi's pajamas and Jin's casual streetwear. They wore matching uniforms—their military gear, Astrea guessed. Leather body armor and harnesses covered their torsos, their undershirts barely visible under their tall bracers and fingerless gloves. Their tight-fitted pants tucked into combat boots, and their heads and faces . . . well, their hoods and masks covered those. All black, too—no identifying insignia, not even an imperial seal. The only thing she could see were their eyes.

This was not the Jin Astrea knew once upon a time. This wasn't Prince Varojin from the imperial dinner. This was Captain Auris, the side of him she had never truly met. The side Adi had hinted at.

They'd even given Astrea an extra mask and hood they had, though it was big on her. She felt absolutely ridiculous, so unlike herself, between that and the dagger Jin had fastened to her belt before they left the house. She didn't know how to use these things, but he'd made her promise not to use anything other than her empath magic. No healing, no light, nothing. If she was attacked, she was to stab. *Stab,* she thought ruefully.

Ridiculous. But she'd agreed to follow his orders, and that had definitely been an order.

If she'd thought the city deserted before, she was wrong. Now, in the few hours before sunrise, it was stone-still. They skirted side streets, crept past gardens, and always, Astrea noticed, stuck to the shadows. At some point, Adi and Jin had sandwiched her between them. Astrea pushed her senses out to the point of painful again, trying to take in anyone else who might be lurking around the city in the middle of the night.

Twice in one night. She was sneaking around in the dark twice in one night. What would Saros think?

It didn't take long for them to reach the right street. Jin stuck his arm out in front of her, stopping both Astrea and Adi in their tracks. He turned, those golden eyes of his shadowed by his hood.

"You ready?" he whispered as he pulled his mask down. "If it's not clear, we go back to the house."

She nodded, and Jin pulled the mask back up. They began moving again, this time down the street toward the house. The same window she and Cressida had looked through was dark now. Jin tilted his head toward it.

Astrea forced out a breath and focused. Jin's wall was up, as it had been since that kiss, and it seemed even Adi had constructed one now, though it wasn't as thick. A hint of focus brushed over her skin like a whisper.

Beyond them. She needed to find whatever was beyond them. The house felt empty, not like the void on those people, though. Simply empty. Still. Quiet.

"Good," she whispered. "Clear."

Adi went to the front door, sliding something into the deadbolt lock. *We really should've brought Cressida,* Astrea thought. But they'd all agreed someone needed to stay at the house just in case Jin, Adi, and Astrea didn't come back by sunrise. Someone to call Zephyrine or Eliana.

Astrea swallowed hard. *It won't come to that,* she told herself. *It won't.*

Adi slid his tools out of the lock. Then Jin tugged Astrea toward the open door, and they all slipped inside.

It was so dark. Her magic itched under her skin, ready to help, but Astrea pushed it down. Jin hadn't summoned any fire; she would listen to orders and not summon her light, either.

The house was smaller than she'd imagined. The narrow foyer was empty. To their left was the window Astrea had been able to look through earlier in the night, and in front of it, a credenza. Adi opened its drawers and cabinet, but they were empty. Jin tilted his head to a closed door. That was where they'd seen people inside; it had to have been. It lined up perfectly with the window.

Astrea's senses remained open, and still, there was nothing. She nodded at Jin again, and he opened the door. It was a sitting room, decorated not unlike the one at Mattina's house. Only here, all of the furniture was knocked over.

Not good.

Whatever Jin and Adi thought, their silent exchange said little: a wisp of confusion from Adi but nothing from Jin. They moved to opposite sides of the room, and Astrea followed Jin to the right.

The room was a mess, knickknacks pushed off the otherwise empty bookshelves and paintings knocked off the wall. What had happened here in such a short time? And where had everyone gone?

Adi rejoined them at a door in the far corner. When Astrea nodded—yes, it was still clear—Jin pushed it open. The door squeaked, and Jin stopped. He held up one hand, his entire body still. Astrea listened, breath held tight under her mask, but still, her magic came up empty. She nodded at him again, and Jin pushed the door the rest of the way open.

He tried to, anyway. Something blocked the door halfway through its motion. Jin pushed again, but the door wouldn't move. A flame flickered to life over his free hand, and he leaned around the door as much as the narrow space would allow. "Shit," he muttered. "Another door?"

"On it," Adi replied.

As Adi retraced their path through the wrecked sitting room and slipped into the hallway, Astrea tapped Jin's shoulder. "What's wrong?" she whispered.

"It's blocked."

Blocked? Was more fallen furniture in the way? Had the whole place been ransacked?

Adi's hand on Astrea's shoulder made her jump. He motioned for them to follow him. They crept back through the sitting room, through the hallway and foyer, and then turned left to a different door. But as Astrea was about to follow Jin inside, Adi grabbed her forearm and pulled her back.

"What?" she whispered, voice so low she wasn't sure Adi would hear her.

"Hey." That was Jin, loitering in the doorway. "How many people did you see come into the house again?"

Astrea's gut sank as she crossed the last few steps to the door, the answer to Jin's question forgotten as her eyes made out shapes on the floor of what seemed to be a kitchen. Human-like shapes.

Bodies, she realized as her magic still came up empty.

Jin had told her not to use her magic, but the tiniest bit of starlight danced around her fingers as she took another step into the room. She pushed her light out low, just enough to illuminate the floor.

At least a dozen bodies, each one of them covered in those same pulsing shadows.

The woman at the museum. Mattina. These people.

This was . . . somehow unexpected. Some of them had been able to control the shadows, right? If that was the case, why were they all dead?

Ice flooded Astrea's veins as she tried to find the marks on their bodies. On a few, she could make out what looked like the tattoo, but the rest she couldn't see. They were either face down or slumped over each other.

Astrea couldn't stop staring. What had happened here? Why would all these people be killed by the very magic they seemed to celebrate? The same thing had happened to Mattina, so was it the same murderer? She was about to turn around to ask Jin and Adi when pain burned through her, so hot she thought she might be on fire. Something stabbed between her shoulder blades, her spine and sternum burning, too. She looked down at her body. Nothing. No wounds, either from magic or weapons. No shadows on her own skin. When she looked back up, though, Astrea's heart nearly stopped.

Oh, little Lightbringer.

That skies forsaken voice was back, the one from her dreams. Here, when she wasn't asleep. Here, in Sezia. Two red eyes glowed in the corner of the kitchen.

You are too late, little Lightbringer, and so, too, is your emperor.

Too late for what? she wanted to ask. *What am I too late for?*

The voice didn't respond. Despite the fact that her feet weren't moving, Astrea felt like she was being dragged forward, stretched beyond comprehension. The darkness of the kitchen fell away, replaced by the Great Library. Fire consumed everything. Before Astrea could react, before she could figure out how she'd gotten back to the city, the image changed. The Nikaphoroses' home, engulfed in shadow. The palace, the white facade so black it looked like volcanic stone. The emperor's throne room. Only instead of Emperor Aelius on the throne, those same red eyes stared back at her.

Someone hauled Astrea back, pulling her flush against their hard body. She couldn't move, couldn't speak.

"Az? Don't just stand there," Jin whispered. How was he here? Was he seeing this too? "We're leaving."

"But—" Nothing else would come out of her mouth. She couldn't breathe.

He'll never believe you, little Lightbringer.

"We're leaving," Jin whispered again. "Now."

Astrea squeezed her eyes shut. This wasn't real. Whatever she was hearing or seeing, it couldn't be real. Jin's hold on Astrea tightened, and she finally opened her eyes. Everything was bathed in darkness again, but she was back in the kitchen. No red eyes. No movement. No Kalama. Just a dozen dead bodies in a small Sezian townhome.

"Now, Az," Jin hissed in her ear. "Come on."

Finally, her feet moved, and Astrea followed Jin into the faint morning twilight. Adi was there, saying something to Jin, but Astrea didn't pay attention to them.

She turned, staring back through the same window she had hours before. There, again, were the glowing red eyes.

What was going on in that house, and why didn't Jin and Adi see it?

Astrea pulled off her mask and hood as soon as they were back inside Cressida's family home. Neither Jin nor Adi had said anything on their way back to the house, and a lump was still lodged in Astrea's throat.

She pushed past the men as they stopped in the foyer to remove their body armor. Astrea headed for the kitchen. Coffee. She needed coffee.

Floorboards creaking overhead had to be Cressida. Several suitcases had already been stacked near the front door when they'd returned. Good. The sooner they could get away from Sezia, the better Astrea would feel.

Never mind the dozen bodies in the house. Was that what her uncle saw when he had visions? Was that why Saros was so afraid of whatever he saw coming for Kalama? Was it just some figment of her imagination, a manifestation of her stress and lack of sleep?

Astrea started a pot of coffee, then slumped into one of the chairs around the rectangular table nestled in one corner. So much had changed in such a short time. Maybe Adi was right about why everything felt so out of control. And maybe that was why she was seeing things. She'd been awake for almost twenty-four hours.

A hand on Astrea's shoulder made her open her eyes; she hadn't realized she'd closed them. Jin sat down next to her, his mask bundled in one hand.

"You did good."

"Thanks," she muttered.

She considered telling Jin about what she saw, but that voice . . . *He'll never believe you, little Lightbringer.* What if it *had* been a vision? Saros had told her once, years before, that getting visions could be disorienting. *I need to talk to Saros first,* Astrea decided. Hopefully he would have answers or at least some idea of what had happened. More questions would do them no good.

Adi wandered in next, heading straight for the coffee. He brought four mugs to the table, then the coffee pot itself. Cressida came in not long after, and only when they were all seated did Jin speak again.

"We need to go to Talmaris."

"What the fuck did you find in that house?" Cressida asked.

As Jin explained everything, Cressida glanced at Astrea, but Astrea forced herself to focus on her coffee. It was terrible without any sugar or cream, bitter and burned. Had she boiled the water too hot?

Once Jin had finished his story, Cressida frowned. "That doesn't ex-plain why going to Novaria is our next step."

"That was the other address in Mattina's journal," Jin said. "And in the letter, he mentioned going there to meet that leader. I think it's safe to assume whoever killed Mattina killed the people in that house, which means it's also safe to assume the killer has those very same addresses as us."

"And you want to go to the same place they're likely going next?" Orange anxiety and dark green concern lit up Cressida's aura. "You think that's a smart idea?"

"I think it's our only option."

"And how do you propose we do that?" Cressida asked. "Ask your father for an airship?"

"We're not telling my father anything," Jin said. He drank the last of his coffee, then pushed the empty mug toward the middle of the table. "He knows we're here. He knew we were looking for Theo's book before we told him about it. And while I may have been able to hide Mattina's body, I cannot think of any way to hide all of the ones in that house. There's no garden to bury them, and I'm not going to set the house on fire and risk the people living around there."

"I don't understand," Cressida said.

"My father is going to know that we know about the bodies," Jin said. "He knows what's going on in Kalama, and when the Sezian police find those bodies in a few hours, maybe in a day, he'll start piecing it together. He's going to know that we've figured out he's connected to void magic. He's going to figure out how much we know, and then he's either going to silence us or force us to cooperate."

Silence us? What, would Emperor Aelius have his own son thrown in prison? Assassinated? Ice settled in Astrea's bones.

"You always say your father never does anything without a very specific reason," Adi said. "Could he have wanted you to discover more about void magic for him for some reason? Is that what your project was really all about?"

"Seems likely," Jin said. "But I don't think it matters anymore. If he already has one void mage on his side, and if he's really going on that expedition back to the Badlands for more meteorite, I can only imagine what he's up to."

"You think he wants void magic for the army?" Adi asked.

Cressida had mentioned that Emperor Aelius wanted her to fuse the meteorite with existing weapons, all in search of something stronger. And if he wanted the book Theo and the void mages were looking for, the emperor obviously wanted to know more about void magic, too. If he was successful in either endeavor, what would that mean for the Corsycan war?

"But why would he want us to put together all of this stuff for the Novarian delegation coming to visit?" Astrea asked. "That was why he started having us research it in the first place."

"Maybe that was just a cover story," Cressida said. "Maybe he just wanted you to find this information for him but needed a reason to ask."

"Whatever his reasons for that, I'm more concerned about what he has planned," Jin said. "We need to stop him, and I think it all goes back to that book. Too many people are looking for it. That can't be a coincidence."

"So . . . we're just going to leave?" Astrea stared at Jin, but he didn't look toward her.

"We're going back to Kalama," Jin said. "You can have an hour to pack whatever you need from home, then we'll go to the airfield. I'll call in a few favors, and we'll leave before my father learns what's happened here in Sezia. By the time he does, we'll be gone."

"What about Ellie?" Cressida asked. "My parents? Saros?"

"Talk to them," Jin said as he stood. "Get them to come with us. There'll be plenty of room on the airship."

The silence stretched on for one heartbeat, two, three, and then finally, Cressida nodded. "We're all packed. We can go whenever you want."

"Let me make those calls, then we'll leave," Jin said. "The more of a head start we can get, the better."

CHAPTER 42

Astrea spent most of the drive to Kalama sleeping in the car. By the time they got back to the city, it was just past the tenth morning bell, and the worst of the morning traffic was clearing out.

Adi pulled the car up to the curb outside the Nikaphoroses' townhome. Cressida climbed out first. She was somber, but when Jin asked her to meet at the airfield in no later than an hour, she agreed.

They were silent for the rest of the ride back to the palace. Astrea played over and over in her mind the image of where the *Myth and Magic* book was in her bedroom and checked twice that Mattina's journal and letter were still tucked safely away in her satchel on her lap. They were. Those were the three most important things she could think to take with her.

When Adi pulled the car into the deserted palace garage, Astrea threw her door open and climbed out. An hour. She had an hour to get what she needed before fleeing the country. What had her life become?

"We'll meet you and Saros by the streetcar stop near the palace gates," Jin said as he handed Astrea her suitcase. "By the eleventh hour. Although," he muttered, leaning out of the garage to look up at the darkening sky, "it looks like it's going to rain."

"Can I leave this here?" she asked, pointing at the suitcase still clutched in Jin's hand. "I only need a few more things from home."

Jin nodded, sliding her narrow brown suitcase back into the car. "Of course. It'll be waiting here for you."

Astrea ran back to the observatory, her satchel bumping against her hip as she went. She needed to find Saros and ask him about the vision. She burst through the observatory door, taking the stairs two at a time up to the apartment.

"Uncle?" she called as soon as she flung open the front door. "Uncle!"

"Astrea?" Saros's familiar dark hair popped out of the kitchen. "What are you doing back so soon?"

As she stepped into the kitchen, Saros opened his arms for an embrace, and she stepped into them. Neither of them were prone to hugging, but Astrea leaned into it, feeling like a child again as her uncle held her. He'd done that often right after her mother had died, and after everything that had happened recently, it was nice.

"What did you find?" he asked as she finally pulled away. "I was just making tea, if you want some."

"No tea," she said. "There's no time."

He frowned. "What do you mean?"

Astrea didn't bother going to the kitchen to chat. She launched into an explanation of what they'd found in Sezia, from the way the shadows were embedded in Mattina's skin to the journal to the people they'd found and their plan to leave the city. "And," she said, "that's not all. I think I had a vision." She explained what she saw and how it felt when those red eyes had pulled her into the vision.

Saros blew out a sharp breath. "So it's true, then."

"What's true?" Astrea asked.

"My visions."

"Of course they're true," Astrea said. "The shadows, the tattoo, everything. It's all true."

"No, no. My visions of you, my dear."

Astrea stared at Saros, then said, "You can explain that to me once we're on the airship." She had so many questions, and while Astrea knew her explanation of everything was patchy, they could go over everything in more detail en route. Right now, they needed to pack and get ready to join their friends. "We need to leave immediately if we're to meet Jin. Cressida and her parents will meet us at the airfield."

Astrea was halfway to her bedroom when she realized Saros wasn't following her. Pausing, she turned and looked over her shoulder. He stood in the kitchen doorway, watching her.

"Come on, hurry," she said. "We need to leave."

"You go ahead and pack," he said. "I'm not going with you."

"You're not . . ." Astrea blinked. "You're not coming?"

"No," Saros said. "Someone needs to figure out what Aelius is doing. I should be here to help figure out what he's done."

"But . . ." She swallowed. "But how will you stay safe? Isn't he going to figure out something's going on when Jin and Eliana flee the country? Won't he know . . ."

"I'm sure he will," Saros said. "But my safety is my own dilemma. You need to go, Astrea. You need to figure out who is looking for you before they find you again."

No. Saros had to come with them. He *had* to. Astrea needed him. She had so many questions. And he hadn't been very open with her these last few weeks, but couldn't he see that now was not the time for this? That she needed his help?

"Uncle—"

"You're not going to change my mind," he said gently. "I need to stay here. I need to figure out what has come to this city. If you go to Novaria and I stay here, we're more likely to find the answers we both need."

The distance between them wasn't more than a couple dozen feet, but the persistence pulsing around Saros was enough to push Astrea away. She turned on her heel and rushed into her bedroom. She snatched the *Myth and Magic* book from her bedside table first. Next was the notebook she'd been using to keep track of her research for the emperor, then she shoved another handful of clothes into her satchel. It was past full, but it would have to do. She double-checked that she'd buckled it closed before slinging the bag across her body.

Saros was still standing near the kitchen door when she returned.

"If you won't come with me," she said, turning and meeting Saros's gaze, "then I'm going to make you."

"Astrea—" he started, but she stormed past him and out the apartment door.

Jin would know what to do. He'd be able to convince Saros, or even pick the man up and drag him to the car if he had to. Adi would help. Saros couldn't stay here. They couldn't get separated. Yes, Saros had wanted Astrea to leave Kalama for months, but it couldn't be like this. They had to go together. They'd been together for years, just the two of them. They were family, and they needed to stay that way. She had so many questions she needed him to answer.

If she left without him, when would they see each other again?

Fat raindrops fell on Astrea's head as she entered the palace gardens. She walked faster, turning into one of the mazes of hedges, flowers, and trees. This was the fastest way. Three left turns, a right, another left, and she'd be that much closer to the palace. She was halfway through when the hairs on her arms prickled, her skin covered in goose bumps.

Astrea's magic reached out first, vibrating under her skin. There it was again, that void in the space around her.

"Are you finally going to embrace the shadows, Miss Sovna?"

She turned, gravel crunching under her shoes. She'd expected to see the shadow man. She'd expected a vision, even. But Victor Nazarov stood a dozen feet away, his dark pinstripe suit a harsh contrast to the green all around them.

"What do you want?" Astrea asked, heart pounding in her ears.

"I asked you a question," he growled.

Even though she couldn't read him, the air seemed to hum around Nazarov. Where she would normally see a change in his aura, a spike of color, there was just vibrating, pulsing air. Something dark and unfamiliar had pulsed around him that night at the Whiskey Dream, so why couldn't she see that now?

"Are you going to just stand there?" Nazarov asked. "Or are you going to say something?"

"I have nothing to say." Astrea took a step backward, then another, but Nazarov followed.

He chuckled, a dark, scratching sound. "I'm sure you have plenty to say to that princeling of yours."

"If you have a problem with me, just say that."

"I don't have a problem with you." Nazarov took a step closer. "Don't you see, Astrea? You are the solution."

"The solution to what?" Was that what Saros meant when he spoke about visions? Surely not. "What am I the solution to?"

"You are here to help us."

"What if I don't want to help you?" The steadiness in Astrea's own voice surprised her, but Victor Nazarov was the last person she wanted to help.

"Fine," Nazarov snarled. "Then we'll just have to do this the hard way."

Dark fire snaked through the air, humming with unfamiliar power as Astrea finally got her feet to move. She was too slow. Nazarov's flames licked her forearm. She hissed but shoved the pain down until she couldn't feel it.

"Why are you resisting?" Nazarov shouted, stalking closer. More dark fire danced around his hands, shadows crawling up his arms until they consumed his face. "Don't you want to see what the shadows can offer? Don't you want to see what we could do together, little Lightbringer?"

Lightning crackled overhead. Thunder rumbled. Astrea was stuck to her spot, watching as Nazarov transformed before her eyes. He had a similar build to the man from Solstice Night, but he definitely didn't have the same lean frame of the person who had killed the woman behind the museum.

How many void mages were running around Kalama? Had Nazarov killed Mattina? Was he going to kill her now?

Dark fireball after dark fireball whizzed through the air toward Astrea as Nazarov stalked closer. She managed to dodge the first two, but the third caught her shoulder, and Astrea suppressed a scream.

What did it matter now if she kept her magic hidden or not? If she didn't, she might very well die here, just as Eliana might have died on Solstice Night. Even if Nazarov didn't kill her, he obviously wanted to take her somewhere far away from her home. Some things were bigger than secrets, bigger than the fear aching in Astrea's bones.

She pulled on the magic now boiling in her veins, almost painful as she concentrated power in her hands. The light swirling around her was white hot, pulsing in time with her heart.

A mean smile pulled at Nazarov's mouth. "Oh, the little Lightbringer's found her fight?"

This wasn't what she was built to do. She wasn't trained to fight. *Doesn't matter,* she told herself. Anything was better than nothing. Even if she could just distract him. Even if she could just do enough to get away.

Astrea pushed her light out from the right first. Nazarov dodged with a chuckle. But Astrea pushed out the light from her left side, straight into his path. He tried to maneuver away again, but her light caught the edge of his torso and burned through his suit jacket.

"You stupid little bitch," Nazarov snarled, the shadows creeping further up his face. His eyes, those copper eyes she'd first seen in the Whiskey Dream, looked almost red, lit from within. "Should've just done this the easy way."

Energy spiked in the air again as Nazarov lunged toward Astrea. Dark fire headed her way. Astrea skidded backward, the gravel path of the garden slick as more rain began to fall. She forced herself upright only to see Nazarov was off-balance, too.

Solstice Night. Temporarily blinding their attackers had been the only way they'd escaped. Astrea pulled on her magic again, light exploding from both of her hands with such intensity even she couldn't see.

Then, she ran.

"You cannot escape the void!" Nazarov shouted over the next crash of thunder.

Rain soaked Astrea's clothes as she tried to keep her footing on the slick gravel. Two more turns and she'd be out of the hedge maze. Two more turns and she'd be at the palace—not ideal but certainly better than whatever Victor Nazarov was trying to do. Astrea's lungs burned with the effort of sprinting across the wet ground, her head and heart pounding.

She started turning the next corner. Almost there. She was almost there. Then the air left her body as someone slammed into her from behind. Gravel and stone cut into her as she landed, but the weight of another body never came. Fear, outrage, and approval crashed into Astrea's senses, disorienting.

Scrambling up, Astrea turned to see Saros skidding to a stop behind Nazarov, light swirling in his hands. Saros attacked. Light whizzed by

Nazarov's head, burning one of the tall hedges. The plant smoked, leaves crumbling to the ground in blackened bits of dust.

"Well," Nazarov said, laughing as he watched Saros, "it seems the somber Stargazer has finally found his spine."

What was Saros doing here? What was he—

Saros's light slammed into Nazarov's shoulder, then chest, leaving behind angry red burns. Nazarov growled, the air around him pulsing in that strange way again.

"Astrea, run!" Saros yelled. "Go!"

She hesitated, but after another bright burst of light, Saros was running toward her. Her feet started moving, and she was just a few steps ahead of him, leading him through the maze. One more turn and they were almost out.

"You can't escape the void!" Nazarov shouted from behind them.

"Go, Astrea," Saros hissed. "Keep going."

They burst free from the hedge maze, Astrea's heart pounding so hard she thought it might explode. Rain fell faster, soaking Astrea down to the bone.

"Now what?" she asked. Did they go into the palace—its entrance was just feet away now—or did they try to outrun Nazarov?

"You cannot stop us!" Nazarov yelled, his voice coming closer. "The Paragon will restore balance!"

Who the fuck were the Paragon?

"Find Varojin," Saros said as thunder rumbled overhead. "I'll hold him off."

"Uncle, you can't," Astrea pleaded, voice cracking. "Come on, you have to come with me." She really couldn't leave him there if that was what he was up against. Nazarov would kill him. The pain Saros would feel . . . "You have to."

"Astrea, *please*," he begged. "Find Varojin and go to Novaria."

"Hey!" Jin shouted over the rain as he pushed his way outside. "Watch—"

Astrea didn't need to hear Jin's warning; she could feel that energy in the air again, the one when Nazarov attacked. She spun. She didn't know what she was doing, but her magic reacted, pushing out in a burst of light that swallowed Nazarov's shadowy flames.

Jin rushed past her and launched himself toward Nazarov. But he met Jin punch for punch, fireball for fireball, one bright orange and the other tinged black. Astrea could barely keep track of their movements, nothing more than a flurry of flame and shadow amid the rain.

Jin stumbled, sliding as the ground became a muddy mess. Nazarov brought his fist down, black flame colliding with Jin's temple. Thunder swallowed Astrea's scream. She sprinted forward, catching Jin's arm as he fell backward.

"Captain!" Adi shouted as he skidded to a stop a dozen feet away.

The ground under the gardens quaked. Not even a foot from where Astrea and Jin huddled on the ground, a chasm split the earth open. Nazarov jumped backward, Adi's magic separating the man from the rest of the group. Astrea didn't know where Adi had come from, but skies, was she glad to see him.

"I'm fine," Jin muttered as Astrea helped him stand. A large burn marred his forehead, but that inky darkness Astrea was so afraid to find hadn't seeped into his skin.

"You don't even know the power we hold, princeling," Nazarov hissed. "Even your father doesn't know."

The shadows dancing around Nazarov consumed him. He disappeared, gone one moment and there the next as he landed on the other side of Adi's widening chasm.

"Did you know we can do that?" he taunted as the shadows enveloped him again. "I told you the shadows had more to offer, Astrea."

Though Astrea knew his name, she didn't know who—or what—Lord Victor Nazarov really was. How did he know about her magic in the first place? How did he come to possess this power of the void?

Her breath came in starts and gasps as she turned in a circle, trying to find Nazarov. He finally reappeared on the terrace steps, his human body taking shape again.

Saros sunk into a low stance, magic once again swirling around his hands and arms. Astrea had never seen her uncle act so decisively. So aggressively. She hadn't even known he could fight.

"Well?" Nazarov called, the hint of a smile in his voice as it rang out over the storm. "You can't be tired already, little Lightbringer. Don't you know about the sun and moon? Or did you never find that book?"

Did Nazarov have the book now? Had he killed all those people in Sezia?

"Go, get out of here!" Saros called over his shoulder.

"Uncle, we have to—" Astrea started, but Saros ignored her.

"You promised me, Varojin." Saros's gaze locked onto Jin. "You promised me."

"Jin," Astrea said, her voice raising an octave as she whirled on him. "Please, you have to help me convince him. He says he won't come."

Adi glanced at Jin, some silent message passing between them. When Adi nodded, Astrea's stomach sank.

"Jin," she begged. "Please."

The hair prickled on her arms again, that hum of energy building in the air behind her. The space around Nazarov vibrated with that energy it seemed only she could see.

"Go!" Saros roared, a shield of light flaring to life in front of him. It started down at the ground, curving all the way up over Saros's head. The light was so bright that Jin and Adi turned away, but Astrea forced her eyes to stay open as Nazarov's dark flames rushed forward. Saros's shield absorbed the shadows without faltering. "Astrea, leave! Find the answers!"

"I'm sorry," Jin said, voice strained as he grabbed her hand and pulled her along the slippery ground. "Az, we have to go."

"No!"

Astrea looked over her shoulder, watching as Saros's light began to falter. Even so, the air around him was clear. Bright. No orange fear or anxiety surrounded him. No white terror. No steel pain. He wasn't afraid, not even as palace guards started streaming out of the side door toward him and Nazarov.

"Stand down, both of you!" someone shouted as Jin and Adi forced Astrea around the corner to the front of the palace.

"We have to help him," Astrea pleaded, her foot landing in a pool of water near the building's front stairs. "Please."

"It's out of our hands," Adi said, his cold shock sharp against Astrea's skin. "The guards will know Nazarov is the aggressor."

If they make it out alive. With power like that, how easily would Nazarov be able to escape whatever cell they put him in? Or would the emperor try to harness it for himself instead?

"You're just going to let your father's men take my uncle?" Astrea snapped. "Take Nazarov?"

A horn honked as an emerald car pulled around the palace's circular driveway. Jin opened the door, Adi climbing in first.

"I made him a promise, Az," Jin said. "This is bigger than Saros and he knows it. It's bigger than Nazarov. Saros made his decision, and I made mine. The best thing you can do now is complete the mission."

Complete the mission. Astrea blinked past the raindrops and tears mingling in her lashes. Jin's control had slipped again. Regret and shame and determination flowed across her skin, heavy and impossible to ignore. Jin didn't like what he'd just done.

Find the answers. Astrea looked at the palace again, and though she couldn't see around the corner, she could hear the commotion. Guards shouting, Nazarov yelling, and a strange, familiar laugh.

If she went back now to try to help Saros, it wouldn't do any good. It wouldn't get them answers. It wouldn't stop Nazarov. Going with her friends was no guarantee, but it was her only chance. It was her only chance to save Saros and Kalama.

Wordlessly, Astrea sank into the car and sat next to a horrified Eliana. Jin followed her and slammed the door shut.

"Go, Nicos," Jin said, and the car sped down the palace driveway.

Astrea watched through the window as more guards and soldiers swarmed the palace grounds, undoubtedly searching for information about what had just taken place.

Her friends were talking about something—luggage, the airfield, if Cressida would be ready in time—but Astrea couldn't think about anything except what she just saw.

Thunder boomed overhead, so close and loud it shook the car. Still, they continued through the palace gates, guards shouting and jumping out of the way as Nicos barreled through the exit.

Find the answers, Astrea thought as she leaned her head on Eliana's shoulder. *Complete the mission.*

CHAPTER 43

Kalama's airfield was set on the northwestern edge of the city, a long stretch of paved ground surrounded by gray metal hangars. It was even emptier than Kalama's rain-soaked streets, no cars in sight as Nicos drove toward the far end of the airfield. The massive hangars that housed the airships were closed except for one. There, a compact gray airship was docked at a mooring station.

"You alright?" Eliana asked Astrea as they got out of the car. Jin and Adi were already coordinating with Nicos, heading down the airstrip toward the ship.

Ice spread to every corner of Astrea's body, outweighing even the sting of burns and cuts marring her skin. She knew she should take a moment to heal herself, but she couldn't. All her mind could do was focus on the fact that Saros had stayed behind. "No, I'm not."

"Me either."

Eliana liked to find solutions to problems, but she remained quiet, lavender surprise and orange anxiety pulsing around her. There was no solution. Saros had been arrested or worse. Nazarov was . . . something else entirely. There was nothing to be done right now, and Astrea hated feeling so powerless.

Jin glanced over his shoulder toward the airfield's entrance. "Where's Cress? We need to leave."

"It's going to be a bumpy ride, Captain," Adi warned as he looked toward the sky. The rain had stopped for now, but the dark clouds promised more. "Let's get this thing loaded."

"I'll do it," Eliana said. When Nicos tried to take a suitcase from her, she sighed. "Please? I just need to do something right now."

Wariness rolled off Nicos, but he nodded. "How about I help?"

Astrea slung her satchel over Eliana's shoulder. "Can you check that nothing in there got wet?" she asked.

"Of course." Eliana flashed a halfhearted smile in her direction before climbing the stairs to the mooring station and following the ramp onto the airship. Nicos wasn't far behind.

"So," Adi said after a few heartbeats, "what the fuck was that guy doing back there? I've never seen anyone able to do that before."

"It's the void," Astrea said.

"But teleportation?" Adi blew out a low whistle. "Makes you think."

"Yeah," she murmured. How could someone teleport between locations? Was that how the murderer in Kalama was getting away sight unseen? What did that mean for them going forward? Would Nazarov simply be able to escape custody?

"Adi," Jin said, "can you see if we need to do anything else before the Nikaphoroses get here? Then we can take off immediately."

"Sure thing." Adi jogged off, his footsteps echoing on the metal ramp. "Nicos!"

Jin shifted, that same mix of regret and determination mingling around him. Was this how he'd felt when he burned down that Zaikudi camp to complete that mission? He sucked in an audible breath, but Eliana's voice cut off whatever he was about to say.

"You've got something incoming, Jin!" she called, her footsteps loud as she pounded down the ramp. "Watch it!"

Two cars raced toward them. One was familiar, the simple black paint job indicating the Nikaphoroses had arrived. Behind them was another car, painted cherry red and gaining on them.

"Kaius," Jin muttered as Eliana came up next to them. "Shit."

Eliana pulled Astrea backward as the black car skidded to a stop just a few feet away. Cressida jumped out of the driver's side, but nobody else exited the car. Astrea's heart sank. First, no Saros and now, no Nikaphoroses.

"You see him?" Cressida asked, metal spikes already hovering in the air in front of her.

"Oh, trust me, I see him," Eliana said.

"He's not going to let us leave without a fight," Jin said quickly. "We need to buy Adi some time."

The red car stopped a few dozen yards away. Prince Kaius climbed out of the driver's side. Stepping out of the passenger's side was Caliban, his ghostly features harsh in the post-storm sun.

"Where do you think you're going?" Kaius shouted as he stalked closer.

"We're leaving, Kaius!" Jin called back. "Whatever Father's planning is bad and—"

"Bad?" Kaius laughed as Caliban came to his side. "You don't even know the greatness Father has planned for Helosia, for *us*. If you would just listen to him for once in your skies damned life, Varojin, then you would know."

Goosebumps prickled Astrea's skin. What was Emperor Auris planning if that was Kaius's impression? Was he merely exaggerating? Astrea didn't think he was this time. Anger and betrayal spiked red hot in the air around Kaius, pulsing in time with what she guessed was his rapid heartbeat.

"Just let us go, Kaius!" Eliana called. "We'll be out of your hair, and you can claim your place in the line of succession. Isn't that what you always wanted?"

"Out of my hair?" He laughed. "Out of my hair? No, the only way you'll be out of my hair, Eliana, is if you're six feet underground. The rebels won't stop until you're on the throne. We both know that. Or is that not what you've been discussing with Count Lorenzi?"

Teal understanding danced around Eliana, mingling with her outrage. Astrea had a dozen questions; there was no time to ask. Something familiar hummed in the air, but none of Astrea's friends moved. They didn't even seem to notice the shift in energy around Caliban. He stood a few feet behind Kaius, unreadable but watching.

"Ellie, get out of here," Astrea said.

"I'm not going anywhere," Eliana shot back. "Kaius can try to take me down if he wants, but it's four against two right now."

Eliana was a strong mage, but she hadn't seen what Nazarov could do. She hadn't seen the darkness eating at Mattina and that woman from the museum. She hadn't seen any of it. And that meant she didn't know what was about to come. Even Cressida hadn't seen what these void mages could do. Not really. None of them had seen it quite like Astrea, Jin, and Adi had.

"Alright," Cressida murmured, "let's buy Adi some time."

She moved, six metal spikes flying through the air and splitting off into two groups. One aimed for Kaius, the other for Caliban. Both men deflected easily, but it was enough to pull their attention away from Eliana.

That invisible warning hummed through the air again as Caliban took a step forward, his fists clenching and gaze trained on Cressida.

No. Astrea pulled on her light, calling it forward and pushing everything she could into it. Her rage and sadness, her frustration, her fear all surged forward with the blinding white light headed straight for Caliban and Prince Kaius. Heat pushed against Astrea's skin. Good. Kaius and Caliban could burn for all she cared. Let them finally see what she could do.

As quickly as she'd brought her magic to life, though, it waned. The light died as it reached Caliban. He didn't have dark fire like Nazarov. Shadows snaked up his arms and dripped from his fingers as a wall of darkness swallowed her light whole.

Astrea didn't even have time to consider it. Kaius attacked. Lightning zapped the ground near her feet, and she danced backward, slow. Jin grabbed her by the shoulders and hauled her farther away.

"Oh." Kaius chuckled as he stalked toward Jin, "I get it now. Father has discovered the void, so you go and fuck a Lightbringer, then bring her in to balance the fight." He clicked his tongue, lightning crackling in the air as gray hate danced around him. "You always were a traitor, Varojin. It's in your blood, just like your whore mother—"

Whatever control Jin still had snapped, blinding hot rage grating against every one of Astrea's nerves. Fire burst again and again, Kaius stumbling backward as he cackled with sickening glee.

"He *is* a fighter," Kaius crowed as he found his footing. "Did I touch a nerve, Varojin?"

Kaius's blue lightning burst through the air. Jin dodged, his flames already headed for his brother.

Cressida's hands stretched out, and an ear-splitting screech made Astrea cover her ears. The metal of one side of Kaius's car peeled back, long, narrow strips shooting toward Cressida and molding around her forearms like armor. Caliban barely reacted. He hesitated, watching as Kaius and Jin traded blows and moved farther and farther down the airfield.

Behind them, the airship roared to life. Nicos rushed down the ramp, orange anxiety flaring bright around him.

"Go," Astrea said to Eliana. "Go, we'll be right behind you."

Eliana's gaze danced between her fighting brothers and Caliban. Her shoulders tightened. "I'm not leaving you." Lightning crackled around her fingertips as she added, "Cress, who do you want?"

"Caliban," Cressida said. Then, she attacked.

Jagged piece after jagged piece of metal flew from Kaius's car, heading straight for the ghostly imperial guard. He reacted slowly, one piece slicing his arm before he moved. Shadows crawled up his face and arms again, copper eyes burning bright as Eliana and Cressida sprinted for him.

This was not buying time. This was not a distraction while Adi finished flight preparations. This was becoming a full-on battle, and Astrea was no use. She turned just as Nicos skidded to a stop next to her.

"What is Ellie doing?" he hissed.

"Help her," Astrea said. "Is Adi—"

"He's almost ready!" Nicos called, already running after his princess.

Even if Cressida, Eliana, and Nicos somehow controlled the emperor's guard, Kaius was going to overtake Jin. He was getting sloppy, his emotions out of control. Even amid their fire and lightning, Astrea could see Jin's aura spiking higher, brighter—midnight blue grief, crimson rage, orange anxiety. They pulsed over and over, tangling with the sickening golden joy that flashed around Kaius.

Jin had followed Kaius farther away from the ship and the others. Astrea followed, too, pulling on whatever magic she had left to give. She didn't know how to move the way Jin did, graceful but strong as he danced around his brother. She couldn't move earth or command fire. She barely had control over her light, but she'd be damned if she didn't get Jin back to that ship in one piece.

"Kaius!" Astrea shouted, welcoming the rage still burning through Jin. His pain was her pain, cutting deep.

"Get out of here," Jin growled as he turned toward her. His back was only to Kaius for a second, but that was all the other prince thought he needed. Giddy anticipation slammed into Astrea, overwhelming and distracting.

She gritted her teeth. Astrea just needed one shot, maybe two. It was all she had left in her. One clear shot.

There. Kaius stalked forward, his entire body served up as a target. Astrea pulled on her own anxiety and the uncontrolled emotions pouring out of Jin, pushing them into her light. It shot forward, striking Kaius on the shoulder.

"You *bitch*," he snarled, staggering back. Red blood and angry welts blossomed on Kaius's shoulder, his arm limp.

Jin closed the distance between him and his brother in two long strides. He grabbed Kaius by the collar with one hand, sliding behind him and kicking the backs of his knees out. Kaius dropped to the ground with a grunt.

"Go ahead, Varojin," he taunted. "You can finally prove yourself. I know you want—"

Jin's fist cracked across Kaius's temple, then Jin shoved him to the ground as his body crumpled. Kaius would live, but he'd need a healer when he woke up.

Jin said nothing as he grabbed Astrea's hand. They sprinted across the airfield toward where Cressida, Eliana, and Nicos were still fighting with Caliban. Even Astrea could see Caliban was on the defensive. Lightning, fire, metal, and earth all battered the void mage. Could he not fight back or would he not? Despite everything, was he not willing to risk hurting Eliana?

It didn't matter. Metal screeched again as another side of Kaius's car peeled away. Strips of red metal shot toward Caliban. They wrapped around his knees, ankles, and wrists, and another tightened around his mouth. Caliban fell to the ground, his eyes narrowing as he looked straight at where Astrea and Jin stood.

Astrea stared back at the void mage, willing her magic to find some emotion, some trace of anything on the man. But he simply watched her, unreadable and cold. The only thing Astrea could feel now was everyone's rampant emotions and pain from their injuries. That and the wind whipping across the airfield.

Jin's hand on Astrea's shoulder made her focus. Nicos herded Eliana right past them, Cressida hot on their heels.

"One more thing," Cressida said as she jogged toward them. She kneeled, hands flat against the ground. A crack split the airstrip's pavement, the earth trembling as it opened. It didn't stop until it was nearly a dozen feet wide. "That should buy us more time."

"Get on the ship." Jin's gaze darted toward Kaius's unconscious form one more time. "Go."

Cressida took the lead, heading straight for her abandoned car. With a flick of her wrist, the passenger door flew open and two leather suitcases reinforced with metal straps soared through the air. Cressida caught both without missing a step. Astrea trailed after her, exhaustion and adrenaline fighting for control as she splashed through puddle after puddle. Jin was right behind her, helping her keep her footing as they climbed the slick metal ramp.

"Come on!" Nicos called from just inside the doors, his voice barely carrying above the roar of the engine. "Careful!"

As soon as they were inside, someone shouted an all clear. The ship rose higher as Cressida pulled the door closed. She twisted some kind of wheel, and the door hissed as it sealed.

Astrea could've collapsed on the floor. Would've had Jin's arm not circled her waist before she stumbled toward the windows lining one wall of the airship cabin. Below them, the evidence of the fight was obvious. The split in the ground. Kaius's ruined car. The prince himself, still unconscious and unmoving. Caliban, who seemed to be staring at their ship as it rose higher and higher.

They'd done it. Now they just had to somehow make it all the way to Novaria.

CHAPTER 44

Though they'd managed to leave Caliban and Kaius on the airfield, and though all six of them had made it onto the ship with their lives, the airship's atmosphere was anything but calm.

Jin murmured something about going to check in with Adi, and he was gone before Astrea could respond. Eliana rushed over, taking his place and hugging Astrea tightly. Astrea didn't flinch when Cressida rushed over and joined them. She didn't even care when her knees hit the hard metal floor or that a swell of painful, messy emotions crashed into her.

All Astrea could focus on was that they were there, on that ship, and headed away from Kalama. She was leaving without Saros and without the Nikaphoroses. She was leaving without three of the most important people in her life, and she hadn't gotten to say goodbye.

"Are you both alright?" Eliana asked as she finally pulled away.

"Fine," Astrea whispered. "We're fine."

"You're not fine." Cressida reached for Astrea's wrists but stopped short. "What is all this?"

The skin on Astrea's hands was raw and angry from Nazarov's burns and all the tiny cuts she'd sustained when falling in the gardens.

"I'll deal with it," Astrea said. "Is anyone else hurt?" When both Eliana and Cressida said they were fine, Astrea nodded. "I need to take care of Jin first." Nazarov had hurt him, too, a burn to the side of his face.

"Go," Cressida said. "We'll sort out everything else after."

With the help of her friends, Astrea managed to get back on her feet and finally look around. She'd never been on an airship before. There was a large sitting area in the middle of the cabin, big enough for maybe a dozen people. Several low tables filled the space between the chairs and sofas. A door near the front of the ship led to the pilot's cabin; Adi was there, Nicos beside him. To the rear of the ship were stairs leading up to another level.

Jin had wandered to the windows again and was staring at the shrinking city below. When Astrea touched Jin's shoulder, he flinched. "Sorry," she murmured.

He shook his head. "I'm fine."

"Jin." She sighed when he didn't look at her. Everyone knew about her magic now—Nicos, Kaius, Caliban. The thought of saying her next words out loud was oddly freeing. "Let me heal you."

"I don't . . ."

"Jin." Eliana's voice, coming from somewhere behind them, was tight. "Come on. The sooner you're healed, the sooner you'll be back at it."

"Fine."

Jin didn't look at Astrea; he simply stalked toward the stairs. She followed him, their metallic footsteps drowned out by the muffled engines.

Upstairs was a narrow hallway, just one window at the far end. Several doors lined each side, and Jin picked one, going inside. The room was small and narrow, too. A round window near the ceiling let in some light, but the clouds zipping past were dark gray and gloomy.

Jin didn't say anything as he sat on the bed and pulled his soaked shirt off. Besides the burn on his face, several bruises and less severe burns blossomed on his chest and back.

"Heal yourself first," he said as Astrea sat next to him. "Please."

"I might not have the energy for them all today," Astrea admitted. She'd done too much, pushed herself too far in the last two days. Every inch of her body ached.

"Then I insist you do yours first."

His jaw was set in that familiar Auris way, and Astrea sighed. Healing her arms was simple. Low white light danced around her hands, and she sighed again, this time in relief as the skin became less tight and angry. She did the same for her shoulder, though that one hurt more.

"There," she said, holding her arms out for him to see. The healed skin was pinker than the rest, but it would even out soon. Jin took one of her hands in his. "Where should I start?"

"Whatever you think is a priority."

The burn to his face was the most severe, the skin bubbling around the edges. Astrea slipped her hand from his. "Lie down."

Jin shifted back, stopping when his head reached the pillows. That soft white light returned as Astrea set her hands near the wound. As her magic began to seep into Jin's skin, Astrea gritted her teeth. The right side of her face burned with the ghost memory of Nazarov's flames. Jin's hand found her thigh, squeezing once.

"You can stop," he whispered.

"I'm almost done."

"I hate that you're doing this."

"Would you say that to another healer?" Astrea challenged, the light dying as she lifted her hands from his face. His skin, though flushed, looked infinitely better.

"Other healers aren't you. I hate that you have to take my pain. I just hate . . ." He cleared his throat. "I hate that you had to see me like that."

Astrea knew that feeling all too well. She'd been so embarrassed crying in front of him—still was—but maybe he'd never been judging her, just like she wasn't judging him now.

"I'm glad I was there to help," she said.

"You don't hate me for keeping my promise to Saros?"

"You said it yourself. He made a choice." The thought of her uncle, probably in one of the emperor's prisons right now, made Astrea want to cry. But Saros thought he was doing the right thing. "I can't blame you for that."

The silence pressed on, grating against Astrea's senses. She wanted Jin's wall to slip again, to know what he was feeling. But his grip on it was iron, and she had the feeling it wasn't coming down any time soon.

"Now that we're all here," Eliana said from her position at the head of the sitting area, "let's get started."

After healing Jin, Astrea had followed him back downstairs to join the rest of their friends. She'd been expecting the Helosian army to give chase, but things had been quiet since takeoff. She dropped into the open seat next to Cressida.

"Get started with what?" Cressida asked. She motioned to the group; it was just four of them. Adi and Nicos were in the pilot's cabin, flying the skies damned ship.

"What, exactly, happened in Sezia?" Eliana asked. "Jin didn't get to really fill me in on anything. All Nicos had to hear was 'danger,' and he threw me in the car."

Jin explained what they'd seen in Sezia. "Father seems to want control of void magic," he continued, "and Kaius says he has big plans. There may be two factions of void mages, or at least one person has split off from the main group and gone rogue."

"The Paragon," Astrea whispered. "In the gardens, Nazarov shouted something about the Paragon. That must be them. He kept shouting about them restoring balance."

"Do you know what he meant?" Eliana asked.

Astrea shook her head. She didn't know what it meant, but surely they could find out. They had to find out. *Find the answers.* Saros had told Astrea to find the answers. She would.

"So, what do we do now?" Cressida asked. "We just wait until we get to Novaria?"

"We rest, and we stay ready," Jin said. "I doubt our father will give up that easily."

"I'll only be able to relax once we've crossed into Zaikudi territory and they don't shoot us out of the sky," Eliana muttered. "And whose airship are we on?"

"Zephyrine's."

Eliana's eyebrows rose. "General Kanakos?"

"Yes."

"General Kanakos lent us an airship?"

"It was a favor. She was my commanding officer, Ellie."

"She's more than that, Jin, and we both know it." His jaw tightened, and Astrea closed her eyes. More than his commanding officer? Jealousy spiked in her throat, then died as Eliana said, "We both know of her rebel . . . sympathies."

Rebel sympathies?

"You know where I stand," Jin said simply. "I know where *you* stand."

Kaius's words from the airfield wormed their way back into Astrea's mind. "*The rebels won't stop until you're on the throne. We both know that. Or is that not what you've been discussing with Count Lorenzi?*"

Yes, before Solstice Night, Eliana had said she thought the rebels made some good points. Yes, it was rumored that the rebels wanted Eliana to be named heir. But had Eliana been making plans for this? Had she been discussing something more than general support?

"I'm sorry," Cressida said. "Zephyrine Kanakos has rebel sympathies?"

"It's not like we're going to be welcomed home after this," Eliana said, a nonanswer. She sighed. "I don't think I even want to be. If Father's trying to harness this void magic, I can only imagine what he has planned."

"He needs to be removed from power, Ellie," Jin said. "You know that as well as I do."

Removing Emperor Aelius from power was a far cry from uncovering the secret of void magic. But it shouldn't have come as such a surprise to Astrea. Of course Eliana would think that. Of course Jin would think that. Of course Emperor Aelius needed to be removed from power. However he was connected to the void, it couldn't be good. They had to find a way to stop him *and* the void mages.

Static filled her veins. Astrea almost didn't feel like she was in her own body. None of this felt real. Maybe it was just a bad dream.

Eliana rubbed a palm across her forehead, steely pain spiking around her. "Skies," she muttered. "This is not how I imagined my day going." But then she huffed out a heavy breath and pushed her shoulders back. "I'll figure out what we tell the Novarians when we get to the border. But I need time to think, so I'm going to eat. Nicos is going to pester me all night if I don't."

"And I'm going to pester *you* if you don't eat," Cressida said, tugging on Astrea's arm. "Come on."

"I'll be there soon," Jin said. "I'm just going to talk to Adi."

Astrea hated the way her half-dried dress was sticking to the soft velvet of the sofa. Her mind couldn't seem to focus on anything else, even as Cressida tugged on her arm again. *If Zephyrine Kanakos can afford her own airship*, Astrea reasoned, *she probably isn't worried about reupholstering this.* Laughter bubbled out of her.

"What's . . . what's so funny?" Cressida asked, half-concerned and half-laughing.

"This!" Astrea gestured vaguely to the cabin. "I'm worried about ruining some woman's nice sofa while Saros is probably being tortured by the emperor right now. While Nazarov and Theo and skies knows who else are probably hunting down any of our friends and family left in the city. And everyone else," she continued, voice cracking as she fought against the tears threatening to spill, "is just getting to work like it's nothing. Cress . . . this is . . . this is not . . ."

Astrea pressed her palms to her eyes, trying to force everything down. This was not the time. This was not the place.

"Alright," Cressida said, rubbing the spot between Astrea's shoulders. "Alright, come on. You need to sleep. Come on, stand up."

"I'm fine," Astrea said, sniffling. "I'm fine. I need to eat something, that's all."

"You need to eat, *and* you need to sleep. You've been awake for a day and a half. If you want, I'll bring you some food while you go wash up and change into something dry."

Astrea nodded. That was a plan. Those were steps she could take. After wiping at her eyes again, Astrea climbed the narrow stairs up to the second floor. She stumbled back into the room Jin had gone into before and found a small bathroom attached.

Thunder rumbled outside as Astrea stared at her reflection in the mirror above the sink. She looked terrible. Her skin was pallid, her eyes rimmed with red despite her best efforts not to cry. A bruise bloomed near her collarbone, though what that was from, she didn't know. Astrea found her luggage and satchel in the bedroom, then changed into the short nightgown she'd packed for Sezia.

She opened her satchel next, pulling out the journal, Mattina's letter, her work notebook, and the mythology book. *Complete the mission. Find the answers.* As she flipped through them, Astrea was glad to see they were all dry. She reached for her bag to put everything back, but the mythology book slipped from her grasp. It hit the floor with a heavy thud. Astrea stooped to pick it up and noticed a piece of paper sticking out the top. Had she left some of her notes tucked in it? She rarely pulled pages out of her notebook like that.

Astrea unfolded the paper. It wasn't her messy handwriting but Saros's. There were only four words on the page.

I'm sorry. Forgive me.

Whatever had been holding back Astrea's tears broke. She dropped to the floor, burying her face in her hands as she cried. The tears came hot and fast, her chest so tight she felt like her heart would explode. Why did he have to be a martyr, sacrificing himself with no guarantee it would give them anything? Why did he make Jin promise to take her away?

Why did Saros have to leave her when she needed him?

When Astrea woke up, the room was dark, the hum of engines far away but persistent.

She was in her bed. *A* bed, anyway; she wasn't sure where she was. Astrea lifted her hand, a tiny spark of light illuminating the space around her. Jin was next to her, asleep. He looked almost comical in the bed. It was barely big enough for both of them, and he was practically curled into a ball.

"Do you have to shine that right in my eyes?" he asked, voice heavy with sleep.

Astrea closed her fingers over her palm, the light dying. "Sorry," she whispered. "I didn't know where I was."

"We should be over Zaikud right now," he said, shifting and stretching. "Headed north."

"Is everything okay?"

"Yes, everything's fine. Nobody's following us."

"Good."

"Are you hungry?" Jin asked, pushing himself up on his elbows. "Cressida said she was bringing you food when she found you. Both her and Ellie have taken turns checking on you."

Astrea didn't say anything. What was there to say? She hadn't expected their departure from Kalama to be smooth, but what happened was far outside her expectations. Nazarov. Kaius. Caliban. Now, her head and body ached, and the words from Saros's note ran circles in her mind.

Jin reached out, his hand cupping her cheek. "He's going to be fine."

"How do you know?"

"Because Saros is a fighter. I think he proved that."

Astrea's eyes fluttered shut as she leaned into Jin's touch.

"At the lunch, just before we left for Sezia," Jin said when she still hadn't responded, "Saros asked to speak with me privately."

"I remember."

"That was when he made me promise."

You promised me, Varojin. You promised. Saros's words echoed in Astrea's mind as lightning flashed in the narrow window on the opposite wall. Thunder rumbled, making the bed shake.

Astrea swallowed hard. "What did you promise him?"

"That no matter what happened in the coming days, I would get you away from Kalama. I thought that meant going to Sezia, but I guess I was wrong."

I'm sorry. Forgive me.

Was that what the note was referring to? The promise Saros had made Jin keep? Of course Jin was going to make that promise, and Saros knew it. Maybe he even foresaw it, foresaw all of this. Maybe Saros knew the choice he was going to make days before the opportunity came.

She hadn't even gotten the chance to ask him more about her vision. About *his* visions of *her*. Astrea couldn't ask him anything now.

"I'm not hungry," Astrea said. That was what Jin had asked before, wasn't it? She *was* hungry, but the thought of food also made her stomach churn. She could eat in the morning.

"Alright. Can you go back to sleep?"

Astrea would have preferred to stay asleep as long as she could, in that dreamless place her mind seemed to go when she slept next to Jin. That would have been best until they had their answers, until they had a solution for how they were going to stop whatever plans Emperor Aelius and Prince Kaius and this Paragon group seemed to have.

But she didn't say that. Astrea finally sank back into the hard mattress and settled her head on Jin's chest. He pulled her close, his lips brushing the top of her head.

"It's going to be alright," Jin whispered when Astrea still hadn't said anything. "We're going to figure this out."

Would they, though? They'd been trying to find answers for days—for weeks—and barely had any clues. How was she supposed to do this? How was she supposed to save her family—save Helosia—when she could barely find the information she needed? How was she supposed to help Eliana overthrow her father and take the throne? How was Astrea supposed to do any of that when she had failed so many times the last few weeks?

As Astrea leaned into Jin's warmth, willing it to overtake the familiar dread settling in her bones, her eyes finally began to close. She let her mind believe that Jin was right, that they would figure it out. Maybe. Maybe they would.

But as sleep began to pull her under, pain scratched between her shoulder blades, and that unwelcome voice whispered, *See you soon, little Lightbringer.*

To be continued

ALSO BY H.E. BAUMAN

Forged by Flames: A Darkened Skies Prequel
Into Whispering Shadows: Darkened Skies Book Two

ACKNOWLEDGMENTS

We often think of writing a book as a solitary activity, but there's so much that goes into it, and none of it would be possible without a variety of people. Family, friends, freelancers, and more. . .they've all played a role in the creation of *Under Darkened Skies.*

To my husband, thank you for bolstering my courage to publish, talking through plot with me on drives to the grocery store, and discussing character motivations while we cooked dinner. Thank you for the little notes on my desk and your unwavering confidence in my ability as an author.

To my parents, thank you for encouraging me to follow my muse from an early age. So many kids aren't lucky enough to have parents who believe in them or their art. I'm forever grateful that you believed in me.

To my brother and sister-in-law, thank you both for your encouragement and enthusiasm. I'm pretty bad at sharing about my work, but every time I finally mustered the courage to do so, you both welcomed my book news with open arms. That means the world to me.

To my friends, thank you for listening to my voice memos about this process, chatting over coffee, liking my Instagram posts, and making me cry over margaritas and tacos when you told me how proud you were of me for chasing my dreams. Thank you for everything.

To my beta readers, thank you not just for your feedback and time but also for believing in my story and loving Astrea, Varojin, and the crew as much as I do.

And to everyone not listed here, know that I'm thinking of you as I finally share this book with the world. Thank you, thank you, thank you.

ABOUT THE AUTHOR

H.E. Bauman is a fantasy author fascinated with all things magical. After spending her childhood writing stories, she went on to receive her bachelor's in English and has continued writing ever since. When she's not reading or writing, she enjoys playing tennis, immersing herself in video games, and spending time with her family.

If you want to get in touch, visit H.E.'s website or follow her on Instagram.